About t

Bronwyn Scott is the aut
2018 novella, *Dancing w*
RITA® finalist. She loves h
forward to the next story. She also enjoys talking with
other writers and readers about books they like and the
writing process. Readers can visit her at her Facebook
page at Bronwynwrites and at her blog at http://www.
bronwynswriting.blogspot.com

Regency Scandals

Regency Scandal:

Saved from Scandal

BRONWYN SCOTT

MILLS & BOON

First Published in Great Britain 2021
by Mills & Boon, an imprint of HarperCollins*Publishers* Ltd,
1 London Bridge Street, London, SE1 9GF

www.harpercollins.co.uk

HarperCollins*Publishers*
1st Floor, Watermarque Building,
Ringsend Road, Dublin 4, Ireland

REGENCY SCANDAL: SAVED FROM SCANDAL © 2021
Harlequin Books S.A.

How to Disgrace a Lady © 2012 Nikki Poppen
How to Ruin a Reputation © 2012 Nikki Poppen

978-0-263-30029-1

Printed and bound in Spain
by CPI, Barcelona

HOW TO DISGRACE
A LADY

Chapter One

Merrick St Magnus did nothing by halves, including the notorious Greenfield Twins. Even now, the legendary courtesans were delectably arranged in varying degrees of dishabille on the drawing room's long Venetian divan. His eyes on the first Greenfield twin, Merrick plucked an orange slice from a silver tray and gave it an indolent roll in powdered sugar, in no way oblivious to the charms of her lovely bosom pushed to the very limits of decency by the dual efforts of a tightly laced corset and a low décolletage.

'One sweet temptation deserves another, *ma chère*,' he said in liquid tones, his eyes meaningfully raking her body, noticing how the pulse note at the base of her long neck leapt in appreciation of his open seduction. Merrick skimmed the orange slice across her slightly parted lips, the tip of her tongue making pretty work of licking the powdery sugar, all the while suggesting she'd be quite apt at licking more than her lips.

He was going to enjoy tonight. More than that, he

was going to enjoy winning the bet that currently filled pages of White's infamous book of wagers and collecting the winnings tomorrow. He stood to make a respectable sum that would see him through a recent bad run at the tables. Certainly men had 'had' the lovely Greenfield sisters, but no man had obtained carnal knowledge of them *both* at the same time.

At the other end of the divan, twin number two gave a coy pout. 'What about me, Merrick? Am I not a temptation?'

'You, *ma belle*, are a veritable Eve.' Merrick let his hand hover over the fruit platter as if contemplating with great deliberation which fruit to select. 'Ah, for you, my Eve, a fig, I think, for the pleasures of Eden that await a man in your garden.'

His literary references were for naught. She pouted again, perplexed. 'My name isn't Eve.'

Merrick stifled a sigh. Think about the money. He flashed a rakish smile, popping the fig into her mouth and giving her a compliment she would understand. 'I never can tell which of you is the prettiest.' But he definitely could tell which one was smarter. He dropped a hand to the expanse of twin number two's exposed bosom and drew a light circle on her skin with his index finger, winning a coy smile. Twin one had her hands at his shoulders, massaging as she pulled the shirt-tails from his waistband. It was time to get down to business.

That was when it happened—his manservant began banging on the receiving room door.

'Not right now,' Merrick called, but the banging persisted.

'Maybe he wants to join us,' twin one suggested, unfazed by the interruption.

His man of all work would not be deterred. 'We have an emergency, milord.' He pressed from the other side of the door.

Damn it all, he was going to have to get up and see what Fillmore wanted. Between lost literary references and intrusive servants, this could be going better. Merrick pushed to his feet, shirt-tails loose. He placed a gallant kiss on the hand of each twin. 'A moment, *mes amours.*'

He purposely strode across the floor and pulled open the door just a fraction. Fillmore knew what he was doing in here, of course, and Fillmore probably even knew why. But that didn't mean Merrick wanted him to witness it first-hand. If he thought too much about it, the whole scenario was a bit lowering. He was broke and trading the one thing he did better than anything else for the one thing he needed more than anything else: sex for money, not that anyone else realised it.

'Yes, Fillmore?' Merrick managed a supercilious arch of his eyebrow. 'What is our emergency?'

Fillmore wasn't the normal manservant. The arched eyebrow affected him as much as the Miltonesque reference had affected twin not-so-smart. Fillmore puffed himself up and said, 'The emergency, milord, is your father.'

'Fillmore, you are aware, I believe, that I prefer my problems to be shared.'

'Yes, milord, as you say, our emergency.'

'Well, out with it, what has happened?'

Fillmore passed him a white sheet of paper already unfolded.

Merrick had another go at the arched eyebrow. 'You might as well tell me, clearly you've already read the message.' Really, Fillmore ought to show at least some slight remorse over reading someone else's post; not that it wasn't a useful trait on occasion, just not a very genteel one.

'He's coming to town. He'll be here the day after next,' Fillmore summarised with guiltless aplomb.

Every part of Merrick not already in a state of stiffness went hard with tension. 'That means he could be here as early as tomorrow afternoon.' His father excelled at arriving ahead of schedule and this was an extraordinarily premeditated act. His father meant to take him by surprise. One could only guess how far along the road his father had been before he'd finally sent word of his imminent arrival. Which meant only one thing: there was going to be a reckoning.

The conclusion begged the question: which rumours had sent the Marquis hot-footing it to town? Had it been the curricle race to Richmond? Probably not. That had been weeks ago. If he'd been coming over that, he would have been here long before now. Had it been the wager over the opera singer? Admittedly that had become more public than Merrick would have liked.

But it wasn't the first time his *affaires* had been conducted with an audience.

'Does he say why?' Merrick searched the short letter.

'It's hard to say. We've had so many occasions,' Fillmore finished with an apologetic sigh.

'Yes, yes, I suppose it doesn't matter which episode brings him to town, only that we're not here to greet him.' Merrick pushed a hand through his hair with an air of impatience. He needed to think and then he needed to act quickly.

'Are we sure that's wise?' Fillmore enquired, 'I mean, based on the last part of the letter, perhaps it would be better if we stayed and were appropriately penitent.'

Merrick scowled. 'Since when have we ever adopted a posture of penitence when it comes to my father?' He wasn't in the least bit intimidated by his father. Leaving town was not an act of cowardice. This was about being able to exert his own will. He would not give his father the satisfaction of knowing he controlled another of his grown sons. His father controlled everything and everyone that fell into his purvey, including Merrick's older brother, Martin, the heir. Merrick refused to be catalogued as another of his father's puppets.

'Since he's coming to town to cut off our allowance until we reform our ways. It's later in the note,' Fillmore informed him.

He'd never been the fastest of readers. Conversation was so much more entertaining. But there they were at the bottom of the letter, the words so curt and glaring he could almost hear his father's voice behind them: *I am curtailing your access to funds until such time as your habits are reformed.*

Merrick scoffed. 'He can curtail the allowance all he wants since "we" don't touch it anyway.' It had occurred to him years ago that in order to be truly free of his father, he could not be reliant on anything his father offered, the usual second-son allowance included. The allowance lay tucked away in an account at Coutts and Merrick chose instead to live by the turn of a card or the outcome of a profitable wager. Usually it was enough to keep him in rent and clothes. His well-earned reputation for bedroom pleasure did the rest.

His father could halt the allowance for as long as he liked. That wasn't what bothered Merrick. It was the fact that his father was coming at all. The one thing they agreed on was the need for mutual distance. Merrick liked his father's jaded ethics as little as his father liked his more flexible standards. Coming to London was a death knell to his Season and it was barely June. But Merrick wasn't outmanoeuvred yet.

He needed to think and he needed to think with his brain as opposed to other body parts. That meant the twins had to go. Merrick shut the door and turned back to the twins with a short, gallant bow of apology. 'Ladies, I regret the emergency is immediate. You will need to leave.'

And so they did, taking his chance at two hundred pounds with them at a point where money was tight and his time was tighter.

* * *

'Fillmore, how much do we owe?' Merrick sprawled on the now significantly less-populated divan. He ran through the numbers in his head; the boot maker, his tailor and other sundry merchants would need to be paid before he left. He wouldn't give his father the satisfaction of seeing to his debt. It might create the illusion his father had room to negotiate.

Damn, but this was a fine pickle. He was usually an adequate steward of his funds and usually a fair judge of character. He never should have played cards with Stevenson. The man was known to cheat.

'Seven hundred pounds including this month's rent on the rooms.'

'How much do we have?'

'Around eight hundred to hand.'

It was as he'd thought—enough to clear the bills with a little left over. Not enough to survive another month in the city, however, especially not during the Season. London was deuced expensive.

Fillmore cleared his throat. 'Might I suggest that one way to cut expenses would be for us to stay at the family town house? Rent for rooms in a fashionable neighbourhood is an extravagance.'

'Live with my father? No, you may not suggest it. I've not lived with him for ages. I don't mean to start now, especially since it's what he wants.' Merrick sighed. 'Bring me the invitations from the front table.'

Merrick searched the pile for inspiration, looking for a high-stakes card party, a bachelor's weekend in Newmarket that would get him out of town, anything that might assuage the current situation. But there was nothing amusing: a musicale, a Venetian breakfast, a ball, all in London, all useless. Then at the bottom of the pile he found it: the Earl of Folkestone's house party. Folkestone was hosting a party at the family seat on the Kent coast. Originally, he'd not considered going. It was three days to Kent on dry roads to even drier company. But now it seemed the ideal locale. Folkestone was a crusty traditionalist of a man, but Merrick knew Folkestone's heir, Jamie Burke, from their days at Oxford, and he'd attended a soirée hosted by Lady Folkestone early in the Season, which explained where the invitation had come from. He'd been a model guest, flirting with all the wallflowers until they had bloomed. Ladies liked a guest who knew how to do his duty and Merrick knew how to do his superbly.

'Pack our bags, Fillmore. We're going to Kent,' Merrick said with a finality he didn't feel. He didn't fool himself into believing a house party in Kent was an answer to his woes. It was merely a temporary salve. London was expensive, yes, but his freedom was proving to be more so.

The road to Kent was clearly *not* to be confused with the road to Hell, Merrick mused grimly later after three days of riding. For starters, there were no good intentions in sight. But there were apparently two highwaymen in broad daylight. Merrick slowed his horse and swore under his breath. Damn and double damn, he'd been a short two miles from the salvation of Folkestone's bloody house party. His hand reached subtly for the pistol in his coat pocket.

It was deuced odd for highwaymen to attempt a robbery at three in the afternoon when the polite world was ready to settle in for tea. But given the state of the current British economy, he wouldn't put it past anyone. It was unfortunate he was alone just now, having ridden on ahead of Fillmore and his luggage.

'Is the road out, my good fellows?' Merrick called, wheeling his horse around in a flashy circle. Their horses looked sleek and well fed. Great. He'd run into a set of the more successful brand of highwayman. Merrick's hand tightened on his pistol. He'd paid his bills and his last pound notes were tucked safely in his pocket. He wasn't about to surrender what financial surety he had left.

The two bandits, masked below their eyes with black scarves, looked at each other. One of them laughed and parodied his politeness. 'It is to you, good sir.' The man waved his more obviously displayed pistol with the casual flourish of a man long accustomed to handling firearms with ease. 'We don't want your money, we want your clothes. Be a good fellow and give us a quick strip.' The green eyes of the second bandit flashed with humour.

The sun caught the glint of the pistol butt. Merrick's hand eased on the grip of his weapon, a slow sure smile of confidence taking his face. Merrick stilled his horse and faced the two 'bandits'. 'Why, Ashe Bedevere and Riordan Barrett, fancy meeting you here.'

The green-eyed man with the pistol yanked his scarf down. 'How did you know?'

Merrick grinned. 'No one else in England has emeralds embedded in the butt of their pistol.'

'Damn it, it was a good prank.' Ashe gave his gun a rueful glare as if the weapon alone were to blame for ruining the gambit. 'Do you know how long we've been sitting here, waiting?'

'Waiting in the sun is dusty business,' Riordan put in.

'What were you doing, waiting at all?' Merrick pulled his horse alongside his two friends and they continued down the road three abreast.

'We saw your horse outside the inn last night and the ostler said you were headed over to Folkestone's for the party,' Ashe admitted with an impish grin. 'Since we're going, too, we thought we'd plan a little reunion.'

'We could have reunited over a pint of good ale and rabbit stew last night,' Merrick put in. Accosting friends with pistols was a bit demented even for Ashe.

'There's no fun in that; besides, we were busy with the barmaid and her sister.' Riordan pulled out a pewter flask and took a healthy swallow. 'There hasn't been any fun all Season. London's been an absolute bore.'

So boring that even a house party in Kent held more charm? It seemed unlikely. Merrick peered closely at his friend. Riordan's face bore signs of weariness, but there was no time to pursue that avenue in the wake of Ashe's next pronouncement.

'How about a bathe?'

Merrick's head swivelled in Ashe's direction.

'What? A bathe?' Had Ashe finally gone around the bend? He'd long suspected Ashe wasn't as sane as the rest of humanity, always the risk taker.

'Not in a tub, old chap,' Ashe replied, easily reading his mind. 'Out here, *before* we get to the house party. There's a pond—a small lake, really—over the next rise and off the lane a bit, if I remember this stretch of road right. It will be a chance to wash off the grime of the journey, a last chance to exist in nature before we embrace the unnatural formality of a country party where…' Ashe paused for effect and went on with great exaggeration '…everything should be natural, but most unfortunately is not.'

'Splendid idea, a bathe is perfect. What say you, Merrick? A bathe before high tea and the ladies?' Riordan voted with his heels, spurring his chestnut hunter into a canter, letting the light breeze ruffle his dark hair. Riordan called back over his shoulder, 'Race you! I've got the flask!'

'But you don't know where you're going!' Ashe and Merrick yelled in unison. This had always been the case; even at Oxford, Riordan had been heedless of the details, seizing the pleasure of the moment, ignoring the consequences. Merrick exchanged a knowing look with Ashe.

'All the better to race me….' The words floated back over the pounding of hooves on packed dirt. They needed no further encouragement to kick their horses up to speed and follow.

They found the pond as Ashe remembered it: a cool, shady oasis fed by a quick-flowing stream and perfect for the odd summer bathe. It was hidden from the casual eye by leafy willows and Merrick raced the others, wasting no time in divesting himself of his clothes, suddenly overcome with a desire to feel the cold water on his hot skin. He dived in, refusing to cautiously test the waters first.

The water closed over his head and he felt absolution. He reached out into the water with long strokes and began to kick, every stroke taking him further from London, from his father, from his ongoing battle for the freedom to be himself even if he didn't precisely know who that was. In the water he was clean. Unfettered joy took him and he surged to the surface, shaking the water from his hair. Ashe was watching him, posed gloriously naked on a rock like a sea-god. Merrick reached up, grabbed Ashe's leg and pulled. 'Come on in, the water's fine.'

Ashe gave an undignified yelp as gravity and Merrick took him sliding into the pond. 'Riordan, get in here and help me!'

There was a swift movement on the banks as Riordan grabbed for a sturdy vine and swung into the mêlée. Chaos ensued—the good kind of chaos that washes away years and trouble. They wrestled in the water; they scrambled up the banks, making the dirt into mud with their dripping forms; they ran the perimeter of their sanctuary with loud whoops of pure exuberance, only to jump back in and start all over. For all the sophistication of London and its entertainments, Merrick hadn't had this much uncontrived fun in ages. London's *haut ton* would cringe to see three of their members behaving with such careless, naked abandon. But why not? There was no one to see.

Chapter Two

Thank goodness no one could see her now. Dressed in a loose, serviceable gown of drab olive and scuffed half-boots, Alixe knew she didn't look at all like a proper earl's daughter. The family would have a fit. *Another* fit. The family wanted to have as few fits as possible. Which was probably why they'd let her go out wandering in the first place, despite guests arriving for the long-anticipated midsummer house party.

At the moment, Alixe didn't care if the king himself was scheduled to arrive. She had a precious afternoon of freedom entirely to herself. The weather was fine and she was enjoying her tramp to the furthest edges of the family property, perhaps a bit beyond because she was feeling a little naughty. She had a destination in mind—an old summer house on the nebulous fringes of the estate, where she could settle in with her books and her work, all carefully packed in a cloth bag looped over her shoulder.

She was getting close to the summer house. The

path was increasingly overgrown with fern and nearly obscured from plain view as she ventured further into the wooded area. She smiled and pushed aside some of the rampant undergrowth. It was cool here beneath the trees. Ah, there it was. She quickened her pace, taking the crumbling steps to the entrance two at a time.

Alixe opened the door and sighed. The old place was perfect. She should make a retreat out of it. She could scavenge odds and ends from the attics. Alixe put her bag down and surveyed the open-air room. It was more like a gazebo than an actual house, but it had infinite possibilities—a place where she could be alone, away from the family's odious neighbour Archibald Redfield, away from everyone and all their expectations for her life. Alixe closed her eyes and breathed deeply. Ah, yes, she was blessedly alone.

Then she heard it: the sound of not being quite alone. Alixe turned her head towards the sound. A bird call? It came again—distinctly *not* a bird. It sounded like a human shout.

Oh, dear.

The lake.

Alixe was galvanised into action. Someone might be in trouble. She tore through the woods, running towards the shouts.

Alixe crashed into the lake clearing and came to an abrupt halt too late to rethink announcing her presence once it became patently obvious the only thing in risk of drowning were her sensibilities. Three men cavorted—really, that was the only word for it—*ca-*

vorted in the water. They dove, they wrestled, they noticed her.

Oh, lord, they *noticed* her.

She didn't want to be noticed. This was not what she deserved for playing the good Samaritan. She'd run pell-mell to the aid of three men swimming nude in a hidden lake. Someone could at least have the decency to actually be drowning.

'Hello, are we making too much noise? We didn't think anyone was around,' one of them said easily, unfazed by her sudden appearance. He separated from his comrades and waded towards the shore, the receding water revealing him inch by marvellous inch until Alixe was sure of two things: first, she'd never seen such a finely made man in her life and, second, the finely made man was undoubtedly naked.

She should look away. But where to look? His eyes? They were too mesmerising. The sky wasn't even that blue. His chest? Too well-sculpted, especially the tapered muscles at his abdomen.

Abdomen!

Oh, lord, she hadn't meant to let her gaze or the water get so low. He was still moving towards her, unbothered by his nudity. She had to put a stop to it or she'd be seeing more than the firm muscles of his abdomen.

All her supposed good breeding failed her utterly. Her eyes remained riveted on the stranger's midsection. It would only be a matter of seconds now before all was revealed. She should say something. What did one say to a naked man at a pond?

She opted for a casual response and tried to sound as if she ran into naked men all the time. 'Don't get out for me. I'll just be going. I heard the shouts and thought someone might need help.'

Good. She sounded mostly normal.

Alixe took a step back from the lake and promptly fell over a log half-buried in the mud of the lake side. She landed hard on her backside. She could feel her cheeks burning. So much for normal.

The man laughed, not unkindly, and kept advancing. He was fully revealed now, his manly parts entirely visible. All she could do was stare. He was so magnificent that for a moment she forgot to be embarrassed, her curiosity unleashed at the sight of him. He was beautiful—*that* part of him was beautiful in a wild, primitive way. She'd not expected it.

'Seems as though someone might need help, after all.' The nameless, *naked* man stood over her with a hand held out, not that she had much attention for the hand when there were other dangling appendages in close proximity.

'No, really, I'm all right.' Her words rushed out in a flummoxed mess, her sense of propriety returning.

'Don't be stubborn, give me your hand. You don't want to fall again.' He held out his hand, insisting.

'Oh, yes, my hand.' Alixe offered it up as if she'd just discovered it and dragged her eyes a little further up his chest to his face. He was grinning at her with his whole visage: his smile wide and laughing, his eyes bluer than the cerulean of an English summer sky.

He tugged Alixe to her feet, not in the least nonplussed by his lack of clothing. 'Your first naked man, I take it?'

'What?' It took her a moment to follow the question. It was hard enough to train her eyes away from the environs of his thighs, let alone follow a conversation. She opted for sophistication in the hopes of recovering her dignity. 'No, actually. I've seen plenty in...' She faltered here. *Where* would she have seen them?

'Art work?' he supplied helpfully, water droplets sparking like diamonds in the pale flax of his hair.

'I've seen the *David*,' she shot back, sensing the challenge. It was true. She had in pictures, but the *David* of pictures had nothing on this stranger, who stood bold and brash in the sunlight with all his worldly goods plainly displayed. Her eyes darted about the shores of the pond, in a desperate attempt to not look at said worldly goods. It was all his fault. He'd made no move to retrieve any of the garments lying close by. What kind of man stood naked in the presence of a lady? Not the kind of man she was used to meeting in her parents' genteel circles.

The very thought sent a tremor of excitement through her even as she reached for the nearest garment. 'You should cover yourself, sir.' Alixe held out the shirt. It would be too bad, of course, but it was an absolute social necessity. No one stood around conversing without their clothes on.

He took the shirt, his eyes were laughing at her. 'Should I? I was under the impression you were enjoying the view.'

'I think the only one enjoying this is you,' Alixe

countered, mustering all the outrage she ought to feel at this affront to her sensibilities.

He cocked an eyebrow in challenge. 'At least I'll admit to it.'

That comment did stoke her temper. Alixe squared her shoulders. 'You are a most ill-bred man.' *With the body of a god and a face of an angel.* 'I must be going.' She brushed at her skirts to give her hands something to do. 'I can see everyone is all right. I'll be on my way.' This time she managed to exit the clearing without stumbling over any errant logs.

Merrick watched her go with a laugh. He thrust his arms through the sleeves of his shirt in a belated overture to decency. Perhaps he shouldn't have done it—shouldn't have teased her so mercilessly. But it had all been good fun and she'd not shied away from it. He knew when a woman was curious and when she was genuinely mortified. This creature in the drab dress hadn't been nearly as mortified as she claimed. Her lovely sherry eyes had been wide with curiosity satisfied as she looked her fill.

Merrick reached for his trousers and slid them on. To be sure, she'd tried to look away, but healthy inquisitiveness is hard to defeat and she'd lost that battle from the start. Not that he'd been bothered by her frank enquiry into the male anatomy. She wasn't the first woman to see him naked. He'd been naked in front of a lot of them.

Women liked his body, with its lean lines and muscled contours. Lady Mansfield had once, quite publicly, declared it the eighth wonder of the world. Lady Fairworth had spent nights staring at him for hours. She'd made a habit of having him fetch things from around the room so that she could watch him walk across the floor stark naked for her.

He hadn't minded. He understood the needs of those experienced women and, in turn, they understood his. But today had been different. There'd been something unsullied in her gaze. He'd clearly been her first. Even now the knowledge fired a low heat in his groin. She'd been surprised, but she hadn't shrunk from her discoveries. She'd welcomed them. Her response to him had sparked a kind of eroticism he was not familiar with. It had been ages since he'd been anyone's first naked man.

More than that, the very directness of her demeanour had appealed to him. He'd known he could push her sensibilities. For all her clumsiness, he'd known she could handle herself. Helpless misses didn't run through the forest to the rescue of drowning victims. He'd not been disappointed. Her sharp conversation had been every bit as enjoyable as her hot, open gaze. Too bad he didn't know her name. He'd just have to burn on his own.

Alixe's cheeks were still burning when she got back to the summer house. She resolutely settled in with her book, determined to not think about the encounter at the lake. But her mind would have none of it. Her mind preferred instead to recall, in vivid detail, the well-muscled torso with its defined abdomen and lean hips tapering down to that most manly part of him. And that smile. Even now, that wicked, laughing grin sent a curious skittering sensation straight to her stomach. He'd been flirting with her. Those dancing blue eyes knew exactly what they were doing, exactly what kind of havoc they were wreaking on her senses. It had been ages since anyone had flirted with her, even if it had been a little unorthodox.

Well, more than a little. It was the most unorthodox thing that had happened to her to date. Until today, she'd never seen a man without his shirt. Probably, if she thought about it, she hadn't seen a man without a waistcoat since her come-out. A gentleman didn't dare remove even his coat in the presence of a lady, while this man had removed quite a bit more than his coat. It begged the question: what did that make him? Certainly not a gentleman.

The blush started again and Alixe was swamped anew with the sensation. She'd seen a real, live, naked man.

Up close.

Very close.

Extremely close. And it had been gorgeous. Which begged the question: what did that make *her*? Curious? Wanton? Something more? The answer would be worth exploring. She was no prude, genteel rearing and shielding aside. She'd partaken as eagerly in the sights as he'd displayed them. Alixe fought the urge to fan herself like an insipid miss. She had to find her focus and be done with this ridiculous mooning. She'd seen no more today than the gifts God had given mankind in general. Every man had one, which was roughly half the population.

There.

She'd taken the philosophical high ground—and failed miserably to dispel the image from her mind.

It was official: she was definitely unsettled. She would get no reading done at this rate. Alixe tucked her book back into the bag. What she needed was a change of scenery. She might as well head back to the house; if she smiled like an empty-headed fool the whole way back, so be it.

By the time she'd gained the safety of her rooms, Alixe had found perspective. She had indeed smiled the entire walk back to the house. She might even continue to smile her way through the tedious evening that lay ahead. If people wanted to believe she was smiling at them, they could. Only she would know what she was really smiling about. Other than that, she'd come to the realisation there was no harm in her secret. The man from the lake didn't know her; she didn't know him; they would never see each other again, except perhaps in her dreams.

But the knowledge did make her feel undeniably more worldly than she'd felt four hours ago and she dressed with a little more care than she might otherwise have done in celebration of it. She had her maid lay out the pale-blue dinner gown with the chocolate-brown trim and the low-cut bodice. The gown was one of a few exceptions in her otherwise 'sufficient' wardrobe. She'd always been more interested in her books and manuscripts than clothes and society; a fact her family was not willing to accept, although she'd achieved the august age of twenty-six and had firmly put herself on the shelf. Despite her most persuasive efforts, not all of the family had despaired of marrying off the controversial, blue-stocking daughter of the Earl of Folkestone just yet. She'd refused to go to London this Season, so her dogged family had brought London to her in the form of a house party peopled with the very best of her brother's acquaintances.

Alixe clipped on her dainty pearl earrings and gave herself a final look-over in the mirror. It was time to go downstairs and pretend she'd never seen a man without clothes. Surely she could do that?

'Alixe, there you are.' Her brother, Jamie, materialised at the foot of the stairs. 'You look pretty tonight; you should wear blue more often.' He tucked her arm through his and for once she was grateful for the assurance of his presence. 'There are some people I want you to meet.'

Alixe stifled a groan. Jamie meant well, but he worried too much about her. As a result, he was always trying to matchmake.

'Alixe, it will be all right. These are friends of mine from university. Now, be nice. Here they are,' he whispered at her ear, whisking her into the drawing room.

A group of gentlemen stood near the doorway. At Jamie's entrance, four pairs of eyes turned her direction. One set she recognised. They belonged to the squire's son. The other six belonged to two dark-haired devils and one angel—one very naughty angel, an angel she'd seen naked.

Alixe froze, her mind racing with all nature of embarrassing scenarios. Perhaps he wouldn't recognise her. In her expensive evening gown she hardly looked like the girl tramping in the woods.

Jamie proudly pulled her forwards. There was nothing to do but brave it out. 'Let me introduce all of you to my sister, Lady Alixe Burke. Alixe dear, these are the old friends from university I was telling you about. Riordan Barrett, Ashe Bedevere and Merrick St Magnus.'

Great, now the angel had a name.

'Enchanté, mademoiselle.' Merrick bowed over her hand, his eyes trained on her face the whole while. He'd learned early how to read a woman. Elegant gowns and complicated coiffures often hid a multitude of sins or truths, depending on how you looked at it. To really see a woman's identity, one had to look at her face. In this case, he was not distracted by the fine gown and the sophisticated twist of hair.

It was definitely *her.*

He'd know those long-lashed sherry eyes anywhere. They'd been the most expressive part of her today. They'd been wide with an intriguing mixture of shock and curiosity. If her eyes weren't enough, there was her mouth. Merrick considered himself a great connoisseur of mouths and this one begged to be kissed. Not that he'd be doing any kissing of Jamie Burke's sister. She was the kind of girl who was off limits and he'd already danced fairly near the fire today, even if by accident.

She gave a short incline of her head, greeted the others in a perfunctory manner and made polite excuses to go in search of a girlfriend. But Merrick watched her leave them only to stand with Lady Folkestone and a group of older matrons near the wide fireplace. He didn't sport with those who didn't welcome it. Ordinarily, he'd feel badly about causing a shy young lady discomfort. But in this case, he knew better. Alixe Burke was no retiring miss, no matter her airs to the contrary. She was due for a little provoking. After all, she'd 'provoked' him that afternoon. Turnabout was fair play.

Jamie noticed his distraction. 'Perhaps I could arrange for you to take Alixe in to supper.'

Jamie was one of those rare individuals who could make wishes come true. At Oxford, they'd had only to voice a want and Jamie would see it granted. In the years since then, that ability had not changed and now, even though there were two gentlemen present who technically outranked the second son of a marquis, Merrick found himself conveniently seated beside the somewhat-aloof person of Alixe Burke. That was about to change. He wanted to see her face alive with surprise, or with any emotion. This expression of bland passivity she wore in polite company did not do her features justice.

'Miss Burke, I cannot shake the feeling that we've met before,' he murmured as the first course was set in front of them.

'That would be unlikely. I am not much in London,' came the short ten-word response followed by a curt smile.

He'd thought that would be her gambit. She was pretending she didn't recognise him. Either that or hoping he didn't recognise her. But it was all pretence. Her left hand lay fisted in her lap, a sure sign of tension.

'Then perhaps we've met around here,' Merrick offered amiably, pushing the subject. She'd been a delightful juxtaposition of emotions that afternoon—part of her trying to pretend naked men in ponds was *de rigueur* while the other part of her had been rampantly excited by the titillating disturbance. He wanted that woman back. That woman was intriguing. This woman sitting next to him was a mere shell for that other person.

She set down her spoon with deliberate firmness and fairly rounded on him with all the chagrin allowed at a dinner table. 'Lord St Magnus, I seldom go out even around here. I spend my time with local historians. So unless you are involved in the work of restoring medieval documents from Kent, we most certainly have never met.' That was the shell talking. No woman with a mouth like hers was as proper as she was pretending.

Merrick stifled a grin. He was getting to her. She was past ten words now. 'But surely, Lady Alixe, you must, on occasion, walk through the woods and visit a pond or two. Perhaps we met there.'

'What an outrageous place to meet.' A blush started

up her cheeks. She must realise the game was up or very nearly so.

Merrick gave her a moment to regroup while the servants removed the first course. The second course arrived and Merrick fired his next salvo. 'Of course, it is possible that you simply don't recognise me. If it's the occasion I am thinking of, you were wearing an old olive-green dress and I was wearing my birthday suit.'

To her credit, Lady Alixe choked only mildly on her wine. 'I beg your pardon?'

'My birthday suit, nature's garb, my Altogether.'

She set her wine glass aside and fixed him with a hard stare. 'I knew precisely what you meant the first time. What I cannot fathom is why you want to recall the event at all. A gentleman would never confront a lady with a blatant reminder of such a difficult and accidental encounter.'

'Perhaps you are making faulty assumptions when drawing that conclusion.' Merrick sat back and waited for the next remove.

'You are familiar with syllogisms, Lady Alixe?' he continued easily after the servants had done their work. 'Man is mortal, Socrates is a man, therefore Socrates is mortal. In this case, gentlemen don't discommode ladies, Merrick St Magnus is a gentleman, therefore, he won't bring up the little escapade at the pond this afternoon. Is that how your reasoning went, Lady Alixe?'

'I had no idea the three of you were taking a splash.'

'Ah, so you do remember me?'

Alixe pursed her lips and capitulated. 'Yes, Lord St Magnus, I remember you.'

'Good. I'd hate to be unmemorable. Most ladies find my "Altogether" quite memorable.'

'I'm sure they do.' She took a bite of her beef in a clear tactic to tersely end the conversation.

'Do I hear another syllogism in the making, Lady Alixe? Most ladies like my "Altogether". Lady Alixe is a lady, therefore...'

'No, you do not hear another syllogism in the making. What you hear is an exception.'

Merrick gave her a lingering smile. 'Then I shall endeavour to change your mind.' This was by far the most interesting conversation he'd had in ages, probably because how it would turn out was not a forgone conclusion. He wasn't use to that. With his usual sort of woman, conversation was *always* a prelude to a rather predictable outcome. That wasn't to say the outcome wasn't pleasurable, just predictable.

Too bad it was nearly time to turn the table and engage the partner on his other side. Even if he didn't recognise the signs that the table was about to shift, Lady Alixe's deep sigh of relief would have cued him. He wouldn't let her go that easily.

With a last sortie of mischief, Merrick leaned close to Lady Alixe, close enough to smell the lemon-lavender scent of her *toilette* water, and said in a conspiratorial whisper, 'Don't worry, we can talk later this evening over the tea cart.'

'I wasn't worried.' She managed to smile through clenched teeth.

'Yes, you were.'

Lady Alixe turned to the man on her other side but not before her slipper-clad foot managed a parting kick to his ankle beneath the table. He would have laughed, but it hurt too much.

Chapter Three

Dinner lost some of its lustre after that. The squire's wife on his left was quite willing to engage in light flirtatious banter, but it was far less exciting than sparring with the stoic Lady Alixe. It had been a hard-won battle to wring the slightest smile from Lady Alixe, who'd been trying so desperately to ignore him. The squire's wife smiled rather easily and laughed at everything, a conquest of moments.

After-dinner brandy dragged on with tedium. Merrick spent most of his time attempting to align the pretty but remote Lady Alixe from dinner with the openly curious girl at the pond. There'd been signs of that girl. Lady Alixe's wit was finely honed and quite humorous in a dry sense when she gave it free rein. But she clearly hadn't wanted to be recognised and not surprisingly so. If anyone got wind of their encounter the consequence could be dire for them both.

For the record, he'd have to be clear on that point with Ashe and Riordan. He didn't truly worry they'd match the girl up with Lady Alixe. They'd been too far out in the pond to get a good look at her today and Lady Alixe wasn't the type of girl either of them would look twice at. Most of that was Lady Alixe's own doing, Merrick suspected. She had many excellent features. She simply chose not to maximise them and her sharp tongue would deter anyone from looking more closely at what was on offer. Ordinarily, he'd not have looked more closely either if it hadn't been for the incident at the pond.

But now that he had, he wanted an even closer look at Lady Alixe Burke, who lived in something of a self-imposed social limbo. She had the potential to be pretty, had the propensity for clever conversation and had her father's money. There was no reason she wasn't up in London dazzling the *ton*'s bachelors or at the very least kicking them in the shins. Merrick smiled to himself. Hmmm. A mystery. If there was *no reason*, then by logical extension there was a *very good reason* she wasn't in London. He was eager to get back to the drawing room.

In the drawing room, Merrick spotted Lady Alixe quickly. She was precisely where he thought she'd be, sitting on a sofa with an elderly neighbour, patiently listening to whatever the lady was saying. He filed the information away. Lady Alixe fancied herself a retiring sort, a bookish sort. What was it she'd said at dinner? She worked with local historians? Intriguing.

He approached the sofa and made the appropriate flattering remarks to the older lady, who probably only heard half of them. 'Lady Alixe, might I steal you away for a moment or two?'

'What could you possibly have left to say to me?' she asked as Merrick manoeuvred them over to ostensibly take in a painting on the far wall.

'I think we need to agree that our encounter is to remain a private event between the two of us,' Merrick said in low tones.

'I do not wish to have you blather about it to anyone any more than you would want me to publicly discover that the girl in question was you. We both know what society's answer to such a scandal would be.'

'I do not "blather".'

'Of course not, Lady Alixe. My apologies. I confused blathering with kicking me under the table.'

She ignored the reference. 'And your friends, they do not blather either, I assume.'

'No, they will not say anything,' Merrick promised.

'Then we have reached an accord and you need not seek my company out again.'

'Why so unfriendly, Lady Alixe?'

'I know men like you.'

He smiled at that. 'What, precisely, is a "man like me"?'

'Trouble, with a capital "T".'

'That might be because you're beginning the sentence with it.'

'Or it might be because you charm women into compromising themselves with you. You, sir, are a rake if ever I've seen one.'

'Have you seen one? A rake? How would you know?

Oh, I forgot, you've seen the *David*. Well, for your information, I know women like you, too. You think you don't have much use for men, but that's because you haven't met the right one.'

That sobered her up. 'You are too bold and you are no gentleman.'

Merrick laughed. 'No, I'm not. You should have known better, Lady Alixe. Don't young misses learn in the schoolroom that you can always tell a gentleman by his clothes?'

Her jaw tightened. 'I must admit, my lord, on that point you have me at a distinct disadvantage.' Lady Alixe turned on her heel and made a smart retreat to the newly arrived tea cart.

In a quiet corner of the room, Archibald Redfield watched the animated exchange between St Magnus and Alixe Burke. It was the second such interaction they'd had that evening. He couldn't hear what was being said, but St Magnus was laughing and Alixe Burke was in a high-coloured huff as she set off for the tea cart. That was nothing new. Alixe Burke was a shrew in his opinion. He didn't have much use for sharp-tongued women unless they were rich or knew how to use their tongues in other ways.

Fortunately Alixe Burke was quite rich and so he tolerated what he classified as her less-attractive qualities. Redfield tapped his fingers idly on the arm of the chair, considering. Things were not getting off to a brilliant start. He'd come to the house party with the specific intention of putting himself into Alixe Burke's good graces. She'd shunned his advances earlier this spring and he was hoping to recoup his losses there. He'd arrived early that afternoon, only to discover she was out somewhere. She hadn't put in an appearance until dinner and then she had been seated too far away from him for conversation. Now, that libertine from London was stealing a march on him.

It was not to be tolerated. He had chosen Alixe Burke as a most specific target. She was the reason he was in this sleepy part of Kent to begin with. He'd done his research in London, looking for 'forgotten' heiresses, or wealthy spinsters on the shelf. In other words, women who might be susceptible to a man's charms, or families desperate to marry them off. That's when he'd heard of Alixe Burke, from a viscount she'd rejected. She hadn't been back in town since. So he'd come to her, pretending to be a gentleman. He'd even gone so far as to buy an old manse in the area to complete the charade. After having done so much, he would not lose his advantage to a golden-haired second son who deserved the title of 'lord' no more than he did himself.

St Magnus—where had he heard that name? Oh, yes, the son of the Marquis of Crewe. Always in the midst of a scandal—most lately it had been something with the Greenfield Twins. Redfield was thoughtful for a moment. Maybe he could use St Magnus and his wild tendencies, after all. He would wait and watch for his opportunity.

Alixe had taken the first opportunity to retire for the night, something she should have done hours ago.

In the privacy of her room, Alixe pulled the pins from her hair and shook the dark mass free, breathing a sigh of relief.

The evening had gone moderately well if she counted the fact that this time she'd managed to stay upright in his presence. Kicking him was probably not the best choice, but, all in all, she had survived mostly intact. Somehow she'd managed to sit through dinner *beside* him and not become entirely witless under the barrage of his clever conversation. While it hadn't gone well, it certainly could have gone worse. If things had gone well, he wouldn't have shown up at all. If things had gone worse…worse hardly bore thinking about. After all, he hadn't shouted their encounter from the rooftops and he'd sworn himself to secrecy.

Her secret was safe with him and depressingly so. If the secret got out, he'd have to marry her and that could hardly be what a man like Merrick St Magnus wanted. He'd want a beautiful, stylish woman who said sophisticated things.

Alixe gave her reflection in the mirror a sultry smile, a smile she'd never dare to use in public. She pulled the bodice of her gown down a bit lower and shrugged a coy shoulder. 'Why, St Magnus, it is you. I hardly recognised you with your clothes on.' She gave a toss of her head and lowered her voice to a purr. 'So you do have clothes. I was beginning to wonder after all this time.' A sophisticated woman would trail a well-manicured nail down his chest, look up at him with smoky eyes and he would know exactly what she wanted. And then he'd give it to her. One had only to look at him to know his body didn't promise pleasure idly. Whereas, she would only be that sophisticated woman in the solitude of her room.

Alixe pulled up the bodice of her gown and rang for her maid. It was time to put the fantasy to bed, among other things. That was precisely what St Magnus was. What he promised was a temporary escape. It wasn't real.

She knew what society said a real marriage was. It was what her handful of lacklustre suitors had seen when they looked at her: a responsible alliance that came with an impeccable lineage, a respectable dowry and a nice bosom. Admittedly, it was a lot to look beyond. No one had made the effort yet. That suited her. She'd seen the reality and decided it was better to hole up in the country with her work than to become trapped in a miserable relationship.

Her maid entered the room and helped her out of the dress and into her nightgown, brushed out her hair and turned down her bedcovers. It was the same routine every night and it would be for the rest of her life. Alixe crawled beneath the covers and shut her eyes, trying to shut out the day. But Merrick St Magnus's face was not easily dismissed. His deep blue eyes danced in her head as her mind chased around the question, 'Shouldn't there be more than this?'

After a restless half-hour, Alixe threw back the covers and snatched up a robe. Sleep was hours away. She could use the time productively, making up for what she'd lost this afternoon at the lake. She'd go to the li-

brary and work on her manuscript. Then, she'd try to
sleep and when she woke up she would spend the day
avoiding St Magnus. A man like him was anathema to
a girl like her. Women didn't want to resist St Magnus
and she was not arrogant enough to think it would be
any different for her. He'd never be more than trouble
to any girl. Heaven help the fools who actually fell in
love with him.

The routine was somewhat successful in its goal.
Over the next few days, she did her best to keep out of
St Magnus's way. She was careful to come down only
after the men had left for whatever manly excursion
had been planned for their mornings while the ladies
took care of their correspondence and needlework. At
dinner, she managed to avoid being seated next to him.
After dinner, she retired as early as courtesy allowed,
to her brother's dismay, and spent her evenings in the
library.

That was not to say she'd been entirely successful
in erasing the presence of Merrick St Magnus. She did
sneak a few glances at dinner. It was hard not to. When
he was in the room he became its centre, a golden sun
around which the rest of the company revolved. She'd
hear his voice in the halls, always laughing, always
ready with a quip. If she was on the verandah quietly
reading, he'd be on the lawns playing bowls with Jamie.
If she was taking her turn at the pianoforte in the evenings, he was playing cards near by, charming the old
ladies. It quickly became apparent her only real retreat

was the library, the one room he had no inclination or purpose to visit. That was all right with her—a girl needed time to herself.

Chapter Four

❦

As house parties went, this one was proving to be exceptionally virtuous. There were guests aplenty of just the right ages and gender to make an excellent population for all the different entertainments Lady Folkestone had meticulously planned. But while the girls were pretty and the widows or other unattached ladies of a certain age happy to flirt lightly with their conversation, they were all respectable. In fact, after three days of taking the party's measure, Merrick concluded the girls in attendance were as notorious for their goodness as the Greenfield Twins were for their badness, a comparison he voiced out loud to the late-night group of gentlemen who'd gathered restlessly in the billiards room after the rest of the company had gone up to bed.

The eight gentlemen laughed heartily at his complaint. It wasn't that Merrick did not appreciate the house party. The affair was brilliant on all accounts. The entertainments were actually entertaining; there had been fishing for the gentlemen just today in the East Stour River at Postling. There'd been cards and billiards with light wagering on the side that had allowed Merrick to add to his stash of pound notes. Certainly not the sums available in London's gaming hells, but something all the same. The food was excellent, Folkestone's easy largesse abundantly displayed on the dining-room sideboards with three meals a day and two teas.

Above all, Merrick was thankful. Whatever was lacking in his usual vices, simply being here offset the loss. Here, he could take double pleasure in having thwarted his father's attempt to rein him in and in having minimised his expenses. For the next two weeks he was free.

All he had to do was please the ladies in attendance. If that pleasing occurred outside the bedroom door, that was a small price to pay. To date, Merrick had done an admirable job of fulfilling his obligations. He'd made himself available to all the ladies present, from elderly Mrs Pottinger to shy young Viola Fleetham. The only lady he'd been unable to charm was the elusive Alixe Burke, whom he had only caught glimpses of since the first evening. It was too bad, really; he enjoyed needling her just to hear what she'd say.

'St Magnus, tell us about some of your scandals in London,' one of the younger fellows present piped up. 'I hear you had quite the curricle race recently.'

'I hear you nearly had carnal knowledge of both Greenfield Twins at the same time,' another rash young pup put in. 'Tell us about that.'

'That's nothing, laddies, compared to his escapade on the way here,' Riordan drawled, swigging heavily from the ever-present flask. Riordan had drunk far too much for Merrick's tastes since they'd arrived, but saying anything about it made him sound like a prude so he'd refrained. 'Tell 'em about the pond.'

Merrick shot Riordan a quelling look. The man was worse than an old biddy. The last thing Merrick wanted to do was talk about the pond. 'That's hardly anything, nothing happened,' Merrick tried to pass it off.

'It's hilarious,' Riordan protested. 'Never mind, if you won't tell it, I will.' He recognised he had the audience hanging on his every word. Riordan leaned forwards hands on thighs. 'We stopped by a pond for a bit of a bathe before we arrived.'

'Which pond?' one asked before another punched him in the shoulder for being a dolt.

'The one on the edge of the property, near Richland's farm.' Riordan said, idly picking up the story again. 'Anyway, *where* the pond is isn't the real tale. It's *what* happened. There we were, stripped down to nothing and splashing away when all of the sudden this girl comes crashing through the woods.' Riordan paused and clapped Merrick on the back in male camaraderie. 'Our man gets out of the pond and startles the poor chit senseless. She's so overwhelmed by the sight of his pizzle she falls over a log and can't get up, so this good chap here offers to help her up. Mind you, he's naked as a newborn babe the whole time and there's more dangling over her than just his hand.'

There was a general uproar of laughter around him,

a few of them slapping him on the back with comments like, 'St Magnus, you're the luckiest devil ever, women literally fall over themselves to get to you.' Merrick tried to laugh good naturedly with them. Normally, he would have laughed the loudest. Riordan was a great storyteller—he'd turned the escapade into the stuff of legends. But knowing the girl in question was Jamie's sister gave the tale a dangerous edge.

Women *did* fall over themselves for him and what he offered, but they were women who could afford the luxury. The Greenfield Twins were courtesans, for heaven's sake. That was the kind of woman he dabbled with. They were like him. He never trifled with women who couldn't afford to play his games, never made them the butt of his wagers. No one suffered for his entertainments. The Greenfield Twins had *wanted* him to take them both. But Alixe Burke had wanted no part of what had happened at the pond. His code of ethics demanded he protect her. That was where he differed from his father. The innocent deserved protection when their paths crossed with those more worldly.

'It's easy to seduce the willing,' came the words from a handsome but sly-eyed fellow lounging on the group's periphery. Redfield was his name. Merrick didn't care for him. He was always watching people. 'Why don't we have you prove your reputation? We'll design a wager for you.'

Merrick raised his eyebrows at that. What in the world could these young rascals design that would actually stump *him*?

'We should all get to wager on it. I'll bet on St Mag-

nus to do just about anything. I'm in.' Ashe withdrew
a money clip from a waistcoat pocket and laid its contents on the table. 'Shall we split the winnings, old
chap?' Ashe winked at him.

Merrick appreciated the show of support, but not the
mounting pressure. Ashe's finances were no more stable than his own. If Ashe was in, there'd be no backing
out. He couldn't let his friend down. To be fair, Merrick didn't want to back out. The money accumulating
on the table was no small sum. He couldn't win that
sum at the genteel wagers made at cards in the next
two weeks. Yet, a very small piece of his conscience
niggled him to be cautious.

Merrick drew a deep breath and fixed the young
cockerel with a confident stare. 'What shall you dare
me to do?'

'Well, since the party is so "virtuous" in your own
words, I think you should steal a kiss before sunrise.'

'You can kiss me right now, St Magnus, and we'll
claim victory before midnight,' Ashe quipped drily
from his corner.

'Rule number one, you must steal a kiss from a *lady*,'
Redfield qualified. 'That means no going belowstairs to
wake the maids, that's too easy.' Redfield looked like
the sort who would know; probably spent too much
time chasing the maids since he couldn't catch anyone
else. Everyone knew the maids were somewhat obliged
to endure such advances if they valued their positions.
Merrick didn't respect a man like that.

'Other rules?' Merrick enquired coolly. He was already thinking of who'd be most likely to put up with such a dare. The attractive Widow Whitely, perhaps.

'Proof, we must have proof,' one of Redfield's chums put in. The wagering had created a clear division between the young bucks and the 'old regime'.

That was potentially dangerous. 'No, I draw the line there,' Merrick spoke up. 'A token might be recognised, thus incriminating the lady. I won't be a party to that. You'll just have to take my word as a gentleman.' That brought a round of laughter as he expected and Redfield had to relent on that account.

Redfield's eyes gleamed wickedly. 'Since we must keep the game decent, I say St Magnus must confine his efforts to the library. There will be no roaming of the house or sneaking into bedrooms.'

There went the idea of enticing Widow Whitely. Merrick had the distinct impression she didn't read much. But neither did he. 'It's a little past midnight, I doubt there's much feminine traffic in the library at this hour.' Merrick shrugged. 'What happens if I sit there all night and no one suitable for kissing shows up?'

'Then no one wins or loses,' Redfield replied too easily for Merrick's liking. Redfield thought someone would be there. Merrick could see it in the confident tilt of his head. The man was an ass and a pompous one at that. He was a silly man, too, if this wager was the best he could do for excitement. But Redfield clearly had something planned. Did Redfield think whoever would be in the library would be immune to his charms? Merrick was equally as confident. He had stolen far more than kisses for far less than the money lying there on the billiards table and no one had had any complaints. Whatever Redfield had in mind, Merrick wouldn't know what it was if he didn't go and find out. With an exaggerated salute to the crowd, Merrick set out for the library.

The library was dark when Merrick arrived. No surprise there. It was late for reading unless someone was having difficulty sleeping. Merrick took his time, lighting a few of the lamps and giving the room some life. It was a well-appointed room with a long reading table that ran down the centre, a green-veined marble fireplace with a cluster of chairs and sofa about it, a few small tables and chairs scattered near the wide windows for reading and walls lined with carefully selected books.

Merrick scanned the titles with modest interest. He could see Jamie's hand in the selection. Jamie had excelled at history while they were at Oxford and his love for the subject was readily evident in the titles on display. For himself, Merrick hadn't the aptitude for history like Jamie, or Italian music like Ashe or Riordan's love of Renaissance art. He'd discovered his own niche in languages, a field where he could excel in conversation.

Merrick plucked a book from the shelf at random and settled into a chair near the fireplace to wait. He'd managed to get through the first five pages when the door opened. The newcomer was definitely female, dressed in a plain-blue robe with the hem of a white nightrail peeping beneath it. Her back was to him, showing off a long thick braid of nut-brown hair as she made great effort to quietly shut the door behind her. Whoever she was, she wasn't supposed to be here or at the very least didn't want to be discovered here. He couldn't help her with that. Any moment now she'd turn around and be surprised to see him.

But then she did turn and the surprise was all his. Damn and double damn, the one person who'd come to the library was the one person he hadn't seen for days: Alixe Burke. Suspicion flicked across his mind for an instant. He'd hardly got settled, hardly begun to read his admittedly boring tome on the history of French kings, and she'd shown up. If he'd stopped along the way, he might have missed his chance altogether. Had Redfield known she'd be here? A simple wager was becoming suddenly more complex.

Merrick grinned. 'So this is where you've been hiding.'

Alixe clutched the neck of her robe closed at the throat out of instinct. 'What are *you* doing here?'

'You sound surprised to see me.' Merrick waved the book he held in one hand. 'I am reading up on the French kings.'

'I'm surprised to see *anyone* in the library after midnight,' Alixe retorted.

'And yet *you're* here,' he replied glibly, those blue eyes of his studying her with a disquieting intensity that stirred up a warm flurry of butterflies in her stomach. That look made a woman believe he was waiting just for her. Yet, that was improbable. He hadn't known she'd be here.

'Why aren't you playing billiards with the other men?' She was surprised, disturbed, dismayed. The list of adjectives was quite long. Three days of avoiding him and he'd still managed to turn her thoughts to incoherent mush in a matter of minutes. She needed him to go away.

She'd hoped to make some progress on her latest translation. She'd promised Vicar Daniels she'd have the translation ready for display at the village fair less than two weeks away.

'I haven't seen much of you since the party began. I hope you haven't been avoiding me?' Merrick said casually. He kicked his booted legs, very *long* booted legs, up on the fireplace fender, dispelling any hopes that he might vacate the premises soon. Apparently the French kings were more scintillating than she'd thought.

'Of course not. Why would you think that?' Alixe said, hoping her lie wouldn't show.

Merrick shrugged. 'I'm glad to hear it. I thought perhaps our encounter at the pond had disconcerted you in spite of my assurances.' He opened his book and returned to his reading.

Dratted man. Why did he have to pick tonight to read? Alixe began to debate the options in her head: stay or go? This was absurd. Conventional wisdom suggested she leave the room immediately. Unmarried women didn't entertain men in their nightclothes. Unmarried women didn't entertain naked men at ponds either and she'd already done that. By comparison, this was by far the lesser of those two evils. She should leave.

But her stubborn nature could not tolerate defeat. The thought of departing the field while her work beckoned galled. No man had ever dictated her choices over decisions far bigger than this. She wouldn't give up ground over something so minor. St Magnus had already cost her an afternoon. She would not let him steal a night, too. There was always a chance she could outlast him.

'Are you going to come away from the door? You needn't worry, I've seen ball gowns far more revealing than your nightwear.' He spoke without looking up from his book, but the challenge was clear. He was daring her to stay.

Alixe made a face at the back of his head. She must look like a silly ninny to him, clutching her old robe and hovering at the door. Is that what he saw when he looked at her? A spinster afraid of being in the presence of a dazzlingly handsome man?

Anger flared. That settled it.

She *wasn't* a spinster.

She wasn't afraid.

She also wasn't leaving.

Alixe stalked towards the long table in the centre of the room and pulled out a chair. She sat down and did her best to get to work. It was clear she'd have to try harder to avoid St Magnus. She had not fought her battles for the freedom to live her own life only to give up those victories to a pair of flirting blue eyes. Still, it was better to know the chinks in one's own armour before one's enemy did. She'd recognised that day at the pond St Magnus's potent appeal and how she'd responded most wantonly. It would not do to keep putting such temptation in her path if it could be avoided.

She'd managed the bucks of the *ton*, but they didn't unnerve her the way he did. St Magnus's witty and overly personal conversation at dinner had made her feel unique, made her feel that she was beautiful enough on her own merits to attract the attentions of a handsome man without her dowry to speak for her. But he was a rake. Nothing good could come from an association with St Magnus. She was smart enough to know that from the start.

Her efforts to work lasted all of five minutes.

'What are you working on?'

Alixe looked up from her books and papers. He'd turned his head to watch her. 'I'm translating an old medieval manuscript about the history of Kent.' That should bore him enough to stop asking questions. 'The vicar is putting on an historic display about our area at the upcoming fair and this document is supposed to be part of it.' She put an extra emphasis on 'supposed', to imply that interruptions were not welcome. Usually, such a hint did the trick. Usually there was no need to resort to that second level of defence. Men stopped being interested much earlier. The words 'translating an old medieval manuscript' were typically enough.

In this case, the effect was quite opposite. St Magnus uncrossed his long legs, set aside the French kings and strode towards the table with something akin to interest in his blue eyes. 'How's it going?'

'How's *what* going?' Alixe clutched at the neck of her robe again out of reflex, her tone sharp.

'Your translation? I take it the original isn't in modern English.' St Magnus gestured towards the papers.

It wasn't going well at all. The old French was proving to be difficult, especially in places where the manuscript had worn away or been smudged. But she wasn't going to admit that to this man who played havoc with her senses.

Three days of assiduously avoiding his company had not met with successful results. All her efforts, and he ended up in her—*her*—library anyway, the one room where she thought she'd be alone. Her avoidance strategies certainly hadn't dulled her awareness of him either. Even at midnight, he still looked immaculate. His shoulders were just as broad, his legs just as long, his hips just as lean as she remembered them. She knew for a fact that well-hewn muscle lay beneath the layers of his clothes, providing the necessary infrastructure for that most excellent physique. But all that was merely window-dressing for the arresting blue eyes that had a way of looking at one as if they could see right through a person's exterior, stripping away more than clothes, making one believe she was, for the moment, the centre of his universe.

She had to remind herself that plenty of women had been the centre of his universe. Jamie's quiet caution ran through her head. St Magnus was a fine friend for a gentleman, but not for the sisters of gentlemen. She had no trouble believing it.

'Perhaps I can help?' He settled his long form beside her on the bench.

Alixe's senses vibrated with warning. She could smell the remnants of his evening *toilette* before dinner, the scent of his washing soap mingling with a light cologne, a tantalising mixture of oak and lavender, with something mysterious beneath.

'I doubt it unless you have some familiarity with Old French.' She meant to be rude, meant to drive him off with her high-handed manner. How dare he walk into her life unannounced and stir things up? And not even mean to do it. He was a stranger who knew nothing about her. He had no idea of what his mere presence had done. She'd just reached a point where she was happy with her choices, with devoting her life to her work. The very last thing she needed was to convince herself a man of St Magnus's ilk appreciated her efforts and not her dowry. In the past, that road had been extremely dangerous, not to mention disappointing, to travel.

St Magnus's next words stunned her. 'It just so happens that I have more than a passing acquaintance with Old French.'

This flaxen-haired charmer with azure eyes was conversant in an obscure language? What he did next was even more astonishing. He shrugged out of his jacket and rolled up his sleeves. He slid closer to her, oblivious to their thighs bumping beneath the table.

She wasn't oblivious, however. Every nerve in her body was acutely aware of each move he made.

'The document isn't that exciting.' Alixe tried one last time to turn him away. 'It's just a farmer who writes about his livestock. He's especially obsessed with his pigs.'

Merrick tilted his head and studied her. She shifted uncomfortably in her seat. '*Just* a farmer who writes? In this case, it's not what he writes about that is important, it's that he writes at all.'

The import of it struck her with a shocking clarity. In her hurry to translate the document she'd forgotten to look beyond the words on the page and into the context of the times in which it had been written. 'Of course,' she murmured. 'A farmer who is literate most likely isn't only a farmer or a tenant renting fields, he's probably of some status in the community.'

Merrick smiled. It was a different smile this time, one full of enthusiasm. 'What's the date of the document?'

'My guess is mid-thirteenth century, about 1230.'

'Post-Magna Carta,' Merrick mused more to himself than to her. 'Perhaps he is a self-made man, an early instance of the gentry class, not a noble or beholden directly to a king, but a man who has determined his own worth.' He sounded almost wistful as he voiced his thoughts.

'In pigs.' Alixe smiled. 'Don't forget the pigs.'

Merrick chuckled. 'Show me the pigs. After all your mentions of them, I want to read about them for myself.'

Alixe passed him the pages on the pigs and he fell to reading them with surprising thoroughness, one long finger moving across the lines one word at a time, his eyes following. Within moments, he was completely absorbed in the reading and Alixe turned her thoughts to the pages in front of her, aware in the back of her mind that something astounding had occurred: she was working on her translation with Merrick St Magnus, London's most talked-about male. More than that, he'd shown himself to be more than a handsome face. He'd been interested, intelligent and insightful. Amazing.

Truly, it was nothing short of miraculous. No one would believe her if she told them. She was starting to see why a friendship had sprung up between Merrick and Jamie at school. Like her, Jamie loved history and Merrick understood its sociological aspects.

Merrick laughed suddenly, breaking the compatible silence that had sprung up. 'It's not his pigs he writes about, Alixe.' His eyes were dancing with good humour. 'It's his wife.'

Alixe furrowed her brow. 'I don't believe you.' She reached across him without thinking for the page. 'There…' She pointed to a line. 'That is very clearly the word for pig. More specifically, "sow".'

Merrick nodded. 'It is. But you're forgetting the use of "like". It's a simile. I think you were reading it as "she is a big sow". But we should be reading it as "she's as big as the sow".' Merrick reached around her. 'Show me the later pages. I want to bear out my hypothesis that his wife is expecting a child in the very near future.'

'Yes!' Merrick crowed a few moments later. 'He's writing about his wife. Have a look, Alixe.' He pushed the page towards her and leaned close, one arm on the other side of her to brace himself as they studied the page together.

'You're right.' Alixe enthused, her excitement evident. Her mind rushed forwards. 'I wonder if there would be parish records. I wonder if we could find him. If we could, we might be able to determine where his land was. We could find out how the story ends, if his baby is born safely.' Alixe bit her lip, realising what she'd done. She'd said 'we'. 'I'm sorry, I'm getting carried away. We'll probably never know what happened to him.'

Merrick smiled. 'Maybe *we* will. I'll be here for two weeks. Surely that's enough time to puzzle out how your farmer's story ends.' For all purposes, he looked as if he was genuinely enjoying himself. He looked as if he wanted to be here with her instead of downstairs playing billiards.

Alixe looked down at her hands, regretting some of her earlier thoughts about him. 'I must apologise. I didn't think it could be like this.'

He covered her hands with one of his own where they lay on the table. It was a gentle gesture and his hands were warm and firm. She didn't think it was meant to be a seductive gesture, but that didn't stop a *frisson* of warm heat from shooting through her arm at the contact.

'It or me? You didn't think *it* could be like this or

that *I* couldn't be like this?' Merrick spoke in low tones, his gaze holding hers.

'You,' Alixe replied honestly, meeting his gaze. 'I didn't think you could be like this. I misjudged you.'

'I'm glad to have surprised you,' Merrick said softly, his voice igniting the tiny space between them with a sharp awareness of one another. Their eyes held and in the cocoon of the moment the briefest of thoughts occurred to Alixe: he's going to kiss me.

That was exactly the same idea voiced seconds later when Archibald Redfield burst into the library with an angry, newly awoken Earl of Folkestone in his wake, still belting his robe and all but bellowing the traditional words of horrified fathers everywhere when discovering their daughters in compromising situations. 'What is the meaning of this?'

To which Alixe managed the most unoriginal of answers, 'It's not what it looks like.' But she knew what it looked like—Merrick sitting so very close to her, his sleeves rolled up, and she in her nightclothes.

To which Archibald Redfield countered unhelpfully with an arrogant smirk, 'It's precisely what it looks like. St Magnus wagered several gentlemen in the billiards room not an hour ago that he'd steal a kiss from a lady before the night was out', then went on to add as if it would improve matters, 'I have witnesses.'

Alixe groaned. He'd bet on stealing a kiss. She should have left the room when common sense had demanded it.

'No, no witnesses, please.' Her father held up the hand of authority. He had his robe belted now and was in full command of the situation. 'We are all men of honour here,' He looked pointedly at St Magnus as he said it. 'We can sort this out and do what must be done in a quiet manner. There is no need to make an unnecessary fuss.'

Alixe had never seen her father so angry. No one else would guess the depths of his anger. He was one of those men whose voice became more controlled when angered. Then he spared a glance for her, taking in her completely inappropriate attire. There was more than anger in his gaze. There was disappointment, which was worse. She'd seen it before when he looked at her. It seemed she'd spent an inordinate amount of her life disappointing him. But this time would be the last time. She could see in his face he'd decided it would be so and that frightened her very much.

Her father jerked his head at her with a dismissing nod. 'Go to your room and stay there. We'll speak in the morning. As for you, St Magnus, I'll settle with you right now. Put your jacket on and make yourself presentable.'

Alixe shot a parting glance at St Magnus, although what help she thought she'd find there she didn't know. He'd never been truly interested in her or her work. She'd merely been his most convenient target. He would have kissed whoever walked into the library. He had no reason to help her and, right now, he'd be more worried about trying to help himself.

St Magnus had risen, arms folded, eyes narrowed and burning like hot blue coals. He was a formidable sight, but he spared not a glance for her departing form, she noted. All his attention was directed at Archibald Redfield.

Chapter Five

Who would have thought the road to nowhere in particular led straight to the Earl of Folkestone's library? Granted the journey had taken the better part of ten years, but right now that only served to make matters worse.

Merrick shifted ever so slightly in his chair. It was one thing to be called on the proverbial carpet by a stuffy peer when one was a young buck about town. It was another when one was nearly thirty and an established rogue. Rogues didn't get caught engaged in minor infractions. One could be caught *in flagrante delicto* with a lovely widow and live it down. But one could absolutely not be caught stealing kisses from an earl's daughter. Yet it seemed he had been and it seemed he was going to pay. The terrible irony was that he hadn't done anything. This time, everything was innocent. Admittedly it looked bad: her apparel, his shirt sleeves, the time of night, their close proximity at the table. Most of all the looming reality of the damning wager with Redfield. All the signs pointed to disaster. In another five minutes it might even have escalated to a real disaster; he might actually have claimed the kiss he was accused of stealing.

'You were attempting to kiss my daughter,' Folkestone spoke, his face a mask of icy contemplation.

'Yes, the key word here is attempting. I had not yet achieved that goal.' Merrick pointed out. Folkestone frowned, not appreciating the clarification.

'I do not care if you were attempting to turn metal into gold. It does not change the fact that you were alone with her at midnight.'

'In the library, sir,' Merrick protested. He'd been about to say the library was the least amorous room in a house, but then he remembered what he'd got up to in the library at the Rowlands' ball a few weeks ago with the lovely Mrs Dennable and thought better of it.

'Thank goodness Redfield is the soul of discretion,' Folkestone commented.

Assuming he has a soul. Merrick let a raised eyebrow convey his question of the assumption. Redfield had set it up, he was sure of that, if not the man's motives. But saying as much would appear petty and it hardly sounded better to say 'any girl would have done as well; it just so happened your daughter walked in first'.

'You've compromised my daughter, but that does not make her an innocent in this. She could have walked out of the room once you made your presence known,' Folkestone mused. His sharp dark eyes, the colour of Alixe's, never left Merrick's face.

'Alixe has always been unconventional. A husband and family would go far, I suspect, in settling her and giving her life some stability.' Merrick sensed Alixe would disagree with her father's assessment, but discreetly kept it to himself.

Folkestone continued. 'Alixe needs a husband.'

It took all of Merrick's willpower to not cringe. He waited for the inevitable. After this evening, Folkestone would expect him to do the right thing and offer for her, a girl he hardly knew.

Folkestone leaned back in his chair and steepled his fingers. 'I am sure you are aware that in most situations of this nature, the gentleman would be expected to marry the lady in question. However, to be blunt, you are not precisely "husband material", no matter who your father is. You have a reputation ten miles' long for licentiousness and general mayhem. Here's what I propose: make my daughter the Toast of the Season.'

Merrick sat a little straighter in his chair, not certain he'd heard correctly or that he'd been reprieved. This option might be worse. 'Sir, it's already June. There will only be six weeks left. I hardly think…'

'Or marry her yourself at Season's end as penance for your failure,' Folkestone cut in. 'You're not the only gambling man in the room, St Magnus. I know all about your reputation. You have no desire to be leg-shackled. I'm willing to bet you love your freedom enough to see the job done. Goodness knows I'd prefer almost anyone else than you as a son-in-law. I think that's one thing you and I just might agree upon. You no more want to be my son-in-law than I want to have you, no matter what Jamie thinks of you as a friend.'

Valiantly ignoring the insult, Merrick tried a different approach. 'Sir, the people I know are not the best, I'm not sure…'

This too was easily dismissed. 'You're here, aren't you?' Yes, dammit, he hadn't meant to insult the earl's sterling reputation.

'You do have connections when you choose to exert them, St Magnus. Exert them now or accept the consequences.' Folkestone rose, signalling the end of the interview. 'There's really nothing else to discuss. This is not your decision to make. You made your choice when you engaged my daughter in the library for your silly wager. You have a little under two weeks here in the country to get her up to snuff and the rest of the Season to make her attractive to gentlemen or else align yourself with the fact that you will be taking a September bride.'

The study door opened, admitting Lady Folkestone, hastily dressed and followed by Redfield. 'I've brought your wife,' he said with a tragic flourish. 'Sometimes a woman's view can soften these things.' Yes, definitely a tragic flourish. Surely a man as astute as Folkestone could see through Redfield's façade of helpfulness.

Lady Folkestone was no shrinking violet. She sailed to her husband's side and demanded an explanation, which Folkestone promptly gave. Afterwards, Lady Folkestone turned her thoughtful gaze in Merrick's direction. 'So, you're to marry our daughter?'

'Not necessarily, my lady.' Merrick replied smoothly. 'I hope to help her find a more suitable match.'

Lady Folkestone laughed. 'There is no such thing as a suitable match for Alixe. We've tried for years now. When I say "we", I mean London society collectively, not just her family. She'll have none of the young men on offer.' The bitterness surprised him. It wasn't the attitude he expected a mother to have.

Lady Folkestone waved a dismissive hand. 'She has no regard for the family's wishes. After the last business with Viscount Mandley, all she wants is her manuscripts and her peace.'

Then why don't you let her have it? Was that so much to ask? Folkestone had enough money to support one spinster daughter. The vehemence of his thoughts shocked Merrick.

'Ah, Mandley. That was an unfortunate business indeed. She'll not see a better offer,' Redfield commiserated from the doorway where he hovered as some post-facto guard to their privacy.

'Hardly,' Merrick scoffed. 'Mandley didn't want a wife, he wanted a governess for his three daughters whom he didn't have to pay.' The man might be handsome for a fellow over forty and have plenty of blunt, but he was legendary in London's clubs for his unnecessary penny-pinching. He'd once asked if his subscription to White's could be reduced for the months he spent in the country.

'There's nothing wrong with frugality,' Redfield retorted.

Ah, that reminded him. There was one score he

could settle tonight. Merrick turned and shot Redfield a hard stare. He couldn't do anything more for his own situation at present, but he could still salvage Ashe's. He rose and approached Lady Folkestone. 'I deeply apologise for the untoward actions which have taken place here tonight. I will do my utmost to see that Lady Alixe's reputation emerges from this thoughtless escapade unscathed.' With that, he bent over her hand with all the charm he possessed and kissed her knuckles. 'If you will excuse me? I will look forward to meeting with Lady Alixe in the morning.'

Merrick brushed past Redfield on his way to the door, stopping long enough to murmur, 'I believe you owe me. I'll be waiting outside and expecting payment.'

Merrick found Ashe and Riordan alone in the deserted billiards room, each of them slumped in their chairs. Crisis always had a way of thinning out the crowd. He tossed down a substantial roll of pound notes on the billiards table. 'There's your portion of the winnings.'

Ashe sat up a bit straighter. 'How did you manage this? Were you faster than Redfield?'

Merrick grinned. Besting Redfield was about the only good thing to have happened tonight. 'I kissed Lady Folkestone's hand right in front of him. He had to be the witness to his own dare.'

Ashe visibly relaxed and reached for the winnings. 'Redfield had it planned all along. After you left, he was bragging he knew a certain lady had been visiting the library the last few nights.'

Merrick stiffened at that. 'Was he careless enough to share her name?' Folkestone was counting on discretion, on the fact that no one but he and Redfield knew Alixe had been caught with him in the library.

Ashe shook his head. 'No, no names, just that he knew.'

Merrick nodded. Good. But it didn't make sense he'd deliberately set up a wager he'd lose. Unless he thought Alixe wouldn't succumb.

'But I can surmise from the presence of Lady Folkestone at the interview that the lady in question was Lady Alixe. Jamie will not be pleased,' Ashe said quietly.

'Jamie is not to know.'

'Are wedding bells in your future?' Riordan slurred, offering Merrick his flask.

Merrick waved it a way with a rueful smile. 'Sort of.' He explained the agreement to hush up the indiscretion if he 'helped' Lady Alixe become the Toast of London.

'Then you have truly become a *cicisbeo*, a man whose status and welfare in society rests on his ability to please a lady,' Riordan slurred, unmistakably well into his cups. 'You know, in Italy it works this way, too. Usually it's the husband who picks a *cicisbeo* for his wife, but in this case, her father has picked you to bring her out into society.'

'I don't think it's an apt comparison at all,' Merrick snapped, eager to cut off Riordan's rambling. He was showing all the characteristic signs of launching into a full-blown lecture on Italian culture.

Ashe idly twirled the stem of an empty snifter. 'Do you remember that night at Oxford when we formed the *cicisbei* club?'

Merrick nodded, losing himself for a moment in the reminiscences of a long-ago time. They'd been foolhardy and a bit naïve. It had seemed a wicked thrill to commit themselves to a lifestyle of 'love', to devote themselves to the pursuit of beauty in all its feminine forms.

'I suppose I've been a *cicisbeo* long before tonight,' Merrick sighed in response to Riordan's comment. He'd made a large part of his living based on charm and romance. He might not be a 'kept' man who was obviously dependent on a woman's gifts to him, but if he looked closely enough at his life, he was dependent in other ways, not that the honesty made him proud to admit it.

A 'life of love' wasn't as glamorous as they'd imagined it all those years ago sitting in a student-populated tavern. Then, the road to the future had been long and untravelled—anything was possible. They'd toasted the fact that they were second sons with no expectations placed upon them. There was nothing to inherit but a future they'd carve for themselves. They'd make great reputations as London's finest lovers. It had seemed like jolly good fun at the time.

'Don't worry about it,' Ashe said rather suddenly, his eyes serious and sober in contrast to Riordan's. 'We've all sold ourselves in some way or another. It's impossible not to.'

Merrick stood, adopting a posture of humour, not

wanting to be sucked into Ashe's maudlin philosophy. 'There's no time to worry about it. I've got a bride to transform and a bridegroom to find.'

Heaven forbid that bridegroom end up being him, Merrick mused, taking himself out into the darkened hallway and finding the way to his room. He wasn't a marrying man. His father had made sure of that ages ago and, in the intervening years, he hadn't done much to improve the notion. He was well aware there were too many rumours surrounding him and his profligate behaviours. While the rumours inspired curiosity they also inspired distrust.

An image of Alixe's face, alight with excitement over the translation, came to mind. Tonight had been an unlooked-for surprise. He'd not expected to enjoy the work so much. In fact, there'd been a point where he'd forgotten about the stupid wager altogether. For Alixe's sake, he couldn't forget himself like that again. To a woman of her standards, it wouldn't matter that while many of the rumours were true, a few of the most damaging were false.

Alone in his room, Archibald Redfield drank a silent toast. St Magnus would be gone by sunrise. A man like him had no particular code of honour. With the matrimonial noose dangling over his head, St Magnus would run as fast as he could, leaving the path to Alixe open. Archibald would be on that path, ready to approach Folkestone with an offer to rescue Alixe. Who knew what kind of rumours St Magnus would spread? It had been an expensive victory, but worth it. In one move, he'd managed to eliminate St Magnus from the house party and he'd put Alixe Burke in a corner from which he would gallantly offer to rescue her.

Archibald took another swallow of brandy. An engagement would scotch any blemish to Alixe's reputation. Archibald was certain after this last *débâcle*, Folkestone would be eager to marry Alixe off to the first man who asked, even if he was a mere mister, and Archibald would be there, only too ready to comply. Folkestone would be grateful and that could be useful, too, in perpetuity. Everything was working out brilliantly at last. He couldn't make Alixe marry him, but Folkestone could.

'You cannot make me marry anyone,' Alixe said evenly, matching her father glare for glare across the expanse of his polished mahogany desk. So, this was his plan, the plan she'd waited all night to hear. Merrick St Magnus was to marry her or find someone else to do the deed for him. It was implicitly understood that was the only reason for being made over into the Toast of London.

'I can and I will. We've tolerated your foibles long enough,' came the reply.

Her foibles? Alixe's temper rose. 'My work is important. I am restoring history about our region. This is as much the history of Kent as it is the history of our family.' Her family knew that. 'You think it's important as long as Jamie's the one doing it.'

'It's not appropriate for a woman. No man wants a woman who is more interested in ancient manuscripts than she is in him.' Her father stood up and strode around the desk. 'I know what you're thinking, miss. You're thinking somehow you'll get out of this, that you'll reject every suitor St Magnus finds and you'll find a way to run him off at the very last. If you do that, I'll cut you off without a penny and you can see exactly how it is for a woman on her own in this world without the protection of a man's good name.'

That was precisely what she was thinking: the driving-the-suitors-away part anyway. The last bit worried her. Her father would do it, too. He was furious this time. If it was possible, he was even more furious over this than he had been about her rejection of Viscount Mandley.

She had to throw him a proverbial bone if she meant to renegotiate this. 'I'll go to London after the house party and finish out the rest of the Season, *without* St Magnus.' That should appease him.

'No. You've had a chance, *more* than one chance, to turn London to your favour.' Her father sighed, but she did not mistake it for a sign that he might be relenting. 'The arrangement isn't all bad. St Magnus has a certain *savoir-faire* to him; he's stylish and charming and he's risky without being a full-fledged black rake, although he skates pretty close to the edge. Being with him will bring you a cachet of your own, it will help others see you in a different, in a *better* light. There's no real chance of actually marrying him, thank goodness. Use him and drop him, Alixe, if he's so distasteful to you. Everyone has a place in this world. It's time you learned yours.'

So much for her father's version of sympathy.

Alixe cast a beseeching glance her mother's direction, only to receive a slow shake of the head. 'Your father and I are together on this, Alixe.' No help from that quarter. Perhaps she could cajole Jamie into pleading her case. There were any number of stories he could likely tell that would persuade her father to keep her as far from St Magnus as possible.

'One more thing,' her father added. 'We are to say nothing of this to Jamie. It would create a grievous rift in his friendship. We've all agreed to keep this incident quiet.' There went her last hope. Now all that was left was to appeal directly to St Magnus. Surely he was no more enamoured of the tangle they found themselves in than she was.

Chapter Six

It was over. Her bid for freedom was truly over this time. Alixe sank down on a stone bench in the flower garden, setting her empty basket beside her. She was in no mood to pick flowers for the vases in the house, but it gave her a useful excuse to be away from the gaiety of the party. Most of the guests were still lingering over breakfast before preparing to ride out on a jaunt to the Roman ruins.

Her father had meant it this time. There would be no reprieve. In all honesty, he'd been generous in the past. He'd tolerated—she couldn't say forgiven—*tolerated* her rejection of Mandley and, before that, her rejection of the ridiculous Baron Addleborough. He'd tolerated—she couldn't say supported—what he viewed as her oddities: her preference for books and meaningful academic work. She knew it had all been done in the hope that she'd come around and eventually embrace a more traditional, accepted life.

Only it hadn't worked out that way. Instead of deciding to embrace society on her own after realising the supposed error of her ways, she'd retreated. The retreat had started simply. At first, it had been enough to stay in the country and devote her efforts to her history. Then it had become easier and easier to not go back at all. Or perhaps it had become harder to go back. Here, she was less bound by the conventions of fashion and rules under the censorious eyes of society. Here she could avoid the realities of an empty, miserable society marriage. Here, she was happy.

Mostly.

The truth was, for all the solace the country offered, she'd been restless even before St Magnus's foolish wager. She'd spent the summer roaming the countryside, looking for...something. Restlessness and loneliness were the apparent going prices for the relative freedoms afforded by the isolation of the countryside. Now, all of that was about to change and not for the better. She should be more careful what she wished for.

'There you are.'

Ah, her unlikely fairy godmother had come to make a silk purse out of sow's ear. She met St Magnus's easy demeanour with a hard stare. In that moment she hated him, truly hated him. After a night that had upended whatever future he had imagined for himself, he looked refreshed and well dressed, a rather striking contrast to the picture she knew she presented with her dark circles and plain brown gown.

She hadn't slept at all and she hadn't taken any pains this morning to disguise the fact. But St Magnus was impeccably attired for riding in buff breeches, polished boots and deep forest-green jacket. The morning sun glinted off his hair, turning it platinum in the bright light. It was the first time that she had noticed his hair was almost longer than convention dictated, hanging in loose waves to his shoulders, but not nearly long enough to club back. Or was it? Hmmm.

'Is something wrong with my face?' St Magnus enquired, lifting a hand tentatively to his cheek.

'No.' Alixe hastily dragged her thoughts to the present. Wondering about his hair would serve no purpose, no *useful* purpose anyway.

'Good. I've come to discuss our predicament.' St Magnus set her empty basket on the ground and sat down uninvited beside her on the little bench. She was acutely aware of his nearness in the small space and of the other time they'd been so close.

'Do you think this is a good idea?' She tried to slide apart, but there was no place left to slide.

'Discussing our situation?'

'No, sitting so close. The last time was a disaster.'

He eyed her with a wry look. 'I think that's the least of your worries, Alixe. It's certainly the least of mine.'

Alixe. The sound of her name on his lips, so very casual as if they were friends, as if working together last night had meant something instead of being contrived to steal a kiss, sent a small thrill through her until she remembered why he was there. She folded her hands in her lap. 'I imagine you're quite concerned about the little matter of your wager.'

'I am and you should be, too.' He stretched his long legs out in front of him and crossed his booted ankles.

'If I fail, your father will see us married. Neither of us wants that, so tell me who you want to marry and I'll see to it that you have him.'

Alixe snorted. This was like a bad fairy tale. 'How do you propose to do that? You can't wave a magic wand and conjure a husband out of thin air.'

'No, but you can. I can teach you what you need to entice your man of preference. So, name your man. Who do you want?'

Alixe stood and paced the path. 'Let me think… He should be moderately good-looking, moderately young. I don't want anyone too terribly old. He should be intelligent. I would want to have decent conversation over a lifetime of dinners. He should be respectful and he should appreciate me for who I am—'

'No,' St Magnus interrupted.

'No? He shouldn't be respectful or able to make decent conversation at meal time?'

His blue eyes flashed with irritation at her recital of characteristics. 'No, as in I don't want a list of qualities. I want a name. For example, Viscount Hargrove or Baron Hesselton.'

'Then we are at cross purposes,' Alixe snapped. 'I don't want a name. I want a man, a real person.'

St Magnus rose to meet her, arms crossed. 'Listen, Lady Alixe, you can play stubborn all summer, but that won't change the outcome, it will only change the husband.'

'And that would be intolerable since it would be you. Don't stand there and make it seem as if all your plans are for my benefit. You're only interested in saving your own precious hide,' Alixe said angrily. 'You're not concerned about me. This is all about you getting what you want, just like it was last night. You didn't care about the translation. You cared about the wager and I was fool enough to believe otherwise.'

Merrick's eyes narrowed to dangerous blue slits. Good. He was angry. She'd managed to shake his attitude of casual insouciance. It was about time he was appalled by what faced them. Goodness knew she was.

His voice was cold when he spoke. 'We are most unfortunately in this mess together. You can either take my help and take charge of how this ends, or you can be saddled with me for a husband. I assure you, such a result will only bring you grief.'

She saw the truth in it. Marriage to a man like St Magnus was perhaps worse than the reality of a traditional society alliance. At least then there would be no illusions like there had been momentarily last night.

'Are you threatening me?' Alixe tipped her chin high. Women who married the fantasy were inevitably betrayed when their husbands created the fantasy with other lovers.

'That's your father's threat, my dear, not mine.' Mischief twinkled in his eyes. 'I think you might enjoy certain aspects of being married to me. It's not as though it's a case of *caveat emptor*. You know exactly what you're getting. There won't be any surprises when the clothes come off on our wedding night, after all.'

Alixe felt the hot blush creep up her neck. This man was impossible. 'Really, you must stop mentioning it.'

St Magnus laughed. 'I probably will when it ceases

to make you blush. Now, we must get you back to the house and get you changed for the excursion out to the Roman ruins.'

This was too much. 'You do not have the ordering of me.'

'I thought we'd established that I do until you choose another husbandly candidate.' There was almost a chill to his tone, cautioning that she'd better be careful about pushing this man too far. His easy manners hid a deeper, angrier soul. It was a surprise to discover it. Nothing in his behaviour to date had suggested such a facet to his personality existed. The glimpse was gone as quickly as it had come.

'I hadn't planned to go on the excursion.' She picked up the flower basket.

'I hadn't planned to get caught in the library with you.'

She turned to face him with hands on hips. 'Look, I'm sorry you lost your wager, but that doesn't give you leave to make my life any more miserable than it has to be under the circumstances.'

'I think you'd better get used to calling me Merrick, and you're wrong about the wager. I won, after all.' He gave her a cocky grin. 'I kissed your mother.'

She knew the look on her face was one of pure astonishment. She couldn't help it. The most incredible statements kept coming out of this man's mouth. 'You kissed my mother?'

St Magnus—no, *Merrick*, chuckled and sauntered down the path back towards the house. 'On the hand, my dear girl,' he called over his shoulder. 'I'll see you in half an hour at the carriages. Don't even think about being late.'

Alixe humphed and stomped her foot. He was infuriating. She had no doubts he'd come looking for her if she wasn't there. She'd tried to avoid him this morning and he'd found her anyway. Well, he could demand she be at the carriages, but he couldn't tell her what to wear. Alixe smiled to herself. He'd soon see what a Herculean labour her father had set before him. When her father realised there was no way Merrick could free himself from marrying her, her father would relent. Her father didn't want Merrick for a son-in-law.

Alixe hummed her way back to the house. For the first time since midnight, she had a plan and it *would* work. Then she'd be right back where she'd begun the summer. Never mind that the two words 'restless' and 'lonely' hovered on the periphery of her thoughts. She'd worry about that later. At present, she had a husband to lose.

She was prompt, Merrick would give her that. At precisely eleven o'clock, Alixe Burke presented herself on the front steps with the other milling guests, ready for the outing to the ruins. It was something of a surprise that she was on time given she looked a fright. Mastering such an unattractive, nay, *invisible* look took time.

If he'd been wearing a hat, he would have tipped it to her in temporary recognition of victory. She wasn't going to concede quietly. Lucky for him, he liked a challenge. Just as long as he won in the end.

Merrick excused himself from the group he chatted with and made his way to Miss Burke's side. '*Touché*, Lady Alixe,' he said in low tones for her ear alone. 'You will have to do much better than that.'

Her eyes flashed, but her chance for a rejoinder was cut short by the arrival of carriages and horses. There were a few moments of organised pandemonium while Lady Folkestone sorted everyone into vehicles and those who wished to ride.

Alixe chose to ride. Merrick watched Alixe mount the roan mare, taking in the leaping head on the pommel of her side saddle. She was something of a serious horsewoman, then. No one would consider jumping without it. That she considered jumping at all said something about the quality of her riding. She reached down to adjust the balance strap on her stirrup, further testimony to her competence. That was when he looked more closely at the hideous habit. Its lines weren't ugly. In fact, the outfit was efficiently cut. It was merely the colour. Where other women wore traditional blue and greens, she'd chosen a mousy grey that did nothing to enhance the amber sherry of her eyes or the chocolate lustre of her hair.

'You don't fool me for a moment, Alixe,' he said casually once the crowd had separated into groups along the road. The road was only wide enough for two to ride abreast and the riders had neatly paired off with the partner of their choice. Merrick would remember what a formidable hostess Lady Folkestone was. No doubt, this outing was designed with matchmaking in mind, the road chosen for this exact purpose. There'd be plenty of chances for the young couples to exchange semi-private conversations while in plain sight of others along the road to the ruins. It was a stroke of brilliance on his hostess's part.

'What fooling would you be referring to?' She kept her eyes straight ahead, her tone cool.

'This attempt to be invisible, not to mention unattractive. It will take more than that to get me to beg your father to reconsider, or to send me running back to London, refusing to honour my agreement.'

'Perhaps I like this habit. Perhaps you err by insulting a lady's dress.'

Merrick laughed out loud. 'You forget I saw your evening gown a few nights back. At least one item in your wardrobe suggests you have some sense of fashion. As for your "liking" the habit, I *do* think you like that riding habit. I think you like being invisible. It gives you permission to sail through life without being noticed and that makes you unaccountable. People can only talk about things they see.'

That made her head swivel in his direction. 'How dare you?' Now she was angry. The earlier cool hauteur had melted under the rising heat of her temper.

'How dare I do what?' Merrick stoked the coals a little more. He liked her better this way—she was real when she was angry.

'You know what I mean.'

'I do and I want to be sure *you* know what I mean. I want you to say it.' The real Lady Alixe didn't think about what she was going to say or do, she just did it, like kicking him under the table. Such a quality would make her unique, set her apart from the pattern-card women of the *ton*. Well, maybe not the kicking part, but there was a certain appeal in her freshness. The real Lady Alixe had a natural wit and a sharp understanding of human nature. The masked Lady Alixe was prim and invisible and quite the stick-in-the-mud. That Lady Alixe thought too much and acted upon too little, tried too hard to be something she wasn't—a woman devoid of any feeling.

Merrick took in the smooth profile of her jaw, the firm set of her mouth. There was plenty of feeling in Lady Alixe. She'd simply chosen to stifle it. It would certainly help his cause if he could work out why. Then he could coax it back to life.

She wasn't going to answer his question. 'It's not in your best interest to ignore me, Alixe,' he prodded.

'I know. Don't remind me. If I ignore you now, I'll spend the rest of my life ignoring you as my husband.' She rolled her eyes in exasperation. If the road had allowed room for it, Merrick was sure she'd like to have trotted on ahead. But she couldn't keep running from this; surely she knew it.

Just when he thought he'd made her squirm a bit mentally, forced her to face the reality of her situation, she startled him. 'You are quite the hypocrite, St Magnus. How dare you accuse me of being invisible for the sake of *unaccountability* when you've made yourself flagrantly *visible* for the same reason. Don't look so surprised, St Magnus. I warned you I knew men like yourself.'

'I warned you I knew women like you.'

'So you did. I suppose that gives us something in common.'

Merrick gave her the space of silence. He wasn't impervious to her feelings. He understood she was angry and he was the only available outlet for that anger. He also understood he was the only one with a chance of truly emerging victorious from this snare. He could turn her into London's Toast and walk away. He'd still be free to go about his usual ambling through society. But Lady Alixe's days of freedom would be over whether he succeeded or not. He did feel sorry for her, but he could not say it or show it. She would not want pity, least of all his. Honestly, though, she had to help him a bit with this or they would end up leg-shackled and her chance to choose her fate would be sealed. She was too intelligent to be blind to that most obvious outcome.

Alixe kept her eyes fixed on the road ahead. St Magnus's silence was far worse than the light humour of his conversation. His silence left her plenty of time to be embarrassed. She wanted to take back her hot words. They'd been mean and cruel and entirely presumptuous. She still could not believe they'd tumbled out of her mouth. She wasn't even sure she truly thought them, believed them. She'd known St Magnus for a handful of hours, far too little time to make such a damning judgement. It might have been the unkindest thing she'd ever said.

She snuck a sideways look at him in the periphery of her vision. Thankfully, he did not *look* affected by her harsh words. Instead, he looked confident and at ease. He'd chosen to ride without a hat and now the sun played through his hair, turning it a lovely white-blonde shade aspiring debutantes would envy. Buttermilk. That was it. His hair reminded her of fresh buttermilk.

'Yes?'

Oh, dear. He'd caught her staring—gawking, really—like a schoolroom miss. But his remarkable blue eyes were friendly, warm even. 'I'm terribly sorry. I spoke out of turn. It wasn't well done of me,' Alixe managed to stammer. It wasn't the most elegant of apologies; needless to say she had had very little practise apologising to extraordinarily handsome men with buttermilk hair and sharp blue eyes that could look right through her if they so chose.

He gave her a half-grin. 'Don't apologise, Lady Alixe. I know what I am.' That only made her feel worse.

Now she'd really have to make it up to him—as if someone like her could ever make anything up to someone like him. But her conscience demanded she try.

She started by giving him a tour of the ruins. The ruins were in two parts. There was an old Roman fort and the villa. Since the fort was closer to the space the group had appropriated as the picnic grounds, she started with that. Afterwards, they joined the other guests on blankets strewn on the ground, where she promptly began a polite but boring conversation about the state of food being served.

'Why is it, Lady Alixe, that people talk about food or the weather when they really want to talk about something else,' St Magnus murmured when she stopped speaking long enough to take a bite of strawberry tart.

'I'm sure I don't know what you mean,' Alixe said after she swallowed. She *did* know what he meant. People had the most ridiculous conversations about absolutely nothing because saying what one honestly felt was impolite. But she'd quickly discovered that when conversing with St Magnus, the conversation grew more interesting when he expounded.

St Magnus had finished eating and taken the opportunity to stretch his long form out on the blanket, propping himself up on one arm, a casual vision of indolence and sin in the early summer sun. He lowered his voice slightly above a whisper just loud enough for her to hear. 'Do you truly believe everyone here *wants* to talk about the ham sandwiches and jugs of lemonade? Yet everyone's conversations are the same if you listen.'

'The ham *is* rather fine and the lemonade is especially cold,' Alixe dared to tease.

St Magnus laughed. 'I'd wager William Barrington over there with Miss Julianne Wood isn't thinking about the ham and tarts.'

'What is he thinking about?' The words were entirely spontaneous and entirely too curious, hardly the right sort of conversational banter for a proper miss. A proper young lady would never encourage what was likely to be an improper avenue of discussion. But St Magnus had a way of encouraging precisely that. She was under the impression that no conversation with him would ever be completely proper.

St Magnus gave a wicked smile. 'He's probably thinking how he'd like to lick that smear of strawberry off her lips.' He gave his eyebrows a meaningful arch. 'Shocked? Don't be. They're all thinking roughly the same thing. Perhaps the place they want to lick varies.'

She was indeed shocked. No one had ever said anything quite so outrageous to her. Ever. But she would not retreat from it. She was fast discovering that being shocked did not have to be the same as being appalled. Since she'd met St Magnus, shock had only increased her curiosity. What else was out there to discover? She'd always thought there was more to life than the veneer society put on its surface. Now, she was starting to discover it, one shocking conversation at a time. Shocking, yes, but intoxicating, too. And, yes, even a little bit empowering, a boost of courage to be the woman in her mind who said witty things, who made challenging statements of her own.

She met his blue eyes squarely, a little smile hovering on her lips. 'I don't know what shocks me more: what you said or how you said it with such nonchalance as if you were indeed discussing something as mundane as the weather.'

'Why not treat it with nonchalance?' St Magnus gave an elegant lift of his shoulder and reached for a last berry. 'It shouldn't be a secret that all men really think about is sex.'

Had he just said 'sex'? In the presence of an unmarried female?

'Oh, yes, Lady Alixe. Males are not complex creatures when you get right down to it. Why not be honest about it? Consider this your first lesson in becoming London's Toast. The sooner you embrace the fact as common knowledge, the sooner you can successfully cater to it.'

'How ironic that you've used a food-related term. We're right back to where we started. Food, the subject people talk about when they're really thinking about licking people's lips for them.' Oh my, oh my. Now was the time to be appalled. She ought to be horrifically shocked by what had come out of her mouth, but she wasn't. It seemed the natural response to St Magnus's comment.

'You can be a rare treat when you decide to employ that tongue of yours for good and not evil, Lady Alixe.' St Magnus was laughing outright now.

'People are starting to look,' Alixe said through the gritted teeth of a forced smile. She was not so given over to the levity of their conversation that she was oblivious to the conditions of their surroundings.

'We want them to look, don't we? We want them to wonder what Lady Alixe has said that has St Magnus so captivated. They're conversational voyeurs. They're only looking because we're having more fun than they are.' He winked a blue eye. 'And do you know why?'

'Because we're not talking about food,' Alixe replied smartly, thoroughly enjoying herself.

'Precisely, Lady Alixe. We're talking about what we want to talk about.'

'Are you always like this?' she asked before she lost her courage, before 'sophisticated woman with witty things to say' retreated. She'd never let that part of her out to play before. She had no idea how long it would last before she stumbled or ran out of things to say.

Something like solemnity settled between them; a little of the hilarity of the previous conversation receded. His eyes were serious now. 'I am always myself, Lady Alixe. It's the one thing I can't run away from.'

She sensed a reprimand in there somewhere, whether for himself or for her she could not tell. Perhaps she'd crossed an invisible line in her heady excitement. She seemed to be an expert at doing that today. 'I'm sorry, I've been too forward. I don't know what's wrong with my mouth today.'

'Nothing's wrong with your mouth except maybe a smudge of strawberry tart, just here.' He gestured to a corner on his own mouth. Alixe's pulse ratcheted up a notch. *He was going to do it.* Merrick St Magnus was going to lick her lips. Perhaps the most irrational and wicked thought she'd ever had, but it was a day for all those types of firsts. She took a deep breath, her lips parting ever so slightly in anticipation, her stomach fluttering with curiosity.

He leaned forwards, closing the gap between them… and most disappointingly reached for a napkin.

He dabbed it against her lips, gently wiping away the stain. She knew it was bold. No man had ever touched her mouth before, not even with a napkin. Yet she couldn't help but feel it wasn't bold enough. After all their talk of mouths and food and what men were really thinking, a napkin seemed far too tame.

There could only be one awful truth. He hadn't wanted to. She'd let herself get carried away. In the end, he was Merrick St Magnus, man about town who could have any woman he wanted any time he wanted her, and she was plain Alixe Burke, with an emphasis on the plain. He didn't want to lick her lips any more than he wanted to marry her, which, of course, was why he was trying so hard so he wouldn't have to.

Alixe let out a deep breath and stood up. 'You should see the villa before we go. It's a bit of a walk, so we'd best start now or there won't be time before we leave.'

Chapter Seven

'The villa probably housed military officers, although the larger Roman defences were built at Dover. The lack of a deep-water harbour made Folkestone an unlikely place of attack from the sea. Folkestone was used only as a look-out point.'

She was seeking refuge in her history again. Merrick didn't think she'd stopped chattering since they'd left the blanket. She'd talked about the local fauna on the walk to the ruin and she'd been a veritable fountain of knowledge once they'd actually reached the ruin. It was undeniably interesting. She was well informed, but he was more interested in what had brought on the change, the reversion. She'd been a lively match for him on the blanket, one that he'd enjoyed far beyond his expectation.

'This main room here was a banquet hall. We know this because shards of pottery have been found...' Merrick moved away from her recitation, his eye caught by a short crumbling stair. He went up, thankful for the traction of his boots on the rubble of the remaining steps. But the short climb was worth it. The upper chamber afforded a spectacular view of the sea and of the current Folkestone harbour in the distance. Merrick let the breeze flow over him for a moment as he took in the panorama. He'd discovered that most things looked peaceful from a distance. Distance was useful that way.

'St Magnus, you shouldn't be up there,' she called. But he ignored her. '*Merrick*, it's dangerous. The steps aren't stable and goodness knows how treacherous the ground up there is.' She was looking up at him, shielding her eyes from the sun's glare.

'The view is spectacular and not to be missed,' he called down. He moved towards the steps and offered her a hand. 'Come up, Alixe. The ground is dry and firm. I don't think we're in any danger of sliding down the cliff side today.'

Alixe gave him a look as if to say 'oh, very well' and took her skirt in both hands for the climb. She tripped on the third step, giving him another look. This one saying 'It's dangerous, I told you so'.

'Don't be stubborn, Alixe. Take my hand.' He came down a few steps to meet her, forcing her to acknowledge his offer. Her hand slid into his, warm and firm, and he tightened his grip, ready to haul her up if necessary. But there were no further mishaps.

At the top, Alixe was transformed. 'Oh, look at this!' she gasped. 'This would have been a splendid look-out. They could see all the way down the coast. Perhaps they could even have sent signals from here. A tower in Dover or Hythe would be able to pick them up.' She turned to him, her enjoyment evident on her face. 'I've never been up here, you know. In all the years I've lived here, I've been to the ruins several times, but I've never come up the stair.'

She turned back to the view spread before them. 'To think it's been here all the time and I've missed it.' The last was said more to herself than to him. The breeze took that moment to be slightly more forceful, toying with her hat. She reached up, hesitated for an instant, then took it off. 'That's better,' she said to no one in particular. Then she closed her eyes and gave her face over to the wind and the sun.

Realisation hit him all at once.

Alixe Burke was a beautiful woman. It was objectively true. He could see it in the fine line of her jaw, the elegant column of her neck, visible only because her head was tilted upwards to the sun. She had a perfect nose, narrow and faintly sloped at the end to give it character. It fit the delicate boning of her face, the slightly raised cheekbones one could only fully appreciate in profile, the generous mouth. Cosmetics could not manufacture a bone structure like that. The grey habit she wore might distract from those finer points of beauty, but a discerning man would see the narrow waist and long legs beneath the bulky skirt. A man wouldn't have to be that discerning at all to note the high thrust of her breasts beneath the jacket, tempting a man to wonder whether or not that was the doing of nature's bounty or the assistance of a corset.

It would be simple work to see her gowned according to her attributes, her beauty fully displayed to the gentlemen of the *ton*. He doubted her earlier debutante wardrobes had done her beauty complete justice. No whites or pale pastels for this lovely creature. She belonged in rich earthy tones, deep russets and golds to show off the walnut sheen of her hair.

Merrick moved behind her, his hands finding a comfortable place at her shoulders. He was used to touching women. He hardly thought anything of the gesture. It was casual and easy. But she tensed at the contact. They would have to work on that. She would want to be comfortable with a casual touch now and then, perhaps even doling out a few touches herself, light gestures on a gentleman's arm. Men liked to be touched as much as women. Touch had enormous effects to the positive; it made a person memorable, it created a sense of closeness and trust even when a relationship was new.

Well, now he might be going too far. She wasn't going to seduce anyone. She didn't need to know *all* of the tricks he could teach her, just enough to be pleasant, to draw London's attention and thus the eye of the right kind of gentleman.

'The view is intoxicating,' Merrick murmured at her ear and was rewarded with a small sigh of wistfulness.

'The sea goes on and on. It makes me realise how little of the world I know. I wonder if the Roman who sat here watching wondered the same thing—what's out there? How much more of the world is there beyond what we've already discovered?'

With one of his experienced lovers he'd have drawn her back against him at this moment and wrapped his arms about her, but he knew better than to dare such a thing with Alixe. 'I wasn't talking about *that* view,' he whispered. 'I was talking about this one.' He tucked an errant curl behind her ear. 'You're a beautiful woman, Alixe Burke.'

She stiffened. 'You shouldn't say things you don't mean.'

'Do you doubt me? Or do you doubt yourself? Don't you think you're beautiful? Surely you're not naïve enough to overlook your natural charms.'

She turned to face him, forcing him to relinquish his hold. 'I'm not naïve. I'm a realist.'

Merrick shrugged a shoulder as if to say he didn't think much of realism. 'What has realism taught you, Alixe?' He folded his arms, waiting to see what she would say next.

'It has taught me that I'm an end to male means. I'm a dowry, a stepping stone for some ambitious man. It's not very flattering.'

He could not refute her arguments. There *were* men who saw women that way. But he could refute the hardness in her sherry eyes, eyes that should have been warm. For all her protestations of realism, she was too untried by the world for the measure of cynicism she showed. 'What of romance and love? What has realism taught you about those things?'

'If those things exist, they don't exist for me.' Alixe's chin went up a fraction in defiance of his probe.

'Is that a dare, Alixe? If it is, I'll take it.' Merrick took advantage of their privacy, closing the short distance between them with a touch; the back of his hand reaching out to stroke the curve of her cheek. 'A world without romance is a bland world indeed, Alixe. One for which I think you are ill suited.' He saw the pulse at the base of her neck leap at the words, the hardness in her eyes soften, curiosity replacing the doubt whether she willed it or not. He let his eyes catch hers, then drop to linger on the fullness of her mouth before he drew her to him, whispering, 'Let me show you the possibilities', a most seductive invitation to sin.

Alixe knew she was going to accept. He was going to kiss her and she was going to let him. She could no more stop herself than she could hold back the tides on the beach below them. There was only a moment to acknowledge the act before she was in his arms, his mouth covering hers, warm and insistent that she join him in this. He would not tolerate false resistance and, frankly, she did not want to give it. His tongue brushed her lips. She opened, instinctively parting her lips, giving him access to her mouth, kissing him back with all the enthusiasm her limited skill in this area permitted.

She felt his hand at her nape, his fingers in her hair, guiding her ever so gently into the kiss, his other hand at her back, guiding her not into him precisely, but against him. The planes and ridges of him were evident beneath his clothes: the structured hardness of his chest, the muscled pressure of his thighs. She had seen all this at the pond, of course, but to feel it, ah, to *feel* a man was heady indeed.

It ended all too soon. Merrick drew back, murmuring, 'My dear, I fear you tempt me to indiscretion.' He stepped backwards, putting a subtle distance between them, his eyes soft with a look that warmed her to the toes of her half-boots and made her feel bold beyond her usual measure of cautious restraint.

'Surely a *little* temptation is tolerable? It is just a kiss, after all,' Alixe flirted, stepping forwards—perhaps this time *she'd* kiss *him*. Her intentions must have been obvious.

Merrick side-stepped her efforts. 'Careful, minx. There are those who would take advantage of your enthusiasm for the art. With the gentlemen of London, you'd do best to let them do the pursuing and to be discriminate in bestowing your favours. The rarer a treasure is, the more sought after it becomes.'

Alixe turned sharply, presenting Merrick with her back. She flushed, furious and embarrassed. She'd let herself get carried away. She'd let herself believe they were two people caught up in the beauty of the moment, the kiss a celebration of having shared the stunning vista together. It was no use. No matter how she tried to rationalise it, it sounded like nonsense even in her head. The point was, she'd got carried away and pretended the kiss was something more than it was, which obviously it wasn't. He was unperturbed by what had transpired while she was all too worked up.

She wasn't ready to turn around and face him yet, but she could see him in her mind's eye leaning with easy grace against the rock wall of the ruins, letting the breeze ruffle through his hair. At least he could be angry.

'Alixe, look at me.'

'Don't you dare be nice and say something pithy.'

'I wasn't going to.'

She could hear him pushing off the wall and crossing the villa floor, pebbles crunching beneath his boots. She blew out a breath. She wanted to vanish, wanted the cliff to swallow her up, embarrassment and all.

'What I was going to say, Alixe, is that if you want to kiss a man, you need to know how.'

Oh. *That* made it better. 'Just for the record, you're not boosting my confidence.' The best kiss she'd ever had and it was entirely juvenile to him, probably no better than the sloppy work of a three year old.

He was standing behind her. She could feel the heat of his body. She couldn't put off facing him any longer. She turned, trying very hard to look irritated instead of mortified. Her eyes darted everywhere in an attempt to avoid looking at him directly. He would have none of it. After a few futile seconds of looking past his shoulder, he gently imprisoned her chin with his thumb and forefinger.

'Look at me, Alixe. There's nothing wrong with your kiss, just your approach. You need finesse. Your suitors will want to feel this was all their doing. You can initiate the kiss as long as they think it was their idea. Here, let me show you.'

That was a dangerous phrase. Alixe made to move backwards, but he captured her hand and continued smoothly with his instructions. 'Touch your gentleman on the sleeve. Make it look like a natural act during conversation. Lean forwards and laugh a little at something he says when you do it. That way it looks spontaneous and sincere. Then, flirt with your eyes.

Give him a little smile and look down as if you hadn't meant to get caught staring. Later, when you're walking in the garden, let your gaze linger on his lips a bit. Make sure he catches you at it. You can shyly bite your lip and look away quickly. If he's any sort of man at all, he'll stop within the next ten feet and steal a kiss. When he does stop, you can close the deal by parting your lips, a sure sign that his affections will be welcomed.

'I should have brought paper for notes,' Alixe mumbled. 'I was not expecting a treatise.'

'Now that's a fine idea. Perhaps I should write a book on kissing as a noble art.' Merrick laughed.

Unfazed by her reticence, he pushed on. 'Now you try it. I already know it works. Sit there and I'll pretend I've brought you some punch.' Merrick gestured to a rounded boulder.

'This is silly,' Alixe protested, but she did it any way.

'I've heard the very best bit of news while I was at the refreshment table,' Merrick began their *faux* conversation.

'Oh, you have?' Alixe widened her eyes in simulated interest.

'Yes. I heard that the Cow is about to run away with the Spoon,' Merrick said in his best conspiratorial whisper.

'Isn't the *Dish* supposed to run away with the spoon?' Alixe corrected.

Merrick didn't so much as blink over his error. He leaned closer, a wicked grin taking his elegant mouth. 'I do believe it is. That's why my "news" is so astonishing. It's entirely unexpected.'

Uncontainable laughter surged up inside her. Before she knew it, she was leaning forwards, her hand on his forearm in gentle camaraderie. 'Oh, do tell,' she managed in gasps between bouts of laughing.

'Well, I heard it from the Cat who heard it from the Fiddle…' Merrick was struggling against losing his composure entirely. It was a fascinating battle to watch on his expressive face—mock seriousness warring futilely with the hilarity of their conversation. In that moment it was all too easy to forget who he was, who she was, as they had in the library.

Alixe's eyes dropped to his mouth with its aristocratically thin upper lip. Merrick's eyes followed her down, his head tilting to capture her lips in a gentle buss. He sucked lightly at her lower lip, sending a pool of warm heat to her belly. This slow, lingering kiss carried an entirely different thrill. There was sweetness in its tender qualities. She wanted to fall into it, wanted to feel it turn into something more passionate. She'd never guessed kissing could be such a lovely pastime.

'That's how you know you did it right. The proof is in the pudding. Top marks,' he whispered playfully. 'You're an apt pupil. Keep this up and we'll have London at your feet in no time.'

The words were said in jest and perhaps reassurance, but Alixe could not take them that way. How had it become this easy to forget what this man was? He was a flirt. No, he was more than a flirt. He was a consummate seducer of women. She'd been warned by her own brother. She knew precisely what his role was in this farce to see her married. And yet that knowledge had not been able to prevent *it*; when he kissed her, it felt real. It didn't feel like a lesson. It was positively mortifying to forget herself so entirely.

Alixe stood up and brushed at her skirts, summoning anger to be her shield. 'Let me make one thing clear. I do not need love lessons. Most especially, I do not need them from you.'

Merrick laughed softly at her indignation, having the audacity to smile. 'Yes, you do, Alixe Burke. And you most definitely need them from me.'

Love lessons, indeed! Alixe fumed. She could barely sit still long enough to let Meg dress her hair for dinner that night. The man was insufferable. He treated the whole shambles as if it were a lark. More than that, he treated *her* as if she were a lark.

He'd merely laughed at her riding habit. If he thought he could laugh away her ugly gowns or cajole her into better looks, he would soon learn she wouldn't give up her strategy easily. Her excessively plain wardrobe had been an excellent defence against unwanted suitors up until now. He was very much the exception. She would remind him of that this evening.

Meg had laid out her second-best dinner gown, but Alixe had opted for an austere beige gown trimmed in unassuming lace of the same colour. Meg had clearly disagreed with her choice. Her maid tugged a braid up into the coronet she was fashioning.

'I don't know why you want to wear that old thing. Lord St Magnus seemed plenty interested in you this morning. He's a handsome fellow. I would have thought you'd want to wear something pretty tonight.'

'He was just being polite.' Alixe sat up straighter and squared her shoulders. Polite enough to trade banter at the picnic, polite enough to show her how to kiss. Polite enough to make her forget he had a job to do and that job was her. But she couldn't confess that to Meg.

Her father had truly humbled her this time, blackmailing St Magnus into this ludicrous proposition. No. She had to stop thinking that way. She had to stop thinking of St Magnus as a victim. *She* was the victim. St Magnus was on her father's side. Perhaps not by consent, but he was on the side that wanted to see her married off and that meant her father's side.

'Would you like a little rouge for your cheeks?' Meg suggested hopefully, holding a little pot.

'No.' Alixe shook her head.

'But the beige, miss, it washes you out so.'

Alixe smiled at the pale image she presented in the mirror. 'Yes, it does do that beautifully.' She was ready to go down to supper. St Magnus would see that she meant business. No matter what kind of love lessons he offered, she did mean to scare him off by revealing to him the futility of his task.

Chapter Eight

In the drawing room, Merrick discreetly checked his watch. Alixe was late and he worried that he'd overstepped himself today with his offer of love lessons. There was some irony in that offer. What did he know about love? He knew about sex and every game that went with it. But love? Love was beyond him. It had not existed in his home. His father did not love his mother. His father did not love him. He was merely another means to an end—a loose end in this particular case. Growing up, he'd loved his mother, a beautiful, delicate woman, but that had turned out poorly. His father had used that devotion with merciless regularity in order to obtain what he wanted until Merrick had finally decided to put as much distance between himself and his family as he could. That had been seven years ago. No, Merrick knew nothing about love and he'd prefer to keep it that way.

There was a rustling at the door and Merrick spied Alixe immediately. He'd been hoping she would not meekly accept defeat. Part of him was intrigued about what she would do next, and he was certain there would be a 'next'. He understood his situation was precarious for a bachelor wishing to avoid matrimony. But regardless of the peril, he'd been intrigued by Alixe Burke again today, proving that his earlier fascination hadn't been a one-day novelty.

She was a beautiful, spirited woman attempting to hide in dismal clothing. He suspected she was hiding not only from the world, but from herself. It had been difficult for her to acknowledge the passionate side of her nature today. The responses he'd drawn from her had surprised her greatly. Watching her let go and simply be herself for even a few moments had pleased him immensely.

Alixe made her much-anticipated entrance and Merrick smiled. She had not disappointed. The beige gown was even 'better' than the grey riding habit because there was less one could technically take issue with. The gown was cut in the latest fashion. She wore very proper pearls around her neck and her hair was done up neatly. But she looked invisible. Everything about her ensemble was completely unassuming, from the colour to the sparse trimmings. She was almost convincing. *Almost.*

Her head was held too high for the kind of woman who would wear that gown and her eyes were too sharp. Her natural disposition betrayed her in ways the gown could not hide. Merrick would be damned if he'd tell her.

Merrick made his way to where she stood surveying the room and probably wondering where best to put herself out of notice.

'You look beautiful tonight.'

'I do not.' She responded proudly. 'I'm the plainest woman in the room.'

He took her arm and tucked it through his own. It was a lovely proprietary act, one that everyone in the drawing room noticed while they were trying hard not to. He was well aware every woman's eyes in the room had discreetly watched him cross the floor to Alixe's side.

'Beauty is often found in the eyes of the beholder,' Merrick replied smoothly, strolling them around the perimeter of the drawing room.

'A very useful cliché.'

'A very *true* cliché. You'll see.' Merrick winked slyly. She was not nearly as seasoned at the games of flirtation as he was. She only knew how to avoid them. He knew how to play them. She didn't quite understand what he was doing. But he did.

A man's undivided attentions were a potent lure for other males. Once other men saw his attentions they would swarm: some out of curiosity, wanting to see what he saw, others out of fear that something of merit might slip beyond their grasp and still others because men were by nature competitive creatures and could not stand to be bested. And the women in the room would make sure the men noticed. Already, a few of them whispered to companions behind their fans.

Ah, yes, Merrick thought. He would pretend the

beige gown was beautiful and by the end of the evening the other men would think so, too.

Merrick was up to something. The knowledge that the 'game was afoot' had Alixe on edge throughout dinner. But she could detect nothing. Merrick sat beside her, solicitous and charming, his manners without fault. She heartily wished she knew more about the games men and women played with one another. She was starting to see the large flaw in her strategies. Her tactics had all been focused on avoiding the game. As a result, she hadn't the faintest idea how to play the game or even what the rules might be.

The 'rules of engagement' was taking on a vastly differently meaning. Before Merrick, Alixe had thought of the term solely in its military capacity, part of the historic vocabulary of war. But now she was starting to see it in a different light, unless one wanted to speculate that love and war were fought on similar fields of battle.

Rules, like the ones Merrick had introduced, were *not* the rules she'd learned from her governesses. Governesses taught a person how to walk, how to sit and how to make polite conversation; all of which were apparently useless skills in spite of society's argument to the contrary. What a girl really needed in her arsenal was the ability to coax a kiss. A man, too, for that matter.

Merrick hadn't said as much, but Alixe suspected the converse was indeed true. Merrick had demonstrated that quite aptly this afternoon at the villa. His allure most definitely did not stem from his ability to make polite conversation or from his talent for sitting ramrod straight. In fact, he was proving it right now across the drawing room while they waited for the games to begin. It was the first time all evening that he'd left her side.

Merrick *lounged* where other men stiffly posed against the mantelpiece. Merrick *said* what he thought while others searched for careful phrasing.

And it was working. The pretty Widow Whitely tilted her blonde head to one side, giving Merrick a considering look, a coy half-smile on her lips, her eyes dropping to his mouth and then to an unmentionable spot just below his waist.

Oh. Alixe felt a blush start to rise on Mrs Whitely's behalf. Had Mrs Whitely really done that? It had happened so quickly, Alixe couldn't be entirely sure of what she'd seen. Merrick was leaning forwards and smiling, a behaviour that sent an unlooked-for surge of jealously through Alixe. He had smiled at her in a similar manner up at the villa today. Jamie had warned her Merrick liked women. But a warning wasn't quite as effective as seeing the evidence first-hand.

Watching him with Widow Whitely was a gentle reminder that these were the tools of his trade. It was also a reminder that he wasn't hers to command. He was merely her unconventional and secret tutor at the moment. If he wanted to flirt with Mrs Whitely, she had no right to countermand him.

As if drawn by her thoughts, Merrick looked up

from his tête-à-tête with the engaging widow, his eyes discreetly finding hers.

Five minutes later, he materialised at her side. 'Did you learn anything, *ma chère*?'

Other than that Mrs Whitely might have a fascination with certain parts of yours? That could absolutely *not* be said out loud. Alixe elected to say nothing. She shook her head.

'I did,' Merrick continued, his voice low at her ear. 'We were noticed at the picnic today and again in the drawing room. I've been approached by no less than three ladies who have commented on it.'

'In a good way, I hope.' Alixe could imagine the ways they might have been noticed. She was not used to deliberately drawing attention to herself. 'The last thing I need before going to London is too much attention.' She would prefer no one had spied them up at the villa or actually heard what they were laughing over at the picnic.

Merrick gave one of his easy smiles. 'There is no such thing as too much attention. Don't be confusing attention with scandal. They are two different animals entirely. One is good and the other is to be avoided at all costs.'

Alixe raised an eyebrow in quizzing disbelief. 'And you're a prime example of avoiding scandal?'

'Scandal is to be avoided at all costs, if you're a woman,' Merrick amended.

'Quite the double standard since it's pretty hard to fall into scandal without us,' Alixe said drily.

'Still, there are ways.' Merrick laughed, then sobered. Alixe followed his narrowing gaze to the arrival of a newcomer to the drawing room. Archibald Redfield entered with Lady Folkestone on his arm, his golden head bent with a smile to catch a comment.

'Your mother seems quite taken with our Mr Redfield.'

'My father, too. They dote on him.'

'Whatever for? He's a sly sort. Surely they can see that.'

'They only see his manners, his standard-bred good looks. He's solid, not the sort to stir up trouble. He's exactly what this sleepy part of England is looking for in a landowner. He took over the old Tailsby Manse last year. It was the most exciting thing to happen in Folkestone for ages. Everyone with a daughter under thirty was thrilled.'

'Do you include your mother in that grouping?' Merrick's eyes followed Redfield about the room in a manner reminiscent of a wolf stalking prey.

'Of course.' Alixe shrugged, hoping to fob off any further inquisition.

'But to no avail?' Merrick probed. This was uncomfortable ground.

'To no avail on my end. I was not interested in Mr Redfield's attentions.'

'But he was?'

'Yes. Yes, he was interested,' Alixe replied tersely. She'd retreated from London to avoid men like Archibald Redfield. Merrick looked ready to ask another question. 'This is not a seemly topic of conversation for a drawing room,' Alixe said quickly. She had no desire to delve further into just how interested Mr Redfield had been or how naively she'd been taken in for a short time.

'Then perhaps you'll do me the honour of continuing the conversation later in the garden after the games. I believe I am to join old Mrs Pottinger and her cronies at whist shortly.' Merrick was all obliging affability at the thought of an evening spent at cards with old ladies.

'I hadn't planned on staying for the games,' Alixe admitted. 'I am behind on my manuscript. I'd hoped to sneak off and get some work done tonight.' She'd lost so much time since the house party had begun and the manuscript was still giving her fits.

'Oh, no, that will not do,' Merrick scolded. 'You can't be noticed if you're not here. You need to stay *and* you need to enjoy yourself. Go over and join Miss Georgia Downing and the young ladies by the sofa. I promise they'll be delighted to make your acquaintance. With luck, you can all make plans to call on one another in London.'

It would be fun to spend an evening in the company of people her age—well, roughly her age. She knew she was a bit older. Still, Jane Atwood was in that group and she was twenty-two. 'But the manuscript…' Alixe protested weakly.

'I'll help you with it in the morning,' Merrick promised.

That coaxed a smile. Alixe could feel it creeping across her mouth. 'So you really do understand Old French?'

'Did you think I didn't?' Merrick feigned hurt. He touched a hand to her wrist. 'You doubted me?'

'Well, I did suppose rumours of your abilities might have been greatly exaggerated in that regard.' Alixe found herself flirting in response to the light pressure of his hand at her gloved wrist. It was impossible to hate him; his charm proved irresistible even when she knew precisely what he was.

'Bravo, that was nicely done, quite the perfect rejoinder—definitely witty and perhaps even a bit of naughty innuendo thrown in. Why, Lady Alixe, I do think you might have the makings of a master yet.'

Alixe let herself be drawn into the fun of conversing with Merrick. She dropped a little curtsy. 'Thank you, that's quite a compliment.'

'Then I shall depart on a good note and take up my chair at the whist table.'

'Do take care. Mrs Pottinger is sharper than she looks.'

Merrick gave her a short bow. 'I appreciate your concern. But I assure you, I can hold my own against county champions of Mrs Pottinger's skill.'

Alixe laughed. 'I wouldn't be so certain of that. She counts cards like an inveterate gambler.'

Damn, but if Alixe wasn't right. He shouldn't have played his heart. He'd suspected Mrs Pottinger was out of them and would trump his jack, but he'd lost count. Apparently there were only two hearts left against his jack and not three. From under her lace cap, the elderly dame gave him a smug look of triumph and led her ace of spades.

Merrick gathered his wandering attentions and focused on the game. If he wasn't careful, he and his partner would lose this rubber. There'd be no living it down in London if word got back he'd lost at cards to a group of old country biddies.

Mrs Pottinger let out a sigh and tossed her last card. 'You're a wily fox, after all, St Magnus. For all my finessing I can't wheedle the eight of spades out of you and it will be my undoing. My poor seven will fall to it and the game is yours.'

'But your skill is not in doubt, Mrs Pottinger,' Merrick said gallantly, tossing his eight of spades on to the trick. 'You are a most impressive player. I was rightfully warned about you.' Merrick rose from the table and helped each of the ladies rise after their long sit. 'Thank you for the game, ladies. It's been a delightful evening.'

He'd done his duty for Lady Folkestone. Now it was time to give his full attention to the interesting situation with Archibald Redfield. He'd meant to confront Redfield about the questionable nature of the wager. 'Rigging' a wager was not honourable conduct among those who gambled and Merrick, as one who wagered rather often, knew it. He was not going to let Redfield slip by on this one. Redfield's attempt at rigging the wager had nearly jeopardised a lady's reputation. It had most definitely jeopardised the lady's future.

Not all of his attentions had been diverted to the 'Redfield situation'. The lady in question had done her share of distracting, too. Many of his thoughts had, in fact, been diverted to the 'Alixe conundrum'. On more than one occasion, his eye had been drawn to her across the room where she'd taken his advice and joined a group of young ladies. Why had she refused Redfield's attentions? Her past association with Redfield put an entirely different cast upon the wager, one that suggested the wager hadn't been about himself, but about Alixe and quite possibly retaliation.

Revenge seemed a long way to go merely because a lady rejected the man's attentions. But perhaps there was more to it. Alixe had seemed loathe to discuss the situation in detail. Originally, he'd attributed her reticence to their circumstances. A drawing room full of people was hardly conducive to divulging secrets. Now, he was starting to wonder if the reticence didn't come from something more.

Merrick strolled towards the wide bay of French doors leading out to the spectacular Folkestone gardens. Games were breaking up and people were starting to mill as they waited for the end-of-evening tea cart. Once he caught Alixe's eye, it would be easy to slip outside unnoticed and wait for her.

Waiting was the harder part. He'd been about ready to go inside and detach her from the group when she finally came out. 'This is dangerous.' She scolded. 'What if someone sees us?'

'I hope they do. There's nothing to hide. I'd have to be completely foolish to try to steal a kiss with the entire house party looking on.' Merrick scowled, tossing a hand to indicate the long bank of French doors. 'I thought you were never coming out.'

'I didn't think we had anything urgent to discuss.'

'I disagree. We aren't done talking about Redfield.'

He recognised defiance. Her chin went up a slight fraction, just as it had at the villa.

'I'm starting to think he made the wager on purpose, that perhaps he wanted revenge. The wager was meant to land you in the suds. I was merely a tool.' Merrick laid out his hypothesis, noticing that she didn't rush to deny the claim. 'Is there merit to that? What might have transpired between you that would cause him to take such drastic measures?'

Alixe smoothed her skirts, another gesture he was coming to associate with her when she was not certain what to say. 'I don't think it has any bearing on our current circumstances,' she replied coolly.

'I do.' Merrick crossed his arms over his chest, studying her in the light thrown from the drawing room. He wished he could see her eyes more clearly. They would tell him if she was as cool as she sounded. 'Redfield tried to fix the bet and not for his benefit. He knew you'd be there; if I succeeded, he would lose money, not to mention the money his friends would lose. Have you thought about why a man would set himself up for a likely failure?'

'Perhaps he thought I'd resist your attempts.' She squirmed a little at that. 'For that matter, how do you know he knew I'd be there?'

'He brought your father, hardly someone who'd be interested in who I was kissing unless it was his own daughter. Your father wouldn't care two figs if I was in there kissing Widow Whitely. Besides, Ashe told me Redfield was boasting he knew someone would be there.'

'Oh.' It came out as a small sigh and her shoulders sagged just the tiniest bit, the only acknowledgement she'd make that he was quite possibly right. 'I refused him when he put the question to me. Needless to say, he was stunned. He should not have been. The daughter of an earl is quite a reach for a man of his modest antecedents. We did not discuss it, but I had reason to believe his intentions were not as true as he represented them to be.'

Merrick believed that. It was how polite society conducted its business. Redfield would never know the reasons she'd refused him. He would have hidden his disappointment just as she'd hidden her true reasons. It did not take great imagination to envision them sitting properly in the Folkestone receiving rooms, voicing polite platitudes of having been honoured by the other's attentions and regretful the outcome could not be otherwise. Then they'd gone about the business of being courteous neighbours because there was no other choice. Neighbours must first and foremost always maintain a veneer of politeness, which often precluded being able to speak the truth.

The situation with Archibald Redfield was untidy beneath the placid surface. It made her anxious to speak of it. Even now, her gaze was drawn towards the doors, looking for distraction. She found it in the tea cart's arrival. 'We should return inside.'

'You go in first and I'll follow after a decent interval.'

He'd wait five minutes before returning and then he'd stay at her side for what was left of the evening. He counted off the minutes, letting his mind wander, mulling over what Alixe had revealed and even what she hadn't.

Redfield's former relationship with Alixe put an entirely different cast on his motives for the dangerous wager he'd made. Redfield had been taken aback by her refusal—so stunned, in fact, that he wanted revenge enough to plan a compromising situation, to see Alixe Burke ruined. But to want revenge seemed an uncharacteristically harsh action.

More questions followed. Alixe had hinted she'd discovered something unsavoury about Redfield's intentions. Did Redfield suspect she'd made such a discovery and did he fear she might expose it? What would Redfield have to hide?

All of it was supposition. But if any of it were true, Alixe Burke might be in danger from more than an unwanted marriage. Whether she realised it or not, she was in need of a champion.

Ashe would be the first to point out the hero did not have to be him. Merrick was not required to champion Alixe Burke against jilted suitors. Yet he could not help but feel a need to champion this woman who had dared to carve out a life contrary to society's preferences. Her daring had left her alone. Perhaps that was the kinship he felt with her. In spite of his notorious popularity, Merrick St Magnus knew what it meant to be alone.

* * *

Archibald Redfield considered himself a man who was rarely surprised. Human nature held little mystery for him. Yet St Magnus had managed to surprise him. He had not expected to see the devil-may-care libertine that morning. St Magnus had stayed. Not only had he stayed, he'd played his role to the hilt at the picnic, never once leaving Alixe Burke's side. It was not what he had expected and that made him nervous.

What made him even more nervous was the sight of Alixe Burke slipping back in to the party, trying hard not to be noticed. No doubt she'd been sneaking out to see St Magnus. He didn't like that in the least. The last thing he needed was for Alixe to decide she actually liked the rogue or for St Magnus to do the deciding for her. It would be death to his plans if anyone caught St Magnus and Alixe being indiscreet.

Redfield knew rogues. He feared that the reason St Magnus hadn't left was that St Magnus wanted to woo Alixe for himself, compromise her if need be and the dratted man was now perfectly positioned to do that, having been given *carte blanche* to act the role of an interested suitor. This was a most unlooked-for complication. Redfield would have to keep his eye on the situation most carefully.

Fortunately for the present, no one else had noticed Alixe's return. She wasn't the 'noticeable' type, not dressed like that anyway, in a beige gown that matched the wallpaper. He was astute enough to know the Earl of Folkestone's well-dowered daughter could afford better, but he simply didn't care what she wore or why.

He didn't care if she'd rather live in the country with her books. He only cared that she came with a great deal of money. Plain women, ugly women, beautiful women—he'd had them all when it served his purposes. In the dark they were all the same. Except that Alixe Burke was the richest prize he'd ever gone after. She'd be the last, too, if he was successful.

Scratch that. There could be no 'ifs' about it. He had to win her. He'd sunk his funds into the Tailsby Manse, the first step in his bid to be a respectable gentleman. The manor was definitely a gentleman's home, but that also meant it was in a certain state of disrepair. The roof leaked, the chimneys smoked and it took servants to run the place. All those things required money. Alixe Burke had money and prestige. Marriage to her would solidify his claim to a genteel life.

But she had turned him down. He had not expected it. A woman on the shelf didn't turn down offers of marriage, earl's daughter or not. It was a setback he could not easily afford. She would find she could not afford it either. He would push the choosy Miss Burke into a corner until she had no choice but to accept his twelfth-hour offer and this time she'd be all too glad to accept.

As long as St Magnus played by the rules and did not compromise her for himself, all would be well. Not even St Magnus could turn her into an interesting woman, the kind of woman who could be labelled a Toast. Yes, there'd be fortune hunters like himself who wouldn't care what she looked like, but she was to be made a Toast precisely to avoid those men and draw the right kind of man to her side. Folkestone would know the difference. Redfield was confident the right man would not emerge.

He was even more confident Folkestone would not want to see his daughter married to St Magnus, a man with his own social ghosts and demons to contend with. That would be when he made his generous offer to marry Alixe, saving the family from the scandal of attaching themselves permanently to St Magnus. It would all be wrapped up neatly by Season's end and there'd be time to have his roof patched before winter set in.

Chapter Nine

Alixe was dressed hideously again in a shapeless work dress when she met Merrick in the library the following morning, her hair left to hang loose in her hurry to make up for oversleeping. There was no one to notice this grooming oversight on her part. The house party had taken themselves off to the village for a day of shopping and touring the local church. But one would have thought the king was coming to call the way St Magnus was turned out in sartorial perfection for the simple and isolated task of working in the library with her.

He was waiting for her, attired in fawn breeches, crisp white linen shirt and a sky-blue waistcoat in a paisley pattern that managed to deepen the hue of his already impossibly blue eyes. He'd been freshly shaved and his hair was brushed to the pale sheen of cream. His morning elan was perhaps a not-so-subtle commentary about her own choice of clothing. But if she'd meant to get a more obvious rise out of Merrick over her clothes, she was to be disappointed.

His comment extended merely to a raised eyebrow. Instead, he turned his attentions to the project at hand and after a few minutes of study to familiarise himself with the text, he said 'I think you're taking the translation too literally again. The sentence makes more sense if *profiter* means taking advantage of. You're using it to mean making money, the way one would use the word today.'

Merrick slid the document back across the long library table to let her look at the section in question, the understated scent of his morning *toilette* teasing her nostrils as he leaned forwards slightly to push the document towards her. He smelled clean, the very idea of freshness personified. Then he pulled his arm back and the delightful scent retreated. She wanted more. Alixe wondered what he would do if she acted on the impulse to lean across the table and sniff him, a great big healthy sniff. A giggle escaped her at the very thought of acting on the notion.

'Is there something humorous?' Merrick was all stern seriousness.

'Um, no.' Alixe blushed and feigned a throat-clearing cough. 'A tickle in my throat, I think.' *I was just thinking about sniffing you.* Alixe hastily shifted her gaze to the manuscript and pretended to read, using the pretence to gather her scattered thoughts. She'd worked on this manuscript for weeks without distraction until St Magnus's arrival. Now, her focus fled at the smallest provocation from him. The isolation of the country must be getting to her. She took a deep breath.

'Better?' St Magnus enquired, needing only a pair

of eye glasses to look the consummate college professor, albeit a very handsome one.

'Yes, much better, thank you.' What was wrong with her? She did not usually think in such terms. Then again, she wasn't in the habit of taking kissing lessons from men she hardly knew either.

Alixe scanned the document. It didn't take long to see his interpretation was correct. 'It seems so obvious now that you've pointed it out. The rest of the document should translate easily from this point.' His translation made perfect sense. Really, it was a marvel she'd missed it.

Too bad swallowing her pride wasn't as simple. She was a historian, even if she had been self-trained. She'd had the benefit of tutors and a fine education up until Jamie had left for Oxford. How was it that a well-educated person like herself had not seen what Merrick had noted immediately? She scribbled some notes on a tablet and then looked up, considering. Morning sunlight streamed through the long windows of the library, turning his buttermilk hair to the pale flax of corn silk. 'How is it that you know so much about French?' It seemed patently unfair this gorgeous male should also be in possession of an intellect. He'd demonstrated on two separate occasions that intellect was quite well developed.

'It's the language of love, *ma chère*.' Merrick flashed her one of his teasing grins. 'I didn't have to be a genius to see all the uses I could find for it.'

Alixe wasn't satisfied. He knew far more than a passing phrase for impressing the ladies. 'Don't trivialise your skill.' The vehemence of her defence startled them both. 'You don't have to pretend you don't have a brain. Not with me anyway.'

An awkward silence followed in the wake of her outburst. It was one of those moments when they stepped outside their prescribed roles of rake and blue stocking and the revelation that had followed was nothing short of surprising. It was difficult to think of her and Merrick having something so significant in common.

'You studied French at Oxford. I hardly think the curriculum there was limited to a few *bon mots*.' Alixe cast about for a way to restore equilibrium to the conversation, not entirely comfortable with what she'd learned.

'Have you ever considered that Oxford might be overrated?' Merrick leaned back in his chair, propping it up on its hind legs, his hands tucked behind his head, an entirely masculine habit. He tried for evasion. 'Rich men send their sons to Oxford to get an education when they know full well we spend most of our days and nights carousing in the taverns and getting up to all nature of mischief. It's a different sort of education than the ones the dons intend for us. Our fathers don't care as long as we don't get sent down in disgrace.' There was a bitterness that underlay the levity of his tone.

'Jamie mentioned there was time for a few larks.' Alixe got up from the table and absently strode to one of the long windows to take in the morning sun. 'But I don't believe you picked languages entirely on whim.' She wouldn't let him get away with skirting the question. Evasion was an unexpected strategy from a man who'd stood on the edge of the pond unabash-edly naked.

'I like to talk and languages are another way to talk. At the time it seemed like a kind of rebellion. I liked the idea of being able to say something that can't quite be said in English.'

'Such as…?' Alixe faced him, her back to the window. She'd not have guessed a discussion of his personal life would send this extroverted man into full retreat, discreet as the retreat was. It touched her in dangerous ways that he would be vulnerable. It made him far more human than she'd like.

Merrick gave a lift of his shoulders. 'Like *esprit de l'escalier.* It means thinking of a retort after the moment has passed. Diderot introduced the phrase in one of his works.'

'The spirit of the staircase?' Alixe quizzed, absently lifting her hair off her neck and then letting it spill through her hands in a careless gesture as she pondered the phrase. 'I'm afraid I don't understand.'

Merrick was studying her with his blue eyes. She shifted uncomfortable with his scrutiny. Something had changed in the moments since her comments. The air had become charged with a sweet tension that implied impending action.

'Do that again,' Merrick ordered, a low-voiced demand edged in sensuality. 'Pull up your hair and let it sift through your fingers.'

She did as he commanded. He'd risen from his chair. He was stalking her now, with his eyes and his body, coming towards her in slow strides, his eyes locked on hers. She did it again, raising her hands to gather up the thick length of her hair, her teeth delicately worrying her bottom lip subconsciously. She wasn't aware she'd even done it.

'Ah, yes, Alixe, very good. Every man likes the innocent wanton,' Merrick whispered, lifting his arms to take her hair in his own hands. She trembled at the feel of his warm hands skimming her shoulders as he dropped her hair. Her stomach tightened in anticipation. He was going to seduce her again as he had the day before. She ought to resist. There was nothing here but another lesson.

'My Alixe, your body is so much more eager than you know.' He leaned in, feathering a light kiss against her neck in the hollow beneath her ear.

A moan escaped her lips and she swayed towards him, all thoughts of resisting vanished in the wake of the curious warmth that spread through her, conjured there by his touch, his kiss, his words. Her face was between his hands and her mouth was open beneath his. With her eyes shut, it seemed all her senses were heightened. She was acutely aware of the feel of his hips pressed ever so gently against hers. The clean smell of him enveloped her—she could make it out now, a light *fougère* layered with oak and moss, a hint of lavender and something else that called to mind grass on a summer day—and the taste of him was in her mouth, the sweetly pungent remnants of morning coffee.

With the morning to guard her, Alixe had thought she'd be safe from him and the wickedness he awoke in her. She had imagined such seduction could not occur in the bright light of day. She should have known better. The afternoon had not served her well yesterday.

Her hands needed somewhere to go and it only seemed right that they should anchor in the buttermilk depths of his hair. The move pulled her closer to him, her breasts pressed against the masculine planes of his chest. This was most wicked of her and in the light of the window, too...

'Oh!' The realisation was enough to make her jump, a hand hastily covering her mouth. 'The window! Anyone might see us.' She knew she was clumsy in her panicked retreat past him to the relative safety of the table.

Merrick only laughed, in no hurry to back away from the window. Why had she thought he'd react differently? It was all a game to him, one of the many games he played.

'Oh, hush!' she scolded.

'I do believe you are a hypocrite, Alixe Burke.' Merrick returned to the table and resumed his seat, eyes full of mischief.

'I don't know what you're talking about.' Alixe seethed. She'd been caught out again by that scoundrel.

'Yes, you do, you little fool.' Merrick gave a warm chuckle. 'Look at you, sitting there with your straight back and folded hands like a genteel angel all worried about propriety when moments ago you were the very devil in my arms and propriety be damned.'

Alixe's face burned. She could not gainsay the truth. He was right. She'd been all hot abandon and it was positively disgraceful. She could not argue otherwise.

'Come now,' Merrick coaxed, 'there's no need to be ashamed. Why not admit you enjoy our lessons?'

'There can be no more lessons, as you call them.' Alixe made an attempt to return her attentions to the manuscript. He'd shown her his vulnerable side and she'd shown him hers. She was certain it was far more than either had intended.

Merrick was letting her stew. She didn't dare look up, but she could hear him rifling through book pages and shuffling papers. She pretended to read and scribble some illegible notes in the margins and waited.

'You do realise you're in an enviable position to combine business with pleasure. You should make the most of it,' Merrick said casually at last, not bothering to look away from his papers.

'I'm afraid you'll have to explain that,' Alixe replied with the aloofness that had staved off most of male London.

It didn't freeze Merrick in the least. If anything, it had the opposite effect, encouraging him to indecently honest conversation.

'Most young women would like to be in your position, privy to the secrets I can teach you.' He leaned back again in his chair, his feet hooked about the front legs. 'Perhaps your father has accidentally started a new fad: coaching one's daughter in the ways of Eve.'

Alixe slammed down her notebook. She was angry at herself for having proved so gullible as to allow herself to be seduced. She was angry at her father for forcing her into this situation and most of all she was angry at Merrick, who refused to be anything but outrageous. 'My father may have blackmailed you into this, but he did not expect you to take such liberties. You were only assigned to raise interest in me. I dare say that can be done without the "lessons" you've apparently designed for my edification.'

Merrick was thoughtful for a moment. 'All right. No more lessons unless you ask for them. However, I do need to raise interest in you and you must allow me to do my duty—'

'Without kissing, without excessive touching beyond what is expected in polite society,' Alixe interrupted.

'Agreed,' Merrick said without hesitation.

'Agreed,' Alixe answered with equal swiftness. But deep down, her confidence faltered. She'd got her terms. There'd be no more moments like the one at the villa, like the one in front of the window. But she was going to pay—she just couldn't determine how.

Or when.

Chapter Ten

Four days into their agreement, Alixe was regretting it. Merrick had kept his word. He'd not kissed her, not tempted her to wanton passions, at least not in any way she could take issue with. He'd kept his part of the agreement, holding to the letter of the proverbial law, if not the spirit of it.

Even the slightest of his touches at her elbow managed to send *frissons* of anticipation through her, reminding her of other, less-decent touches, and of possibilities that existed if she would only ask for them. Mostly those touches reminded her that this was all her fault. The frustration that plagued her late at night alone in bed was of her own doing.

He was doing it on purpose, but she couldn't prove it, just as she couldn't substantiate the niggling feeling that the other shoe still hadn't dropped.

And then it did with a resounding clatter bright and early one morning when she'd least expected it. Of course, that was how it always happened. She should have known.

Alixe awoke to a sun-soaked room, well aware that today held both excitement and danger. Today was the day she was to take her completed translation to Vicar Daniels and help set up the historical society's display for tomorrow's fair in the village. That was the exciting part. The danger was what the fair stood for—a day closer to the departure to London and the fate that awaited her there.

She was keenly aware the house party had reached its zenith and was careening towards its conclusion: the fair in the village followed two days later by her mother's much-anticipated midsummer ball. And she had failed to stop it—not the ball, but her imminent departure.

It wasn't all she'd failed at. She'd failed to shake Merrick from her side and where she'd failed, he'd succeeded magnificently. She might not be the Toast of London yet, but she'd become the Toast of the house party. Merrick's presence at her side ensured a heightened interest in her that not even her plain, unobtrusive garb could counteract. Being in his company made her visible to others.

She had not noticed until it was too late that he'd orchestrated their days into an easy pattern—mornings spent in the quiet seclusion of the library working on the manuscript where they were joined at times by Jamie or Ashe pursuing their own projects. During the afternoons, she and Merrick were taken up with various groups until no one even considered inviting Merrick without her. They played lawn bowls with Riordan and the young bucks he'd gathered whom he felt met his standard of debauchery. There was croquet and a badminton match against Ashe and Mrs Whitely. Merrick cheered from the sidelines for her at an impromptu archery contest among the young ladies and he saw to it that she stood beside him while he and Ashe engaged a pair of bragging riflemen in a friendly competition of marksmanship.

She had never lived like this before. She'd never allowed herself to as part of her self-imposed exile from society. She was discovering it was fun to be the centre of a group, to play and to laugh. Most of all it was fun to be with Merrick and it was easy to forget why he was with her.

Such forgetfulness was her biggest failure. He was luring her to London and then he'd disappear when his job was done. It had to stop. Today would be a day to start afresh in her campaign of resistance. The first thing to do was get dressed. She had a dress in mind, a sallow-yellow muslin that did nothing for her complexion.

With renewed determination, Alixe threw open the doors to her wardrobe, expecting to be met with the usual chaos that lay inside, stockings and ribbons peeking out of drawers where she'd haphazardly stuffed them. But there was nothing. It took a moment to digest the vision. Her wardrobe was entirely empty.

She had no clothes.

The olive dress she'd worn to the summer house was gone. The grey riding habit was gone. The pale-blue

dinner gown she'd worn the first night was gone. There
wasn't even a dressing robe she could throw over her
nightrail. Alixe reached for the bell pull and yanked.
There was something odd about all this. Wardrobes
didn't simply disappear and Meg was far too experienced of a maid to do all the laundry at once.

Meg arrived in record time, having trouble hiding
a smile. Alixe eyed her suspiciously. 'You seem happy
today.'

'Yes, I suppose it's the prospect of the fair tomorrow.' Meg nearly giggled. 'Lord St Magnus's man,
Fillmore, has asked if he could walk down with me.'
Wonderful—now Merrick had got his well-manicured
claws into her maid.

'I'm looking forward to the fair, too, only I'm afraid
I won't be able to go since I haven't anything to wear.'
Alixe gave a dramatic sigh. Meg had the good sense
to look slightly sheepish.

'My wardrobe is empty, Meg. Do you know anything about that?'

Meg's sunny smile returned in full force. 'That's
because you have all new clothes, my lady. Isn't it exciting?'

Alixe sat down hard on the bed. 'How is that possible? I haven't ordered anything.'

Meg opened the door and gestured out into the hallway. Her room began to fill with a procession of maids
carrying box after box in all assorted shapes and sizes.
'It's all Lord St Magnus's doing, although I helped him

a bit since he couldn't very well go rummaging around a lady's bedroom.'

Alixe listened, stunned. With Meg's help it hadn't been difficult to determine sizes. Nor had it been difficult to spirit her old gowns away, which had apparently been done last night while she was down at dinner.

Meg held up a white-muslin walking dress sprigged with pink flowers. 'This will be perfect for today, my lady. There's a light shawl in pink and a matching parasol to go with it.'

The gown was lovely in its simplicity, but it was not drab. She wanted her gowns back. She felt comfortable in them. She knew her limits in them. She needed them. Without them, her plans would fall apart. How could she convince St Magnus she was hopeless if she showed up wearing that pretty creation?

Yet what choice did she have? If she didn't put it on, there was nothing else to wear. She'd spend the day in her room, an unpalatable option. She'd miss the fair, miss seeing her manuscript on display and she'd have to explain why. The explanation sounded petty even to her. She couldn't very well argue she wasn't going downstairs because she had nothing to wear when there were boxes piled up in her room full of new clothes.

This all assumed Merrick would allow her to remain in her room. She fully expected he wouldn't. If she failed to appear for the departure to the fair, he'd come charging up here to demand the reason why. There she'd sit in her nightclothes without a robe to cover herself. Those blue eyes of his would run over her body and he would say something provocative that would make her blush, then something that would make her laugh and forget his insolence. At which point, she'd give up being angry. She would dress because she had no good reason not to that didn't sound childish and they would go about their day.

'My lady, should we dress?' Meg was still standing there, holding out the pretty muslin.

'Yes,' Alixe decided. She would not wait for the fight to come to her. The only way to stop Merrick would be to best him. 'Where is Lord St Magnus, Meg? I want to thank him, personally.'

'I believe Fillmore mentioned he was already at breakfast with Mr Bedevere on the verandah.'

Alixe grinned. Perfect. She knew exactly what to do. A stop by Merrick's rooms was in order. She was about to redefine sartorial elegance for him and return the 'favour'.

Ashe and Merrick sat at a small table on the verandah, enjoying a leisurely breakfast. Most of the ladies had opted for trays in their rooms. Other male guests ate in the breakfast room or at small tables nearby, taking in the coolness of the summer morning before the heat of the day.

'Riordan's not up yet?' Merrick enquired.

Ashe shrugged. 'We won't see him until noon and when we do, he'll be as growly as a bear. Celibacy and hangovers don't mix well for him.'

'It's barely been a week and a half.' Merrick laughed. 'Surely Riordan can manage that long.'

Ashe slid him a sly look. 'We haven't all had the

company of Lady Alixe to keep us occupied. Billiards and fishing lose their ability to keep a man fulfilled after a while. It'll be good to get back to London in a few days and the bountiful supply of willing women. This house party is a bit too chaste for me.' Ashe nudged Merrick with an elbow. 'Perhaps you and I should throw a house party, males only, at my hunting box after the Season. We can have Madame Antoinette send over her French girls. We can have a little competition, lay some wagers while we're laying the girls. How many are you up to, by the way? Have you hit two hundred yet?'

This was an old score. He and Ashe had long competed for who could claim the most conquests. Actresses, willing ladies of the *ton* and skilled courtesans of the *demi-monde* peopled the list of past lovers. But this morning, the claim was somewhat awkward. The lustre of the brag had become tarnished. It didn't seem to be a point of pride. What would Alixe think? She would not respect such behaviour. What others thought had never bothered him before, but this morning it did, especially when it came to a particular someone. 'What about you, Ashe? Up to fifty yet?'

'You're surly, Merrick.' Ashe laughed. 'Is the parson's mousetrap getting a bit dangerous? You've been spending a lot of time with Lady Alixe. Is there any hope of getting her up to snuff?'

Merrick tensed at Ashe's tone, wanting to defend Alixe. 'She's quite decent once you get to know her. You have to understand how difficult her predicament is. She's being forced to marry. None of this is of her choosing. I find I've come to admire her fortitude in the face of adversity.'

Ashe leaned forwards in deadly earnest. 'Listen to yourself, Merrick. You make it sound like a Drury Lane drama. *She's* being forced to marry? We're all forced to marry when it comes down to it. It's the price for being born noble. You and I are the lucky ones. We're second sons. We might escape that particular fate as long as our brothers don't see fit to die too soon. But Lady Alixe was fated for the altar the moment she was born. If you're not careful, you'll end up as her "predicament".' He paused and added a considering look. 'Unless that doesn't bother you? There are certain benefits to marrying her. She would solve your cash-flow issues.'

'I don't have a cash-flow problem.'

'Yes, I suppose that requires the possession of money to start with.' Ashe laughed. 'You are the slyest old fox, Merrick. I think you will marry her, after all, with just the right amount of remorse to convince old Folkestone you hadn't planned it this way all along.'

'That is hardly my intention,' Merrick ground out, fighting a rising urge to take a shot at Ashe's perfect jaw. He didn't like thinking of Alixe in those terms. She was more than someone to be bartered away. She was full of passion and life, intelligence and spirit. He didn't want to see that quashed by a heartless marriage to him or to anyone not of her choosing.

'You're not really her protector, you know,' Ashe drawled. Merrick recognised that drawl. Ashe was about to make some profound statement. 'Don't fool yourself into thinking you're a knight in shining armour awakening her to her true self, that whatever you've been doing with her these past days is in her best interest. You're not on her side. You're leading her away from everything she professes to want in order to save your own freedom. If she's as smart as you say she is, she'll work that out eventually. Be ready for it. Don't kid yourself into thinking otherwise.'

Because she'll hate you for it. Merrick heard the unspoken message. He pulled out his pocket watch and flipped it open. She was probably upstairs hating him right now. By his calculations, Meg should have presented the new wardrobe already. It would be enough to get Alixe started in London. The other half would be waiting for her once she arrived. After the debacle with the riding habit, he'd sent measurements and style notes to a dressmaker in London for evening wear and ball gowns. The other gowns had been supplied by a local draper. It had been rather enjoyable spending someone else's money and the earl had been all too glad to pay the bill.

Alixe would look stunning in her no-expense-spared wardrobe. But Ashe's comment gouged. He wasn't Alixe's protector. More honestly, he was her betrayer. Thanks to his efforts, she was well garbed and, with her funds, she'd have the choice of the right kind of husband this go-round, a choice she couldn't refuse for a third time. He didn't want to betray her. He was not a malicious man by nature, but if he didn't help her find a decent husband, it would be far worse to be married to him and his family full of secrets.

'Look at that,' Ashe murmured appreciatively, nodding at a point over Merrick's shoulder. 'Exactly what have you been doing with Lady Alixe? You might just be free of the parson's mouse trap yet.'

Merrick turned. Alixe stood on the verandah, wearing the sprigged muslin he'd told Meg to lay out. She looked exquisite. The pink-ribbon trim beneath her breasts drew the eye ever so subtly upwards to the high, firm quality of those breasts while the tiny lace trim on the low-scooped neckline of the bodice reminded the looker those breasts belonged to a lady. Her hair had been simply styled into a soft chignon at the base of her neck. Everything about her was cameo perfect. Alixe did look beautiful. She also looked angry.

Chapter Eleven

'May I have a word with you?' Alixe approached the table, her colour high and flushing her cheeks delightfully.

'You must know it is highly unorthodox for a young lady to approach a gentleman,' Merrick began in low teasing tones, noting with a surreptitious sweep of the verandah the amount of eyes turned in their direction.

'*You* must know it is highly unorthodox to take a lady's clothes,' Alixe hissed.

'Oh, my, Merrick, whatever have you done now?' Ashe stifled a chuckle.

Alixe shot Ashe a quelling look. 'Well? Might I have that word?' She trained her gaze on Merrick, her foot tapping. 'I must speak to you right away.'

Merrick scanned the verandah. He didn't want a scene. His best option for privacy was the gardens that lay at the foot of the shallow verandah stairs. 'Perhaps a walk in the garden would settle my breakfast. Would you care to join me?'

'I want my clothes back,' Alixe began the moment they reached the bottom of the wide stairs.

'Why? You look perfectly lovely in this ensemble. You cannot argue that this outfit is less fetching than that olive sack you tramp around the countryside in.'

'Because they're mine and you had no right to take them!'

Tears threatened in her eyes, a reaction that made Merrick feel decisively uncomfortable. This was one area of the female mystery he'd not yet solved with any great success.

'You couldn't go to London looking like a farmer's daughter,' Merrick offered. No woman he'd ever known would balk at the size of the wardrobe he'd had delivered to Alixe's room. He'd counted on that assumption to overcome any opposition.

'That's just it. I don't want to go to London at all.' Merrick heard the frustration welling up in her voice. She'd all but stamped her foot. This wasn't about clothes. This was about all the things that had been taken from her in the last two weeks. The urge to protect surged strong and hard within him. Alixe Burke was getting to him in the most unexpected ways. He'd not expected to care so deeply about what happened to her. He'd always thought of himself as a selfish creature. It was surprising to realise otherwise.

'Alixe…' he began, looking for a way to apologise. But Alixe was too impatient.

'No, don't say anything. There's nothing you can

say. There's nothing you can do. This is all your fault, you and your stupid wager with Redfield. You never should have taken it.'

'If not me, then it would have been someone else.' Merrick stopped strolling and turned her to face him. 'Don't you see? Redfield was out to get you. Someone that night would have taken the wager.' He had yet to gather up any substantial proof of that. Redfield had spent the house party dutifully charming the matrons and putting on a well-mannered performance that suggested he was all he purported to be. But Merrick's instincts were seldom wrong.

'So it is inevitable. I am to accept my fate and go meekly to London.'

'Quite possibly, my dear, although it gives me no pleasure to say it. However, no one says you have to hate it.'

Alixe's brow made a small furrow. 'Isn't the expression "no one says you have to *like* it"?'

'That's what *everyone* says. It's not what *I* say. Why not enjoy the experience? Enjoy the beautiful clothes, enjoy the glittering parties. Enjoy each day, Alixe. Don't fret too much about the future, it spoils the present.' Merrick looked around the garden. 'Here's a perfect example. We have this glorious day spread before us and no plans. Let's drive down to the village and help with your historical society. Fillmore and your Meg can come to make it decent. We can pack a picnic to enjoy on the way home.' He didn't wait for an argument. 'Go get your things and meet me on the drive in twenty minutes.'

* * *

The fair itself was to be held on the green, a wide
space atop the west cliffs. The cliff end of the green
was edged by a promenade overlooking the sea and
Alixe couldn't imagine a more striking setting. With
the blue sky overhead and the bustling excitement of
friends and neighbours on the green, it was hard to
stay angry at Merrick for spiriting away her clothes,
especially when she felt wonderful in the new sprigged
muslin. She'd dressed in her plain gowns for so long
she'd forgotten how much fun it was to dress up.

Merrick helped her down from the gig and a group
of workers waved them over to the booth being assembled by the historical society. It was a heady moment
to be swept up into the group, everyone exclaiming
over her translation. Headier still were the hours that
followed. Alixe put an apron on over her gown and
threw herself into organising the displays with the other
women while Merrick joined the men in constructing
the wooden frame for the booth and hanging bunting.

His willingness to join in came as a surprise. He
was always immaculately turned out and building fair
booths was not the immaculate work of a gentleman.
But Merrick had not hesitated. His coat had come off
and his shirt sleeves had gone up. She caught sight of
him with a hammer in one hand and nails clenched between his teeth. She could not help but stare.

It was hard to imagine London's premier rake engaged in such work. Then again, it was hard to conceive of London's premier rake doing most of what
he'd done in the past two weeks. He had not balked at

playing cards with Mrs Pottinger's group or cringed at donating himself to the cause of charming wallflowers at the house party. Neither had he shied away from his pledge to her father. In their own ways, these were the actions of a man who was more honourable than he might first appear.

'Your fellow's a handsome man,' Letty Goodright commented beside her, sorting through a pile of sixteenth-century bonnets someone had donated to the display.

'He's not my fellow.' Alixe quickly returned her gaze to the items in front of her where her eyes should have been all along.

'Isn't he?' Letty reached for another pile of miscellaneous clothing. 'A man doesn't spend the day sweating in the sun for no good reason. Other than you, I can't see what reason he has for helping out. He's not from around here. This village fair is nothing to him. I know men, my dear, and this one is interested in you.'

'Well, maybe.' What else could she say? She couldn't very well explain the arrangement between her and Merrick. At least it wasn't an outright lie. Merrick was interested in her, just for different reasons than the ones Letty presumed. Letty did know men. She was one of those lush-figured, earthy women that managed to be pretty while possessing a rather robust figure. She'd had her pick of men in the village at sixteen, had married a local farmer of good standing in their little community and now, ten years later, trailed a string of seven rambunctious children behind her whenever she went to market.

'There's no maybe about it. He's smitten with you. Look at him.'

Alixe looked up to see Merrick flash her a smile, nails and all. It was a ridiculous grin and she couldn't help but laugh.

'He's a charmer.' Letty clucked. 'Let me give you some advice. Don't give in too soon. The charmers all like a challenge whether they know it or not.'

'I don't mean to give in at all,' Alixe retorted. But the idea was secretly tempting. He played his role so convincingly, it would be easy to believe Merrick was falling in love with her.

Letty tossed her a coy look. 'Giving in is all the fun. Of course, you'll give in, just don't do it too soon.'

'I'm leaving for London when Mother's house party is done. I expect I'll meet some other, more suitable men,' Alixe said with a touch of primness.

'Unsuitable men are more fun and they make the best husbands once they've reformed. Take my Bertram, for example, a scalawag if there ever was one. Why, before he met me, he was in the public house every night, drinking and playing cards. His father had despaired of him ever becoming a serious landowner. But then he met me…'

Alixe smiled politely. She'd heard the stories about Bertram and Letty before. Her thoughts could safely meander from the conversation. There was soundness in Letty's counsel. There was no one more unsuitable than Merrick and he was extraordinary amounts of fun. Her life had been considerably more entertaining since he'd entered it. But she mustn't forget the price. She must *never* forget the price. He was going to entertain her all the way to the altar where he'd leave her to another man. For which she should be thankful. There was no amount of reform that would make him into an exemplary husband who did not stray from his wife. Jamie had said as much when he'd warned her. Based on what she'd seen of Merrick, she was inclined to believe her brother.

Merrick came striding towards them, his shirt splotched with sweat and his hair tousled. He'd never looked more handsome or more real than he did at that moment. The realness of him was far more intoxicating than any sartorial manufacturing could create. His grin was easy. 'The booth is complete, if you would like to start bringing your displays over.'

A half-hour later, the displays were arranged to satisfaction, her translation in pride of place at the front in a glass case Vicar Daniels had taken from the church.

'I hope *that's* not the church.' Merrick pointed to a large ruin on the edge of the Leas and everyone laughed.

'No, that's the church of St Mary and St Eanswythe,' Vicar Daniels explained. 'What you're looking at are the ruins of the original Abbey. It was destroyed around 1095. But there's a priory now and monks still live there, although I suspect they will be moved in the near future to a less-ancient home.'

'We are hoping to do some restoring of the Abbey. The project will be extensive. We've been raising money for quite some time,' Alixe put in. This was a project dear to her. St Eanswythe was not only a local saint, but a woman who had challenged a king for the right to found and rule an abbey in a man's world. 'We're nearly there. We're hoping this display will help generate the last few donations.'

'I don't think I've ever heard of St Eanswythe,' Merrick admitted with a grin.

'Our Alixe can tell you all about her. She's made the saint a special point of study.' Letty smiled mischievously. Alixe would have pinched her if she'd been standing closer. 'You should show Lord St Magnus the ruins and tell him the stories of Eanswythe's miracles.'

Merrick complied, immediately understanding Letty's game. 'I would love to see the ruins. Perhaps you and I might find a place to picnic in the shade while we tour your landmarks.'

'We can't abandon everyone when there's work to be done,' Alixe protested. The last time she'd picnicked with Merrick had been disastrous for her. He'd kissed her at the Roman villa.

'Off with you.' Letty made a shooing gesture with her hands. 'There's hardly anything left to be done and you've worked through lunch.' The group agreed, making short work of Alixe's last line of defence.

'Resistance is useless, my dear,' Merrick said smugly, tucking her arm through his and leading her away from the safety of the group. 'Relax, it's just lunch, Alixe. We're going to talk about ham sandwiches and lemonade. What could happen?'

'Plenty happened the last time we picnicked,' Alixe reminded him sharply. Being in a group of her mother's house guests had not protected her from her flight of fancy at the villa.

'Yes, but now you have your agreement in place. What could possibly happen with your friends a mere shout away and Fillmore and Meg to hand? Really, Alixe, you make me out to be a wolf.'

Merrick-logic was all too persuasive. He made it sound safe and reasonable. What could happen indeed? Regardless of the facts, she knew better. Even the most usual of events turned into adventures when Merrick was around. A naughty, rebellious part of her could hardly wait to find out—the part that wanted to take his advice and not worry about the future, the part that wanted to appreciate the present. Perhaps Merrick was right. If she couldn't change the inevitable, she might as well enjoy the journey. Why shouldn't she enjoy the fact that she was wearing a new dress, the weather was fine and a handsome man wanted her attentions? Why shouldn't she dice with the devil just a little, just once?

'You shouldn't have done it,' Merrick said between bites of cheese. 'You should have followed your instincts and resisted. You have very fine instincts about people, Alixe.'

They'd found a place under the shade of a leafy maple in the corner of the ruined churchyard. Their picnic lay spread out before them: a cheese wheel of cheddar, a loaf of brown bread and a basket of pears. Merrick had stretched his long limbs and lay back, hands behind his head. Alixe wished she could afford the luxury of doing the same. It would be heaven to lie back on the blanket and look up at the sky through the leafy canopy of trees. But a lady did not indulge, especially not when it would mean lying next to a man.

'Why do you say that? Especially since it's far too late for me to go back now.'

'Because I am a wolf, contrary to my protests otherwise.' Merrick took a savage bite from a pear to illustrate his point.

Alixe took a more delicate bite of her food. 'You may be a wolf, but you are not a ravenous wolf. You are in complete control of yourself and for that reason, I have nothing to fear from you.'

Merrick rolled to his side, propping himself up on one arm, his eyes alight with his special brand of mischief. 'I have been coaxing women off the paths at Vauxhall since I was sixteen. Coaxing a well-bred lady into a churchyard is child's play by comparison.'

He was teasing her, but there was a hard truth lurking around his humour. 'Why do you think that is?' she queried.

'Women know what can happen in the dark shadows at Vauxhall. They're warned about the possibilities. But well-bred virgins never believe anything untoward could happen in a churchyard.' Merrick took another crisp bite of his pear and chuckled. 'As if God pays more attention to what is happening in his churchyards than he does to the dim paths of Vauxhall.'

Really, he'd gone too far there. A scold was in order, but she barely got the words out before her own laughter bubbled up at the image his words created. 'Merrick, you shouldn't say things like that.'

'No more than you should laugh about them and yet here we are doing both.' Merrick finished off his pear and tossed the core towards the base of a tree trunk for the birds to find later.

'Now, tell me about St Eanswythe in the hopes that we can redeem ourselves with a more suitable subject for our surroundings.'

The request took her by surprise. No one had ever asked her to tell them about St Eanswythe. She'd delivered a talk about the local saint to a few clubs and the historical society, but no one socially in the course of polite conversation had ever asked her about her favourite topic. She began tentatively at first, giving Merrick a chance to interrupt, to show any sign of uninterest. But no sign came. Instead, his blue eyes remained attentively fixed on her, his head nodding in attention.

'She performed three miracles and won the king's approval to establish the first convent in England,' Alixe concluded.

'You sound impressed with her,' Merrick commented.

'I am. She fought for what she wanted. She turned down marriage to a king.'

'Ah, correction.' Merrick wagged his finger, throwing his recently acquired knowledge back at her. 'She offered the king a chance to win her. She wagered and she would have had to pay if she'd lost.' He reached for another pear. 'Not unlike yourself.'

'I did not wager.'

Merrick shrugged a shoulder. 'A slight discrepancy, I should think. Like her, you have also given up the complications of life for a simple one and, like her, you have devoted yourself to thwarting suitors for your hand.'

'She did it on purpose,' Alixe said to be contrary.

'So have you,' Merrick countered readily enough. 'You're pretty, you're smart, you're titled and you're rich. You've merely taken pains to hide all that and make yourself difficult to obtain.'

Merrick inched closer to her on the blanket and reached out a hand to tug at her chignon, his hand softly sweeping the gentle curve of her jaw. 'Do you think it worth the sacrifice, pretty one? The world of man is not as bad as you think.'

Alixe's breath caught at the sound of his voice, low and personal in the quiet of the afternoon. Meg and Fillmore had taken themselves off a while ago to see if they could spot France from the cliff-walk promenade.

Her hair came loose with another tug and spilled down her back. 'Would you die as your Eanswythe did? Without knowing the touch of a man? Without knowing the secret pleasures she was made for?' His hand tangled gently in her hair, pressing her forwards to him, his mouth taking hers in a kiss. She thought fleetingly of their agreement, but those words seemed to provide inadequate protection at the present. Instead, she gave herself up to the kiss, a small moan escaping her. She was all heady compliance.

She would never remember quite how it progressed from there. Had she drawn him down to her, or had he pressed her back on to the blanket? Somehow she was beneath him, her hips moving in rhythm against his, his sex heavy against her thigh where trousers met skirts and neither of them thinking much beyond the moment. His hand was at her breast, tracing teasing circles through the cloth. She arched against him, intuitively looking for release from the frantic heat pulsing through her, knowing he possessed the answer, the ability to assuage her. Her hands were at his shoulders, kneading the muscles beneath his shirt, wanting to do more. Then her fingers were working his buttons, pushing the halves of his shirt back, finding the muscled expanse of bare skin underneath. Her palms skimmed the planes of his chest, her thumbs running over his nipples much as he'd done for her. He groaned his delight, his hips pressing harder against hers in response. His mouth was devouring her now, his hands shoving up her skirts so that she would be bare to him and it was still not enough. She was hungry, so very hungry for this, for his touch.

She was aware of his hand at her most private place, of his hand unerringly parting her damp curls and stroking the secret nub until the sensations he ignited drowned out any thought of reality, of recognition over what they were doing. Then he took her beyond all thought where she bucked hard against his hand and he lay beside her, crooning soft words of encouragement until she gave herself over entirely to the pleasures that swamped her.

She was a long time recovering. Alixe wanted nothing more than to lay beneath the maples in a well-sated stupor for ever. Merrick seemed content to lay there, too, propped on an elbow, looking down at her face, an idle hand stroking back an errant strand of hair.

'What was that?' Alixe said, her voice coming out slightly hoarse.

Merrick smiled. 'The pleasures of the world of man, my dear. Did you like it?'

'You know I did.' It was an embarrassing admission. From what she'd been told, a lady didn't like such things.

'You should. There's nothing wrong with liking it. You were made for it, I was made for it,' Merrick said softly.

'Is this what happens to virgins in churchyards?' Alixe quipped, her wits coming back to her as the haze of sated desire receded.

Merrick chuckled. 'Yes, except your Eanswythe.'

A wave of sadness and reality swept over Alixe. She turned to face Merrick, acutely aware they lay side by side in such close proximity. It would be entirely shocking if anyone found them this way. 'Is that why you did it? To show me what she missed?'

Alixe didn't want it to be the truth, that this most incredible experience, most intimate experience, had been another of his lessons.

'No, pretty one, it's not.'

Chapter Twelve

Merrick cut through the water, cleaving it with powerful strokes in the hopes that if he swam hard enough, long enough, he could exorcise the heat *she* raised in his body, the turmoil she raised in his mind. Alixe Burke had become dangerous to his sense of well-being.

He had not meant for things to progress as they had that afternoon. He had not risen in the morning with any thought of showing Alixe pleasure on a picnic blanket beneath a summer sky. Merrick flipped on to his back and began a long, methodical stroke that took him across the lake. If it had been an instructive interlude or a love-game of the type he played with his myriad women, he would have a proper perspective for understanding what had transpired—the generating of physical pleasure. But that had not been what had happened.

She had roused to him with a natural passion devoid of coy artifice. Those sherry eyes of hers had widened in awe and amazement, her untutored hips had sought release against his with no concept of what they were asking of him; the artlessness of her wanting had been a heady aphrodisiac to his jaded sense of sexual conquest. And it had fired him beyond reason, driven him to answer the calls of her body in ways she wanted, but could not imagine without him.

His body remembered every moment of her pleasure, of her body arching into his, her hips bucking against his hand. Even now, hours later, the memory of it was burned into his body, the simple recalling of it enough to bring to life a hard-suppressed erection. He had told her the truth. Touching her had nothing to do with lessons. He had touched her because he'd wanted to, because he was enchanted with her storytelling. Her face had come alive as she'd spun her tales of Eanswythe. He could have lain on the blanket and listened to her all afternoon. His London cronies would have laughed to see the sophisticated Merrick St Magnus captivated by the simple tales of country saints. For that matter, they would have laughed to see him with hammer in hand building fair booths.

But it had seemed right. He'd spun a fantasy for himself today with Alixe at the centre of it. It had been a lovely escape to imagine himself a country squire working with his neighbours, casting a glance every now and then to where his pretty wife chatted with other women. It was a perfect image, free of the entanglements of his debauched ways. The man in his fantasy didn't wager on how many women he could bed in a year. The man in his fantasy needed only one woman and had the ability to remain constant. That man would not grow bored in the country as Merrick most certainly would.

Merrick floated on his back, his body exhausted, his mind still restless. It was an escape, nothing more. London waited and with it his regular life, his social rounds, his endless search for wagers and women that would keep his pockets lined. And his father waited. Reality waited. Alixe Burke would see him for what he was behind the clothes and easy words. In London there would be no hiding from the rumours. Even if he did nothing outrageous for the next six weeks of the Season, there were rumours enough from his past to convince her most thoroughly of his unsuitability.

That would be for the best. He'd not been the only one caught up in his little fantasy today. He'd caught her watching him in the same manner he'd been watching her. For all her protestations, Alixe was not immune to him. He'd initiated her into the pleasures of physical intimacy. That would count for something with a woman like Alixe Burke.

Merrick snorted up at the dusking sky. It was laughable really, the idea of he and Alixe together. Rakes didn't marry good women who wanted to rebuild churches and translate old documents. And yet Merrick could not dismiss the idea that Alixe would be a perfect lover, that hard-to-find mix between untutored honesty and a curiosity in her own sensuality that overrode any annoying pretence towards modesty and embarrassment. He had no use for any woman who was too shy to admit to her own longings.

Merrick gave up on the pond. The heat of the afternoon had faded to the pleasant warmth of a summer evening. He would be missed and Lady Folkestone had entertainments planned for the evening—an alfresco dinner on the lawn and fireworks. Merrick towelled himself dry with his shirt and reached for the clean change of clothes he'd stopped by the house to get before setting out. He thrust his hand through the sleeve, tugging at the shoulder, and stopped, the sleeve coming off in his hand. What the hell…?

Merrick slid the ruined shirt off his body and studied the seams. They'd been ripped out so that only the basting remained. No wonder the sleeve had torn so effortlessly. He'd have to speak to Fillmore. He'd also have to walk home shirtless. Not that he cared. The evening was warm and he knew enough back paths to avoid encountering anyone.

He reached for his trousers and pulled them on. He bent to collect his boots and heard an ominous rip. Merrick straightened and laughed into the evening sky. It wasn't Fillmore he needed to speak with. It was an amber-eyed minx who'd wanted a little bit of revenge for his having stolen her clothes.

The west lawn looked like a fairyland with coloured lanterns strung from poles and candles under glass shields lighting the tables. Around Alixe, guests exclaimed over the summer magic her mother had created for the alfresco dinner. The meal would be the talk of London when the guests returned to town in a few days. But Alixe had little time to appreciate the summer splendour. Her eyes were busily quartering the guests for any sign of Merrick. He'd returned her to the house and abruptly left again. To her knowledge he had not returned yet. When she'd asked Fillmore where he might be, Fillmore had merely said he'd taken a change of clothes and left for a swim.

Now she was worried. And she was feeling a little bit guilty. What if he had picked up the clothes she had altered that morning? She had meant for him to discover her little prank in the privacy of his room. If he'd taken those clothes to a swimming hole... The image of a naked Merrick striding through the forest like a primordial god, tattered clothes in hand, brought a hot flush to her cheeks. He would act as if it didn't matter, as if roaming around in his 'altogether' was a perfectly natural experience. She had not meant to embarrass him, just to show him that she would not submit easily.

It seemed a poor prank after what had happened that afternoon. The simple pleasures of the outing had become complicated in the wake of what had occurred on the picnic blanket. He said he hadn't done it to teach her a lesson and she had found comfort in those words as long as she didn't examine them too closely.

If it hadn't been a lesson, what had it been? She knew without doubt that she was harbouring a perilous fascination with him. The interest she held in his life, the attraction she felt, the frantic wildness he raised in her when he touched her could no longer be explained away as general curiosity. There had been suitors before, but none with whom she'd felt this level of allure.

None of them had inclined her to even a kiss, let alone risk the temptations he'd presented her with today.

Those temptations went beyond the intimacy of what he'd done for her, although that had been exquisite and extraordinary in the sense that nothing had prepared her for the possibilities of such pleasure. She was still awash with the sensations. But there had been other temptations, too. He had listened to her tell the tales of Eanswythe with a sincerity that could not be faulted.

Today, she had been the centre of his attentions, not just during the stories, but throughout the entire afternoon. He'd built those booths for her, helped with the historical society for her. She could not recall the last time anyone had been so entirely devoted to her and she hadn't even asked. The greatest temptation of all was to fall for the fantasy he'd created: a fantasy where she wasn't being carted off and paraded on the marriage mart, a fantasy where he was not the greatest lover of women in all of London and had likely pleasured countless women the way he'd pleasured her. In this fantasy, he was hers alone.

And for all that, she'd ripped the seams on his clothes so that they wouldn't hold when he put them on. She wished she hadn't.

Couples were pairing up at the round dinner tables set out across the lawn. The house party had been a success. Several matches would come of these two weeks. Alixe's gaze darted through the groupings, searching for Jamie. She was feeling distinctly *de trop* without a partner. She had not realised how implicitly she'd come to rely on Merrick's presence at her side throughout the week. If he was absent, walking around naked out there in the summer night, she had only herself to blame.

Gentle hands skimmed her bare shoulders and a familiar scent enveloped her. 'Missing me yet?' came Merrick's voice at her ear.

'Please tell me you're wearing clothes,' Alixe whispered back.

Merrick's warm chuckle was all the reassurance she needed, bringing with it a sense that rightness had been restored to her world. 'I am, no thanks to you, minx.' It was a playful reproach. He was not angry.

'I am sorry.'

'Don't be, I rather enjoyed the joke.' He leaned in, the delightful smell of his cologne wrapping around her. 'You could have enjoyed it, too, if you'd been there. I did have to walk back half-naked.'

'I am sorry, truly.'

'To have missed it? Of course you are. Most would be.' His voice was a naughty whisper against her neck. 'But you are already familiar with my altogether, so perhaps you feel the loss more keenly.'

Alixe laughed. 'If I had a fan, I'd smack you for that.'

Merrick made a small bow and pulled something from his inner pocket. 'But you do.'

He presented her with a small ivory-boned fan done in lace on the points and the fabric of the body painted with delicate multi-coloured flowers. 'Oh, there are even sequins sewn on the petals,' Alixe exclaimed over the little details, delighting in how the sequins caught the play of the candlelight. 'Merrick, it's lovely. It might be quite the loveliest thing anyone has ever given me.' She looped the ribbon strap about her wrist and let it dangle experimentally. 'Thank you.'

'I am glad you like it. Now, shall we find a table?'

Merrick's hand was warm at the small of her back and she could feel the fantasy rushing back. 'I see Ashe and Mrs Whitely over there. We could join them and seal everyone's suspicions.'

It would be the smart thing to do. Her mother had most adroitly allowed her guests to sit where they'd like. It allowed the gentlemen to declare their preferences most subtly, a very fitting gesture as the party came to a close.

Merrick guided her through the maze of tables, his hand a constant light pressure at her back. She was well aware of people watching them. She was sure many had seen him give her the fan and many more were watching to see if he'd 'declare' himself the way others had tonight with their seating preference.

Merrick held out the chair for her and helped her arrange her skirts before sitting beside her. Riordan and Jamie joined them, Jamie bringing over a distant cousin who'd come for a few days to take in the ball before going on to London.

They made a merry group. Wine flowed freely, but carefully, and the gentlemen indulged them by telling stories from their college days that Alixe was certain were heavily edited for public consumption. This was a side of Merrick rarely seen, although she had glimpsed it on brief occasions, a Merrick who was at ease the way he'd been earlier today. This was not the cynical Merrick with his jaded innuendos, nor was it the Merrick whose proper behaviour was almost so perfect among society it seemed to subtly mock that same society.

Merrick was the life of the table, engaging the quiet cousin, and ribbing Riordan when his manners flagged. *My word, he is truly the sun they all revolve around,* Alixe thought. He really was remarkable.

After cheese and summer fruit had been served, Jamie rose and took his leave. Fireworks would be starting and he had hosting duties that required him to circulate among the tables. Soon, candles would be doused to make the most of the summer darkness. In anticipation of that, couples were making their way to viewing locations around the lawn.

'Come with me,' Merrick said in hushed tones. 'I have it on good authority from Jamie that the best viewing will be on the rise over there.'

Discreetly, he led her apart from the larger group. He'd planned well. A blanket awaited them, already laid out, pinned to the ground with a small woven basket. The location was indeed ideal. It put them at the back of the crowd. Everyone else would be facing away from them when the fireworks went off and it was just dark enough to not be noticed.

Alixe seated herself on the blanket and opened her fan, still touched by the unexpected gift. 'It is very pretty.'

'Not nearly as pretty as the one who holds it.' Merrick smiled. 'How do you like your wardrobe now that you've had time to become accustomed to it? You've chosen well tonight—the gold silk de Chine is deeper than a yellow, it sets off your hair wonderfully.'

'It's magnificent. You chose well.'

'I chose for *you*. Enjoy it even if you cannot bring yourself to enjoy the reasons for it. I liked thinking of all the money your father was spending. It served him right for putting you in this position,' Merrick said slyly with a wink that made her laugh. He reached over and captured her hand where it held the fan, his voice dropping. 'But this was not something your father paid for.'

A true souvenir, then. More complications. What did it mean that he'd chosen this token of his own accord? Jamie had insinuated Merrick's pockets were thinly lined and yet he'd spent his limited funds on a trinket for her. Was it merely his custom to give ladies presents? Did it mean anything? She wanted it to mean everything, that he'd fallen for the fantasy, too. A dangerous truth began to take root in her mind: after fighting it for so long, she might be falling in love.

A hushed pop and the soft hiss of liquid being poured into a glass called her back to reality. 'Champagne, Alixe?' Merrick passed her a flute.

'So that's what was in the basket!' Alixe took the glass. 'This is a rare treat indeed.'

Merrick clinked his glass against hers, his eyes on her, burning with their intensity. 'A toast, Alixe, to all a man can ask for: a beautiful woman to himself on a lovely summer night.'

Alixe sipped the cool liquid to dissipate the lump

that welled in her throat. If the afternoon had been magical, the evening had quickly become astonishing. She had not missed the import of the fan, and now the champagne and—oh, my, was that a bowl of strawberries he was laying out? All for her. He was making it so easy to believe.

'Open, Alixe,' he commanded huskily, popping a juicy berry in her mouth. She could feel the berry dribble on her lip and flicked out her tongue to catch the droplets.

'Allow me.' Merrick leaned forwards, taking her mouth in a kiss.

'No, allow me,' Alixe said, seized with a sudden daring. She offered him a strawberry and he took it in his mouth, teeth bared, and bit, his eyes never leaving hers. She drew a sharp breath, struck by the sensuality of it.

'I could do that to you, too, Alixe.' He gave a wicked smile. 'My mouth at your breast, suckling and perhaps the tiniest of nips to heighten the sensation.'

The mere suggestion sent a thrumming heat to the core of her and she felt herself rouse as she had that afternoon. Madness surged.

'And you? What could I do for you? Can I pleasure you the way you have pleasured me?' A dangerous wildness edged her voice. He was holding her with his eyes and she could not look away. The future could be damned in exchange for this moment, this adventure.

'You can, if you're willing. You could take me in your hand.'

His hand covered hers, guiding it to where his length

pressed against the fall of his trousers. He was fully aroused beneath the fabric and Alixe knew to touch him this way was not enough.

'I want to feel *you* against my hand, not the cloth,' she murmured. She could be astonished by her own audacity later, but not now. She did not want to think here in the summer night. She fumbled with the buttons and sought him in the darkness. Her hand closed over the length of him, hot and hard within the circle of her fist.

Merrick gave a small moan as her hand clasped him and began to move over the thick extent of him. Above them the first fireworks fractured the sky with their colours. She experimentally stroked the wide tender head of his manhood, eliciting a gratified exhalation from Merrick. This was glorious power indeed to know she could excite him so thoroughly. Merrick wrapped his hand about hers once more, settling her into a rhythm as her hand moved up and down his shaft. Then he leaned back, giving himself over to her ministrations while fireworks sprayed their colours across the night's dark canvas.

Alixe felt him surge once more against her hand, spending himself in warm release, and she knew she would not forget this, no matter what happened in London, no matter what happened for the rest of her life. She would not forget the evening she pleasured *him* beneath a summer sky with champagne and fireworks.

She could not expect to hold him beyond the few days that remained, but she could make the most of what time she had. There would be plenty of time later to sort through the foolishness of falling for Merrick St Magnus.

Chapter Thirteen

'**W**hat the hell do you think you're doing?' Ashe threw back the curtains, letting sunlight splinter mercilessly against Merrick's eyes.

Merrick threw up a hand to ward off the bright glare with a groan. 'More to the point, what the hell do you think you're doing?' Merrick opened one eye a crack. Ashe was dressed for riding, a fact worth noting given Ashe's penchant for late nights and later mornings. By the look of things from the one eye he'd managed to open, the morning was not far advanced.

'*I* am leaving, something I'd advise you to consider as well. Toss your necessities into a valise and we can be on the road before breakfast.' Ashe was already tearing through the wardrobe on the hunt for his travelling valise.

'Whatever are you talking about?' Merrick groused.

'I'm talking about last night. You're damned lucky I was the only one who saw you up on the hill last night with your champagne seduction and Lady Alixe's hand on your cock.'

Merrick sat up, instantly awake. It was funny how shocking news could do that to a body. Merrick's mind raced even as his words fumbled. His first instinct was to protect Alixe. 'I can explain.' The words sounded ridiculous. He couldn't come up with a plausible alternative for Alixe's hand between his legs.

Ashe laughed outright at his poor effort. 'Explain? I assure you, I don't need an explanation for what I saw. There was no mistaking it.'

Another panicked thought swept him. 'Did anyone else?' He'd been fairly sure the location would not draw attention.

'No, I told you already I was the only one out that way. You weren't the only one with seduction on your mind.' Ashe was impatient. 'Now, let's get you packed and be off.'

'I can't leave. I've got to take Alixe to the fair and there's the masquerade ball tomorrow night—'

Ashe cut him off in mid-list, disgusted. 'All of which are reasons you should be leaving today. Listen to yourself, Merrick.'

'Why are you leaving?' Merrick opted for a different tack. 'There's only two days to go and there's entertainment aplenty.' He eyed Ashe with a speculative gaze. 'Is it Mrs Whitely?'

Ashe was not forthcoming. 'I prefer to leave before things sour,' he offered, purposely obtuse. 'You ought to prefer it, too. You've done your job for Folkestone. The party is winding down, no one has exposed Alixe for being discovered in the library with you and she's ready to lay siege to London. You can meet up with her there, dance a few times and call it square with Folkestone. Whatever you still need to do for her relies on being in town. There's nothing more that requires you here. Tell Folkestone you want to go on ahead and prepare the way with a well-placed comment here and there.' Ashe paused, carefully considering his next words. 'Leaving now will make it clear your time with Alixe is nothing more than discharging a gentleman's agreement. Even I can see things are starting to get "confused" if last night was any indicator.'

Merrick shook his head. 'Alixe is counting on me today.' Alixe would be devastated to wake and find him gone. She would think his departure had to do with last night. He could not bear for her to think he'd fled because of *that*.

'Dear lord, I have a fool in love on my hands.' Ashe faced him, hands on hips, a challenge to deny his claim. 'You've gone and fallen for your own creation.' Ashe shook his head. 'It's impossible, you know. For one thing, Jamie will kill you. For another, his father will kill you. Either way, you'll end up dead. You weren't meant for her.'

Ashe gave a scornful laugh. 'Men like you and me aren't supposed to marry the virgin daughters of earls. There's only marriage if you continue down this road, Merrick. Surely you know that? You cannot expect to dally with her and play at love simply to walk away when you get tired of this little fantasy. You will get tired. You're not made for monogamy and you know it.'

Merrick shoved back the bedcovers and rolled out of

bed. 'Thank you for the sermon, Vicar.' He was cross with Ashe and with himself. He hardly knew what the truth was any more when it came to his feelings for Alixe Burke. He had gone far beyond being sympathetic for her. Sympathy had long ago morphed into admiration and admiration had turned into something much more powerful. He had only a few days left with Alixe and it would be a hardship to say goodbye. He would prolong it if he could.

'You're upset because I speak of reality,' Ashe said from the bank of windows. 'A gentleman knows when to make his exit.'

Merrick snorted at that. 'You and I have never pretended to be gentlemen.'

Ashe relented, his tone softening. 'Stay if you must, but see things as they are, not as you wish them to be. I am off and I am taking Riordan with me.'

Merrick gave a rueful smile at the notion of Ashe playing nursemaid to Riordan. Ashe was hardly the tolerant nurturing sort. 'Try to sober him up. He's been drinking too much.'

'I will. London has its distractions, if nothing else.' Ashe was all seriousness. His tone provoked Merrick's curiosity, but there was no time for that conversation at present.

'Godspeed, then, Ashe.' For a moment Merrick prevaricated. Perhaps he should go. If Riordan was in true need, he should be there for him. But Alixe needed him, too. There were things that needed sorting out between them for his own peace of mind and Riordan might simply be being Riordan.

'I will see you in London.' Ashe saluted with the riding crop and exited the room, leaving Merrick with the chaos of his thoughts.

Merrick dressed himself with care, gingerly testing the seams of his second-best day shirt in case Alixe had tampered with more than one set of clothes. He let out a sigh of relief when the sleeves held.

Ashe was right. Things had gone far off course where Alixe was concerned. He was no longer a social tutor to her. In all honesty, that role hadn't lasted much beyond the outing to the Roman ruins. He'd kissed her that day for himself because beautiful things should be kissed. She'd been uncertain and trusting in his arms, but not naïve. Even then, she'd questioned his motives as he should have done. It had been too easy to explain his actions to himself as an act of good will, part of some secret curriculum to turn Alixe Burke into a social sensation.

He knew now that she didn't need to be turned into anything. Ashe had called her his creation. But he had not created Alixe Burke, he had not even refashioned her. All she'd become had already been there. He'd merely uncovered what she'd chosen to hide and now he was about to turn all that over to another man.

The very thought made him sick.

He did not want to turn Alixe Burke over to another. But any other answer was impossible as Ashe had so adroitly argued. To not turn her over to London's fine young men meant marrying her himself, a prospect he was not fit to fulfil. He had secrets. She didn't really know who he truly was. If she did, she would despise him. She would demand faithfulness, something he wasn't sure he was equipped to give. Even if he could give her that, he had no means of supporting her.

He'd be completely reliant on her dowry and whatever her father saw fit to endow them with. Those were invisible chains that would chafe him every day. He would have become a kept man in every sense of the concept. There would be no wagers to hide behind, all disguises for what he was would be stripped away. Society would whisper behind their hands that he was Alixe Burke's pet. He would not bear the brunt of society's scorn alone. Alixe would share it. Society would say Folkestone had bought his daughter a husband. He and Alixe would live in a kind of cruel exile without ever leaving town.

Merrick reached inside the wardrobe for his boots. The travelling valise Ashe had sought tumbled out. He could still follow Ashe and Riordan. No. That was the coward's way and it would serve no purpose. His feelings, his confusion, would still exist. It was best to stay here and wait them out. If this was infatuation, it would pass. He never stayed infatuated for long. If it was something more, that would have to be sorted out, too. Better to do it without the rosy glasses of distance to diffuse it.

Alixe was waiting for him downstairs in the main hall among the other guests taking carriages over to the Leas. Merrick halted for a moment on the stairs to study her. The apple-green muslin walking dress she wore gave her the appearance of a summer goddess, the white-ribbon trim at the bodice adding a hint of virtue to the lush charms on display. A bonnet of matching green moire fashioned in the new French shape dangled by its ribbons from her hand. She looked up and her face lit with pleasure at the sight of him. It was a kind of genuine pleasure he was not used to seeing on a woman's face. It had nothing to do with coy calculation about how to get him in to bed and how to exact the thrills he could coax once there.

Yet he felt his arousal stir at the sight of her wanting him. He thought of her touch on his phallus, the otherworldly expression on her face when she'd come against his hand. And the burning started all over again. He highly suspected there wasn't enough swimming in the world that would quench that particular fire. And yet he could not have her, not completely. That was one thing he could not take from her. He was not a rake who trifled with virgins.

Merrick made his way to her side and swept her hand into the crook of his arm. She felt natural beside him, being with her an easy sort of companionship. It would take some getting used to being without her when the time came. But that day wasn't today. He must not let the future ruin the present. She was his for today, and for tomorrow and a little time beyond, that was all that mattered. 'What shall we do first?' Merrick asked.

'Let's see the animals. The animal pens smell better in the morning.' Alixe laughed and let him lead her to a waiting gig. He helped her up and they set out on the road to the Leas.

The fairgrounds were bursting with people who'd come to enjoy the June treat. Excitement trembled on the light breeze and Merrick felt himself get caught up with it. Today was not a day to worry about what might come. Alixe felt it, too. Her smile was contagious and she squeezed his arm as they strode towards the animal pens to see who had the biggest pig or the fattest calf.

He bought her a pasty and ducked her behind a tree to lick a juicy droplet off her lips with his tongue. She laughed and sank into him. 'How is it that you always smell so good?' she murmured, her eyes dancing up at him with mischief. 'You smell like lavender and oak and something else I can never quite name.'

Merrick chuckled. 'It's the coumarin. I have a perfumer on Bond Street make it especially for me. It's supposed to simulate hay after it has been cut.' The cologne was one expense he hadn't been able to force himself to forgo. It reminded him of innocent summer days before his life had become corrupted with all its various vices.

'What's it called?' Alixe made a show of burrowing her nose into the collar of his shirt and breathing deeply.

'The scent is *fougère*. Many perfumers can mix a *fougère*, but I have a place I prefer.' Merrick winked. 'Perhaps the *fougère* is part of my charm.'

'I think your charm is more than that.' Her eyes

turned misty. 'What are we doing, Merrick?' Her arms
were settled about his neck, his own hands were settled
at her hips, resting as if they belonged there.

'We're doing the best we can, all we can.' There was
no sense pretending he didn't understand what she was
asking. It was the very same thing he'd been grappling
with himself. He moved to kiss her again. She turned
her head and evaded the gesture.

'What sort of answer is that supposed to be?' she
challenged softly.

'The only answer we can make. What do you want
me to say, Alixe? Do you think I can save you?' He
dropped his voice to a husky growl. 'Or do you think
you can save me? I'll tell you neither is possible. We
have shared time. We have found pleasure together.
We have come to care for one another beyond what
we expected when we began this association. We are
caught in the throes of those feelings, but that doesn't
mean we should marry.' Merrick stroked the curve of
her jaw with the back of his hand. 'Marriage to me will
not save you and it certainly won't save me, my dear,
although I do appreciate the thought.'

Alixe shook her head and laughed up at him. 'Are
you really as bad as you make out?'

'I'm probably worse.'

'Not at all. There's a streak of honour in you whether
you admit it or not.'

Merrick cocked an eyebrow. 'There are many who'd
disagree with you. I am not the heir, so I am not learning to run the family holdings. I am not the current
marquis, so I am not taking up a seat in Parliament.

I am not a military man, so I am not considering my next post in some godforsaken region of the empire. I am not a man of the cloth contemplating the philosophies of religion or how to best bore my parish from the pulpit on Sunday. In fact, I follow none of the pursuits that make a man honourable.'

His speech made her uncomfortable. He could see the slight furrowing of her brow. 'You're right to be uncomfortable, Alixe. The truth often is. Better to know it now than before you delude yourself into thinking I'm something I not. Here's another truth. I'm a bounder. I follow the money, I live from one wager to the next.'

'Then why didn't you leave? The man you describe wouldn't have stayed under the conditions my father laid out. That man would have been out of Folkestone as fast as he could saddle a horse,' Alixe countered.

Merrick favoured her with a fond smile. Apparently, she was not willing to be swayed just yet. 'It's nice to think someone still believes I can be redeemed.' That it was Alixe Burke, a woman who had little to gain from an association with him, touched him beyond measure. This was dangerous ground for them both. Her feelings did not go unreciprocated. For the first time with a woman, he wished it could be different, that *he* could be different. That was when he knew it. Alixe Burke was in love with him. The realisation was overwhelming. He had to protect her from that before it went any further. He had no business encouraging sentiments he could not return, no matter how he felt.

'Alixe, you don't want to get bound up with me.' He groped for words to make her see that his failings were far too big for her to solve. 'My family doesn't know how to love.' He voiced his worst fear. 'Why would I be any different?' He'd never said it out loud, this nagging concern that he would only create an empty, cruel marriage like his father had. But now that he'd started, the words poured out.

'My father married my mother for her money.' He put up a hand to stop any questions. 'I know a lot of people marry for money, but many times it's mutual and people understand what they're getting into. They have rules about how to deal with their "arrangement". But not my mother. She loved my father and I think she thought he'd love her, too, eventually.' Merrick shook his head. 'She died still hoping, still believing. Perhaps she even died of a broken heart. She never got over her illusions.' He drew a deep breath. 'When I look at you, I fear the same will happen. Don't love me, Alixe. I'm not worth it.'

Alixe wouldn't budge from her position. 'If there is no hope, why didn't you leave with Ashe this morning?'

'I wasn't ready to leave you yet. I can't have you beyond a few days, but I will take what I can if you will have me.' He could see her debating the options in her mind. He pressed on, his groin tightening at the prospect that she hadn't refused yet. 'It's hardly a fair proposition.'

Alixe held his gaze with all seriousness. 'It's the only proposition, though, isn't it, Merrick?' Then she gave a smile that took him entirely by surprise. 'Well, now that's settled, we can get back to having a good time today.'

'Alixe Burke, you astonish me.' Merrick grinned. 'I'll make it worth your while.'

She nudged him with her elbow. 'You had certainly better. I have expectations.'

It was better this way. They knew where they stood with one another. Merrick's disclosure had put the fantasy into perspective and now she could enjoy it for what it was. There would be no gallant offer of marriage for which she would eventually be thankful. She had not really expected one. He wasn't the marrying type and he'd gone to great lengths to explain why. She could not bear the idea that he might have offered out of pity or a sense of misguided honour to save Jamie's sister from her unwanted fate. She was in love with him and there was nothing worse than unrequited love. That kind of love had the power to enslave. He understood that and wanted to protect her from falling victim to it. What he could offer her was the pleasure of his company and the pleasure of his body for a limited time. If that was all, so be it. She would reach out and take it with both hands, then she would set him free. It would be her gift to him. She would accept the first decent offer she received in London and set him loose from any further obligations. Merrick St Magnus was a wild creature and wild things were meant to be free.

But that was for later. For now he was hers and she was his by mutual consent.

They returned to the fairgrounds and strolled the

booths. He bought her pretty ribbons to match her dress and she laughingly tied them to her bonnet. They stopped at the historical booth where she accepted praise over her work on the medieval document. They wandered over to see the games. Targets were being set up for a knife-throwing contest and the men were coaxing Merrick into joining the line of contenders.

'All right, all right.' Merrick gave in and laid aside his coat. He began rolling up his sleeves while the instructions were announced. Three knives per thrower. The top scores would move on to a final round.

Alixe stood on the sidelines with the other spectators. She recognised several of the contestants, but she held her breath when Merrick stepped up to the line, hefting the first knife in his hand. Archibald Redfield sidled in beside her, finished with his own throws. 'Don't worry, St Magnus is supposed to be a dab hand with throwing knives.' His tone was jovial, but Alixe sensed something smug lurking beneath. Merrick's first throw landed in the ring that preceded the bullseye and she straightened her shoulders with pride.

'I have it on good authority he was involved in a knife-throwing wager at a high-class bordello in London. The winner won a certain lady's favours for the evening,' he said in quiet tones for her alone.

Alixe's skin crawled. 'I cannot believe you thought such a rumour fit for my hearing.' Merrick's second knife found the bullseye. The crowd applauded.

Redfield was not subdued. 'I cannot believe you wouldn't want to know such a thing about someone with whom you've spent so much time recently.'

'If I have, that's your fault,' Alixe dared to reference the odious wager. 'You've put him in my path.'

'And I regret it,' Redfield said. 'I had hoped he'd play his end of the wager with honour, although your father is more to blame than myself for those particular conditions.'

Merrick's last knife found the bullseye, making him an easy candidate for the final round. 'A fair opponent for me,' Redfield said cockily. 'I'll enjoy facing him in the finals. He owes me for last time.' He leaned close. 'Surely you know he woos you for himself. He doesn't care if you succeed in London. He'll gladly marry you. Your father misjudged him there. He's a whore of the highest order. If the price is right, he'll sell himself in marriage. You would solve a lot of problems for him and after you have, he'll leave you alone and carry on with his usual debaucheries.'

Alixe blanched at Redfield's coarse warning. It wasn't true. She and Merrick had just discussed the improbability of marriage. Surely Merrick couldn't ensure her failure in London—only she could do that. If she chose, she would dazzle every last bachelor in town. Redfield was wrong. A horrible suspicion came to her: unless Merrick had lied. No. It wasn't possible. She simply wouldn't believe it.

Archibald Redfield stepped up to the line and waited his turn while St Magnus threw. A rough childhood on the docksides of London had served him well today. His own throws had been excellent and the competition was down to him and St Magnus now, the other

finalists having been eliminated. He'd sown his seed
of doubt well. He'd been pleased with how the conversation with Alixe had gone.

She was a smart woman and smart women usually
had a healthy streak of cynicism, always overthink-
ing things. Just when she'd started to believe in the
bounder, he'd come along and punctured that fragile
bubble of hers. Oh, he knew she wanted to believe St
Magnus—what woman wouldn't want to believe him?
But she hadn't completely allowed herself to give up
all logic yet and he'd played havoc with the small piece
that remained. She'd not said as much, but he'd seen
it in her face.

Best of all, he'd done it without really telling any
lies. If she asked around, she'd find the story of the
bordello readily confirmed and probably much more
he'd not yet uncovered.

Those kinds of rumours would lead her to the conclusion he'd already put before her. St Magnus needed
her money. He had nothing of his own and enjoyed an
estranged relationship with his father. She would easily put all the pieces together and conclude St Magnus was using her for his own ends. That was when
he'd be there to make his offer of marriage for the second time. This time, he would deal through her father.
Folkestone would see that he was the only way out of
facing St Magnus at the altar.

The crowd applauded. St Magnus had struck two
more bullseyes, beating his own single and two near-
misses. The bastard was as lucky as they came. St
Magnus strode to the sidelines and swept Alixe Burke

into his arms and kissing her full on the mouth in a victor's kiss. Too bad, Redfield thought, he couldn't bury those knives in St Magnus's heart instead of hay targets. But he could beat St Magnus to the prize and he would do that tonight.

Chapter Fourteen

❧❧❧❧

A subdued tension underlay the rest of the afternoon like the heavy stillness that precedes a thunderstorm until Alixe was ready to burst from the anticipation. He'd kissed her in public. Word of it would reach her father and there would be the devil to pay for Merrick's indiscretion. One could kiss country lasses like that, but one could not kiss the Earl of Folkestone's daughter. Archibald Redfield's warning rang through her head. Perhaps Merrick had kissed her on purpose, knowing full well her father would not be able to let it pass.

While her mind cared a great deal about being manipulated by Merrick's flirtations, her body cared not at all, only that it was aroused with an adventurous curiosity. Her body wanted again the pleasures he'd shown her. With every look, every smile, every touch, her body was drawn taut with wanting until she thought she couldn't stand it a moment longer.

Merrick was not oblivious to the presence of mounting tensions as they finished touring the booths late in the afternoon. Alixe noted a growing tightness about his mouth when he smiled, an agitated distraction to his gestures. They had promised each other to enjoy the time they had left, but that had changed since the knife throwing. They were both avoiding something, although Alixe doubted it was the same thing. Merrick had been nearly giddy with the win and the small purse that came with it. She had been more restrained, her enjoyment of Merrick's victory tainted by Redfield's accusations.

Their amblings took them to the place Merrick had left the gig and he helped her up, both of them implicitly finished with the fair. The gig gave under his weight as Merrick took his seat next to her and grabbed up the reins. Alixe was extraordinarily sensitive to the nearness of him, of every brush of his thigh against hers. There was nothing for it. She knew the tight proximity of the bench seat demanded such touching be permissible.

'What did Redfield say to you?' Merrick asked once the fairgrounds were behind them. The grimness of his tone caught her unawares. She'd become accustomed to his usual laughing tones, or his low, sensual murmur. This grimness was a not something she'd come to associate with Merrick.

'Nothing of merit.' Alixe shrugged. But she was not convincing in her nonchalance. Merrick eyed her speculatively with a raised eyebrow and a sideways glance that said he didn't believe it.

'Clearly it was something of note. It has upset you.' He paused. 'Unless it was my kissing that upset you?'

'No, it was not your kissing,' Alixe confessed. She looked down at her hands, searching for the right words. 'You do know my father will hear of it, though.' Alixe gathered her courage. 'Is that what you intended? Do you mean to force my father's hand to see you as an acceptable suitor?'

Merrick gave a sharp bark of laughter. 'You know it's not. Did I not assure you of that very thing this morning?'

She felt his eyes on her, his gaze strong and probing. 'Ah, I see. That's what Redfield told you while he was over there, whispering his poison in your ear.' He had nothing but disdain in his tone now and not all of it was for Redfield. A healthy dose of it was reserved for her. 'You believed him. You believed him over me.'

Alixe felt her cheeks burning. She had not seen it from his point of view, of how it would appear to Merrick.

'For shame, Alixe—only this morning you thought I might still be redeemable. How fickle is a woman.' Merrick clucked to the horses and that was the last sound either of them made until they arrived home.

Alixe was in tears by the time she reached the sanctuary of her room. Meg wouldn't be back until evening to help her dress for dinner and Alixe was glad for the privacy. She wanted to be alone with her misery. She had behaved shabbily towards Merrick. For all his reputation to the contrary, he'd not treated her poorly. Nothing had happened without her consent and he'd shown her a sincerity no suitor before him had.

Yet, at the first hint of chicanery, she'd been influenced by a man whom she'd previously turned down, who might possibly be bent on taking revenge for that rejection. Archibald Redfield might not be a scandalous rake with an obvious history of womanising and wagering, but neither was his reputation without tarnish, mostly because no one knew much about him. He'd simply arrived in the neighbourhood. All anyone knew was that his antecedents were of the murky country-gentry sort with a baronial great-grandfather buried somewhere in his past. He was polite to the ladies and good-looking. But *she* knew that, at least in one thing, Archibald Redfield was not honest.

Alixe gazed up at the ceiling. It shouldn't have been enough to sway her from Merrick's standard. She *knew* Redfield was not a genuine man. Redfield had been after her money. She'd overheard him talking with his solicitor when she and her mother had come to call at the manor. Her mother had been outside, having forgot something in the carriage. It had been the day before Redfield had proposed to her in private. Wanting her money wasn't precisely scandalous in the way Merrick's knife wagers in a bordello were, but it was still intolerable to her. Up until that overheard conversation, she'd thought Redfield had genuinely liked her. She'd known he wasn't in love with her, but he'd liked her, respected her work. It had all been a ruse.

Which was why it had been so easy to believe Redfield today. Didn't it take one to know one? Like Redfield, Merrick, too, pretended to like her, had shown respect for her work and he'd been entirely convinc-

ing. Much more convincing than Archibald Redfield
had ever been.

Even now, it was hard to believe Merrick had designed all this for his benefit while stringently main-
taining that he was unattainable. But his presence
marked her room. The fan he'd given her lay on her
vanity. The ribbons he'd bought her dangled from her
bonnet. The faint smell of coumarin-laced *fougère* lingered on the gown she'd worn to the alfresco party. In
small ways, he'd made himself unforgettable and ever
present while agreeing to all her demands. He'd acquiesced to her silly requirement that he teach her no more
of his unconventional lessons. But that hadn't stopped
them, merely changed their context. In hindsight, lessons would have been better. She could have understood their place. There would have been no confusion.

He loves me, he loves me not. If she'd had a rose
handy, she would have denuded it. A thought occurred
to her in the midst of her melancholy: she was working
the wrong end of the equation. Perhaps it didn't matter
if he loved her or how much. Perhaps what mattered
was whether or not she loved him.

The dangerous idea that had begun to bud last night
amid champagne and fireworks was in full bloom now.
She loved him. It was hard to say when precisely it had
happened. But one thing she was certain of: this was
not an impulsive decision, not something that had occurred overnight. In spite of her best efforts, it had
crept up on her. Alixe sat down hard on her bed, letting the discovery rock her very being.

She loved the murmur of his voice enticing her to

wickedness. She loved the feel of his body beneath her hands. She loved his laughing eyes that took nothing too seriously. It wasn't just his good looks. It was his soul, which wasn't nearly as dark as he liked to pretend. He was a good man who'd worked beside villagers, who shared her interest in history, who didn't despise her mind, who carried with him a thoughtful intellect. He was extraordinary in ways London had not recognised.

Most of all, she loved how she felt when she was with him. He made her feel... She groped for the word in her mind. Alive. He made her feel alive in a way she'd never felt before and, for that, she loved him and it didn't matter if he loved her.

All she knew was that she felt ashamed of her doubt, ashamed of the way she'd treated Merrick. He deserved so much better. She wanted to apologise. She wanted things back the way they'd been that morning when she and Merrick had kissed behind a tree and he'd pledged all he could offer. If she'd believed in him, she might be off somewhere right now with him, indulging what time they had left instead of moping about her room, wallowing in her regrets.

A frenzy of resolve engulfed her. Within moments she was striding out of the house. Merrick had not stayed once he'd dropped her off. But she knew where she could find him and what she'd do with him once she did.

Merrick dived into the water, letting the water close over him, letting the cool rush of it drown out all else.

He wanted to forget. He'd momentarily been a fool and it hurt. Alixe Burke had made him believe he was finer than he was, for a few hours at least. But Alixe had not believed him over Redfield's lies. The knowledge of it stung.

This was the problem with virgins. With his usual women, it was all straightforward: pleasure for pleasure with no complications afterwards, no expectations. No one mistook those encounters as a prelude to love. Everyone involved knew the rules of those engagements.

Alixe Burke did not play by those rules and yet the pleasure she'd brought him had far superseded any he'd known. There'd been an indescribable completeness to the release she'd given him. But it hadn't been enough. It had merely whetted his appetite for more. After the fireworks, he'd entertained indecent thoughts of her all night and most of the day. Walking beside her at the fair had been an exquisite sort of torture. Limiting himself to a kiss behind a tree had been another when all he'd wanted to do was toss up her skirts and bury himself in her until he was cured of the wanting.

The coolness of the water did nothing to subdue his arousal. He could imagine her writhing against the tree trunk near the shore, screaming her release as he took her. She would be glorious in her abandon, her hair streaming about her. She would call his name…

'Merrick.'

His imaginings were getting fairly vivid. Her voice sounded as if it were here in the grove with him.

'Merrick!' The call came again, more insistent this time.

Merrick opened his eyes. There stood the object of his musings on the bank of the swimming hole, beckoning him with the curl of one outstretched hand.

He neared the shore and she raised her arms to her hair where it lay in the loose chignon she preferred on warm days. She tugged and it fell loose about her, a coy smile on her lips. His heart thumped at the universal signs of a woman with seduction on her mind.

Merrick grinned, arms crossed as he floated on his back in the water, his head up just enough to keep her in view. 'Why, Alixe Burke, did you come here to seduce me?'

Her smile widened. Her hands dropped to the fastenings of her gown. 'Absolutely, although I might need you to get out of the water and help me.'

'With the seduction? Gladly.'

'No, my dress. Perhaps I should have planned better and worn something a little easier to get out of.' Alixe gave a charming laugh of helplessness.

He rose up out of the water and Alixe sucked in her breath. A warm sense of pride filled him at her admiration. He spun her about and set to work on the dress, his wet hands leaving watery tracks down the back of her gown. 'Are you sure you want to do this?' he murmured in her ear, pushing her long cascade of hair to one side, leaving her neck bare to his kisses. He hoped the question was merely rhetorical, but he had to ask. That streak of honour Alixe was convinced he possessed was hard at war with his desire.

He pushed the dress off her shoulders and she turned in his arms to face him, her own arms wrapping about his neck, her head thrown back to look up at him. 'I want this and more, Merrick. This time I want it all. With you. No more individual pleasure, Merrick. I want us to find pleasure…together.'

Her words would undo him before they even got started. His erection pressed against the thin fabric of her chemise. 'Alixe, I am flattered by your offer, but I cannot ruin you for a few hours of pleasure.'

'I do not care,' she said with a confident ferocity that made him smile.

'Your future husband might.' He had to know she understood what she was asking, what she was doing. God knew he wanted her beyond reason, but he had to cling to the shreds of that reason as long as he could for her sake.

'I've enough money to make him forget,' she whispered, reaching a hand between them to cup him with a light squeeze that sent a jolt of fierce, raw desire ricocheting through him.

There was nothing for it. He would give her something to remember. And himself, too.

The dusky summer evening closed around them as he took her down to the ground. At his kiss, she'd begun to burn; now she was fully consumed, revelling in the weight of his body over hers, the muscled sinews of his arms where they bracketed her in the place between her shoulders and head. His pale hair had darkened from the water and dripped erotic droplets on her breasts. She could feel his erection pulse against her thigh and she arched against him in her hurry to find relief from the building inferno. But Merrick would not be rushed, his damp skin cool against the heat of her own. His hand was at the juncture of her thighs, massaging, stimulating her body into ready compliance for what came next, his mouth at her breast, teasing with his tongue until she could bear the twin points of pleasure no more.

'Open a bit more for me, my love,' Merrick whispered at her ear, his knee gently widening the space between her legs and then he was there, poised at her entrance. She strained towards him, her heat rising again, her breath coming in gasps as he plunged.

She could feel him sliding inside her until the easy sensation stopped, replaced by a razor-sharp stab of pain. She cried out. She'd not expected that. There'd been no allusion to pain in their previous encounters.

'Shh,' Merrick hushed her. 'Be still, it will pass in a moment and then the pleasure will come. I promise. It only hurts the once.'

Already the pain was ebbing, her body relaxing around him, a new sensation starting to grow as he began to move inside her. Merrick took her mouth in a kiss, his hips pressed to hers, coaxing her body to join him in the rhythm. She moaned, her body moving with his, her need rising. Merrick's blue eyes were midnight-dark with passion, his body straining as his own desires spiked. Her body careened towards release, Merrick thrust once more, surging them over an unseen edge and they soared. There was no other word for it.

Somewhere, somehow, they were flying in a world that had fractured into a kaleidoscope of sensation.

Her only thought as she floated back to earth was that she'd been right. She'd been right to do this most intimate act with Merrick. It was nearly inconceivable to think of doing this with another. Yet when Merrick rose and held out a hand to her, she took it, letting him lead her to the pond, neither of them abashed by their nakedness.

In the gathering dark, they swam and bathed, basking in the sunset filtering through the trees. There were more kisses and gentle love play in the water, but Merrick did not take her again no matter how she pressed him. She would be too sore, he said.

At last, Merrick rose from the water and searched for his clothes. *This is what Eden must have been like,* Alixe thought, taking her fill of his nakedness while he dried, appreciating the lean curve of buttock descending into long thigh. Lord, how she'd become wanton. Two weeks ago, the sight of his nakedness had sent her stumbling over logs. Now, she could not get enough. He pulled on his trousers and she made a disappointed mewl.

'Sorry, love. Convention demands I wear trousers.' Merrick shifted his hips, adjusting the fit of his trousers, his hands at the waistband to work the fastenings. Alixe sucked in her breath. Even the way he put on his trousers was erotically fascinating. It was as sensual and intimate to watch him dress as it was to watch him undress.

Merrick threw her a knowing smile. He'd done that

on purpose. 'I should splash you for that,' she scolded. 'You were teasing me.'

'I was teasing *you*? My dear, I think you have that wrong. You're the one who's still naked.' Fully garbed, Merrick walked to the pond's edge and held out a hand. 'I'll play lady's maid. Let's get you dried off.'

Twenty minutes and several kisses later, they walked out of Eden, hand in hand. Everything had changed and nothing had changed. Merrick could not marry her, or want to marry her, any more than he had that morning. But Alixe suspected he most definitely had ruined her for other men far beyond the technicalities of having lain with her.

The house came into view and Merrick squeezed her hand. 'Shall you go on? They'll be missing you.'

'I'll tell them I stayed at the fair. No one saw me come back.' They were the first words they'd said since they'd left the pond.

Merrick nodded. 'It's as good an excuse as any.'

Silence followed. She wasn't ready to go in. The moment she crossed the lawn, everything would revert to normal. She wanted to ask if he would come to her again, but she feared sounding too desperate. Perhaps it would have to be she who went to him. She searched for something to say, but found nothing.

'I'll see you inside.' Then she started walking.

Straight into hell.

Chapter Fifteen

Alixe's mother saw her first as she was 'just coming down' to join everyone in the drawing room. Alixe had wisely opted to use the servants' stairs and return to her room undetected. She was doubly glad for the decision now that it was clear her mother's sharp eyes had been on the lookout for her.

'There you are, my dear.' Her mother beamed at her and Alixe's suspicions rose. Alixe smoothed the front of her skirt, thankful she'd had time to change into one of Merrick's new gowns, a lightweight summer silk in deep apricot that highlighted the healthy glow of her skin and the rich walnut hues of her hair.

'You look lovely, the new wardrobe is perfection itself.' Alixe could not recall the last time her mother had complimented her clothing. She searched her mother's smiling face for clues to this transformation. Ever since she'd turned down the last offer, her mother had treated her with an air of polite disregard. She'd been left to her own devices once it became clear she did not mean to return to London, her mother in clear despair of seeing her daughter married.

Tonight was a most glaring exception.

'I came back late from the fair and lay down for a moment. I must have dozed off,' Alixe improvised hastily to explain her tardy arrival.

Her mother shooed away the need for apology with a wave of her hand. 'No matter, you're here now. Your father and I have exciting news for you. Come join us in the study. Jamie can play host in our absence.'

Her father was already there, having taken up his customary place behind the massive desk where all important business was conducted. But he was not alone. Sitting comfortably in a chair in front of the desk was Archibald Redfield. Redfield had not spent the last few hours rolling about a swimming hole. He was turned out in his country finest, looking neatly barbered and self-confidently handsome with his dark-gold hair and alert hazel eyes. He rose when she entered and strode forwards to take her hand. 'My dearest Alixe, you look ravishing. I dare say a day at the fair has put some colour into your cheeks. When I saw you earlier, you looked a trifle pale.'

What was going on? Alixe's first thoughts were that Redfield had reported Merrick's kiss from the fair or, worse, that Redfield had somehow known what she and Merrick had been up to at the swimming hole. But her mother looked far too happy for anything calamitous to have occurred. Redfield was a rat, but not tonight. Tonight he was playing the indulgent gentleman to the hilt and that worried her greatly. She preferred the rat.

'Have a seat, my dear.' Her father gestured for her to take an empty chair. 'We have fabulous news. Just this afternoon, our Mr Redfield has asked for your hand in marriage.'

'This is wonderful,' her mother gushed. 'He's our neighbour, after all, and you won't live far from home. It's the most perfect of arrangements.'

Redfield smiled and humbly studied his nails while her mother outlined the benefits of the match. Alixe listened in growing horror.

'What about St Magnus?' She managed to slip the words in when her mother stopped to draw breath.

'You're absolutely correct, darling.' Redfield looked up from his nails with a benevolent smile that bordered on patronising. 'He should be told immediately. You and I have much to thank him for.'

Alixe bristled, but Redfield acted quickly. 'If it's all right, I would like a moment alone with my fiancée.' He gave a wide, white-toothed grin as he said the word, looking every inch the pleased bridegroom.

He dropped his act fast enough once her parents had exited the room. 'I know what's going through your pretty head, Alixe Burke,' he began. 'But you needn't worry. St Magnus can't harm you now. I won't allow him to slander my wife. I explained the entire situation to your father, how St Magnus was overly exuberant after winning the competition.'

He was talking about Merrick's ill-advised kiss, but that was merely the tip of the iceberg. 'St Magnus has been "overly exuberant" before this, I suspect, hasn't he? But I don't care, such is my regard for you.'

Alixe was not fooled about the nature of his 're-gard'. It had nothing to do with his affections. 'You've become quite desperate for my fortune.' She held his gaze steadily.

'Your parents have become quite desperate to see you married. Far more desperate than they were this spring. St Magnus has surprised us all. To my way of thinking, this works to both our benefits. I am desperate to wed, they are desperate to see St Magnus as far from you as possible.'

Redfield made an off-handed gesture. 'You should not be so surprised. This is how these alliances are made, my dear. Driven by my regard for you, I went about it all wrong this spring by asking you first. If I had gone straight to your father from the start, this might all have been settled long before now. I could have saved you from the ignominy of St Magnus's attentions.'

'I am not "your dear",' Alixe ground out.

'You're not St Magnus's either.' Redfield gave a mirthless laugh. 'He will be disappointed I've beaten him to the prize. But that is all. Men like him don't care to lose. He played a deeper game with your father's terms and lost. I'll have your money, he'll have his freedom. I suspect in the end, he'll be happy enough knowing that he's "lived to fight again another day" and all that. He will recover from this. There's always another woman ready to support the St Magnuses of the world.'

His cold analysis was revolting. She wanted to flee this room, wanted to throw herself on her parents' mercy for whatever it was worth and tell them Redfield only wanted her money. More than that, she wanted to throw herself into Merrick's arms and hear him tell her it wasn't a lie, that he hadn't wooed her for himself with the intention of claiming her dowry for his own, that he hadn't used her body against her.

'You disgust me.' Alixe turned on her heel. But Redfield caught her fast, his face close to hers.

'When you realise I'm being honest, you'll thank me. You know precisely why I want you. St Magnus, on the other hand, has served you a platter of lies. This isn't the first time he's traded pleasure for funds and tried to dress it up as something more. Ask him about the Greenfield Twins some time.'

Alixe wrenched her arm free. It wasn't true and she would prove it just as soon as she could find Merrick.

Merrick scanned the gathering in the drawing room. Alixe was nowhere to be found. It was not lost on him that the earl and countess were not present either. He hoped there hadn't been any difficulties. Lost in his concerns, he startled at the sound of Jamie's voice beside him.

'Looking for Alixe?' Merrick didn't care for the tension in Jamie's tone. It wasn't like him.

'Is she not here?' Merrick queried carefully.

'I need to tell you some news, news I hope you'll be happy to hear.' Jamie was drawing him outside onto the verandah, away from the other guests.

'I know you've been spending a lot of time with Alixe these past weeks and I haven't said anything.

She's been happy and she's starting to dress as she should again. You've been good for her, although I can't fathom why you've done it. She's not your type of woman.'

'Ashe doesn't think so either,' Merrick said with a touch of grim cynicism. He was getting tired of hearing about how unsuitable Alixe was for him. Did people actually think he didn't know that? Even so, did anyone think knowing it could stop him from wanting her?

Jamie shrugged in agreement and then elbowed him playfully. 'It's no secret what type of woman you like.'

A walnut-haired one with sherry eyes who swims naked and cries her pleasure to the sunset skies. But he could not say that to Jamie, nor could he seek Jamie's counsel about what to do next. He was feeling Ashe's absence keenly.

'Your news?' Merrick pressed.

'Archibald Redfield, our neighbour, has asked for her hand.'

The news was like a physical blow. He should not have been stunned. He knew Redfield coveted her fortune. 'But she's to go to London and have her pick of the Season.' Merrick managed to get out the words without exposing the scheme behind it. 'Surely she will decline.'

'Not this time. My father will not tolerate her refusing any offers at this point. He's over the moon about it. They're in the estate office discussing it right now. Redfield came right after his return from the fair.'

Merrick supposed there was veiled reproach to his poor behaviour at the knife-throwing contest in there somewhere, but he was still reeling. He wasn't ready to lose her so soon. He'd thought there'd be more time. He'd thought losing her in London would be easier, surrounded by his usual entertainments. Merrick placed a pleading hand on Jamie's arm.

'Do not allow this, Jamie. If you have any influence with your father, let her go to London and find someone better. The man is a fortune hunter. Do any of you know a thing about him?' He was thinking quickly now. He couldn't save himself, but perhaps he could still save Alixe. At the moment, it was the only thing that mattered.

Jamie stiffened at the request, the reference to fortune hunting finding purchase with him. 'What do you know, Merrick? Do you know something unsavoury about him?'

Merrick shook his head. 'Ask Alixe. Did you know she refused his overtures last spring? She didn't say anything about it out of fear of your father's wrath.' Merrick drew a breath and pressed on. 'The man doesn't even have a title. What is your father thinking to marry Alixe to him without trying London once more?'

'He's thinking of his daughter's well-being,' a harsh voice broke in. Redfield emerged from the drawing room, shutting the French doors behind him. 'Better to marry her to an upstanding landowner of the county than turn her loose in London where you can continue to lead her astray with your debauched ways and useless promises.'

'That is libellous!' Merrick roared.

'What is this?' Jamie looked from Redfield to Merrick. 'What have you done?'

'Do you have to ask? You know him better than any of us,' Redfield accused smoothly, arms folded confidently over his chest. 'What do you think he's been doing with your sister all this time? He's used your friendship to gain entrance to this gathering of decent people. In return, he's paid court to your sister in hopes of claiming her for himself and all the money that goes with her. He accuses me of what he's done himself.'

'You're a liar!' Merrick had enough. He was not the villain here. He lunged at Redfield, forcing him back to the wall with a body-jarring thud against the sandstone. He landed a solid punch to Redfield's gut before Jamie got a hold of him and dragged him off the other man, pulling him on to the lawn, away from the light.

Redfield was bent double, panting in his pain, milking it for all it was worth when the earl barrelled out on to the verandah, bellowing a phrase Merrick was coming to associate with him quite readily. 'What is the meaning of this? James?'

'There seems to be a difference of opinion over Alixe's engagement,' Jamie managed, fighting to keeping a restraining grip on him, much to Merrick's disappointment. If that scum Redfield wanted to moan in pain, he'd damn well give him something to moan about.

Folkestone raised his greying eyebrows and focused his cool gaze in Merrick's direction. 'Oh? Is that true? St Magnus, your work here is done. You've fulfilled your end of the agreement. You've won your freedom.

That is all you were promised. I have bargained with you in good faith; I trust you have returned the favour and not reached above yourself.'

'What is going on?' Jamie demanded. Merrick felt his heart sink. It was all going to come out and Jamie would not forgive him.

Redfield sneered, managing to stand upright at last. 'Your precious friend was caught with your sister in dishabille in the library. To avoid paying a gentleman's price for his indiscretion, your father allowed St Magnus to "help" Alixe find a more appropriate husband instead of marrying her himself. After all, why would anyone want Merrick St Magnus for a son-in-law if it could be avoided? However, there was a provision, that if St Magnus failed, he would marry her anyway. The longer St Magnus thought about it, the more appealing the idea of failure became. Why not claim her for himself? Why fix her up with pretty clothes and manners for someone else when he needs the money as much as the next man?' Redfield spat out. 'Your *friend* is as low as they come. Fortunately, I have offered for Lady Alixe to save her from being duped by St Magnus here.'

Jamie's grip relaxed slightly, probably out of stupefaction. Merrick took advantage and twisted free. 'You're a conniving rat.'

Merrick lunged again, but this time Redfield was ready for him and they both went down on the lawn, punching in a full-blown brawl.

It took both Jamie and the earl to separate them. 'Stop this, Merrick, for Alixe's sake,' Jamie murmured at his ear. 'This will only make a scandal for her.' It was the only argument that carried any weight with Merrick. Onlookers were starting to gather. Jamie and Folkestone would have to skilfully hush this up if they hoped to staunch any nasty rumours. Lady Folkestone would kill him for this. Instead of her house party being remembered for all the successful matches made, it would be remembered for this breach of propriety right at the last and it would be attributed to him.

'Let me speak with Alixe,' Merrick asked, tugging his waistcoat into place and relenting.

The earl shook his head. 'As I said, your work here is done and most admirably so. I would advise you to pack your things and leave. You can take rooms at the inn for the evening and then go on to wherever your kind goes when you aren't disturbing decent society.'

Merrick was gone. Alixe knew it without Jamie having to tell her, although he had quietly taken her aside before the dinner bell and told her Merrick had left on urgent business.

Redfield had taken up residence beside her for the duration of the evening. He'd been late coming into dinner and when he had arrived, he'd been wearing a different shirt than the one he'd worn in her father's study. Alixe couldn't help wonder if Merrick's urgent business was in some way connected to Redfield's change of clothing, as was the after-dinner disappearance of Jamie and her father into the study.

The only good to come of the evening was her father's decision to hold off announcing a formal engagement. She expected she had Jamie to thank for the reprieve. They would go up to London as planned instead of announcing the news at the midsummer ball the next evening. The delay would give Alixe a chance to enjoy the Season before the wedding and time to put together a fashionable trousseau. Besides, her father said, the contracts still had to be drawn up and there was no hurry now that things were settled.

Redfield had agreed to the arrangements with a tight smile that suggested he wasn't truly pleased. Alixe smiled at him smugly behind her father's back as they shook hands, but Redfield was not content. He cornered her on her way up the stairs, a proprietary hand on her arm that tightened painfully.

'St Magnus has left and I am still here, my dear. I defended your honour tonight with my fists and my proposal when that scoundrel St Magnus would have defamed it. You owe me. Don't ever forget it.'

Alixe fell asleep to sobering thoughts. It was hard to believe she'd lain in Merrick's arms just six hours ago. It was harder still to believe he'd only been part of her life for two weeks. She'd felt more alive in those two weeks than she had in the last two years and now it had all come to an end. Merrick had deserted her. Whatever his reasons, he was gone and she was alone once more. She wished she'd told him what she'd so recently discovered: that she loved him. But it was too late now. It was all over.

Chapter Sixteen

The juicy truth was all over London. Merrick St Magnus had been expelled from the Folkestone house party for brawling over a lady. *Brawling,* mind you, the matrons said behind fast-fluttering fans. Gentlemen might covertly duel, but gentlemen *never* lowered themselves to an all-out fist fight on a host's lawn, over the host's daughter none the less. It just went to prove Merrick St Magnus was no gentleman, no matter who his father was—a fact that made those fast fans reach gale proportions. More than one matron was entertaining libidinous fantasies behind those fans. What would it be like to be in the arms of a man who gave full vent to his passions? To his tempers? Women shivered in London's hot ballrooms at the very prospect.

It was the same wherever he went. Their minds were fairly transparent, as were the charms of some of the more forward ladies, Merrick noted, striding through Lady Couthwald's ballroom with Ashe at his shoulder. He returned the inviting smile of a popular lush-figured widow with a curt nod of his own. There was little variation in their thoughts except that some of the more ambitious entertained ideas of having both he and Ashe warming their beds.

'The conquering hero returns,' Ashe murmured. 'Is there a woman in the room who doesn't want you?'

'Only the ones who want you,' Merrick replied drily. Such lust was not as amusing as it had once been.

'The widow wanted us both. It might have been fun. We haven't done that for a long time.' Ashe Bedevere was the only person Merrick knew who could talk about a *ménage à trois* with the same casualness he spoke of picking out a new waistcoat.

'*We*'ve never done that,' Merrick corrected.

'Are you sure? What about the time—?'

'I'm *very* sure.' Merrick cut him off, not about to argue in the middle of a ballroom about whom Ashe had engaged in one of his *affaires*. Ashe had been his constant companion since he'd returned to town three days ago. Ashe had opened up his rooms to share and Merrick was grateful, but not *that* grateful. Ashe's debaucheries weighed on him. Somewhere between Kent and London, his friend's habits had become tiresome.

'Are you in danger of becoming a prig?'

'Just because I don't want to "share" with you doesn't mean I'm becoming a prig.' But maybe it did. Maybe Ashe was right. He was changing and it frightened him. He didn't know what to make of it. It was why he hadn't hurried straight back to London after the fight with Archibald Redfield.

He could have come earlier. He'd delayed in the

hopes that time would dull the edge of scandal that was sure to precede him. But absence had only heightened the anticipation of his arrival and London society was certain he would arrive. Alixe Burke was here, after all, looking lovely and dazzling the young men. Surely St Magnus would not have risked a brawl only to retreat from the field, not when he'd been dancing attendance on the former jilt for two weeks in Kent, depriving the women of London of his presence? He didn't need a great sense of intuition to know this. The betting book at White's was full of wagers: when would he arrive, when would he seek out Alixe Burke at a venue and when he did would he stake his claim?

He had yet to see Alixe. There was no reason to. He'd done his duty for her and for her father. She was the Toast of London. His fisticuffs had ensured her initial popularity. Everyone was waiting to see the woman who'd brought two men to undignified brawling. Alixe Burke must be transformed indeed from the girl society remembered.

The rumours told the rest of the story. She'd gone from being on the shelf to being a highly contended prize. Men wanted to win the woman who had made St Magnus "decent" for even a short time. The last bit was Jamie's invention. Merrick wasn't convinced he'd been decent where Alixe was concerned. That was the other reason he hadn't hurried back to town. He'd hoped his ardour might have cooled and brought perspective.

It hadn't. The remedy had failed miserably. If anything, it had only increased.

He needed to see her. He wanted to assure himself she was well—that was what he told himself. In his more honest moments, he knew he wanted her—craved her, in fact; craved her dark eyes, her hair slipping through his fingers, her body pressed against his. That was not all he craved. He craved sitting in the library with her, talking with her, listening to her stories of history. But that was a craving he could not succour. There was nothing honourable he could give her in exchange for what she gave him. Because of that, he could not seek her out. People could speculate on what happened in the country away from society's collective eye. But what happened in London became fact. He could not indulge with her here.

Fate decided to tempt him and his hard-won logic. The crowd thinned at the far end of the ballroom and there she was. Alixe Burke in her newfound glory, gowned in soft peach with pearls at the base of her neck, a familiar fan dangling closed at her wrist and surrounded by gentlemen. She gave a laugh at something the gentleman to her right was saying. She leaned towards him, a gloved hand skimming his sleeve ever so lightly. There was nothing improper about it. The gentleman beamed, encouraged.

Merrick felt his gut tighten. He'd taught her that little trick. She'd been loathe to practise such measures that day, but this evening she employed it with enviable ease. He'd not anticipated feeling a proverbial blow to the stomach when she used it on someone else. Merrick recognised the gentleman with her, a Viscount Fulworth, who'd just happened to bet at White's that

Merrick would ask her to dance before the sixth of July. He wanted to pummel the man for wooing her while betting on her next move.

Behind him, Ashe cleared his throat. 'I think I'll see if the widow would settle for just one of us. Excuse me.'

Merrick nodded absently. By now others had noticed that he and Alixe were in close proximity to each other. The swell of conversation faded and covert glances darted his way. Alixe looked away from the gentleman she was conversing with, her gaze following the trail of silence until her eyes found him, wide and full of warm emotion for a brief instant before it was replaced with wariness.

He moved towards her. He had to act quickly, naturally, before onlookers started to speculate what any hesitation on his part might mean. On his periphery, he saw Jamie start to move, too, detaching himself from the nearby group he'd been with. He was grateful for it. Jamie's presence would sanction the interaction. But he knew, too, that Jamie would be there to protect Alixe. Merrick didn't imagine he was anything but *persona non grata* in the Folkestone household these days.

'Lady Alixe…' Merrick bowed over Alixe's gloved hand '…it is a pleasure to encounter you here.' He mentioned nothing about any prior meeting.

'Thank you, are you enjoying the ball?' Alixe replied.

'Yes, and you?'

'Yes. The decorations are quite fine.'

The banality of the conversation was stultifying. He didn't want to talk about the ball or the decorations. He wanted to ask her how she was, whether or not she regretted their decision at the swimming hole and did she understand why he'd left the house party; he wanted to explain he'd had no choice, that it had been in her best interest that he leave. He wanted to apologise for not being able to contact her, assuming she wanted to hear such things from him.

There was only one place that provided any privacy at a ball. He doubted she had any dances left, but he had to try. The orchestra was striking up the early refrains of a popular waltz.

'Would you care to dance, Lady Alixe?' Merrick asked.

Alixe looked flustered for a moment. She sought refuge with a glance to her dance card. 'I'm afraid this dance is spoken for.' She cast a quizzing glance at Fulworth.

Merrick's sharp eyes moved to the viscount. 'I don't mean to intrude, forgive me.' He was all politeness, but he could afford to be. He was about to help Fulworth win. Fulworth had a large sum riding on the wager.

Fulworth bowed. 'If Lady Alixe would not mind, you may take this dance, St Magnus. I find my supper has not settled as well as I'd hoped. My dear Lady Alixe, would you forgive me?'

What a ninny the man was. But Merrick merely offered Alixe his arm and swept her on to the floor before Fulworth invented another lengthy show of chivalry.

'He's no good for you, Alixe,' Merrick began, fitting his hand easily to the small of her back.

'Why is that?' Alixe enquired.

'He bet on you at White's. He wagered that I would dance with you before the sixth of July. Lucky for him, tonight's the fifth.' Merrick swung them through a turn, taking the opportunity to draw her closer.

'I'm coming to discover men are not so very different from one another, regardless of station,' Alixe said with a touch of coolness.

'How have you been?' Merrick moved to safer conversational territory.

'Do you mean, how have I been since you left so abruptly?'

'I understand you're upset. I would like to explain.'

'There's nothing to explain.' Alixe sighed. 'I'm not even sure I'm angry at you, precisely, except that you left without saying goodbye. But you'll be glad to know that Jamie picked up the pieces admirably.'

'And Archibald Redfield?'

'He has been temporarily thwarted. I have been given a London Season to enjoy the city and put together my trousseau while my father draws up the contracts and looks into Redfield's background. Father and Redfield stayed in the country, but I expect them to arrive any day.'

'London agrees with you. You look lovelier than ever.'

'I have to. It's my last chance to find someone better than Redfield.' She looked up at him, her gaze touching him at his core. In that brief moment he acknowledged what he'd been avoiding all those days on the road, putting off his return to London. He *loved* Alixe Burke.

'You were right, Merrick, I have only the freedom to

choose who my husband will be. Redfield tried to take that away from me. He may still succeed unless I find someone else. A titled young gentleman with a decent background would sway my father, I think. So you see, marriage has become a jail and an escape all at once.'

'You could marry me.' The words were out before he could stop them, before he could think about all the reasons he was unsuitable for her, before he could think about his fear that he would fail her.

Alixe stumbled against him in her surprise.

'My father has released you from your obligations. Jamie told me. You're no longer the husband in waiting.' Alixe shook her head. 'I don't mean to be cruel, but you haven't any money, no title. You are no better a candidate than Redfield, perhaps worse. My father would not accept you.'

'I'm not marrying your father. I'm marrying you. Would you accept me, Alixe?'

Her face froze, her whole body tensing in his arms. 'I cannot discuss this here.'

'Then where?' He unashamedly leaned close to feather her ear with a soft sensual breath. He would fight with everything in his arsenal, be it a sin or no. 'Name the place and I'll be there. I've thought of nothing else but you since I left Folkestone. I dream of you, I wake hard and ready with the wanting of you. Tell me you don't think of me, that you don't remember the magic we can make together.'

Her pulse leaped beneath the strand of delicate pearls and Merrick smiled. 'Admit you want me, Alixe Burke.'

'I will admit no such thing.' But she trembled as she said it and her eyes could not help but fall on his lips.

'You don't have to. Your body has done it for you, my dear.' They passed the doors to the verandah. 'Shall I sweep you outside and kiss you senseless?'

'Merrick, please don't,' Alixe begged. Her fingers had buried themselves in the fabric of his jacket at the shoulder. She was wavering.

'Why not? Why should I not ask for what I want? Why should you not take what you want?'

'Because wanting is not marriage. Marriage is for ever, Merrick, and wanting is…' She moved her bare shoulders in a delicate shrug. 'Wanting is not for ever, Merrick, and you know it better than any of us.'

Merrick gave her a final turn and the music ended. They stood facing each other, Merrick unwilling to release her. 'What if you say yes and we find out if you're right or wrong?'

'No more wagers, Merrick. Why don't you return me to my court of gentlemen?'

'And then what? Shall we make conversation about things we don't want to talk about? All the while I'll be making love to you in my mind and you'll know what I'll really be thinking.'

He returned her, but he didn't get a chance to flirt any further. Jamie quickly removed him from the circle of admirers moments after their return under the pretence he wanted to catch up with his old friend. Merrick wasn't fooled.

Outside, Jamie did not spare words for niceties. 'I think it would be best to leave her alone now. You've made your appearance to satisfy society's curiosity. There's no more reason to patronise her court.'

'Is this a warning?' He'd expected no less. Jamie had a sister to protect and Jamie knew what he was. But his tone was sharp with Jamie. His own emotions were on edge. In the last fifteen minutes he'd discovered he was in love, proposed marriage and been refused. It was quite a full evening even for him.

'Merrick, we're friends. This is an awkward spot for me to be in. She's got a decent proposal from Redfield and all these fellows to choose from now if she doesn't want him.'

'Don't forget my proposal,' Merrick added.

'You haven't proposed to her,' Jamie countered.

'I have, too—just now on the dance floor.'

'The dance floor?' Jamie breathed in disbelief. 'Merrick, really.' Then he paused, groping for the right phrasing. Merrick felt a stab of sympathy for his friend. Jamie was struggling to find proper words for a most improper betrayal.

'As friends, Merrick, tell me—is Redfield speaking the truth? Did you think to claim Alixe for yourself?'

Merrick leaned against the balustrade. 'No. I would never play such a game with your sister.' Or with any woman. That was his father's style, not his.

'Then why?'

Why propose to Alixe Burke when he could have any woman of the *ton* for any myriad pleasures without the office of marriage?

'Because, Jamie, when I look at her, I can't imagine her as anyone's but mine.' It was the single reason that had overcome years of reservation and belief that he'd never be suitable in that capacity for any worthy woman.

Jamie's hand was strong on his shoulder in commiseration. 'Then I am sorry.'

Sorry that he wasn't a better sort of man, a man who hadn't lived his life earning a reputation for questionable behaviour. Sorry for not having the funds to afford a wife like Alixe Burke. Sorry for falling in love with the one woman he could not attain.

Alixe couldn't concentrate on anything Fulworth was saying. Whatever wit he'd possessed before the waltz had vanished upon her return. Merrick and Jamie had gone out to the verandah. Only Jamie had come back in. She hoped they hadn't quarrelled. She hoped Merrick hadn't gone to seek comfort somewhere else. She hoped so much, the list was getting rather long and distinguished by the time she dragged her attention back to the conversation. Fulworth was going on about lobster patties on buffet tables.

Was that what he was truly thinking? Surely the very proper Fulworth wasn't thinking improper thoughts. If Merrick had been there, she was certain he would have flashed her a private look, one of his half-smiles that sent a hundred messages at once, all of them sinful. She couldn't help the small smile that crept across her mouth at the thought of Merrick. He'd been outrageous on the dance floor, but it was hard to stay angry with him for long. Even when she should.

He had proposed! She had refused and rightly so.

The idea was preposterous. It took more than wanting to make a marriage, just as it took more than connections and money. Redfield would say the proposal proved Merrick was after her money and had been all along.

'By my calculations, at two lobster patties a piece at an attendance rate of two balls an evening, the average gentleman consumes two hundred and fifty lobster patties a Season,' Fulworth said with a flourish.

'Oh, that's quite a lot,' Alixe exclaimed with enough verve to hopefully sound impressed with his mathematic prowess.

The other gentlemen were arguing now—was two really a fair approximation? Wouldn't three be better? What was he considering as the start of the Season, the week after Easter or the Academy art showing?

Did they care that much? They were certainly putting up a grand impression of caring greatly about the consumption of lobster patties among English peers. Alixe mumbled an excuse about visiting the retiring rooms to Fulworth, who hardly gave her a glance, and slid into the oblivion of the ballroom, glad to have made her escape.

Alixe found a quiet retreat in the dark haven of the Couthwald library. She sank on to the sofa and kicked off her slippers, flexing her toes in relief. She was tired of dancing, tired of smiling, tired of pretending any of London's finest held an iota of appeal. They were nothing but a way out of a bad situation and into a mediocre one. She would resist marriage to the fortune-hunting

Redfield however she could, even if meant taking one of those lobster-patty experts out there.

You could marry Merrick. To his credit, he had seemed in earnest tonight. But that didn't change facts, and she knew all too well every reason Merrick should be refused, from social considerations to her own personal happiness. It would kill her to watch him stray once the 'wanting' had waned.

But until then, it could be wonderful, came the dangerous counter. Perhaps a little bit of pleasure was better than none at all.

Alixe took a deep breath to relax. It was the first clue she wasn't alone. She caught a faint whiff of *fougère*.

'We have to stop meeting like this,' came the familiar seductive tones of the devil himself. Merrick emerged from an alcove hidden from view of the sofa. His very stance was one of insouciance. His cravat was off, his waistcoat unbuttoned, a snifter of brandy dangling casually in one hand.

Fleeting panic struck. Alixe stood up in a rush, slippers forgotten. 'Please tell me you're alone.' Alixe's gaze travelled past him to the alcove, praying no one else emerged. She didn't want to see him with another woman tonight.

Merrick gave a wicked grin and stepped closer. He gave the brandy an indolent swirl. 'I could, but it would be a lie since I'm here with you.' Blue hunger raged in his eyes. This was not the tamer, flirtatious version of Merrick St Magnus who talked a harmless scandal on a picnic blanket. This version was wild, a barely leashed original of the other paler imitation. His hunger was for her and it roused her most outrageously. A wanton heat pooled between her legs, tingling and sharp.

When he spoke, his voice was nothing more than a growl, hoarse with desire. 'You've refused my decent proposal. Can I offer you an indecent one?'

Chapter Seventeen

One three-letter word and he would be her lover. It would be rough and beautiful and there would be no going back. Once could be excused as spontaneous, but twice was deliberate. Alixe lifted her hands to her coiffure and pulled the pins from her hair until it shook free. 'Yes.'

Her voice was the slightest of whispers but it was all the confirmation Merrick needed, all she needed. She was in his arms, her hands working the fabric of his shirt loose from the waistband of his trousers as his hands worked the folds of her gown up her thighs. It would be folly to disrobe. This decadence would have to be enough. Alixe strained against him, hands slipping beneath his shirt, palms running up the planes of his chest, revelling in the feel of him beneath her fingers.

His mouth was buried against her neck, his kisses sending a *frisson* of heat through her. She offered up a moan of both desperation and completion. Nothing had been right since she'd left his arms. Everything was right now. In this moment nothing mattered but the feel of him, the taste of him, the smell of him.

'I missed you so much,' came the simple words, the inadequate words. Would he understand all they entailed? Were there words enough to convey what he'd meant to her?

'God, Alixe.' Merrick breathed against her, hands tangled in her hair, pulling her head up to meet his hot gaze. 'Wanting you is killing me.' He lifted her against him, whispering hoarse instructions. 'Wrap your legs about me.'

She did so, tightly, as if she could hold him for ever. The library wall was at her back, a bulwark against the rough onslaught of passion that followed. He took her in a single stroke, hard and forceful, and she welcomed it. *Welcomed him.* She could do nothing but moan her pleasure as he claimed her again and again, branding her with each thrust, his own need for her every bit as great as her need for him. Alixe thought dimly, as their desire crested, how would once, twice, three times, ever be enough, how would she ever get over the wanting of him? She knew only one thing: she was lost. Lost to pleasure, lost to want, lost to him and she could do nothing about it except give in for however long it lasted.

With a final thrust, Merrick surrendered to the madness of want, letting the sensations of ultimate release thunder through him as he poured himself into Alixe. This was what he'd sought during those interim days while he roamed aimlessly between Kent and London. He'd been waiting for something and this was it. This was definitely it: loving Alixe.

Alixe's face was dreamy as she lifted her head from his shoulder where she'd buried her cries, but her eyes were questioning. 'What shall we call this, Merrick?'

'Madness, utter madness.' It was the only answer he had for her. He couldn't fully explain any of these feelings to himself, let alone another, and certainly not while he was still deep in the throes of satiated climax. 'We could end the madness with marriage, Alixe,' Merrick ventured.

'A most proper option under the circumstances. I am surprised, Merrick, but only a little,' came a cynical voice from the door. The door shut with a quiet snick behind the intruder. 'Tsk, tsk. I would have thought after the incident with Lucy the upstairs maid you would have learned to lock the door.' The figure stepped forwards into the dim light of the room.

'Perfect timing, as always.' Merrick made no move to restore his dishabille, his voice barely veiling the sneer of contempt beneath it.

'And this must be the ravishing Alixe Burke. Or would it be more accurate to say the "ravished" Alixe Burke?'

Merrick balled his fists. He was going to hit someone. Soon.

To her credit, Alixe didn't flinch. 'Unfortunately your reputation doesn't precede you. You would be?'

Merrick stepped in. 'This is Martin St Magnus, my brother.'

'I've had the devil's own time tracking you down—' Martin began.

'There's a reason for that,' Merrick cut in swiftly. He wanted Martin out of the room as quickly as possible. He and Alixe had things to work out. Now was not the time for a family reunion.

'If you ran from scandal the way you run from Father, your lot in life might be considerably improved.'

'I do not run. I have made it clear to him that he does not have the ordering of me. I go where I please, when I please.' This was not proving to be an expedient exit.

'From your tone, I must deduce that you think I do not enjoy such luxuries.' Martin flicked his dark gaze towards Alixe. 'You've outdone yourself this time, Merrick. Debauching an earl's daughter? You may have overreached yourself at last. You have to marry this sort of girl.'

He felt Alixe tense beside him and his protective instincts surged. She did not need to be dragged into the mire of his distorted family. Merrick crossed his arms and widened his stance. 'You may insult me all you like, but you will not slander Lady Alixe.'

'Or you'll pummel me the way you pummelled that Redfield fellow at the house party? If you keep it up, Merrick, you won't be invited to any decent places.' Martin feigned a sigh and took up residence in a chair with a wave of his hand. 'Then again, that list is probably fairly short as it is. I hear you aren't even keeping your own rooms these days. You're sharing rooms with that degenerate Bedevere. That's got to be a pit of depravity if ever there was one.'

'Don't get too comfortable in that chair, Martin. You need to leave.' Merrick took a menacing step forwards. 'Lady Alixe and I were having a conversation before you interrupted.'

Martin's eyes roved over Alixe. 'Perhaps, Lady Alixe, I could escort you back to the ball before any more damage is done. Surely you know you shouldn't be without a chaperon under such circumstances.' He stood and held out a hand to her. 'Come with me. Walk away from this folly while you still can.'

Merrick's gut clenched. Would she take that hand? Would she take a look at him and realise how reckless they'd been? Would she regret it? *Don't go with him, Alixe,* Merrick willed her in his mind.

Alixe did not hesitate. 'I believe you've been asked to leave.'

Martin nodded knowingly. 'I see. You're in love with him. I pity you, Lady Alixe.' He strode to the door, calling his message over his shoulder. 'I came looking for you because Father has asked you to call on him tomorrow at three. Show up. I believe there's money and property to discuss. You shouldn't miss it.'

At the door he paused and turned back. 'Lady Alixe, make sure you know what you're getting into. There's nothing but heartache down any road he leads you. He's not capable of anything more. You know it's the truth.' Then he was gone, leaving a malevolent silence in his wake.

'His interruption doesn't change what I'm asking you, Alixe.' Merrick pressed what was left of his advantage. Martin may have been right in one respect.

He had overreached himself this time. A woman of Alixe's calibre would think twice about taking on a man with his history. That history was staring her in the face. It was easier to disregard rumours in the country when London was far away. Somehow, they seemed less real than messages delivered in person by heirs to marquisates.

Alixe offered a wry smile and shook her head. 'Am I supposed to say it doesn't matter? What about all the things you said in Kent about not being able to love? What has suddenly changed you to a marrying man capable of faithfulness? Which one is the real you, Merrick? The faithless rogue or the solid family man?'

Of course. Alixe Burke would demand complete faithfulness from a husband. She would not tolerate dysfunction in any guise. Merrick did not like the coldness of her tone. She was slipping away from him; the heat of their passion had chilled.

She moved to push past him. He could not let her leave just yet. She would not seek him out after tonight. She would try to avoid him as she'd tried to do at the house party.

Merrick took her arm in a gentle grip. 'Alixe, I will always be at your disposal should you need me.'

'I won't. Don't you see, it's not enough for me. I would avoid being the wife you've tired of as you pursue the latest woman who's caught your very fleeting attentions.' She drew a deep breath and gathered herself. 'I could not live with myself, knowing I sold myself so cheaply. I don't know how you do it.'

* * *

At promptly three o'clock, Merrick presented himself at his father's town house, a magnificent Greek Palladian structure four storeys high on Portland square. He had not set foot inside the family residence in seven years. It had not changed from the images in his memory. The huge urns in the entry were still filled with enormous amounts of fresh flowers. The marble tile of the floor was enviously devoid of any scuff marks left by errant boots.

In short, the place still felt like a museum. It made him want to stomp his foot on the floor just to leave a clod of dirt behind. But there would only be short-lived victory in that. A servant would immediately sweep it up and pristine order restored. Messes of any sort were not tolerated in the St Magnus household. Which was why he'd bothered to come at all. There was one mess that had lingered overlong and Merrick meant to see himself extricated from it.

The butler ushered him to the study where his father liked to conduct business. Merrick did not miss the message. He'd been relegated to 'business'; perhaps he even rated a 'family business' label.

The walnut doors pushed open into the earl's domain. Gareth St Magnus, the fifth Marquis of Crewe, sat behind his massive carved desk, imposing and austere. Merrick had forgotten how big everything in the house was. The desk, the chairs, the vases in the front foyer.

'Merrick, it's so good of you to come.' Gareth rose halfway from his chair and gestured for him to take the chair set opposite—the business side of the desk. The rules for the interaction were clearly established. There was no 'son', no welcome home embrace. His father might have been talking to an investment partner or a casual acquaintance.

Gareth pushed a packet of papers towards him. 'A great-aunt on your mother's side has left you a small bequest. Apparently, she found you to be quite charming. The papers are all in order, although you can have a solicitor of your own choosing look through them. The property is near Hever. There is one stipulation.' There was a challenging glint in Gareth's eye. 'You cannot sell it to cover gambling debts and you must be wed to inherit it.'

There was a moment's elation. He was a landowner, something he'd never thought he'd be, something he'd never aspired to be. Alixe would be pleased. Then there was a moment's deflation. There was no more Alixe. Alixe had left him last night, hurried towards the inevitable by his brother's cold reminder of reality.

'Perhaps now you can properly offer for the Burke chit.' A curious flame sparked in the marquis's blue eyes, far too like his own. He and his father were genetic imprints of the other. Even at fifty, with gold hair fading to the dull sheen of harvested wheat, his father bore a remarkable resemblance to him. He'd always resented that resemblance. He had spent most of his life fighting against it. He did not want to be his father—a man who'd made marriage miserable with his faithlessness for a decent woman like his mother.

'You wish to marry her. Is she breeding or are you after her money since you refuse to spend mine?'

'That is none of your business.'

'Has she refused you?'

He must have betrayed himself with a slight movement of his eyes.

Gareth crowed, 'She has and rightly so. She's far too good for a wastrel like yourself. This is rich. The infamous lover of London has been refused. Perhaps you're losing your touch? It's not been a good year for you. I hear you can't pay your rent, that you've moved in with Bedevere. All that money in the bank would set your world to rights.'

'I won't touch a penny of it. I want nothing to do with you or anything that's yours.' Of course, his father knew. His father knew everything.

The marquis gave a cold smile. 'Take your estate and go. Find a bride if anyone will have you without my money. Remember, it's fine to have a poor man in bed, but don't fool yourself, Merrick. No woman wants a poor man for ever.'

Chapter Eighteen

It had been two weeks since she'd seen Merrick and Alixe was starting to fear she was going to need him, after all. Alixe pushed a needle through the fine Irish linen she was embroidering with a delicate border of flowers. Her bravado had been only that the night she'd left him in the Couthwald's library. She'd been angry and stunned, although in hindsight she shouldn't have been.

Alixe rummaged in her bag for a strand of blue silk and carefully threaded her needle, letting the routine of the activity and the warm sun in the garden soothe her rampant thoughts. Her mother had offered to sit with her and sew, but Alixe had wanted to be alone, afraid she might betray herself in the company of another. Her mother would be mortified if she knew the direction of Alixe's thoughts, nearly all of them bent on the person of Merrick St Magnus.

She'd known the truth about Merrick from the beginning. Jamie had seen to it with his discreet warnings. Even without Jamie's warnings, London had seen to it. Merrick's reputation could not be hidden in town. She'd heard about it in juicy bits and pieces behind fans at teas where the ladies would pretend to report his antics in appalled tones when they were really titillated. And she'd seen what he was for herself. He was handsome, charming, wickedly dashing in his behaviours and a second son with no other prospects than the ones purchased by his searing blue gaze and well-displayed physique.

She knew men like that. She'd been warned about them all her life. Every heiress possessed of a fortune the size of hers knew who was acceptable and who was not. But she'd wanted to believe Merrick was different. For a time that had been possible. No one expected or wanted her to marry him. He'd not been thrust in her path as a suitor. He had been given a very defined role to play in her life for a very brief period of time. That made him safe.

Then he had kissed her and everything had changed, for her at least, and nothing had been safe any more: not her dreams of freedom through self-imposed spinsterhood, not her determination to avoid fortune hunters and not her determination to avoid a marriage for the convenience of an alliance. If she married at all, she had her standards: respect, fidelity and perhaps even love.

Those were not items Merrick could offer and yet she found herself willing to forgo them in return for the extraordinary pleasures he did offer and the astonishing moments of connectedness that came with them.

In fact, she'd already risked forgoing those ideals twice and it appeared there were going to be consequences.

Oh, yes. Alixe feared she was going to need him very much. She was late. It was early days yet, only five days past the expected arrival of her monthly flow. She could still pretend there were any number of reasons for it: the hectic stress of the Season, the personal stress of her own matrimonial drama, the heat of London in July. There was no reason to panic. But she needed to make plans for the worst, of which there were only two possibilities. Accept Merrick's offer of marriage or accept Archibald Redfield's and push to marry quickly, which shouldn't be a concern in either case.

Archibald wouldn't care; perhaps with his own blond looks, he wouldn't even notice the child wasn't his. He wanted only her money and all the prestige she represented. There was security in knowing what that marriage would be from the start. There would be no illusions, no pretences towards romance, no wounds to heal later when the pretences were stripped away. But that marriage would represent all that she'd fought so hard to avoid.

If she had to choose, would marriage to Merrick be any better? There'd be pleasure, to be sure. There would be moments when all would be well. But there'd be moments of heartache, too, when the reality, once obscured by bouts of pleasure, would shine through and she would realise Merrick didn't love her. There would be doubt, too. Had he engineered this from the start? Had he seen the opportunity to snare her fortune for himself as Redfield had so inelegantly suggested?

Perhaps he'd even hoped she'd become pregnant and forced to marry him. But she was hard pressed to view him in such a devious light. No matter what the scandalmongers said about him, she did not think many of his pranks were undertaken with malicious intent or with those who didn't understand the risks.

What to choose? Illusion or reality? Merrick or Archibald? How could she choose either and still be true to herself? Alixe prayed she wouldn't have to choose at all. But it might be too late to escape all damage. She highly suspected Merrick had already broken her heart.

'Miss, you have a caller. Will you be receiving?' It was Meg and Alixe noted immediately that her maid's colour was high. Her voice quivered ever so slightly with excitement and her hands were clasped tightly together at her waist. Alixe's suspicions rose, her own pulse leaping irrationally at the prospect that Merrick St Magnus was waiting in the foyer, further proof that she had not escaped unscathed.

Alixe smoothed her skirts with her hands, gathering calmness. 'You may send him to me, Meg. Bring him to the garden and ring for lemonade,' she said in her most placid tones.

'Shall I tell your mother?' Meg asked.

Alixe thought quickly. 'No. You shall be our chaperon and that will be enough.' Merrick had a certain amount of audacity to come calling at the town house after her father had summarily dismissed him at the house party. She also suspected Jamie had reiterated that same dismissal in, she hoped, more polite tones at the Couthwalds' ball. Merrick had fulfilled his purpose and the Earl of Folkestone had no more need of him.

It also raised the question of what could possibly bring him here. He was not oblivious to having been given his *congé*. He knew the reception he'd likely receive. A small flicker of hope leapt low in her stomach. Had he come for her? What a wonder it would be if a twenty-six-year-old heiress, relegated to society's shelf, had stirred the honourable passions of a veteran rogue like St Magnus. What a wonder indeed. If he could love her, it might change everything.

If she would accept him, it would change everything and for that, Merrick was willing to risk it all. It had taken some time to wrestle his answer to Alixe's question. Who was he? But now that he had, the path seemed straight, although no less dangerous for its simplicity of direction.

Merrick strode behind Alixe's maid, who was beaming with barely contained excitement. She hurried him out to the garden with all the haste decorum allowed. He understood the reason for it and it both inflated his hopes and reminded him of the risk he took in coming here. Alixe had consented to see him, but he was still *persona non grata* in the Burke household. He was not Folkestone's choice of a proper husband for his daughter.

But he was through the door. He'd been received. One hurdle overcome. One risk conquered. The next was Alixe. He must conquer her inhibitions in regards to marrying him. To that extent he'd taken great pains in the past weeks. Merrick gave his waistcoat a final tug and followed Meg out into the sunlight of the Folkestone garden.

Alixe was sewing at a stone bench, surrounded by lush roses. Her dark head was bent to the needlework and she looked the veritable portrait of genteel English womanhood in a light muslin gown of celadon: beautiful, refined and calm. The illusion brought a smile to Merrick's lips. His Alixe was so much more than that and seldom was she calm. His boots crunched on the gravelled path and she looked up, her sherry eyes unable to hide the questions bubbling beneath the calm surface.

'Why, Lord St Magnus, what brings you out so early in the day?' She rose and let him kiss her hand, all a great show for Meg's benefit. Her gown did her figure all sorts of favours. The neckline enhanced the fullness of her breasts and the skirt flared ever so slightly over the curve of her hip. She looked entirely womanly and he felt himself stir at the sight of her.

Merrick made a show of his own, consulting his pocket watch. 'It's not as early as all that, Lady Alixe. It's nigh on eleven.'

'Not too early for lemonade at least.' Alixe sent Meg a not-so-subtle look and the maid scurried off. The moment she was gone, Alixe dropped all pretence.

'What are you doing here? Surely you know you're not welcome.' Alixe took up her needlework, keeping her hands busy.

'By you?' Merrick sat beside her, drinking her in.

Two weeks had seemed an eternity, but he could not see her until he'd been sure of himself.

'You know what I mean. My father has dismissed you.' Alixe bit off a length of string between her teeth. Merrick found the motion delightfully erotic.

'But *you* haven't, Alixe. I find that I am not satisfied with our last conversation. We have not finished it. I asked you a question and you have not answered it,' Merrick forged ahead. Lemonade would only keep Meg occupied for so long.

'Correction, I did answer your question. You simply did not care for it.' Alixe stabbed the linen with uncharacteristic roughness.

'Hence, my dissatisfaction with our conversation.' Merrick reached over and took the embroidery hoop from her hands. 'Lay this aside for a moment, Alixe. You'll kill the cloth otherwise.' His hands closed over hers to forestall any of her fidgets and it gave him strength, too, to feel the warmth of her skin beneath his.

'You asked me a question at the Couthwalds'. I've come to answer it. You asked me who I was, the rogue or the husband,' he began. He could feel her hands clench beneath his as she tried to pull away. 'You were right to ask. I had no answer that night.'

Meg returned with the lemonade. Merrick waited for her to set the tray on a nearby table and take herself off a discreet distance before continuing.

'I believed because I looked so much like my father I would act like him, too. I would only be capable of being like him. But I'm not him. He has no hold over me. I haven't spent a penny of his allowance and I hadn't set foot in the family town house for seven years, until two weeks ago.' Merrick paused here to pull out a sheaf of papers from inside his jacket. 'I haven't been a perfect gentleman…'

Alixe squeezed his hands. 'I've told you once before I don't believe you're as awful as all that.' Something born of innate goodness shone in her sherry eyes, a refusal to believe someone was so inherently flawed.

'You should. There's plenty of proof.' He was tempted to tell her about the Greenfield Twins, but an errant sense of decency poked at him.

'Could this be enough for you, Alixe? This chance that I could be a better man *for* you, *because* of you?' He handed her the papers he held. 'I hope this is further proof that I can be redeemed. I want to be redeemed, I want to be all you need.'

Alixe took the papers and scanned them. 'You've come into property?'

'From a great-aunt. It's mine upon marriage,' Merrick began. He wanted to be honest about the conditions, but he didn't want Alixe to think he'd come begging for her hand simply to get his hands on the property with the added benefit of her money. 'It could be ours, Alixe,' he said. 'I would have something of my own. I wouldn't be entirely reliant on your fortune. It's not a big estate, but it would be our place. It's not too far from Folkestone. You would be able to keep an eye on your historical projects.'

'What are you asking me, Merrick?' Alixe ventured cautiously, handing the papers back.

'I am asking you to reconsider. In all fairness, I have overcome your initial objections at no small risk to myself.'

'You would have made a fine barrister, Merrick.' Alixe smiled softly in the wake of his closing arguments.

'Well?'

'I am fully cognisant of the honour you do me.'

His heart sank. She was going to refuse. That's how refusals started. Not that he knew firsthand, but he'd heard others talk about it at the clubs. No one had ever refused him. Then again, he'd never proposed anything honest like this to a decent woman before.

'It will not be enough,' Alixe said sadly. 'I wish I could accept, but it will not be enough.'

'Then tell me what it will take.'

'Love and fidelity, Merrick. That is my price.' Alixe squared her shoulders, her chin going up in piquant defiance. 'Can you be faithful to me, Merrick St Magnus?'

How could he promise permanently something he'd barely experienced temporarily? The right answer would be yes. But the honest answer was, 'I'll try, Alixe.'

'There can be no "try" in this, Merrick.'

'I will not bind you to me with a lie, Alixe. Would you prefer I say "yes" for the expedience of gaining your agreement without knowing it absolutely for the truth?'

'No, of course not.' Alixe rose, signalling it was time for him to leave. But she rose unsteadily and swayed. Merrick caught her by the arm and righted her.

'Are you unwell?' Merrick gestured for Meg. 'Pour some lemonade, please.'

'It's just the sun.' Alixe attempted a smile. She sat down and took the cold glass from Meg.

But Merrick thought differently. 'Meg, perhaps a parasol might help. Would you be so kind as to fetch your mistress one?' Surely Alixe would have said something.

'Alixe, is there something you'd like to tell me?' he said gently, although his insides were a sudden roiling mess.

She shook her head and sipped the lemonade. It occurred to him that she might not know. He tried again, forgoing any delicacy. 'Alixe, have you bled since we've made love?'

She looked up, startled by his bluntness. 'No.' It came out in a rueful, breathy little sigh.

'Is there a chance you may be pregnant?' Merrick pressed.

Alixe would not look at him. She kept her gaze fixed on the trellis of climbing roses across the path. 'It is too soon to know. I am not so very late.'

But she was late and Merrick had seen other signs: the smallest of changes in her body barely visible to the casual eye beneath her gown. He would wager her courses would not come. 'You should have told me.'

She looked at him with eyes that threatened to tear and it stabbed him to his core that his Alixe should be suffering. He'd been careless with her, caught up in the magical madness of her and now she had no choices left. It seemed she'd have to settle for 'try', after all. He'd speak to her father this afternoon whether she liked it or not.

Chapter Nineteen

Admittedly, Merrick had little experience with being proper, but women were mainly the same whether they were proper or not when it came to courtship. He presented himself sharply at four o'clock at the Earl of Folkestone's town house, flowers in hand for Lady Folkestone and a box of chocolates for Alixe. Gifts usually went a long way in smoothing rocky paths, as did a clean appearance. A clean, well-kempt man bearing gifts was hard to refuse.

Always careful with his grooming, Merrick had taken extra pains that afternoon to be turned out at his sartorial best. A sapphire stick-pin glinted in the snowy folds of his cravat and a thick band of antique gold adorned the middle finger of his left hand—both pieces a quiet testimony to what he hoped would be perceived as his 'wealth'.

Lady Folkestone received him first in the front parlour, offering him a polite, albeit empty, smile as she took the flowers. But mamas were women, too. Merrick employed a compliment about the wallpaper and the general good taste of the room, drawing her into a lively discussion of the latest trends towards more ornate furniture. 'Being a man, naturally, I prefer a sturdy chair. Those spidery-legged baroque pieces are lovely, but they're hardly able to support a man's weight. Every time I sit down in one I find myself waiting to hear it crack,' Merrick confided in a conspiratorial tone, letting his eyes smile with the sharing of a secret. 'They're not at all like these chairs. Now, these chairs are hardy and yet elegant with the upholstery you've chosen. The light colours of the striping detracts from what might be seen as their heaviness.'

'That's precisely what I was thinking. My husband did not agree. Folkestone thought the lighter colours would show wear and dirt more quickly, but I insisted,' Lady Folkestone exclaimed, obviously thrilled to have a male divine her reasoning *and* agree with it. She was warming to him, although Merrick thought such warmth might fade if she knew what her daughter and he had been getting up to. But surely Lady Folkestone, with all her matchmaking abilities, was not oblivious to the reasons he was here in a home where he'd been all but banned.

A footman arrived to announce the earl was ready to see him. Merrick rose and bowed graciously to Lady Folkestone. 'It's been a pleasure speaking with you. I've enjoyed your insights on decorating very much. I hope to have some property of my own shortly in which I might employ your talents.' Lady Folkestone smiled, a much more genuine smile than the one she'd given him upon his arrival.

The earl was another matter. Folkestone couldn't be wooed with chocolates or flowers or comments about cushion colours. He sat stoically behind his desk, not unlike Merrick's own father, and glared. 'You are not welcome here,' he said baldly.

Merrick took the empty chair across from him, acutely aware he'd not been invited to sit. He sat anyway and crossed a leg over his knee. 'I am here to offer an honourable proposal of marriage to your daughter.'

Folkestone drew a deep, irritated breath. 'You're not what I want for her, as you have been made aware on several occasions now.'

Those were harsh words to hear to one's face, but Merrick merely smiled to show the haughty earl he was not bothered by the rude comments. 'Things have changed since then.' That was putting it mildly. 'I have come into a property, a modest estate near Hever. It passes to me upon my marriage. I would be able to give your daughter a home on my own terms.'

There. Let that quash any concerns over fortune hunting. There was a slight flicker in Folkestone's dark eyes. He had not known about the inheritance. It *did* make a difference, but only a slight one.

Folkestone toyed with an obsidian paperweight. 'A property is important. A man does not want to live off his in-laws' largesse.' What he meant was a 'real' man. 'But there are other implications besides the practicalities of supporting Alixe.' He gave Merrick a hard stare.

'There are social considerations that cannot be swept away with a property.'

'Such as?' Merrick enquired in a blithe tone. He knew full well what Folkestone was hinting at, but he would be damned if he'd give way to implied meanings. If Folkestone wanted to point out his inadequacies, the man would have to do it in explicit terms.

Folkestone's face hardened. 'Don't play games with me, St Magnus. We both know what social concerns I speak of. Your relationship with your family is strained, to put it politely.'

'That's by choice, sir,' Merrick said levelly.

'You have no title of your own, nor any prospect of coming into one. She's the daughter of an earl. Marriage to a second son is a step down for her, especially when you come to her with nothing.'

Merrick stiffened at that. He'd not ever been a direct recipient of the negotiating process Alixe claimed to abhor. He could see why she despised it now. He was being sized up for his assets as if that was all that mattered. 'Is my genuine regard for Alixe such a small thing, then?' Merrick replied.

Folkestone coughed at this. 'St Magnus, your sense of "genuine regard" for a lady is legendary among the *ton*. You've held quite a few ladies in this so-called genuine regard and you've married none of them. It does lead me to wonder why you'd want to marry my Alixe. She's the richest, of course. Perhaps that is what appeals to you?'

'What appeals to me is her intelligence, her compassion, her beauty.' Those were not things he could prove to Folkestone. How could he explain how Alixe made him feel? How did he convey that when he was with her, he was a better sort of fellow than he'd ever been. When he was with her, he didn't miss his old life and its misguided revels.

Folkestone set down the paperweight. 'It seems to me that there are other women who might be glad of the chance to be recipients of your genuine regard and, in turn, save your new-found estate by marrying you. However, my daughter isn't one of them. Even if I found your suit appealing and trustworthy, I would decline. As you also know, there is a very nice and legitimate proposal on the table from Mr Redfield, whose situation I find acceptable. He already has a manse. He doesn't need marriage to claim his property and he'll live nearby so that Alixe will be close to family. I think, under the circumstances, Mr Redfield is exactly the kind of grounded countryman Alixe needs as a husband.'

'He has no title, no wealth of his own. You are holding me to a double standard here,' Merrick argued. He could feel hope slipping away.

'He is a self-made man, which is more than I can say for you. He started with nothing and from it has created something. I find I respect that. You, on the other hand, are the son of a marquis, with many options open to you. But you've chosen none of them.' Folkestone's eyes narrowed.

'Then Redfield has truly fooled you. He may have fashioned something for himself, but at whose expense? How many women has he ruined or exploited to climb this high?'

'None that I know of. The same cannot be said for the Greenfield Twins.'

And that was that. Merrick heartily wished he'd never heard of the Greenfield Twins. His notorious wager was all over town and he hadn't even done anything, technically speaking. He managed to exit the town house with a show of dignity, but his heart was sinking.

He'd hoped Folkestone would have accepted his suit and allowed things to follow their proper course. It would certainly have avoided difficulties. He and Ashe had failed to turn up anything shady on Redfield. Whoever he was, the man had covered his tracks exceedingly well. That option had come to a dead end. The other option was exposing Alixe's pregnancy. It would force Folkestone's approval of the match, but the costs were enormous. Folkestone would never believe after such a revelation that Merrick had offered in good faith. There would always be doubt that Merrick had deliberately seduced her for her fortune and to claim his estate. Under such a cloud, what kind of future could he and Alixe expect to build?

He said as much to Ashe at White's in the quiet of the late afternoon. They had a corner of the main room to themselves. Most gentlemen wouldn't put in appearances until after seven and the evening entertainments began. Merrick was glad for the solitude.

'You have two choices,' Ashe said thoughtfully,

swirling brandy in a crystal snifter. 'You can forget about her or you can marry her.'

'Have you been listening? I don't have Folkestone's permission *and* she's pledged to Redfield.'

'Have *you* forgotten how to play outside the rules?' Ashe shook his head ruefully. 'Spare me the idiocy of fools in love.'

He drank and swallowed. 'You don't need permission to marry her, you dolt. I'm talking about elopement. She's twenty-six, for heaven's sake, and you're thirty. It's not like you're two green children come to town for the first time.'

'There will be a scandal.'

Ashe sprayed his brandy in a choking fit that brought a footman running to his side. 'A scandal? You're afraid of a little scandal *now*?' He coughed. 'It wouldn't be your first and it certainly wouldn't be your worst. This would be your most "decent" scandal, however, since it ends in the noble state of marriage.'

But it wasn't what he wanted for Alixe. He wanted to prove to her that he could be decent. He didn't have to live surrounded by scandal and notoriety. Merrick St Magnus could be something more than the *ton*'s most charmingly wicked rake. He'd liked the man he'd discovered inside himself at Folkestone. He'd liked translating the manuscript, and building fair booths and exploring ruins. That man could build a life worthy of her.

No, he wouldn't embarrass Alixe with an elopement. A dash to Gretna Green in the dark would only confirm suspicions that he'd been hunting her fortune.

A baby appearing early would be the icing on a very bittersweet cake. Society would dine out on the two of them for years. But Ashe had given him an idea. There was a way to decently marry Alixe, but for that he'd need two things: a special licence and her consent. He was certain he could get the former. He wasn't as sure about the latter.

Alixe sank gratefully on to her bed and kicked off her dancing slippers. The night had been beyond tedious. The best thing that could be said about it was that it had ended early. She was thankful. Her feet hurt and her mind had been in a constant state of turmoil since Merrick's surprise visit the day before.

He'd shown up that afternoon, too. He'd left chocolates for her, but apparently the focus of the visit had been to see her father. She'd been apprised of Merrick's proposal over dinner that night before her father's assurances that she'd be safely married to Redfield as soon as the banns could be called.

That meant three weeks. Not very much time at all. Alixe reached up and began pulling pins out of her hair. She'd dismissed Meg, wanting to prepare for bed in private, a decision she might regret when trying to get out of her gown, but not yet.

If she didn't act soon, she'd be married to Redfield and carrying Merrick's child. She was growing more certain of it by the day. It was the stuff of Gothic novels or a theatrical drama. Her life had been so very ordinary, so very predictable and staid not that long ago.

One fateful act had led to another and here she was, so far from the path she'd laid out for herself.

But that path was devoid of love, of certain elemental human experiences. Yet the price of love was exorbitant and it came with no guarantees, not even the guarantee her love would be returned. Merrick loved her for now, but what of later? That very doubt had stopped her tongue at dinner, from declaring she preferred St Magnus over Mr Redfield, after all.

Lost in her thoughts, Alixe struggled with the fastenings at the back of the dress, a summer night's breeze catching her bare skin where the dress lay undone. She turned sharply towards the draught and stifled a yelp of surprise just in time. Standing in the doorway of the little balcony that led off her room with an air of casual confidence, shirt sleeves rolled up, cravat undone, was Merrick.

'What are you doing here?' Alixe hissed in a hushed whisper.

'That's quite a greeting,' Merrick said with his usual casual ease. 'Not "how did you get here"? Or how glad you are to see me?'

'It's rather obvious how you got here.'

'Obvious doesn't make it easy. I will admit climbing up to your room is a bit ill advised. It will be a while before I try it again.' Merrick stepped into the room, filling the feminine abode with his masculine presence.

'No maid?' He looked around for Meg.

'No, you're lucky,' Alixe scolded. 'What would you have done if she was here?'

Merrick gave a cocky shrug, drawing her attention to the broadness of his shoulders. 'She likes me. I wouldn't have done a thing except let her go to bed early. It does look like you're in need of some help, though. Perhaps I could stand in for your maid.'

He swept the long skein of her loosed hair forwards over one shoulder, the feel of his warm hands against her skin, intimate and relaxing as they worked the remaining fastenings. 'Lock your door, Alixe,' he murmured at her neck once he had finished.

'I locked it earlier,' Alixe managed. She was already trembling for him.

'Good, I want to look my fill of you.' He slid the gown off her shoulders, letting it cascade to the ground in a spill of sea-green silk.

That drew her out of her stupor. 'You can't mean to stay! Redfield is downstairs talking to Father.'

Merrick chuckled, a warm soothing sound that reeked of his confidence. 'Are you expecting him?'

'No, of course not. *I* wasn't even expecting you,' Alixe retorted.

'Then we won't be interrupted. Stop worrying, Alixe.' His whisper was at her ear, his kisses light on the column of her neck.

She arched her neck to the side, giving him full access to it, startled by the glimpse of them in the vanity mirror. Merrick stood behind her, a veritable Adonis in the evening light of the room, his attire less than perfect, the mussed quality only enhancing his sensuality, his buttermilk hair a pale halo, his eyes devil-dark with desire. She barely recognised the wanton princess in the reflection as herself: her hair loose and hanging to one side, one shoulder of her chemise falling down her arm, the outline of her breasts visible through the thin material, Merrick's hands just below them, tantalisingly close. It was a provocative image.

Flustered by the sight, Alixe moved to turn into his arms, but Merrick held her fast. 'Watch us, Alixe. Watch how good we are together.'

And she did watch. It was wicked and yet riveting. Merrick pulled the chemise over her head, leaving her entirely unclothed. His hands cupped her breasts, his thumbs moving up and over the fullest part of them, caressing and stroking in a languid rhythm that had her leaning into him with a small moan of delight.

But after a while, it seemed patently unfair that he should be clothed and Alixe turned in his arms. This time he permitted it. She stripped away the cravat and made short work of his waistcoat and shirt. He sat down briefly to pull off his boots and allowed her to slide his trousers down his hips.

He was naked beneath the clothing and she revelled in the sight of him. The lamplight limned the fine sculpture of his chest, the square bones of his hips and abdomen. Alixe ran her hands over the flat of his stomach. 'I think this is the best part of a man.'

'Truly? I would have thought you might prefer other parts,' Merrick said mischievously, moving her hand lower.

Alixe grinned up at him. 'I like this part, too.' And she did. She liked that part of him very much. 'Did you come here to seduce me?'

'Most definitely.' Merrick turned her back to the

mirror, his voice husky with wickedness. It sent a shiver of anticipation through her, her need rising. 'Brace your hands on the vanity, my dear, I will show you how I mean to seduce you.' The moment of play was gone; he was all serious lover now as he bent her to him. 'I shall be your stallion.'

Oh, this was wickedness unleashed! He was hard against her backside and she felt her body respond, wanting him in her. Her gaze was riveted on the mirror now, watching him mount her from behind, watching him drive deep inside her, a warm hand splayed on her stomach to offer support. Again and again he drove until she could feel the surge of passion grow in its intensity, pushing them higher towards some enigmatic apex and then shatter like thin crystal against a wall. He fell against her in his completion. She could feel the pounding of his chest at her back, the heat of him wrapping her in the blanket of his body.

He found the strength she lacked to guide them both to her bed. She nestled against the hardness of his chest, her head at his shoulder, his arm around her, drawing her near.

How easy all this was with him. Being with him, naked and playing, sharing the intimate pleasures of their bodies, was entirely natural. She could not fathom how it would be with Redfield or another.

'You were right when you said this was madness,' Alixe said slowly after a while. She drew a tiny circle around the flat aureole of his breast.

'We have a whole lifetime to work it out, Alixe, to see if it is truly madness.'

Alixe shook her head. 'It's more complicated than that, Merrick. I know my father has refused you.'

'Will you allow his decision to stand? I came here tonight, Alixe, for you. I've never been one for convention and tradition. I don't need his permission. But I do need yours. There's a special licence in my trouser pocket. I would come for you tomorrow night and take you to Folkestone and marry you at St Eanswythe. Alixe, will you have me?' He was all seriousness. She could feel his body tense beneath her as he awaited her answer.

'You don't have to do this for the baby, it's still too soon to tell,' Alixe murmured, trying to stall until she could make up her mind. Did she dare risk it all on Merrick St Magnus?

'Whether there is a child or not is immaterial to me. I came here tonight for you. I would have come anyway.'

'Why?' Alixe breathed, daring to hope.

'Because, Alixe Burke, I have discovered that I love you. It's not a discovery a man makes every day.'

There could be no doubting him. The honesty of his confession brought tears to her eyes. 'Well, that changes everything,' Alixe managed, trying for levity.

She felt him relax beside her. 'I should hope so. But I still want to hear you say the words.'

There in the darkness, Alixe gathered all her courage. She was a smart woman who'd thought much about what she demanded from a marriage and what she demanded of herself. She understood the world even though she'd chosen to shun it in the hopes of a

better life. Her hero, St Eanswythe, had attempted the
same. But St Eanswythe had died at twenty-six and
Alixe Burke was going to choose to live. She whispered the two most important words of her life for
better or worse.

'Yes, Merrick.'

Chapter Twenty

⁓⬦⁓

Alixe stretched, a long languid movement that started in her toes and went all the way up to her arms. She arched her back and let the morning sun bathe her in its warmth. Everything was right with the world for the first time in weeks. She pushed her eyes open. Today was her wedding day.

Sort of.

Today was the day she'd embark on the journey that would culminate in her marriage to Merrick. He was gone already. He'd left at dawn, waking her briefly for a kiss before departing out her window. But he'd be back tonight with a carriage. Twelve hours to wait. He would send instructions this afternoon regarding where to meet.

A trill of excitement coursed through her at the prospect. She would simply disappear. After tonight she would no longer be Lady Alixe Burke. She would be Lady St Magnus. There was a certain fairy-tale quality to it; the self-proclaimed spinster with her shapeless gowns had captured the attentions of London's most sought-after lover.

Alixe blushed in the morning light, recalling the wicked passions of the night. She was most thoroughly ravished. She dropped a hand to the flat of her stomach. Child or not, she was ready to take on whatever lay ahead. She did not fool herself that marriage to Merrick would be perfect. There would be social shoals to navigate. The circumstances and haste of the marriage would be much talked about. She did hope timing might be on their side. The Season would wind down in a couple of weeks. People would return home to their country houses and forget about the events of the Season. By next spring, their marriage would be old news and there'd be juicier bits of gossips to occupy society.

Society wasn't the only hurdle they'd face. There would be her family's outcry to contend with as well. Her father would be furious that she'd gone against his efforts to see her married to Redfield. Her mother would consider this a blow to her social status, having a daughter married to a scoundrel. She didn't know what Jamie might think. She hoped he might forgive her. She hoped he wouldn't blame Merrick for this. This was her decision. She was going to have a try at love and see where it led.

With conviction in her choice, Alixe tossed back the covers and rang for Meg. It was time to embrace the day. Nothing would stand in her way now.

Nothing would stand in his way now, Archibald Redfield thought smugly, his booted toe tapping impatiently on the tiled reception-hall floor of Lambeth Palace. In a few minutes, he'd have the special licence in hand and the road to claiming his heiress would be clear of its last hurdle.

The traditional Folkestone talked of calling the banns, but Redfield wanted a surety should anything go awry. Banns meant three weeks of waiting. A special licence meant instant permission to marry should he need it and he just might. Nothing had gone according to plan where Alixe Burke was concerned and he would not take any chances here at the end with his goal nearly attained, especially not with St Magnus in town.

It had been galling to hear St Magnus had been in town while he himself had been detained with the earl, drawing up a marital contract. But it had been important that he be there. He couldn't be in two places at once and he couldn't risk the earl uncovering anything questionable about his past that might skew the acceptance of his proposal. If he was present, he could explain away any unpleasant discoveries. There were benefits to drawing the papers up in Folkestone, too. The country solicitor was competent, but less likely to have access to the information networks of London. The last thing Redfield wanted to do was draw up papers in London where the risk was larger that someone would know something unsavoury about him. So he had stayed with Folkestone to secure his match. Meanwhile, Merrick St Magnus hadn't given up. Which only meant one thing: the man must feel there was still some hope.

That fear was confirmed last evening when he'd driven home with the earl's family from an early night out at Lady Rothersmith's musicale, a venue he'd not been disappointed to depart. Folkestone had let it drop over brandy after the ladies had retired that the disreputable St Magnus had had the audacity to make an appointment. Of course, the earl had assured him, St Magnus had been refused out of hand. To which Redfield had politely reminded Folkestone with a smile that they had an agreement complete with legal papers. But just in case, perhaps with circumstances being what they were, a special licence would be a useful precaution.

He needed Folkestone's approval on this. An ordinary fellow like himself couldn't simply walk into Lambeth Palace. He'd need a letter of introduction from Folkestone to expedite his case. He had elegantly pleaded a gentleman's prerogative: a poor man might have to wait three weeks while banns are being called, but a man of funds could forgo that necessity. It was an especial honour for the bride to be married by special licence and while money was exceedingly in short supply for Redfield these days, he considered the twenty-eight guineas well spent if it meant procuring Alixe Burke's dowry. Folkestone had seen reason and acquiesced.

At last the heavy doors opened and the clerk reappeared, bearing papers in his hand. 'Do be careful, sir, the ink is barely dry,' he warned, handing over the papers. 'There must be something in the air. This is the second one that's been requested in as many days,' the clerk said congenially.

Redfield didn't care if it was the fifth. He only cared he had what he wanted. But he could afford to be generous in his success so he made polite conversation anyway. 'Who might the lucky fellow be?'

The clerk chuckled at that. 'Someone we'd never thought to see enter these hallowed halls.' He lowered his voice. 'I suppose it's not discreet to tell you, but we all had a good laugh after he left. Lord St Magnus.'

The elation of victory faded. Redfield kept a smile pasted on his face. 'St Magnus, that old dog? What does he want with a special licence?' he said with a congeniality he no longer felt.

The clerk shrugged. 'No idea, but he's got one now. Came in yesterday, late afternoon, and caught the archbishop at tea.'

Right after the visit to Folkestone, Redfield thought. He made a hasty exit. His instincts had been right. St Magnus hadn't taken 'no' for an answer. A new game was afoot. He could guess what it was. St Magnus meant to take the decision away from Folkestone. A *frisson* of anger shook him almost visibly as he strode down the pavement. All this trouble for snobbish Alixe Burke, who thought she was too good for the likes of him. She hadn't even dressed well until St Magnus had forced her to it. He did have to admit, she looked lovely these days. Bedding the shrew would be less of a hardship than he'd originally thought. St Magnus might have taught her some interesting tricks there, too.

Archibald Redfield was a practical man. Love

couldn't buy you a thing, but money could. He wasn't so much troubled by the thought that St Magnus had been tupping Alixe Burke behind the scenes as he was about the prospect that Alixe Burke had permitted it. Therein lay the danger. Such permission implied she preferred St Magnus over him. If so, St Magnus wouldn't have to steal her away, she'd go willingly unless he could stop it.

Archibald Redfield would not go away, Alixe thought with no small amount of irritation that afternoon. He'd taken her out for a drive in Hyde Park, which she'd hadn't been able to refuse, and now they sat in the shade of the garden with her mother, sipping lemonade and talking about the various improvements he wanted to make at Tailsby. The list was long, which no doubt accounted for the lengthy conversation.

'A gentleman's home must mirror his values,' he told her mother. 'I want a place of light and beauty, a place that will be a perfect setting for my family.' He looked her way with a warm smile that she was sure was affected. 'A prospective bridegroom must be indulged in his own fancies.' He laughed. 'While the ladies talk of gowns and flowers, gentlemen plan their home.'

Gentleman, my foot, Alixe thought. If he used the word 'gentleman' one more time, she was going to throw her lemonade glass at him. Then they could see what a 'gentleman' did with lemonade all over him. He might aspire to be a gentleman, but he had not attained such status yet.

'A gentleman?' Alixe queried perversely. 'I was unaware there was a title in your family.'

Her mother shot her a tiny frown of disapproval and quickly moved to restore tranquillity. 'Didn't you once say, Redfield, there was a baronetcy among one of your great-grandfathers?'

Redfield gave a casual lift of his shoulders. 'The family tree is so very tangled I can scarce keep it all straight for three generations, let alone four. I leave that sort of work for nimbler minds such as yours, Lady Folkestone.'

The compliment worked well in placating her mother. Her mother gave her a smile as if to say 'what a nice fellow, he wasn't even put off by your snide and inappropriate remark'.

'Lord St Magnus has a title,' Alixe continued her needling. 'That definitely makes him a gentleman.' She watched Redfield's smile tighten infinitesimally.

'I should like to think it takes more than putting "lord" in front of a name to make a gentleman,' Redfield responded. 'It takes knowledge of certain nuances, demonstration of certain behaviours, a certain restraint. Gentlemen are the bedrock of good society. I do not consider St Magnus to be a model citizen.'

'My brother cares for him a great deal,' Alixe shot back, letting Redfield know he was in grave danger of offending Jamie.

'Your brother is kindness itself.'

Alixe knew what that comment really meant and she neatly turned the tables. 'As you have been. Surely you have other obligations than dancing attendance on the two of us.'

'We are to be married. Nothing gives me greater pleasure than spending time with my fiancée. The only greater joy would be allowing me to announce that happiness tonight.' He was asking her mother for permission, but he was looking at her, his eyes hard and assessing as if he was searching for something, as if he knew something.

Alixe tensed, panic taking her as her mother glanced between them and said, 'Yes, I think tonight at the ball would be perfect. If we wait too much longer, the Season will be finished and there won't be a chance to celebrate.'

He did leave after that. But the damage was done. Alixe's first reaction was to run straight to Merrick. But if Redfield suspected anything, he would also suspect that. He meant to flush her out. She must do nothing to give away her anxiety. That meant she could only wait until evening and hope nothing else went awry.

Even if she'd thought it safe to send for Merrick, there was no chance for it. Her room was the scene of chaos. She was not alone for a moment. Meg was there with her mother and her mother's maid. 'It's not every night my daughter gets engaged!' her mother all but crowed as she bustled about Alixe's room, giving instructions for her hair, her gown, her slippers. Three gowns already lay discarded on Alixe's bed, none of them deemed right for the occasion.

'Meg, bring out the deep-cream gown with the forest-green sash.' It had been one of Alixe's favourites when it had arrived and she hadn't worn it yet. 'I think that one will do nicely, Mother,' Alixe put in, trying not to swivel around while her mother's maid put up her hair. How would Merrick get word to her when she couldn't contrive to be alone? She had thought word would have arrived earlier. It was after seven and no word had come.

A thousand thoughts rioted through her head, adding to the chaos. Had Merrick changed his mind? Had he been delayed? At last she was proclaimed 'ready'. The woman in the mirror looked dazzling, if not a trifle pale.

'I'll just help her with some powder and rouge,' Meg said, shooing the others out. 'She'll be downstairs in just a moment.'

Alixe was grateful for the quiet that followed. She let Meg touch up her face with a light application of cosmetics. 'I don't know what's been going on, miss,' Meg began as she worked. 'But Lord St Magnus sent a boy to the back door asking for me today. Asked me where you'd be tonight and I told him. He said a carriage would be waiting at ten o'clock outside the back-garden gate.'

Relief washed over her. Merrick hadn't forgotten, hadn't changed his mind. Now it was up to her. All she had to do was elude Redfield. She didn't fool herself into believing it would be an easy task. Redfield suspected something was up. How he could have guessed, she didn't know. It was immaterial. The only thing that mattered now was getting to Merrick.

'Is everything all right, miss?' Meg eyed her carefully in the mirror.

'Everything will be all right, Meg. You didn't tell anyone, did you?'

Meg gave her a solemn look. 'No. Are you sure this is what you want? Lord St Magnus is a handsome fellow, but…'

'It's what I want, Meg.' Alixe smiled and rose, giving the maid a quick hug. 'Everything will be fine, you'll see. But if anything goes wrong, tell my brother what you know. You can trust Jamie.' She hoped she was right on that account.

Alixe swept up a matching green wrap and gave her room a final survey. It would be a long time before she was back here and by then everything would be different.

She was late. Merrick checked his pocket watch a fourth time. The minute hand had slipped past the three, edging towards half past the hour. He didn't want to ponder what could be keeping her. There were plenty of doubts that were taking up residence in his thoughts. Had she changed her mind? Had she started her courses and decided against marriage now that the danger had passed? Had the clear light of morning altered her passion-influenced decision the night before? Or was she in need? Had something occurred to prevent her making their appointment?

He hadn't been able to get close to the house today. Redfield had been there nearly the entire afternoon. He'd opted for sending a message through Meg. Had she been able to deliver it? Originally, he'd planned to slip a note into a bouquet and leave it for Alixe, but that seemed too risky with Redfield's presence. Redfield's presence had concerned him greatly, especially with what Merrick had learned that morning. His enquiries had turned up unsavoury information at last. Redfield made a habit of preying on middle-class women of comfortable means. He'd not aimed so high before and Merrick would see to it he wouldn't again by whatever means necessary. The proof was in his pocket.

But that didn't allay his present worries. Had the messenger boy got the time right? The sooner he had her out of Redfield's clutches, the better he'd feel.

There was no way to know short of going inside. That was one thing he couldn't do. He wasn't dressed for it. He was dressed for travelling. For another, he hadn't been invited. Besides, making a scene would hardly assist a discreet getaway.

That line of logic held until ten-thirty. To hell with discretion. He was going in there. Whatever happened inside would be far better than the not knowing going on outside. Merrick climbed out of the coach and called up to the driver, both of which were borrowed from Ashe, who'd called him a fool but loaned them anyway, saying, 'My driver's a good shot if it comes to that.'

'Bring the carriage around to the entrance. I'll be leaving by the front door. And, John, be ready to drive.' He tossed up a bag of coins. 'Bribe 'em for a good spot at the kerb if you have to and have the lanterns lit.'

'Will do.' The coachman nodded, having been fully

briefed on their purpose. 'But pardon me saying so, how are you going to get in? You're not invited.'

Merrick winked, the prospect of action raising his spirits. 'You don't need an invitation when there's a perfectly good fence to climb.' With that, he leapt up on a pile of discarded crates, scaled the railings with an agile ease born of too much practise escaping forbidden boudoirs and disappeared.

Merrick jumped down on the other side, thinking how odd it was to climb railings to get *in*. Usually he climbed them to get *out*. The garden was nearly deserted and he kept to the shadows to avoid drawing attention to himself. The verandah was another matter. Footmen abounded with trays of champagne and lobster patties. It wasn't long until the butler, accompanied by two tall footmen, cornered him at the back of the ballroom and demanded to know his business.

'I have a message for Viscount Knole,' Merrick replied, using Jamie's title. If Alixe was here, there was a good chance Jamie was, too.

The butler's narrowed gaze suggested doubt, but he sent someone in search of Jamie and Jamie turned up quickly, looking less than pleased. 'It's all right,' Jamie dismissed the butler, but the stare he fixed on Merrick told a different story. 'You're not wanted here, Merrick.'

'Where's Alixe?'

'She's up front.'

Merrick stepped forwards, determined to cut a swathe through the ballroom to reach her, but Jamie put a restraining hand on his chest. 'I don't pretend to know what happened between you and Alixe. Whatever it was, it's over now. You need to accept that. She's chosen Redfield. They're going to announce the engagement momentarily. You have to let her go.'

All Merrick said was, 'No.' The woman who'd writhed in his arms the night before would not be swayed from her promise so easily. He plunged into the crowd, making his way to the dais. Folkestone was ringing his champagne flute for attention and Alixe stood pale and desperate beside a beaming Archibald Redfield, her eyes darting through the crowd, searching for something, for someone. That someone was him. *Hold on, Alixe, I am coming*—although he had no idea what he'd do when he got there.

Chapter Twenty-One

〰〰〰〰〰〰

Alixe searched the crowd for a last-minute miracle. Fate had conspired against her in the most agonising of ways. Redfield had not left her side all evening. He'd even escorted her to the ladies' retiring room and waited for her. She'd watched the hours slip away. Ten o'clock came and passed and she remained tied to Redfield. She wanted to kick him, wanted to rail at him for ruining her plans, but that would admit there'd been plans at all. Now it was too late. Unless Merrick guessed at her distress and came for her. Even then, there'd be a scandal to pay. There would be no quiet getaway that her family could choose to unobtrusively hush up. Instead, there would be public drama. She would have succeeded in giving her family fits again after she'd tried so hard to avoid it.

Her father was tapping his goblet for attention. Redfield had her arm in the discreet vise of his grip, firmly holding her rooted to him on the dais. Her mother was smiling and, somewhere in the back of the ballroom, there was a surge of movement swirling through the press of people, the crescendo of murmurs rising as the motion moved forwards. She caught a glimpse of pale-gold hair and broad shoulders pushing forwards.

Merrick.

He had come.

Her father cleared his throat. 'My dear friends, I want to thank you all for joining us this evening and allowing us the opportunity to make a most heartfelt announcement. At long last, I am pleased to share with you the engagement of my daughter to Mr Archibald Redfield, lately of Tailsby Manse. I have been proud to call him neighbour and now I will be able to call him my son-in-law as well.'

Polite applause broke out. Redfield preened. Alixe shot a desperate look at Merrick. He neared the dais, but looking at him was a mistake. Redfield followed her gaze, his grip tightening on her arm. 'My dear, he is too late if he means to claim you. Whatever plans you might have had, they've been successfully rerouted,' he whispered at her ear.

Alixe wrenched her arm to no avail. His grip held. 'Don't make a fool of yourself. You'd look ridiculous up here struggling,' Redfield said in low tones.

'You're late, St Magnus,' Redfield called out. 'Too late, some would say.'

There was some nervous laughter at the base of the dais, but Alixe noted wiser souls stepped back, clearing the space between Redfield and Merrick.

Her father's gaze flicked to Merrick. 'How dare you come to disrupt good society.'

'I come to oppose this announcement.' Merrick's voice rang out, silencing the murmurs that seethed behind him. 'If you ask the lady in question, I think you will discover she prefers another.' Merrick held out his arm, his hand so near she could almost touch it. His eyes turned to her, blue and blazing. 'Come with me now, Alixe.'

'You go with this blackguard, Alixe, and you won't see a penny of your dowry,' Folkestone hissed. Alixe could see the fans near the dais flutter faster. This was rich drama indeed. Drury Lane could do no better. 'Do you want her, St Magnus, now that she hasn't a penny to her name?'

Merrick's eyes held hers, his hand beckoning. 'I'll always want her.'

Tension eased from her shoulders. Alixe stepped forwards. She wanted only to get to Merrick and scandal be damned. She didn't care a whit for what anyone was thinking. Merrick had come for her. Merrick had publicly declared his affections in front of all these people. Nothing else mattered.

But Redfield didn't release her. Instead, he yanked her hard to him, an arm imprisoning her against his chest. The cold press of steel swept across her throat and Alixe gasped. Dear God, he had a knife. Those in the front row screamed in alarm. She vaguely heard her father attempt to reason with him. 'Redfield, what are you thinking?'

It was Merrick who answered. 'He's thinking his chances are gone. Once Alixe is lost to him, he won't be able to pay his bills.' Merrick waved a sheet of paper. 'Archibald Redfield is one of his many names. Under the name of Henry Arthur, he's wanted for defrauding three widows in Herefordshire and two older ladies in York.'

Redfield tightened his grip and Alixe shuddered. 'Don't do anything foolish, St Magnus, or I'll cut her and we'll both be the poorer for it.'

He marched them down the steps, using her as a constant shield, heading towards the garden door where there'd be no one to impede their progress once they gained the street. Alixe tried to struggle, but her efforts were short lived. He hauled her against him with a vicious tug. 'As for you, if you'd like to end up dead, keep it up.'

Alixe could feel the alarming trickle of blood work its slow way down her neck. Her struggles had done that, causing the blade to nick her. He meant business. Something inside Redfield had snapped. He'd become more than a fortune hunter. He'd become lethal.

What was supposed to have been an escape had now become a rescue and an inept one at that. Pandemonium reigned in the ballroom once Redfield slipped out the door. People raced every which way to depart, impeding Merrick's ability to follow Redfield into the night. 'Jamie!' he shouted above the din. 'We cannot let him leave the premises.' With a mixture of fear and hope, he thought of his carriage parked in the street. Ashe's coachman could be a surprise ally. But the last thing he wanted was Redfield to find the carriage and take Alixe into the night.

Jamie nodded and they pushed through the crush together, gathering a phalanx of supporters as they went. Merrick's concern for Alixe fuelled him. The man had shown his true colours tonight. Whatever hopes Redfield had of living the life of the country gentleman and rubbing elbows with the peerage had vanished the moment he'd drawn the knife. Merrick understood what the others present might not. There was still a chance Redfield could earn a ransom if he could get away.

They gained the verandah steps and Merrick caught a glimpse of Alixe's light-coloured gown. 'Over there!' he called to Jamie, dipping down in a fluid motion to retrieve his own weapons. Some men carried a knife in their boot. Merrick carried two, one for each boot. He carried them out of habit. One could never be too careful in the gaming hells or with jealous husbands. Tonight he was glad for it. There might be twenty men behind him, but it wouldn't matter if there were sixty. This confrontation was about who would die first, not about how many. Merrick wondered if anyone else understood that.

Redfield had reached the railings, but was slowed down by the cumbersome task of unlatching the gate while still holding Alixe captive. Merrick threw his first knife with unerring accuracy, sending the whistling blade over Redfield's shoulder and effectively pinning the gate shut.

'You're trapped, Redfield.' Merrick halted with twenty feet between them, the mass behind him stopping as well. He could see the madness in Redfield's eyes and the fear in Alixe's. He would kill the man for that alone. Then he caught sight of the trickle of blood seeping down Alixe's neck. Killing the bastard wouldn't be enough. He palmed his second knife and let cool clarity flow over his red-hot rage.

'You're the one who's trapped,' Redfield sneered. 'My freedom for her life. That's the only deal we have now. I've already cut her once.' The blade pressed again and Alixe gave a gasping scream.

'You're wrong, Redfield.' Merrick considered his options with lightning speed of mind. There was a square section of Redfield's shoulder not protected by Alixe's body. It was his best chance of a good throw. 'There are too many of us. You won't get out of the garden alive.' Perhaps Redfield hadn't realised the game wasn't about numbers yet.

'She'll be dead first,' Redfield countered. 'Or maybe it will be you. Care to bet on that?' Something shifted ever so slightly in Redfield's eyes, Merrick barely had time to react. In an enviously fluid move, Redfield shoved Alixe away from him and threw the knife. Merrick's own response was hasty, but no less accurate. His blade found purchase in Redfield's body just as Redfield's blade embedded itself in his right side. He heard Alixe scream his name as he fell, the force of the blow bringing him to his knees, and then he knew nothing, only that Alixe was safe.

In the week that followed, the Folkestone town house thrummed with stealthy activity. Doctor's orders were for peace and rest, but even those strict commands couldn't keep the halls empty while London waited with a communally held breath to see if its latest hero would survive.

Redfield's knife had struck dangerously close to a lung and Merrick had lost copious amounts of blood along with consciousness. Alixe had taken charge from the start, scrambling to Merrick's side in the garden and ordering he be taken into the house. She'd seen he was given the best bedroom, although her mother had feared the sheets would never recover. She'd seen him tended and had not left his side for any extended period of time since, except for an occasional rest and to update the visitors who seemed to throng the reception rooms.

Ashe Bedevere was there constantly, although he remained in the drawing room playing endless games of chess with Jamie while he worried over his friend. Her father was still in a state of disbelief: how could they not have known about Redfield? The other regular company haunting the drawing room was Martin St Magnus. He sat by himself for hours, usually reading, but he would look up expectantly whenever she entered the room, hungry for news. He was tired and drawn, as they all were. Alixe had not forgotten the disdain he'd shown Merrick at the Couthwalds', but his concern was sincere. She regretted she had no better news to give him day after day. Merrick remained the same: unconscious except for the briefest, most unpredictable moments of lucidity, which lasted only seconds.

Nursing was tiring work. There were those who would help her and at times Alixe accepted their assistance, but for the most part, she insisted on being

his caregiver. He had nearly died for her. He might die
for her yet and there was no deeper proof Alixe could
ask of his fidelity. He'd faced Redfield in the garden,
knowing full well what the risks were, and he'd taken
them fearlessly, never questioning what might be required of him. All for her.

Alixe knew as she toiled over his broken body that
she had not guessed at the depth of affection he held for
her or the tenacity to which he clung to it. She'd been
too caught up in her own feelings to see that he was
struggling with the same emotions. Merrick St Magnus loved her. Truly loved her. Every time she thought
of it, the incredible and undeniable truth of it washed
over her anew. It was a staggering realisation to make
at a staggering time. *You can't die now, not now that I
know,* ran like a litany through her mind day and night.

But she had to prepare herself for the worst. The
doctor had told them that morning if Merrick didn't
rouse to more complete consciousness soon, it wouldn't
be his wound that killed him, it would be the lack of
nourishment. He would grow too weak. It had been five
days since he'd last eaten. They'd made efforts to feed
him, necessarily. But there was only so much broth
that could be delivered via a hollowed-out reed, only so
much water they could force past his unresponsive lips.

The doctor came that evening and she watched him
check the bandage. He shook his head as he rose. 'It
won't be long now. His pulse is not as strong as it was
this morning and even this morning it was less than
what it had been.' He put a kindly hand on her shoulder.

'If he wakes, those who need to say goodbye should be ready.'

No. It wasn't possible. He couldn't die now. Not when he loved her and she loved him. Not when they had a lifetime ahead of them. Not when they had a child on the way. She was very sure of it now.

Alixe locked the bedroom door with slow determination. She had wanted to do this all week, but decency didn't permit it. She crawled in bed beside him and lay next to his good arm. There was solace in being with him like this, physically close. She carefully laid her head on his shoulder and closed her eyes. She imagined they were back at St Eanswythe, lying beneath the trees and he was very much alive, his body thrumming with vitality and passion.

She let the tears come, let them fall on his bare chest in her grief. He had changed her and for the best. They'd talked of his redemption, but they'd never once talked of how he'd redeemed her. He'd reclaimed her from a life of isolation, she saw that now. He'd taught her about the transforming power of love, whether he'd intended to or not. There would be those who might say St Magnus was the one transformed, but in her heart she knew it was the other way around. If only she could tell him.

Damn him. How dare he leave her, she thought not for the first time, but this time the thought was tempered with anger. How dare he, she thought again, her temper rising. Then Alixe Burke did the unthinkable. She kicked him.

'Ow! Always…kicking…me,' came the hoarsest of murmurs.

Alixe screamed and shot bolt upright. She had not expected an answer and yet there it was after days of silence. It was a raspy answer to be sure, but it would do. 'You're awake!' she crowed exultantly before panic set in. 'You mustn't go back to sleep,' she babbled. 'If you do, the doctor says you won't wake up again.' Alixe pressed a hand to the side of his throat like she'd seen the doctor do. The pulse that met her touch was solid and stronger. She breathed a little easier.

'How do you feel?' She studied his face. His blue eyes seemed more alert than they had on prior occasions. She touched his forehead, feeling for the dreaded fever, but there was none.

'Hungry.' One-word answers were all his voice could stand at the moment after his initial outburst.

Alixe grabbed for the bell pull and yanked with ferocity. She didn't dare take her eyes from him for fear he'd slip away if she blinked. She felt the touch of his hand on hers and looked down. His touch said what his voice could not. 'I'm here, Alixe. It will be all right now.'

Her tears fell afresh. She was still sobbing when she unlocked the door to let the food in. But the worst was over. Merrick was going to live.

Over the next few days, Merrick improved steadily, defying the doctor's earlier prognosis. He was able to receive visitors for brief periods of time. Ashe came. Jamie came. Martin came; although the words they exchanged were few, both were affected by the reunion of sorts. Alixe had hopes that whatever differences lay between the brothers, this might mark a new chance for them. Last of all, her father came.

'It seems I owe you an apology,' Folkestone began, settling himself wearily into a chair. Alixe had never seen her father look so very worn out. The ordeal had taxed him not so much physically, but mentally. Merrick's actions had challenged her father's assumptions and required him to draw new conclusions, a task Alixe knew was not easy for him.

'I may have misjudged you. You did my daughter a most honourable service. You saved her life nearly at the expense of your own. That is not something I can overlook. If you still intend to marry her, you have my permission.'

Merrick nodded and shifted on his pillows to sit up straighter. He shot her a warm look. 'I do intend to marry her as soon as I am able. I find now that I have a future to look forward to, I am anxious for it to begin as soon as possible.'

'Well…' Her father coughed, uncomfortable with the level of emotion suddenly present in the room. 'I'll leave you two to work out the details.'

Merrick smiled at her and beckoned, patting a space on the bed beside him. 'Come, let me hold you. That's at least something I can do with one good arm.'

Alixe sat quickly beside him, revelling in the feel of him. After almost losing him, she knew she'd not take the presence of his body for granted again. They had not talked of the evening in the garden since his recovery, but she ventured it now. She traced a circle around his nipple, watching it tighten in response, and smiled softly to herself. 'You're London's latest hero, you know,' she began. 'Everyone's talking about how brave you were, how bold. I think there's even a bit of verse circulating. I was so frightened and there you were, taking charge. You knew exactly what you were doing.' She paused.

'He would have killed me, Merrick, if it hadn't been for you. He was different that night. Something had snapped in him, I could sense it. I couldn't tell you what it was, but it was something. I think now, he'd never been right in the head from the start. He was always watching people.'

Merrick's arm tightened about her. 'I was scared, too. I didn't think about being brave. I only thought about you.' His hand reached up to trace the tiny white scar left by Redfield's knife. 'When I saw that you were hurt already, my only thoughts were to set you free, it was all that mattered and then I realised nothing had mattered for a long time. There'd been nothing to fight for. Now there was—there was you.' He played with her hair, a twinkle in his eye. 'I do believe, Alixe Burke, the London gossips have it all wrong. It was not me who saved you. It was you who saved me.'

Alixe shook her head. 'I disagree. You have saved me in ways far beyond what happened in the garden.'

'Well…' Merrick sighed happily '…then it looks like we're even.'

Chapter Twenty-Two

The ruins of the church of St Eanswythe was hosting its first wedding in centuries. The early autumn sun shone pleasantly through the leaves of the trees and the small gathering of guests hummed with excitement as they sat amid the crumbled stones of the cathedral.

The handsome groom, Merrick St Magnus, stood impatiently at the impromptu altar with Vicar Daniels. Jamie Burke stood beside him along with Ashe Bedevere, who was looking far more decent than he actually was, a fact not lost on several ladies in attendance.

Local flowers and ribbon looped down the aisle on poles mounted into the dirt between the old flagstones, making a pretty setting. But Merrick had eyes only for the woman who waited at the far end of the aisle, gowned in a dress the colour of gold leaves, a wreath of autumn flowers crowning her dark head. In Alixe, he had his very own saint. Not bad for a sinner of such glorious proportions.

The vicar gave a slight nod and she began a slow

procession towards him. He offered her his hand and held it throughout the service, barely hearing the words of the ceremony. His hands trembled a bit when he slipped the gold band on her finger. She was his. The enormous wonder of it was not lost on him. He bent to kiss her, sweeping her into his arms and kissing her full on the mouth until even Ashe felt the urge to intervene. If anyone thought it unseemly, Merrick didn't care. He wanted the world to know he loved his wife, a fact he demonstrated quite publicly throughout the wedding breakfast that followed and more privately later that night.

'I have something for you.' Merrick rolled over to snatch a scroll tied with a small ribbon from the bedside table. They'd chosen to spend the night at an elegant inn on the road to Hever.

'What is this?' Alixe asked, her eyes lighting up at the prospect of a gift. She slid the ribbon off and unrolled the paper. Merrick waited for her reaction. He'd thought a long time about what would be most meaningful to her. The usual gift of jewels didn't suit her and, even if they had, Merrick was determined not to spend her dowry so frivolously.

'Oh!' A gasp escaped her. 'How did you ever manage this, Merrick?' Her eyes moved to his face.

'It looks like your farmer lived happily ever after with his "sow".' He reached over to gently push the hair back from her face where it had fallen forwards.

Alixe put the paper aside. 'It's the perfect gift. How did you know?'

'Because I know you,' Merrick said, pleased the gift

had touched her. He wanted to spend his life pleasing her. She was beautiful in the candlelight of their room.

'How did you ever find out?' she began again.

'I managed a few visits to the village and helped Vicar Daniels go through some old records.' Merrick shrugged, making little of his efforts. He didn't want to talk about a Norman farmer in detail at the moment. His mind was already on wanting to take her again.

Alixe snuggled next to him. 'It's the ideal wedding gift. Thank you.' She traced circles on his chest, her favourite pastime while she waited for better things to come. 'I have a gift for you, too.' She stretched up and whispered one word in his ear.

'Are you certain?' Merrick felt his heart thud.

'Yes. I met with a doctor in London before we left.'

The pronouncement might have undone a lesser man. But Merrick St Magnus threw back his head and laughed.

Twins.

Of course.

He didn't doubt it for a moment. He was Merrick St Magnus and he did nothing by halves.

* * * * *

HOW TO RUIN
A REPUTATION

For my dad and Nancy, just because it's been a long time since I've dedicated a book to you.

Hugs and love to you both.

Prologue

The dim interior of the sickroom bristled with contentious silence. 'The will must be changed.' The old earl fairly shook in his chair with the force of his statement.

'I heard you the first time,' Markham Marsbury, solicitor to the Earl of Audley over the past ten years, responded with a patience born of long practice. The earl wasn't his first client who'd had last-minute doubts about his final arrangements. But the earl's requests might be the most irregular.

'You disagree with my decision,' the earl challenged, sounding more like his usual irascible self than he had in months. Perhaps it was a good sign, Marsbury thought hopefully. Perhaps the old man would get better one more time. Goodness knew the earldom could ill afford to lose him now. On the other hand, he knew better. Anyone who had been around lingering death knew the signs: a sudden rally, a brief explosion of energy that might last a day or two—then nothing.

'Yes, I disagree, Richard.' They'd become friends

over his decade in Audley. 'I can understand wanting to make the inheritance into a regency, a trusteeship of sorts. After what happened to Alex, it's a logical course.' Marsbury shook his head. 'But to divide the governance into shares and leave fifty-one per cent to *her* makes no sense. You have two viable male heirs hanging on the family tree, one of them your second son. For goodness' sake, Richard, she's not even British. She's American.'

'She's what the estate needs. She's already proven it in the year she's been here,' the earl broke in with vigour, unwilling to hear his position maligned. 'Some American thinking will rejuvenate the place and she's become the daughter I never had.'

And maybe even a substitute for the son who had not come home in ten years. 'Ashe will come home,' Marsbury put in. But he got out his papers and his ink and began to write. He recognised the signs of early intractability. There would be no dissuading the earl.

'Not while I'm alive,' the earl said matter of factly. 'We quarrelled and he made his position very clear.'

Then the son was a lot like his father, Marsbury thought privately as he finished the codicil and brought the paper to the earl. He held the older man's hand steady as he signed. The earl hadn't been able to write on his own for some time. Even with help, the signature was a barely legible scrawl.

Marsbury sanded the document and carefully placed it with the other papers. He reached out to shake his friend's hand. 'Perhaps there will be no need for this, after all. You look better today.' He offered a smile.

The smile was not returned. 'There is every need for it,' the earl barked. 'I've done what needs doing to bring my son home. I know my son. What he wouldn't do for me, he'll do for Bedevere. He loves Bedevere and he will come for that reason alone.'

Marsbury nodded, thinking of the other two names on the codicil, the other two 'shareholders' named in the trusteeship. His father's death would bring the errant son home, but knowing Bedevere was surrounded by enemies who had been positioned to snatch it up should he falter, might be enough to make him stay.

'I'll see you tomorrow.' Marsbury snapped his writing case shut.

The earl gave him a wan smile, looking more tired than he had a few minutes prior. 'I rather doubt that. If you mean to say goodbye to me, I would suggest you say it now.'

'You are far too stubborn for such maudlin talk,' Marsbury joked, clasping the old man's hand one last time.

Stubborn as the fourth Earl of Audley was, Death was ultimately more so. It was with no surprise that Markham Marsbury received word over his morning coffee the next day that the earl had passed away shortly before sunrise surrounded by family and one Genevra Ralston, the American in whose hands the fate of Bedevere now resided. Markham called for his writ-

ing things and dispatched a note to London, hoping it
would find Ashe Bedevere and bring him home with
all possible haste.

Chapter One

Sex with Ashe Bedevere was one of the 'Great Pleasures' of the Season and not to be missed, which explained why Lady Hargrove was favouring him with a splendid pout and a peek-a-boo glimpse of her bosom beneath a carefully draped sheet in hopes of persuading him to stay.

'Surely a few more minutes will not matter,' she protested with a coy look, letting the sheet slip ever so provocatively over the curve of her hip.

Ashe shoved his arms through the sleeves of his shirt, dressing rapidly. Whatever he'd found appealing about Lady Hargrove's feminine assets earlier in the evening had vanished in the wake of the note that had come for him. He pulled on his trousers and favoured her with a sinful smile designed to placate. 'My dear, what I had in mind for us takes more than a few minutes.'

The promise of deferred pleasure was enough. Ashe eased out the door before she could argue, all his thoughts fixed on one goal: getting to Bedevere, the Earl of Audley's family seat. Never mind that Bedevere was three days' ride away. Never mind he hadn't any idea of what to do once he got there. Never mind he could have answered numerous requests to return home in the past years and hadn't. Never mind any of it. This time it was different. This time, the solicitor had written two desperate sentences. 'Come home. Your father has died.'

Ashe sprinted the last few streets to his rooms on Jermyn Street, fuelled by a sense of urgency and impotence. He'd always thought he'd have more time.

Three days later

God and the devil in the details! Ashe swore none too softly and pulled his bay stallion to a jolting halt. *This* was Bedevere land? More to the point, this was his father's land? He could hardly reconcile the weed-choked fields and broken stone fences lining the roadway with the once-fertile fields and immaculate roads of his youth. He'd seen plenty of the devil since he'd ridden on to Bedevere land and not much of God. How had it come to this?

A sharp pang of guilt stabbed at him deep and hard. He knew the answer.

It was his fault.

The current summons home wasn't the first, but it would be the last. Ashe could have come home long before when the first bout of illness had settled in four years ago. He could have come home when his brother had gone round the bend two years ago for reasons still unclear to him. But he hadn't and an extraordinary consequence had occurred as a result: the timeless fortitude of Bedevere had faltered, proven fallible at last. He'd waited too long and all this ruin could be laid at his feet.

It seemed an ironic twist of fate that he was now poised to be the curator of a place he'd so willingly fled in years past. The place had been perfect then, so unlike his imperfect self. It was less perfect now and he was still flawed—a broken king to rule a broken Camelot.

There was no use in putting it off. Ashe kicked his horse into a canter for the last ride home. His trunks would have arrived yesterday, signalling that he was not far behind. The aunts had probably been up since daybreak, anticipating his coming, and they would all be waiting.

All *four* of them. He was their protector now, a role he felt ill suited to play. He supposed that was part of the Bedevere legacy, too; the Bedevere women didn't marry men who had the foresight to provide beyond the grave and the Bedevere males hadn't much luck in living long enough to do it for them.

The rough-kept lands preceding the park were a blessing of sorts in that they prepared him for the sight of the manor. Ivy crawled rampant across the formerly pristine sandstone of the hall's façade. A shutter hung loose from a second-storey window. Flowerbeds were overrun with plants that had long outgrown their intended shapes. Nature was having its way with the once-orderly estate.

Years ago, it had been a point of pride that Bedevere Hall, seat of the Audleys for four generations, was the gem of the county. It might not have been the largest home—Seaton Hall was bigger just a few miles to the south—but Bedevere was by far lovelier with its comely gardens and well-appointed views. From what Ashe could see trotting down the drive, there wasn't much of that left now.

Ashe dismounted and steeled himself for what lay inside. If the outside looked this bad, he could only imagine what had taken place inside to allow such decay to be permissible. A lone stable boy ran up to take his horse. Ashe was tempted to ask him about the state of things, but decided against it. He'd rather see it all with his own eyes.

Ashe doubted he'd even finished knocking before the door swung open and time stalled. Gardener stood there, as tall and sombre as Ashe remembered him, perhaps a bit greyer, a bit thinner, but very much the same. Growing up, Ashe had thought it was funny to have a butler named Gardener and a gardener named Smith, who looked to be long gone from the state of things.

'Mr Bedevere, welcome home.' Gardener bowed, 'I am sorry for the circumstances, sir.'

For a moment, Ashe almost looked behind him to see who else had followed him home—the greeting had been so very formal.

'This way, sir,' Gardener said. 'You are expected.'

Ashe followed Gardener down the hall to the drawing room, making mental notes as they went: bare hall tables, faded rugs and curtains. There was a shabbiness to the house. But most striking was the emptiness. There were no maids polishing the staircase, no footmen awaiting errands. The usual bustle of the hall was silent. There was Gardener and the stable boy. Presumably there were more, including a cook, hopefully, but Ashe didn't want to presume too much. It didn't look promising.

Ashe paused outside the drawing-room door and took a deep breath. Beyond those doors lay a responsibility he'd eschewed for years. He had his reasons. It was a mean act of fate that all his efforts to avoid it had come to naught. The Bedevere legacy, the one thing he'd tried so hard to escape, had landed quite squarely in his lap anyway. Perhaps it was true that all roads lead home in the end.

'Are you ready, sir?' Gardener enquired. With years of impeccable service behind him, Gardener knew how to read his betters and had given him a few seconds to prepare himself.

'Yes, I'm ready.' *Or not.* Ashe squared his shoulders.

'Yes, sir, I believe you are. Ready at last.' Gardener's eyes held the twinkle of approval.

'I certainly hope so,' Ashe replied with a nod of his head. He could see Gardener's rendition of the tale below stairs already, full of admiration about how the young lord had ridden in, taking no time to fuss over his appearance after a long ride. Instead, he'd gone straight to his aunts.

Gardener had made a habit of seeing the best in him

in his youth. Gardener would make him out to be an angel by evening. But if he was an angel, he was a very wicked one. Heaven forbid anyone at Bedevere ever learn what he'd been doing the moment the message of his father's demise had arrived. In hindsight, 'aggressively flirting' with Lady Hargrove seemed akin to fiddling while Rome burned.

Gardener opened the door and cleared his throat. 'Ladies, Mr Bedevere.'

Ashe stepped into the room, noticing the difference immediately. The curtains were faded, but the best of what was left in the house had been brought here. There were vases filled with flowers on the side tables, pillows on the sofas, little knick-knacks set about the room for decoration. Ashe saw the room for what it was: an oasis, or perhaps bastion was a better word—a *last* bastion of gentility against the bare realities that lay outside the drawing-room doors.

His eyes roved the room, taking in the surprising amount of occupants. His aunts were not alone; Leticia, Lavinia, Melisande and Marguerite were settled near the fireplace with a man he didn't recognise, but it was the woman seated just beyond them, by the window overlooking the garden, who held his attention. She was of uncommon loveliness—dark-haired with wide grey eyes framed by equally dark lashes against the creamy backdrop of her skin. Even in a crowded London ballroom she would stand out. Ashe suspected she'd chosen her seat away from the others in an attempt to be discreet, a task her beauty no doubt made impossible under the best of circumstances. Today, in a room peopled by elderly ladies and a middle-aged man, there was no opportunity for obscurity.

Ashe approached and gave his aunts his best bow. 'Ladies, I am at your service', but his gaze kept returning to the corner. Her comeliness was not all due to her good looks. It was in the way she held her slender neck, the straightness of her shoulders, both of which said, 'Notice me, I dare you.' For all her delicate beauty, she was no shy maiden. He could see it in the jut of her chin and the frank stare of her gaze in spite of her efforts at anonymity.

Leticia swept forwards, white-haired, regal and perhaps more fragile than Ashe remembered. They were *all* more fragile than he remembered, except for the siren at the window. She'd been watching him since the moment he'd entered the room, no doubt wondering and assessing, just as he was now. She was no one he recognised, but apparently she was important enough to be invited to his homecoming. More importantly, she'd been invited into the household in the aftermath of a significant death.

Ashe was cynical enough in his dealings with the world to be suspect of such an invitation. The aftermath of funerals were private matters for families, a chance for the bereaved to mop up the particulars of the deceased's life, re-organise and carry on. The weeks after a funeral were intimate times. Strangers were not welcome, although strangers invariably came in the hopes of grabbing a scrap from the table. Lovely, dark-haired females aside, Ashe had a word for those importunistic people: carrion.

Leticia took his hand. 'Ashe, it's so good of you to come. I am sorry we could not wait to bury him,' she said softly.

Ashe nodded. He knew that, counting the time it had taken for a message to reach him in London, at least six days had passed since his father's death. Even with all haste, he'd known he'd miss the funeral. One more regret to heap on an already laden platter.

'Come meet everyone. This is Mrs Ralston, our dear Genni.' She gestured fondly to the lovely creature at the window. 'She's been our rock in our time of need.'

Genni was far too girlish a name for the woman. She rose and extended her hand, not to be kissed, but to be shaken. 'It is good to meet you at last.'

Ashe did not miss the note of censure in her tone, so subtly hidden no one would notice it except the intended recipient—or was that his own guilt-plagued imagination imposing its own frameworks?

'Mrs Ralston, a pleasure, I'm sure,' Ashe returned drily. Whoever she was, she'd already inveigled her way into the aunts' good graces. He doubted she was a companion, at least not a successful one. Her demeanour was far too confident to play that submissive role and her clothes too fine. Even the simple lines of her afternoon gown of forest-green merino were cut with the perfection of a high-class dressmaker; the lace trim at her collar and cuffs was demure, but expensive. From the looks of Bedevere, affording that calibre of companion made the point moot. But it raised others. If she was not a companion, what was she?

'Genni has bought Seaton Hall for restoration.'

'Is that so?' Ashe said politely, but his speculations ratcheted up a notch. That probably wasn't all she meant to take advantage of. A woman choosing to take on the responsibilities of an estate alone was quite unusual. Perhaps there was a husband at home? Leticia didn't make it sound as if there were and there was no more information forthcoming. A young widow, then. Interesting. *Young* widows often had the most peculiar histories, some of which didn't necessarily include husbands.

Leticia moved on to complete introductions. 'This gentleman is your father's solicitor, Mr Marsbury. He's generously stayed on until your arrival so the estate can be settled.'

Ashe extended a hand, taking Mr Marsbury's measure. He was an older gentleman, bluff and florid, reminding Ashe of a country squire. 'Thank you for your timely note. I hope you haven't been unduly inconvenienced.'

Marsbury's demeanour was as firm as his handshake. 'It's been no trouble. It made more sense to wait for you to arrive since everyone else involved is already here.'

Ashe gave 'Genni' a cool glance. Did the unfamiliar beauty have a stake in his father's estate? A kaleidoscope of unpleasant scenarios ran through his mind— if she was a widow, was she a late-life lover his father had taken? Did she hope to be provided for?

With that pile of satiny black hair and the delicate sweep of her jaw, Ashe had no trouble believing she could entice even the most resolute of men into a proposal, a difference of thirty years in age notwithstanding. Ashe raised his eyebrows in query. '*Everyone* else?'

Marsbury met his gaze evenly. 'Your cousin, Henry Bennington.'

Cold suspicion took up residence in Ashe's stomach. 'What does my cousin Henry have to do with anything?'

'Henry has been a great support these past months.' The beauty spoke up from her station by the window. Ashe imagined he saw the quicksilver lightning of emotion flash in the depths of those grey eyes. Did the beauty carry a *tendre* for Henry? Henry of the blue eyes, golden hair and manipulative manners?

Ashe met her gaze evenly over the heads of the others. 'Forgive me if I find that hard to believe. Cousin Henry's only notable distinction, other than his penchant for collecting literature, is being the nearest male heir should my father die without surviving issue; a prospect, I assure you, he has long dined out on.' Most especially, Ashe knew from London gossip, in recent years when Ashe's brother, Alex, had no longer been a contender and Ashe's own lifestyle seemed destined to place him on the explosive end of a jealous husband's pistol.

Marsbury folded his arms across his broad chest and coughed to indicate his disapproval of Ashe's comment.

'Mr Bennington will join Mrs Ralston and ourselves in the study where we can discuss everything privately.'

Ashe noted Mrs Ralston looked up with surprise that was rapidly masked. An act, perhaps?

Ashe turned his hard stare on Marsbury, his voice firm with command. 'Yes, we certainly shall.'

So, the reading of the will was to involve the three of them. Certainly not the *ménage à trois* he was used to, but the dynamics were the same: two on one. Ashe wondered if the delectable Mrs Ralston and Henry had cooked something up together. She'd been quick to defend him and that had raised Ashe's suspicions.

Whatever webs his cousin had been weaving in his absence, Ashe wanted it understood that Henry Bennington had no authority here, nor did pretty, dark-haired Americans. Ashe Bedevere had returned.

Chapter Two

The elusive Mr Bedevere had returned. The room fairly vibrated with the evidence of it even after he'd departed with Marsbury. Genevra was not sorry to see him go. In a span of minutes he had unnerved her as few people could. She needed time to gather her thoughts and settle her surprise over the summons.

Genevra turned her attentions out the window, giving the aunts some time to digest their own excitement over Bedevere's arrival. He was the kind of man who stirred excitement wherever he went. Power sat on his broad shoulders as comfortably as his travelling cloak. But she'd met powerful men before. What had disturbed her most was the sensual potency of him. He wasn't just confident, he was seductive. His devil-dark hair had been windblown and rakish, his green eyes as hard as jade when he'd looked at her, his very gaze seeming to penetrate her innermost thoughts with an intensity that had sent a *frisson* down her spine.

If she could get through the reading of the will, she

would make sure to avoid Mr Bedevere when at all possible. Perhaps there'd even be enough chambers done at Seaton Hall for her to move back home. That would certainly help her keep Mr Bedevere at a distance.

'We shall have a party!' Lavinia exclaimed to the others. 'Cook can fix pheasant and we'll put flowers on the dining-room table.'

A party at which Mr Bedevere would be the guest of honour. Genevra turned from the window, her hopes of quick and immediate avoidance sinking a bit further.

Melisande gasped. 'Do you think we should? We're in mourning.'

'It will be private, no one will know and it's not as if there will be dancing afterwards,' Lavinia said staunchly.

She held out a blue-veined hand to Genevra. 'Isn't our nephew a handsome one? I told you he was.'

Genevra smiled and took Lavinia's hand. If the ladies wanted a party, she'd give them one. The past months with the ailing earl had taken a toll on them and not one of them was a day under seventy. She'd ridden over daily to help and had eventually moved in to stay over the winter to be of assistance while Seaton was undergoing renovations. Henry had already taken up residence by then and she'd meant it when she'd said Henry had been a support, which was more than she could say for the errant Ashe Bedevere.

Perhaps the allure of an inheritance had finally been the carrot to bring him home. Whatever had brought him, he was here now. Having taken his measure, she'd do best to keep him at arm's length. Forewarned was forearmed. She'd finally got her life back together. She'd learned her lesson. She wasn't about to let a handsome man turn her life upside down again.

The study was getting crowded, Ashe thought uncharitably. He'd barely seated Mrs Ralston when Henry made his entrance, striding towards him, hand outstretched, a wide smile on his face. 'Cousin Ashe, it's so good of you to come.'

Ashe didn't trust that smile for a moment. Most of the trouble Ashe and his brother had ever found themselves in could be laid at Henry's feet. Henry had a habit of making others pay for his misdeeds.

'So Aunt Leticia has already told me.' Ashe replied drily. Had there really been that much doubt? Ashe made no move to shake the offered hand. He was gratified to see that his lack of a polite response gave Henry a slight pause.

Henry regrouped and took an empty chair, smoothing his hands on his trousers in a nervous gesture. 'I would have been down sooner to greet you, but I was taking care of some estate business.'

'It's my home, *cousin*, I don't need to wait on an invitation.' He would not tolerate being treated as a guest in his own house. Nor did it sit well that Henry had sailed in here and commandeered the estate. Well, no more.

Ashe moved to take the upper hand. 'Marsbury, let's get on with your business.'

Marsbury settled a pair of spectacles on the bridge

of his nose and folded his hands on the desk. 'Gentlemen, Mrs Ralston, as you are aware, circumstances are somewhat unusual in this case. The earl has died, but his oldest son has suffered a nervous breakdown that has left him incapable of overseeing the estate. The title will, of course, transfer to the legitimate heir. Mentally incapable or not, he is still a recognised peer. Alexander Bedevere is officially the fifth Earl of Audley until his death. Should he die without a legal son, the title will pass to you, Mr Bedevere. This is all very regular. However, in the meantime, there is the estate to consider.' Marsbury eyed them over the rim of his spectacles. 'In his present condition, the current earl cannot be expected to manage the estate or its finances.'

Ashe was listening intently now. He'd known the title wouldn't be his, he hadn't wanted it. He was perfectly happy being Mr Bedevere, London's finest lover. But now, he sensed that Bedevere itself was in danger. The cold pit in his stomach spread a little deeper.

On either side of him, Mrs Ralston and Henry had their own reactions; Henry's eyes contained a barely concealed expectation while Mrs Ralston's hands were white from their iron grip on the arms of her chair. Henry was excited, but Mrs Ralston was cautious, perhaps even alarmed and trying to hide it.

Marsbury went on, 'The former earl petitioned the crown for a regency to be granted, not unlike the regency granted during King George III's illness. The petition was granted a few months before Audley's death.

Under a regency, your father was free to appoint any guardians or trustees he saw fit.'

'What the hell does that mean?' Ashe growled.

'It means, cousin, that Bedevere, in the common vernacular, is up for grabs.' Henry was all nonchalant insouciance.

Marsbury cleared his throat in censure of the indelicate translation. 'Not exactly, Mr Bennington. I think it will become clearer if I read the settlement straight from the will.'

Marsbury withdrew a sheaf of papers from his valise and began to read. 'I, Richard Thomas Bedevere, fourth Earl of Audley, being of sound mind and body on the twenty-fourth day of January, eighteen hundred thirty-four...'

The date pierced him. This codicil Marsbury read from was not some long-standing document. The alteration had been made the day before his father's death. Ashe shot Henry a speculative look. Had Henry talked his father into something absurd? Had Mrs Ralston? Sick, desperate men were fallible creatures. Perhaps more than one person had got their talons into his father.

The first part of the reading covered what Marsbury had already relayed concerning the transfer of the title. It was the second part that garnered Ashe's attention.

'During Alexander Bedevere's lifetime, the Bedevere estate shall be managed under a regency overseen by the following trustees who have been allotted the following shares of influence: to my son, Ashton Bedevere, with whom I regretfully quarrelled and have not seen since, I leave forty-five per cent of the estate in the hopes this will inspire him to embrace responsibility. I leave to my nephew, Henry Bennington, four per cent of the estate in the hopes he will understand he has got his due reward. Finally, to Genevra Ralston, who has been like a daughter to me in my final days and who has inspired me with her vision of a profitable estate, I leave fifty-one per cent of the estate.'

Ashe went rigid at the implication. The estate he'd been reluctant to assume had suddenly been lifted from his shoulders, but Ashe did not feel relief. He felt anger. He felt resentment. Had his father thought such an arrangement was what he'd want? Or had his father thought something else altogether less altruistic? He could divine those reasons later. Right now his brain was calculating at lightning speed and discarding scenarios about this particular three-way regency. Had he been meant to align with Henry?

Henry's four per cent did nothing for him. Aligning with Henry would only give him forty-nine per cent. Clearly his father did not mean to achieve a reconciliation between him and his cousin from beyond the grave. It served as further proof that Henry was no good and his father suspected it. From the insult-red beet colour of Henry's face, Henry knew it too.

'Four per cent! That's it? After all I've done this past year?' Henry burst out. 'I gave up a year of my life to come here and look after him.'

'No one asked you to make that choice,' Marsbury said calmly. 'Surely you chose to look after your uncle out of a sense of familial duty and not out of misplaced avarice?'

Well done. Marsbury rose a notch in Ashe's estimation. Henry glowered and stood up, making a hasty departure on the premise that he had a meeting elsewhere. That left only Mrs Ralston. She was beautifully demure, her gaze downcast, effectively hiding what must be a barrage of thoughts. She'd just inherited, at least temporarily, a controlling share in the governance of an English estate. Was she shocked? Was she secretly pleased that all had come out as she'd perhaps so carefully planned?

'Mrs Ralston, I would like a word with Mr Marsbury,' Ashe said, assuming she would be well-bred enough to hear the implicit request for privacy. She did not fail him.

'Yes, certainly. Good afternoon, Mr Marsbury. I hope we will have the pleasure of your company on happier occasions.' Mrs Ralston seemed all too relieved to quit the room. Perhaps she was eager to go up to her rooms and do a victory dance over her good fortune. Or perhaps she was eager to sneak off and celebrate with Henry at his supposed meeting. Together they could rule Bedevere at least during Alex's life, which should by rights be a long one. It had not escaped Ashe's mathematical attention that fifty-one plus four gave Henry a lot more control of the estate through Mrs Ralston. Of course, forty-five plus fifty-one maximised his own control of the estate quite nicely.

It was all becoming clear. Whoever wanted to control Bedevere had to go through Mrs Ralston. His father must have thought highly of Mrs Ralston indeed.

Marsbury set down his papers and folded his hands calmly as if he told sons of earls every day how they'd been essentially cut out of their father's will.

'Mr Bedevere, I think you come out of this better than you believe at present. You will inherit in due course should your brother's life end prematurely, whereas Mrs Ralston's tenure will terminate at some point.'

Marsbury had said absolutely the wrong thing. Ashe fought the urge to reach across the desk and seize Marsbury by the lapels in spite of his earlier favourable outlook towards the man. 'Is that supposed to console me? Because I assure you, it does not. There's nothing I'd like better than to have my father alive and my brother restored to his right mind.'

'Mr Bedevere, I can see you're disappointed.'

'I'd say disappointed is an understatement, Mr Marsbury. Let's be clear about this. I am mad as hell and, for the record, nobody takes what's mine, not an upstart American who has somehow weaseled her way into the family, nor my cousin.' Growing up, Henry had always been a snake in the grass as far as Ashe was concerned. He was *not* getting his hands on Bedevere. Henry would run through the estate within a year.

Apparently most of Marsbury's clients took bad news sitting down. Having no idea how to respond to the blunt remark, Marsbury cleared his throat again and glanced meaningfully at the documents. The man was positively tubercular. If he cleared his throat one more time, Ashe thought he just might leap across the desk anyway.

'Don't think I cannot see what my father has done.' Ashe fixed Marsbury with a hard stare. 'He is mandating marriage without saying the words. The man who weds Mrs Ralston will gain control of her shares upon marriage.'

'That is your construction,' Marsbury said firmly.

'And Henry's too, no doubt, once he arrives at it,' Ashe said coldly. Henry had never been quick. 'It will be a race now to see who can woo the lovely American to the altar.' He paused in contemplation. Every scrap and speck of human nature went back to motives, his father's nature notwithstanding. 'Can you tell me, Mr Marsbury, why my father would have wanted that?'

Marsbury cleared his damned throat. 'Bedevere needs an heiress, sir.'

Marsbury's announcement was the final *coup de grâce*. Ashe felt the quiet words like a blow to the stomach. Bedevere was debt ridden? How was that possible? His father had always been a strict and diligent steward of the funds. Sometimes too strict for a young man about town, but Bedevere's coffers had always been full.

'How bad is it?' He'd not anticipated this. But neither had he anticipated contesting Henry for his own inheritance.

Marsbury met his gaze, his tone matter of fact. 'The money is all gone. Your brother went and lost it a few years ago in some fool land investment that turned out to be a swindle.'

'The Forsyth scandal?' Ashe said with no small amount of disbelief. Three years ago, London had been rocked by the land swindle. It had dominated the newspapers. Shares of a Caribbean island had been sold to merchants and nobles looking to invest in New World property. The problem had been that the island did exist, but it had turned out to be swampy and infested with tropical disease. The shares were valid, but worth nothing. Ashe knew several people who'd lost money, but he'd never imagined his brother would be caught up in it. Alex had always been too intelligent, too reserved for rash behaviours.

Marsbury nodded in confirmation. 'That was the major one.'

Lucifer's stones, there'd been others? The sensation of guilt returned. If he'd come home when first asked, he might have caught his brother in time. Three years past would have put the incident right before Alex's breakdown. Perhaps his brother's faculties had been failing even then to have taken such an unprecedented risk.

'Are you sure there's nothing left?' Ashe put the question to Marsbury.

'I've looked over the books. Mr Bennington has looked over the books. No stone has been left unturned, or in this case, bled.'

Henry had looked over the books? Henry had known Bedevere's assets and worth right down to the last farthing and done nothing? Arguing Henry had known and done nothing made Ashe look like a hypocrite, even to himself. In the years of Bedevere's demise, he had done nothing either. Yet it seemed as though Henry's crime was the worse. He had been unaware, but Henry had *allowed* it to happen.

'Can I challenge this will?'

Marsbury sighed and shook his head. 'You can appeal the process, of course, but this was a special dispensation from the crown and there is legal precedent for it no matter how unusual the situation. I do think it will be a waste of your time and energies.'

'Energies better spent pursuing Mrs Ralston?' Ashe supplied with a dose of sarcasm.

'Yes, if you want to keep Bedevere.'

Ashe clenched and unclenched his fist at his side in an attempt to hold on to his temper. Again, there was the subtle implication that he did not have to assume Bedevere unless he chose to. He could leave it to Mrs Ralston and Henry. It would stay in the family and perhaps Mrs Ralston's American ingenuity would protect it against Henry's inherent stupidity.

Ashe sighed. It was time to talk about the American. 'What did Mrs Ralston do to earn my father's regard? Did she think to marry him at the last moment, but having failed to do that decided to influence the will with her apparent fortune?' His tone left no mistake as to what kind of 'influence' she might have wielded; the kind women had wielded against men since Eve.

Marsbury, who'd managed to stay cool throughout

the difficult interview, did look nonplussed at that comment. He was from the old school. One could talk about money baldly with other men, but one did not bandy about slanderous consideration regarding the fairer sex.

'Mr Bedevere, Mrs Ralston could buy Bedevere ten times over if she had a mind to.' Marsbury's voice was cold as he gathered his papers into a folder. 'Her "apparent" fortune is quite tangible, I assure you.'

'You have to understand this all comes as a shock to me.' Ashe held the man's gaze.

Marsbury took off his glasses and leaned back in his chair. 'Shock or not, it boils to one common denominator. You, Mr Bedevere, are in great need of an heiress and there's one practically living next door with a shipping line and a hundred thousand pounds to her name. I'd call that a pretty piece of serendipity if I were you.'

'That's where we differ, Marsbury.' Ashe fixed the solicitor with a hard stare. 'I'd call it suspicious.' This was starting to look a lot like a conspiracy: an estate that had been allowed to fail, coffers that had suddenly become prey to a string of bad investments, a recently altered will and a rich American living in Henry's pockets.

The next question was—at whose door step did he lay the blame? Mrs Ralston's? Henry's? Were they both in it together? Maybe he was too cynical. Maybe the conspiracy was his father's—one last attempt to order his wayward son's life to specification. His father had thrown down the gauntlet even on his deathbed. Marriage to a woman of his father's choosing was to be the price for Bedevere, for his wildness, for ever having left. Ultimately, whose conspiracy this was didn't matter. The only thing that did matter was what he was going to do about it. Would he sell himself in a marriage of convenience to save Bedevere?

Chapter Three

The aunts were all in it together. Genevra had seen their conspiracy for what it was: matchmaking. She would do almost anything for the old dears, but she couldn't do that. The last thing she was looking for was male attention even if it came with a set of broad shoulders and mossy-green eyes.

Genevra smoothed the skirts of her evening gown one last time before she entered the drawing room. The gunmetal-silk gown was one of her favourites and she'd need all the confidence it afforded if she was going to withstand the probing gaze of Mr Bedevere and the romantic hearts of the old aunts.

Dinner would be a polite battle on two fronts, even if there wasn't the issue of the estate between them. The announcement this afternoon had been most unexpected. Not once had the old earl offered any indication of his thoughts. He'd been intrigued by the American management practices she'd shared with him and she'd known he held her in high esteem. But to leave her the majority share in the estate had not occurred to her.

She appreciated the honour the old man had done her and she would do her best for him. He had been a father to her when she had no one. But taking on the estate also meant taking on other complications, not the least of which waited for her on the other side of the drawing-room door. Mr Bedevere would not be happy or complacent about the current arrangements.

Genevra stepped into the room and her eyes fixed on the man standing at the fireplace mantel. Surely the old earl had not been blind to the implications created by giving her fifty-one per cent. He'd all but set her up to be a target for his errant son should the son decide he wanted the estate. She liked to think she was sighting her enemy straight away, but she would have noticed him regardless. How could she not? He stood there surveying the room, surveying *her*, like a king from his throne. Washing away the road dust had done nothing to diminish his aura of power. It was the hands she noticed first. Long, elegant fingers negligently wrapped about a preprandial drink in a way that conjured up the most decadent of thoughts. She couldn't help but wonder what else he could do with those hands.

Quite a lot if his eyes told the wicked truth. She'd stared too long and he'd caught her. Genevra blushed. A slow smile on his lips said he was making her accountable for it. She looked away from his face with its straight Grecian nose to avoid the forthright heat of his gaze only to find her eyes travelling down the length of his well-apportioned body. Good lord, she couldn't look him in the eye, and no self-respecting lady should look at him *there* where her efforts had landed. She'd try his face again—that was where *normal* people looked at each other, after all.

Then he spoke without a hint of animosity, his tone more reminiscent of bedrooms than drawing rooms. 'Mrs Ralston, allow me to properly welcome you to Bedevere. There wasn't time earlier.' He might as well have said, 'Mrs Ralston, allow me to properly welcome you to sin.' How many women had he led astray already with that voice? She'd never encountered such a blatant sexuality before. Yet she knew precisely what it was; it was dangerous and it drew her as thoroughly as a magnet draws iron filings.

Years of hostessing for her father and then for Philip saved her from an utter loss of words. 'I am pleased to make your acquaintance at last, Mr Bedevere. Your aunts have spoken of you often.'

Genevra managed a curtsy, determined to do her best for the aunts. Tonight was to be a party. The ladies were dressed in their best silk dinner gowns that had seen more fashionable days, but their spirits were high. The aunts, herself, Henry—all of them deserved a slightly festive occasion. Henry! Genevra's mind tripped back over its thoughts.

She'd been so distracted by the handsome newcomer she hadn't realised Henry was missing. 'Will Mr Bennington be joining us tonight?' Genevra's eyes swept the room guiltily in case she'd simply overlooked him. Not that anyone would overlook Henry with his good looks and guinea-gold hair.

'No, dear, Henry had an appointment to dine with the Brownes at the vicarage,' Leticia offered.

Genevra furrowed her brow, trying to recall the appointment. 'Mr Bennington didn't say anything yesterday about it when we went out walking.' Nor had Vicar Browne when they'd stopped by to deliver some items for the sewing circle.

Leticia waved a hand in airy dismissal. 'He said it came up rather suddenly this afternoon. But our Ashe is here now.' There was no chance to say more. Gardener announced dinner and there was a potent moment when Genevra thought the dark god at the fireplace was going to offer her his arm to go into supper. Instead, he turned to Leticia. 'Shall we, Aunt?'

The regal Leticia giggled for a moment like a young girl. 'It's been an age since anyone's taken me into supper, young scamp.' She took his arm and said with a wink, 'You have two arms, don't you, my boy?'

'Mrs Ralston, would you do me the pleasure?' He was all polished English manners in his dark evening clothes, but the eyes that held hers weren't mannerly in the least. Those eyes seemed to be studying her from the inside out, a decidedly uncomfortable predicament that left her feeling as if she was standing there naked.

The Bedevere dining room was turned out in its best; the long dining table was set with the Bedevere china and crystal and a vase of hothouse flowers graced the centre, courtesy of Lavinia's greenhouse efforts.

In the friendly light of candles, one could forget the worn surroundings. There was a whisper of Bedevere's past glory here, of what it must have looked like in more prosperous, happy times, Genevra thought. Mr Bedevere seated them all, giving her the spot on his left and Leticia the seat on his right. At least the devil had manners aplenty, she'd give him that. But manners and good looks made her wary. Philip had had just such a way about him and, in the end, he'd not been so very fine.

'Are you enjoying Seaton Hall, Mrs Ralston?' Mr Bedevere enquired politely after a creamy bisque had been set down in front of them.

Genevra smiled. Seaton Hall was one of her favourite topics. 'Very much. There's been quite a bit of work to do on the gardens, but I hope to have them finished in time for summer.' The gardens were the first stage in a much larger plan she had to turn Seaton Hall into a tourist business. If Mr Bedevere was willing, she could do the same here and help the estate generate funds. He really shouldn't object. The estate was in need and his ten-year absence made it plain that he didn't live here. The experiment would hardly inconvenience him.

Bedevere cocked a dark eyebrow her direction. 'Won't you be going up to London for the Season in a month or so? I would have thought the entertainments of the city would be vastly more appealing, especially after a long winter in the country.'

There was no question of being in London. There was too much work to be done here. It was an excuse she'd long relied on and in time it had become the truth. Besides, the only reason to be in London was to catch a husband. In London, she would attract too much attention and someone was bound to dig up the old scandal. Genevra shrugged and said with a great show of nonchalance, 'London holds little allure for me, Mr Bedevere.' London could keep its prowling bachelors. Her brief marriage had not recommended the institution worth repeating.

He held her gaze over the rim of his wine glass for a second longer than was decent, long enough to cause a note of silence. When he spoke, his words were deliberate and commanded everyone's attention. 'Why is that, Mrs Ralston? London is generally held to be one of the finest cities in the world. For myself, I've lived there for several years and have yet to grow bored with it.'

Genevra had the vague feeling she was being quizzed, tested. There would be more questions she'd rather not answer if she didn't take the offensive now. She shot him a quick smile, 'Well, that's just it, isn't it? We can't all live in London. Someone has to hold things together in the country.'

There was the slightest movement of his dark brows in acknowledgement of her sweetly delivered barb. '*Touché*, Mrs Ralston,' he murmured for her ears alone, leaving Genevra to wonder if her subtle attack had done her more harm than good.

Genevra turned her attentions to the aunts. It was far easier talking to them than it was their nephew, but that didn't mean she wasn't aware of Mr Bedevere's eyes on her, seeking answers as if he intuitively knew the answers she'd supplied were blithe smokescreens for the truth. It was impossible. He'd only just met her.

He couldn't possibly guess she was here because this was her refuge, because the rural backwaters of Staffordshire was one place where scandal couldn't find her.

The rural backwaters of Staffordshire were full of surprises these days, not the least of them the elegant young woman on his left with her piles of dark hair and exquisite figure shown deliciously in a gown of gunmetal silk.

Ashe decided by the fish course that Mrs Ralston would have been a pleasant delight under other circumstances. Watching her converse with his aunts about their watercolours and embroidery had pleased him.

By the time pheasant was served, however, all that pleasantness had begun to work against her. Her answers about her presence here had been vague earlier and far too non-committal for his tastes combined with the fact that she was almost too good to be true.

Ashe watched her with stealthy objectivity as she cut into her pheasant; here she was, beautiful, rich, apparently disposed to a genteel temperament that pleased his aunts, and living practically next door *precisely* when he needed an heiress to save Bedevere.

His father's intentions couldn't be more blatant. The only thing more transparent was his aunts' matchmaking efforts. If the efforts hadn't been aimed at him, he would have found them humorous. The old dears weren't even trying to be discreet as they flaunted Mrs Ralston's charms shamelessly course after course. But always Ashe's thoughts came back to the one idea: when things were too good to be true, they probably were.

All through dinner, he'd looked for a defect: a nasty table manner, a poor conversation ability, an annoying habit. He was disappointed to note that, in spite of her American upbringing, she used the correct fork, carried on flawless conversation without the slightest stutter and hadn't a single bad habit visible to his critical eye.

It all begged the question: what was an attractive heiress doing *here* of all places? In his experience, such a paragon of marriageable womanhood should be in London, American or not. There was no reason for her to be in the country. That in itself was a point of intrigue. Why would she be here when she didn't have to be?

There were really only two answers that came to mind: she was hiding, which carried all sorts of unsavoury implications, or the likelihood that she was fortune hunting—title-hunting, to be exact. That was the only fortune Bedevere had to offer these days and she had to be well aware of it.

Beside him, the mysterious Mrs Ralston laughed, a wonderful throaty sound with a hint of smoke, a laugh made for evenings and candlelight. She shook her head at something Melisande had said and the candles caught the discreet diamonds in her ears. *Expensive* diamonds. It had been a long time since he'd been able to afford to give a woman such a gift. They sparkled enticingly, lending her an air of sophistication.

It was all too easy to see how his father might have

been fooled by her. It was also all too easy to see what she might have been after with her diamonds and elegance; perhaps she'd thought to marry his father before he passed away, no matter what Marsbury thought. That strategy having failed, she'd now opted to stay on and wait to snare the title eventually through the sane second son. It wouldn't be the first time someone had traded themselves for a title. One didn't have to be a sick man to find Mrs Ralston's charms appealing. His own growing fascination with their dinner guest was proof enough of that.

Ashe drained the rest of his wine and set his glass aside. Wedding and bedding aside, it was time to uncover her secrets before things went any further, a task Ashe thought he'd might enjoy just as much as uncovering her.

'Mrs Ralston, perhaps you'd do me the pleasure of a stroll in the conservatory. I seem to recall it used to be lovely by moonlight.' No time like the present to start with that uncovering.

His suggestion was met with great enthusiasm from his aunts and he had a sudden vision of all of them traipsing through the conservatory, a scenario hardly conducive to seducing one's secrets.

'Genni has made so many improvements to the conservatory,' Lavinia put in. 'She saved the roses last summer when they came down with aphids. She mixed up a special spray.'

'Well then, Mrs Ralston, I don't see how you can refuse. Shall we?' Ashe rose and offered her his arm.

Walking brought her close to him, her skirts rustling
against his trouser leg with the sway of her motion. She
smelled of lemongrass and cassia as she walked beside
him. It was a telling scent, not the standard lavender
or rosewater worn by so many of London's débutantes.
The sharp spicy edge of lemongrass was not an innocent's perfume. It was a woman's perfume: a smart,
confident woman's.

At the entrance to the conservatory, he moved his
hand to the small of her back and ushered her ahead of
him. He left his hand there, comfortably splayed. Touch
invited confidences and he wanted hers very much.

His intuition hadn't been wrong. The conservatory
was beautiful. Moonlight streamed through the glass
roof and the scent of orange trees lingered enticingly.
A small fountain trickled in the background.

'This is my favourite place at Bedevere.' Mrs Ralston
tried to walk ahead of him, a step too fast for his hand
to remain at her back. Ashe closed the gap with a long
stride, his hand remaining unshakeable at her back. He
was making her nervous. Good.

'I can see why, Mrs Ralston, it's very lovely.'

Chapter Four

He was most definitely making her nervous. Not even an innocent débutante would believe he was talking about the conservatory with a remark like that. Especially not after the way he'd studied her with his eyes all through dinner, stalking her without moving from the table or after the way his hand had loitered so deliberately at her back. What was worse, his attentions had aroused her. She was honest enough to admit it, to herself at least.

'This place holds the heat in winter. The glass makes it possible to trap the heat from the sun.' She was rambling out of some desperate need to minimise the tension that had sprung between them. 'Your father liked to come here when he was well enough. Henry and I would bring him and spend the afternoons reading.'

She stopped suddenly and faced him, realising she hadn't offered any condolences. It had seemed the wrong thing to do amid the gay atmosphere of the aunts' dinner party. 'I am sorry for your loss. Your father was a good man, a brave man.'

'Was he?' Mr Bedevere's green eyes narrowed in dangerous disagreement. 'Pardon me, Mrs Ralston, I don't need a stranger to tell me about my father.'

A person of less fortitude might have flinched under the cold words. She squared her shoulders and met his gaze unswervingly. 'Forgive me, I thought perhaps it would ease your grief to know he died well.'

'Why? Because I wasn't here?'

There it was, the crime she'd charged him with at the dinner table—absent Ashe Bedevere who couldn't be bothered to come home. It seemed wrong that she, a mere stranger of a neighbour, had seen more of the earl in his last days than his own son had.

'Surely you knew how grave his situation had become.'

'Is the pun intended, Mrs Ralston?' There was a terse set to his finely carved jaw and a hardness to his gaze that matched his rigid posture.

Genevra bristled. Handsome or not, it was ill mannered of him to think she'd engage in witty word play in the midst of a delicate conversation. 'No. The pun is not intended. Was your absence? Intended, that is.'

His eyes glittered dangerously, his tone forebodingly quiet. 'I must inform you, Mrs Ralston, I find this an unsuitable topic of conversation between two people who have barely met.'

Genevra tilted her chin upwards a mere fraction, letting her cold tone convey just the opposite. 'My apologies for any untoward assumptions.'

His eyes were studying her again, the hardness

gone now, replaced by something else more feral. 'You shouldn't say things you don't mean, Mrs Ralston.' The faintest hint of a wicked smile played on his lips. The dratted man was calling her out, fully aware she hadn't really apologised.

'And you, sir, should know better than to scold a lady.' Genevra opted for the high road.

'Why is that?' He stepped closer to her, the clean manly scent of him swamping her senses, his nearness hinting of the muscled physique beneath the clothes. He was all man and there was no place for her to go. She'd backed herself against a stone bench. This was nothing like being with Henry. Henry was the consummate companion, comfortable, never imposing. There were no prickles of awareness like the ones goose pimpling her skin right now.

'Because you are a gentleman.' At least he was dressed like one. Up close, she could appreciate his impeccably brushed jacket stretched elegantly across an impressive breadth of shoulder and the rich cabernet hue of his waistcoat. But other than the clothes, she had her doubts.

'Are you sure?' His voice was low and she was acutely aware of the long curling strand of hair he'd wrapped around one finger. He gave her a sensual half-smile, his eyes roving her face, flicking down ever so briefly to her throat and perhaps slightly lower. His attentions were perilously arousing.

'No,' her voice came out in a hoarse tremor. She wasn't sure of anything in that moment, least of all how they'd arrived at this point. They'd been talking of his father. But the conversation had wandered afield from the comforting solace she'd intended to something else far more seductive and personal.

'Good, because I can think of better things to do by moonlight than quarrel, can't you?'

His next move startled her entirely. Before she could think, his hand was at the nape of her neck, warm and caressing, drawing her to him until his mouth covered hers in a full kiss that sent a jolt of heat to her stomach.

The kiss was all hot challenge and she answered it without provocation. The arrogant man was far too sure of himself. He needed to know he wasn't completely in charge. His tongue sought hers and the kiss became a heady duel. He tasted of rich red wine against her lips. His hands were warm against the fabric of her gown, massaging, pressing her to him, making her aware of the hard lines of him and the most sinful invitation his body issued. She arched her neck, letting his kiss travel the length of her throat. This was not the hesitant kiss of a moonstruck dandy. This was the kiss of man proficient in the art. The kiss promised fulfilment. If she took the invitation, she would not be disappointed.

Her arms were about his neck and she breathed deeply of him. If temptation had a scent it would be this: the understated mixture of sandalwood and vanilla combined with the clean smell of freshly laundered clothing. Genevra nipped at his ear, eliciting an entirely male growl of appreciation. She was not the only one intoxicated by the duel.

Without warning, Ashe stepped back, releasing her, his eyes a smoky green. It was his eyes that held her attention. They were surrounded by long soft black lashes, but the green orbs were hard and assessing when he looked at her. They were not the eyes of a man in the throes of desire, although his body argued that to the contrary.

'I don't know what you're doing here, Mrs Ralston, but I will find out.'

'What makes you think I'm doing "anything"?'

'A woman doesn't kiss like that unless she wants something. Badly.'

It took a moment to comprehend, so unexpected was the comment. 'If I were a gentleman, I would call you out for that.' Genevra fairly shook with rage. She'd never been so insulted. If he wasn't careful, she'd call him out anyway.

'We've already established there are no gentlemen here at present,' he drawled. 'And you, Mrs Ralston, are no lady.'

Genevra stiffened, her temper rising. If she couldn't call him out, there was one thing she could do. She slapped him right across the face.

In the retrospection of a sleepless night, Genevra understood she'd slapped him as much for her behaviour as for his. She *should* have been indifferent to that kiss. Instead, she'd been so flustered that she'd ordered her carriage and set out for home, finished renovations or not. She'd not spend a night under Ashe Bedevere's roof.

She had still been berating herself as she tossed and turned through a sleepless night until she'd finally given up and risen at dawn, her mind more than eager to ponder her behaviour while she watched the sunrise from her window.

There were several reasons she could offer as to why she'd given in. First, there was the element of surprise. She hadn't been expecting such an audacious move on his part. Second, she was lonely. Except for the company of Ashe's aunts and Henry, this part of Staffordshire wasn't exactly a hotbed of society.

These were good excuses for her momentary lapse, but none of them could disguise the reality. She'd let her independent streak get the better of her. He'd baited her and she'd taken the lure, unable to resist the challenge. He'd been testing her again as he had at the table, but it hadn't been the test she'd expected. She'd thought he'd been testing her mettle. It hadn't been until afterwards when he'd spoken those insulting words that she'd realised he'd still been probing for answers as to why she was here in this place of all places and why his father would give her controlling interest in the estate. Answering his challenge as she'd done had not been the best way to allay his concerns.

She hoped the slap had conveyed her intentions as readily as his hot gaze had conveyed his. He was a seducer of the first water, used to getting what he wanted. But in this case, he would not succeed in seducing her fifty-one per cent out of her. His game was far too obvious, even if his kisses had been nothing short of dazzling. Never had anything roused her so thoroughly or so immediately. The stirrings of such emotions was a risky pot. Kisses could cloud a woman's mind, make her forget certain realities. She'd learned her lesson with Philip. He'd only wanted her for her father's money. Bedevere only wanted her share of the regency.

Genevra rose from her chair and prepared to dress. Debating herself over Mr Bedevere's kiss was accomplishing nothing. What she needed was activity to purge last night's memories. Time in the garden overseeing the new landscaping would be just the thing to distract her.

kind, No, nothing seemed to hold the interest today of

especially when he had bad news to report. All eyes at

Chapter Five

Henry heartily wished for a distraction—a bird hitting
the glass panes of his benefactor's prized French doors,
a servant spilling hot coffee on someone's lap. Really,
anything would do as long as it took the gentlemen's
eyes off him. Breakfast wasn't his favourite time of day,
especially when he had bad news to report. All eyes at
the well-set table fixed on him. The meal had long been
finished. It was time to discuss the business for which
their host, a Mr Marcus Trent, had invited them all.

'Well, Bennington, we've had our kippers and ham.
Tell us how the will went yesterday. Are you in full possession of the trust?' Trent was a florid figure of a man
with blunt manners honed in a merchant's world. His
sense of competition and honour had been honed in a
different world—however, a darker, more dangerous
world where one took what one wanted at the point of
a knife if need be. For all the wealth and fine trappings
surrounding Trent, he was no gentleman. Henry had
noted at the beginning of their association not to run

afoul of Trent's good humour. He very much feared he was about to do so.

'There is good news,' Henry began cheerfully. 'My uncle did indeed set up a trusteeship for the running of the estate, as I told you he would.' They needed to remember he had been right about some things. If it weren't for him, they wouldn't even have this opportunity to begin with.

Trent's eyes narrowed dangerously. 'Who is the trustee, Bennington?'

Henry looked at the four other men assembled, sensing their growing worry and, with it, their growing distrust of him. Of them all, he was the outsider. These five men had done business together before. 'Three of us were named trustees: my cousin, Ashe, myself and the American, Mrs Ralston. We've all been given a share of influence when it comes how the estate is to be managed.'

'What precisely is your share?' Mr Ellingson, the group's accountant, spoke up from the far end of the table.

'Four per cent,' Henry offered with feigned pride. He'd been livid over the slight all night. How dare his uncle reward him with so little after a year of his devotion. But Henry would be damned if he'd let this group of cut-throat investors see that disappointment. He went on to spell out the details of the other portions given to Ashe and Genevra while Ellingson stared at him thoughtfully, doing sums in his head.

'This is not what we agreed upon,' Trent put in after

Henry had finished. 'You said Bedevere wouldn't come home, that he'd want to sell his shares, that he'd be lucky to receive any shares at all when you got through kowtowing to your uncle.' The others murmured amongst themselves up and down the length of the table. Henry fought the urge to squirm. He'd been wrong about Ashe and therein lay the crux of his troubles. He'd wagered Ashe wouldn't come home.

Ellingson spoke up. 'There's only one thing for it. Bennington needs to wed the Ralston widow. Marriage will secure him the majority interest in the estate. Her control will pass to him upon marriage and give him fifty-four per cent.'

Trent nodded with approval. 'The Ralston chit is perfect.'

Henry's blood chilled a degree at the potential direction this conversation was heading. They were going to mandate marriage, *his* marriage, as if it were of no major import. 'There's always a possibility she'll refuse me.' Henry hedged.

The table roared with congenial laughter. 'You're too handsome to be refused, Bennington.' The man next to him clapped him on the back and Trent tossed a bag of coins on the table. 'Buy her a pretty bauble and be done with it, Bennington. We're an "I do" away from untold wealth. It would be a shame to falter here at the last.' Trent surveyed the group. 'Let's meet again in a week and see how our young Romeo is progressing.'

Henry smiled and pocketed the bag of coins, but he didn't miss the implication of Trent's dismissal. He had one week to secure the promise of matrimony to a woman he'd not choose to marry of his own volition. Since yesterday, his prospects had been steadily going downhill.

Henry took the long road home, giving plans a chance to settle in his head. He would change clothes, then he would call on Genevra. The thought of pursuing her left a sour taste in his mouth. He had cultivated her friendship of course during the earl's illness because it pleased the earl. The old man had doted on the pretty American. But Henry had seen right away how outspoken she was, how she would be the most non-compliant of wives. She would never give him full control of her money, even if she did happen to fall in love with him. He'd have to beg every shilling from her. It would be like asking his father for an allowance all over again. But it would be worth it, he reminded himself. There was much to be gained.

On his suspicions, a bore hole dug four years ago on the outskirts of Bedevere land had produced a promising sampling of lignite, indicating a rich deposit of coal beneath the land. It stood to be the most plentiful coalfield in Audley, a piece of Staffordshire known not only for its hops and gardens, but for its coalfields as well. The possibility of attaining such wealth demanded extraordinary effort and the men he'd partnered with weren't afraid to go to extremes. But so far, the extremes were all his. Aside from the money Trent's cartel had put up, the risks had all been his. They hadn't spent a year currying favour with the old earl, nor were they now facing a forced marriage.

He had to keep his eye on the goal. He would go courting today and keep in mind the purgatory of those consequences would last only a short while.

It had been a hell of a day and it was only two o'clock. Ashe pushed a hand through his hair, not caring that the action caused his hair to stand on ruffled ends and leaned back in the leather chair. At least here in the study he had the privacy he needed to think. There was so much to think about, it was hard to know where to start.

He'd spent the morning going over the estate books, trying to get a sense of where to start first, assuming he'd come up with some funds. Did he start outside with the gardens or inside with the most-used rooms? Maybe he didn't start with the house at all. Maybe he should start with the tenant farmers in ways that would generate income.

Ashe sank his head into his hands. He didn't know the first thing about managing an estate and there was no one to ask, unless one counted Henry. It would be a cold day in hell before he took that option. Ashe shut the leatherbound ledger. The numbers in the columns didn't add up and there were bills to pay. Surely the horses listed as sold last autumn hadn't gone for so little. The value posted in the ledger was half their worth. His father had kept prime cattle and knew their value.

Ashe pushed back from the desk. The morning

hadn't been an entire waste. He'd done what he could with regard to bills, which had amounted to writing assurances to those who held Bedevere's outstanding accounts telling them all would soon be remedied. He wasn't sure *how* he would see it remedied, but they didn't need to know that.

He'd also sent off letters to London. One was a private message to his closest friend, Jamie Burke, asking him to look into Genevra Ralston's background on the off chance that someone had heard of the American. That much money surely wouldn't go undetected by society no matter what its nationality. If he was required to marry her, he wanted to know who she was and if there was any detrimental scandal attached to her name. It wouldn't have been hard to hide such a thing from his father, but Mrs Ralston would find he was a bit more worldly than his father.

The second was about money as well. He'd enquired about the potential of a loan, as futile as such an enquiry seemed. Ashe was under no illusions. If he could not prove he was the predominant regent, no bank would advance him any funds.

Why does it matter? ventured the devil on his shoulder. *If you don't get the estate, why do you care if it goes to rack and ruin? If Henry wants it, let Henry figure out a way. If Mrs Ralston wants it, let her buy your shares and be done with it.*

Because it's the right thing to do, regardless, answered the angel on the other.

Because it's my home, Ashe thought. Because he'd

spent his life proving his father wrong. He wanted to prove his father was wrong here, too. His father and he had had their differences. Those differences had driven him away years ago, but he could not believe his father hated him that much, believed in him that little, to wrest Bedevere from him. Then again, his father had not planned on losing Alex. There'd never been a need for his father to consider leaving Bedevere to him. If only he could talk to his father one more time, try to explain why he'd had to go.

The devil on his shoulder wasn't satisfied. *If you want to save Bedevere stop brooding over books you can't make sense of and start wooing that pretty heiress at Seaton Hall. You need money and she's got 'piles' of it.*

Genevra Ralston.

All his thoughts seemed to come back to her. In and of herself, she was enough to keep a man busy with all her mysteries. Woman in hiding or brazen fortune hunter, it hardly mattered which. Both spelled trouble. It was a matter of how much trouble he was willing to tolerate along with her money. And trouble was a surety. Last night had established that without equivocation.

He'd not dreamed she'd respond so ardently to his advances. He'd meant to warn her that she played with a man who was out of her league. He knew women and he knew their games. Just because he loved women didn't mean he trusted them. They were as brutal as men when it came to getting their way.

His head ached. The estate wasn't the only thing that

needed sorting out. There were emotions he hadn't expected to feel, and answers he desperately wanted. What had really transpired at Bedevere in his absence? What had really happened to his brother? He would have to find time to see Alex soon, although the prospect was one he dreaded.

A knock interrupted his thoughts and Melisande poked her head around the door. 'There you are, Ashton.' Only his aunties called him that. Not 'Ashe' like the ladies in London, who claimed he could burn them to cinders with one smouldering look of his green eyes.

'You've been cooped up in here for hours.' She clucked disapprovingly. 'You should go for a ride. You never know when the weather will take a turn for a worse this time of year.' She settled herself in a chair across from him at the desk. The chair was large and gave the impression of swallowing up his petite aunt. Old age had made her appear even smaller than he remembered, but no less sharp. She eyed the ledgers.

'Are you making sense of it all?' There was hope in the question. She wanted to hear that all would be well, that things would be better. She wanted to hear he'd found a hidden cache of money or a mistake in the ledger that suddenly rendered them wealthy again. He didn't fault her for it. It was what he'd hoped, too, when he'd sat down with the books that morning, still in disbelief that the Bedevere largesse could all be gone.

Ashe offered her a warm smile. 'There were no miracles in the ledgers. But we'll make our own miracles, I promise.' He would find a way to keep this promise, never mind the string of broken, half-kept promises that littered his past. He had a lot to make up for. He was only just beginning to understand he wasn't the only one who'd borne the consequences of his choices.

'Genni will be our miracle, Ashton,' Melisande said with a straightforward confidence that bore none of Ashe's own cynicism on the subject.

Ashe didn't wish to argue with his aunt, neither did he know how much they knew regarding the will. Was this a comment she made because of their less-than-subtle matchmaking efforts, or because she knew 'Genni's' business acumen would save the estate? Ashe merely shrugged.

The non-committal shrug wasn't enough for his aunt. Melisande leaned forwards and said with force, 'Genni. We all like her and your father thought highly of her. She's the one we want.' He'd never heard his delicate flower of an aunt sound so demanding. At least the outburst had confirmed her motives. She was strictly about matchmaking. She didn't know about his father's arrangement, only her own.

'She might not want me,' Ashe ventured.

'She will. You can be irresistible when you choose, Ashton.' That shamed him. Aunt Melisande meant it with all the goodness of her heart, remembering the pretty child and the handsome youth. She had no idea how 'irresistible' the man had become or how he'd bartered those charms for a price.

Melisande pushed a soft package in brown wrapping paper across the desk at him. 'Since you're going for a ride, I thought you could take this to Seaton Hall. It can be your reason to visit and then you can apologise.'

'Apologise for what, Aunt?' Ashe drawled obtusely.

'For whatever you did to her last night. She's too much of a lady to say anything, but she left so quickly we knew something had happened. I hadn't even had time to give this to her.' A scolding and guilt all rolled into one.

Melisande patted his hand. 'A good apology is never wasted on a woman's heart, Ashton. Your great-uncle could always turn my head with one. Women are capable of great forgiveness if men ask for it.'

'And if we don't?' Ashe teased, taking the package.

Melisande winked. 'Then we're capable of a great many other things.' She rose and made to leave. 'I'll tell the groom you'll want your horse brought around in twenty minutes.'

She shut the door behind her and Ashe let out a laugh. He'd been thoroughly manoeuvred by his seventy-three-year-old aunt. So much for delicate and fragile.

Twenty minutes later, Ashe swung up on Rex. Seaton Hall wouldn't have been his destination of choice after last night. But, Ashe thought with a touch of mischief, it would be rather interesting to see how the stunning Mrs Ralston would follow up last night's slap.

He spurred Rex into a canter and gave the big horse his head through the meadows. He took a jump over a stone fence and revelled at the wind in his face. He took another and let loose a cry of pure enjoyment. There weren't fences like this in London. Anyone could ride in London as long as they could walk a horse through Hyde Park, but this kind of riding across open fields took an accomplished rider.

Ashe came to the road leading to Seaton Hall and reined Rex to a walk. No one in London thought of him as a country gentleman. It had been a long time since *he'd* thought of himself that way, but, buried and ignored, that was the stifled truth. Behind the fancy clothes and elegant manners, he was a product of the quiet rural lands of Staffordshire. Like himself, Staffordshire often struck him as a place of contradictions. The land was riddled with mining and industry, yet a large part of the land had also maintained its rural nature with fields for farming, and its proclivity for beautiful gardens; a proclivity Bedevere had apparently let slide in the last few years, but one that Seaton Hall had embraced with success from the look of things. Roles had been reversed. Under Genevra Ralston's money and careful eye, Seaton Hall had emerged as the belle of the county while the once-elegant Bedevere strangled in weeds.

Ashe turned up the drive, noting with an appreciative eye the trimmed grass of the parkland, the organised flower beds showing early shoots of spring flowers poking through the soil. In a few months, those beds would be vivid with colours. Bedevere had looked like that once. Jealousy stabbed. He wanted Bedevere to look like that again. But that was foolishness, at least this year. One did not waste efforts on pretty gardens when there were bills to pay and mouths to feed. Perhaps if he could get a loan. Right now, everything hinged on money, even his own potential marriage. On his own, with no funds to speak of, what he could do was extremely limited. Once married to Mrs Ralston, an infinity of possibilities lay open to him—one more reason to sell himself in this marriage of his father's choosing.

Ashe sighed. The reasons for marriage were mounting. His desire for freedom, to make his own choice when the time came were starting to look petty and stubborn next to the gains the marriage would give him.

At the door he was told Mrs Ralston was in the back gardens and was shown to a brightly done sitting room at the front of the house where he could wait. If the room was indicative of Seaton Hall's recent fortunes, the American was doing very well for herself indeed. The creamy-yellow paint was fresh, the white-plaster moldings newly painted. Dusky-blue curtains framed the long windows overlooking the front drive. The pillows on the blue-and-yellow sofa were invitingly plump. Best of all, there was a pianoforte along the wall.

Ashe ran his hands along the keys experimentally, noting the full, mellow tones. It must be new if it had the Babcock strings. Curiosity piqued, Ashe gently lifted the lid of the case and peered inside, the old excitement rising. Ah, yes, the soundboard was cross-strung. He couldn't resist.

Ashe sat down and began to play. It felt good, it felt *liberating*. There was no one to judge, no one to impress. This was just for him.

Chapter Six

Bedevere was *here*. The very thought brought a flutter to her usually stable stomach. What did one say to a man one had previously slapped? 'I'm sorry?' 'I hope your cheek isn't terribly sore today?' Obviously the slap had not achieved the desired effect. He'd come to Seaton Hall, clearly undeterred. And here she was, gardening in an old gown in a desperate attempt to forget last night had ever happened.

If she was going to face Ashe Bedevere, she had to look decent. Genevra slid one of her favourite afternoon gowns over her head, a green-and-white sprigged-muslin affair that made her feel pretty and confident. She gave her hair a quick brushing to get rid of any garden debris she might have acquired. It wouldn't do to give that green-eyed rogue a reason to touch her hair again, even if it was under the auspices of picking out a leaf.

Genevra was still trying out possible greetings on the stairs when she heard the music. It was lovely. Perhaps a lieder? It was far beyond anything she could produce. No one had mentioned Mr Bedevere had brought a guest.

At the doorway, Genevra halted in surprise. There was no guest. The musician was Bedevere himself. His back was to her and she took advantage of it, reacquainting herself with the broad shoulders and wavy black hair that skimmed decadently over his collar, too long and too full for fashion's dictates, but just right for him.

The piece ended and Genevra clapped. He started at the intrusion and turned on the bench. 'Please, continue.' Genevra took up a seat on the sofa, relieved that the music had offered a neutral entrée into their meeting. She could smoothly avoid any awkwardness over last night now.

'I am afraid the piano doesn't get much use, but I thought I should have one anyway for musical evenings. Although I must confess, we haven't had one yet for all our good intentions.'

He shook his head. 'I've played enough. It's a fine instrument. It's new, I can tell from the strings. Do you play, Mrs Ralston?'

'Only moderately,' Genevra confessed. 'But I am glad the instrument is a good one.'

'Come here, and I'll show you how good it is.' Bedevere moved to the side, gesturing for her to join him. She crossed the room, unable to refuse the irresistible excitement that hummed about him as he peered into the case. He smelled of wind and vanilla, an entirely intoxicating combination when associated with a man.

'These strings are Babcock's. He patented them a few years back. They're thicker than the old strings, allowing for increased volume.' Bedevere plucked a string inside the case for demonstration. 'And now piano makers are cross-stringing the soundboards to create more resonance.'

With hands like that, she should have guessed. 'You're very accomplished, Mr Bedevere. I didn't know.'

'Please, call me Ashe if you don't mind.'

Genevra recognised the dangerously quiet tones from last night. 'Of course.' She decided not to enquire. She didn't want to spoil this pleasant truce after last night's unpleasantness. 'Will you stay for tea?' She didn't wait for an answer. She went straight to the bell pull. This was England. Everyone stayed for tea.

'I must apologise for dropping by unexpectedly, but I have something for you.' Ashe took a seat and handed her a soft package.

A gift from him? An apology, perhaps, for his prior conduct? Certainly a gentleman would make the effort. A little flutter took up residence in her stomach as she played with the string. In the daylight, he seemed so civilised.

'Melisande asked me to bring it.'

'Of course.' The flutter disappeared. Naturally it wasn't from him. He was no gentleman and slapped men didn't bring gifts. Genevra smiled to cover her mental error.

'It must be Melisande's latest embroidery pattern.'

Genevra held up the cloth. 'Tell her it's lovely. It will do well at the markets this spring.'

'I beg your pardon?' This time he was the one caught off guard and it did things to his face. His dark brows winged upwards, his eyes narrowed in speculation.

'Didn't they tell you?' Genevra folded the cloth up. 'She and your other aunts sell their handiwork at the local markets. Cook even sends some jams. They did quite well last summer.'

'My aunts *sell* crafts at the market?' The look on Ashe's face was incredulous bordering on furious. 'Like *merchants*?'

Genevra replied evenly, 'Yes, like merchants. Like most of the normal world, in fact. Not all of us live in such rarefied circumstances as a British gentleman, dashing around London looking for entertainment.'

A tight tic began to pulse low on Ashe's jaw. Whatever tenuous truce they'd had over the music had evaporated. 'Whose idea was this?' he ground out, thankfully choosing to overlook the other insinuations she'd so carelessly made.

'It was mine,' Genevra said, grateful for the arrival of the tea tray to derail this line of conversation.

But Ashe wasn't ready to let it go like a self-respecting gentleman. 'Why ever would you suggest something like that?' His disbelief was tangible as he took a tea cup from her. She took care to make sure their fingers didn't touch.

'They had no money and you were nowhere to be found.' Genevra allowed her temper to spill over. 'They had to do something and it was a very good something. They were too proud to take so much as a farthing from me. If you must know, people like to buy things that represent the peerage. It's a good advertising angle. It's far more exciting to buy a handkerchief embroidered by a real lady.'

Ashe's dark eyebrows rose. 'And a good deal more expensive too, I hope? Still, they'd have to sell quite a lot of handkerchiefs and jam to support Bedevere.'

Genevra frowned. He was missing an essential component to the effort. 'It's not just about the money. We're expanding to Bury St Edmunds this summer and the aunts are excited.'

'No, *we* are not. I'm home now—those kind of measures won't be necessary,' Ashe said firmly.

Genevra set down her tea cup and fixed him with a stare. She hadn't meant to argue again. She'd meant to behave herself. 'I disagree. It is necessary, even if weren't about the money. Those ladies need to feel useful. This gives them purpose, it helps them feel as if they're contributing.'

'They're English ladies, Mrs Ralston. I don't know that you quite comprehend what that means.'

'They're *people*. I wonder if you comprehend what that means?'

The sound of horses' hooves on the drive broke the ensuing silence. She looked past Ashe's shoulder and felt a wave of relief. 'It's Henry. I'll ring for another tea cup.' Surely Henry would know how to deal with his prickly cousin. She'd certainly made a mess of it thus far. It probably had something to do with a pair of hot green eyes and a wicked smile that only had to flit across those aristocratic lips of his to conjure up illicit memories of a stolen kiss. Goodness knew it was hard to think straight under those conditions.

Henry stepped into the parlour, all smiles and charm until he spotted his cousin. 'I didn't expect to see you here. I'd stopped by to see if Genevra wanted to ride into the village with me.' Henry turned towards her, excluding Ashe from the conversation. 'My monthly shipment of books from London has arrived. I thought you'd enjoy looking them over. But I see you have company.' If she thought Henry would be a neutral buffer between her and Ashe, she was quickly proven wrong. His resentment was barely veiled. In the months she'd known Henry, she'd never seen a poor show of manners until yesterday. Since then, she'd seen two.

Genevra offered Henry a smile, trying to smooth over his lapse in good behaviour. 'I *do* have company. But you're welcome to join us for tea before you go on. I've already called for another cup.'

'Genevra likes Gothic novels.' Henry explained to Ashe with a friendly wink in her direction as he took a seat in the other wing-backed chair. 'I always try to surprise her with a couple in the shipment.'

Ashe was looking at her again in that steady way of his. 'So you like a good romance, Mrs Ralston?'

Even his polite conversation was sensual. She guessed at his innuendo and a hot blush crept up her cheeks. 'I do on occasion,' Genevra managed evenly. He could make of that response what he wished.

'*Mrs Ralston*? When have we ever been so formal among friends?' Henry laughed at his cousin. 'This is Genni, or Genevra if you prefer. I stopped calling her "Mrs Ralston" ages ago. We've practically lived in each other's pockets these past few months, caring for Uncle.' Henry smiled fondly at her and reached across the short distance to cover her hand with his. It was meant to be a friendly, touching gesture, but Genevra sensed undercurrents of something else, as if the display wasn't necessarily spontaneous. It certainly wasn't characteristic. Genevra hated to think this unusual outpouring of affection was motivated by Henry's meagre four per cent. Even more she hated that she was forced to think that way.

'Tragedies have a way of bringing people closer together.' Henry's smile softened as he looked into her eyes for a brief, meaningful moment.

Or tearing them apart. Genevra was distinctly uncomfortable. She and Henry had been perfectly good friends until yesterday. Henry had never intimated he wanted anything more from their association, which had made him all the more attractive to her. He was exactly what she was looking for: an intelligent companion who wouldn't demand more than she wanted to give. She'd tried marriage once and found it not to her liking. She was in no hurry to try it again, even to the amiable Mr Bennington, and certainly not to his less-amiable cousin, Mr Bedevere, no matter how well he kissed.

'We read to your father for hours on end.' Genevra returned the conversation to Ashe, acutely aware that this was the second time Henry had excluded him.

'How cosy,' was all Ashe said.

'Do you enjoy books as well?' Genevra tried again.

'I like picture books.' Ashe gave a wicked grin that left no room for misunderstanding.

'Good lord, Ashe. You're even worse than I remembered.' Henry scowled his disapproval, unwilling to let the second edgy comment pass without censure.

'So are you,' Ashe shot back.

Whatever expectations she might have had of familial love between the cousins were completely vanquished in that single line. Tension thickened like the piano's Babcock strings and Genevra looked about the room for a polite, neutral subject of conversation. Her eyes fell on the instrument against the wall.

'Your cousin played the piano for me just before you arrived,' Genevra told Henry. 'He's amazing.'

Henry arched an eyebrow at Ashe. 'You're still playing? Well, that's something at least. Your rebellion wasn't a complete waste then, was it?'

The tic in Ashe's cheek began to throb again. It was time to get Henry off on his errand before there were fisticuffs in her parlour. Henry hadn't made anything better, but he'd certainly made them worse. 'I'd offer you a second cup, but I fear I've delayed you long enough.' She rose and offered her hand to Henry. 'Thank you for the invitation. It was kind of you to think of me.'

'Then I am always kind.' Henry bowed over her hand and made his exit.

Ashe rolled his eyes, looking entirely at home in the wing-backed chair with his leg crossed over one knee, smashing any hope *he* would be leaving soon. 'That's the most beefwitted line I've heard. My cousin thinks himself a poet. It's ridiculous.'

'It was sweet.' Genevra busied herself stacking the tea things on the tray. Perhaps Ashe would get the message that the interlude was over.

'Do you think so? Do you fancy him?' Ashe asked point blank.

'We are merely friends.' A cup nearly slipped out of her hands at his frankness.

'It seems he'd like to be more than friends.'

'And you?' Genevra faced him, hands on hips. If he could be bold, so could she. 'What are you sniffing around here for? I am sorry if I gave you the wrong impression last night.'

'I assure you, I got the right impression. I can't afford not to. I only have two cheeks to slap.' He followed her with his eyes to the bell pull as she rang for someone to come and remove the tray.

'Is this the part where you regret to inform me I must leave because you have to get back to your projects, but in truth it's because I've spoken too boldly and made you uncomfortable?' Ashe was laughing at her with his eyes, and his mouth, which curved up into a wry, challenging smile, dared her to deny him.

'Only if you don't perceive the need to leave without being asked.'

'And here I was, thinking I might get a tour of your
gardens. After all the talk last night of landscaping, I
did have hopes of sneaking a glimpse.'

He had her there. Her gardens were her weakness.
She loved to show them off. 'Give me a moment to
change my shoes.' Genevra smiled. This would be the
perfect way to show him his assumptions the night before were unfounded. She had *legitimate* reasons for
eschewing London, starting with her gardens.

She showed him the topiary garden first with its
trees shaped into exotic animals. There was a giraffe
and a horse and an elephant, each set in a corner and
surrounded by pansies that would bloom later in the
spring. Even without the added colour of the flowers,
this garden attracted the eye with its designs. Set between the sculpted animals were spiral-cedar topiaries
set in large wooden planters.

'I've tried to copy some Italian designs I've seen in
pictures of the Boboli Gardens,' Genevra explained.
They walked side by side, but she'd been careful not to
take his arm. She did not want to risk rekindling any
of the flames from last night.

Ashe stopped to look at one spiralling tree in a
planter. 'You've managed to capture it exactly right.'

Her breath caught. 'You've been to Florence?'

Ashe nodded, bending down to look up through the
tree's shape. 'All over Italy, actually. After Oxford,

some friends and I went. We were all interested in the Renaissance and I wanted to see Cristofori's pianos.' He paused and she thought she saw a flicker of hesitation before he continued. 'My father hadn't wanted me to go. He loved England and didn't see a reason to venture so far from home.' One piece of the puzzle, Genevra thought. One brief insight into the inscrutable, mysterious past of Ashe Bedevere. She waited for more. It would be all she'd get.

'I would love to travel,' she offered to fill the silence. She'd only come to England because her circumstances demanded it in the wake of Philip's death. If things hadn't gone poorly, she might never have left Boston.

'Then you should, Mrs Ralston.' She wasn't sure if that was an affirmation of her desire or a suggestion that she act on it with the utmost immediacy. Was he warning her off? All the better to gain control of her shares.

They came to a patch of garden still under construction. He offered his hand and this time she took it as they navigated the little piles of rubble. 'This will be a corridor of orchard trees and knot gardens, all leading to the fountain,' she explained with a wide gesture of her free hand to indicate the water feature at the end of the lane. She was well aware he'd kept her other hand trapped in his even though the need was no longer there. His grip was warm and solid.

'Gardens are a lot of work for someone who wishes to travel,' Ashe murmured.

She saw the contradiction too late. 'The future is an uncertain creature. There's no sense in *not* doing something in the present simply because the future might provide a different opportunity. If it doesn't, then much has been lost waiting for what might be.'

They'd reached the wide bowl of the fountain. There was no one about, only the sound of the water splashing as it landed in the basin. They might have been the only two people in the whole world. One of his long fingers had begun to trace slow circles on the back of her hand, conjuring up a reminder of how his hands had drawn small circles on her back last night while he'd trailed kisses down her neck.

'It sounds, Mrs Ralston, as if you know a thing or two about loss.' The invitation to confess was quietly issued. The temptation to do just that was potent. Good lord, this was a man who knew how to touch a woman. His eyes were searching her face and, against all logic, she wanted him to kiss her again, to take away the responsibility of answering him. But he didn't. He merely waited, his lips hovering tantalising inches from hers, reminding her of the possibilities.

'I do,' she whispered. She could give him that much at least. Admission wasn't confession.

'Is that why you're here, Mrs Ralston? To seize the opportunities of the present or to hide from the past?'

Chapter Seven

⟨ ❧ ⟩

Silver-grey eyes looked away to a spot over his shoulder and then back, a small smile taking her lips. 'Is that what *you're* doing here?'

'I'm not hiding from my past, Mrs Ralston.'

'No, I was incorrect there. You're atoning for it.' The words were not meanly said. Her voice was softly reflective as if she'd just come to the revelation herself.

Her mouth was only inches from his, pink and inviting, her face tilted up to his, so close he could see the obsidian flecks of black in her deep-grey eyes. At this proximity, one might believe she was a well-tempered Pocket Venus. But Ashe had seen her quicksilver eyes flash with temper and other more tempestuous emotions. Yet up close, one could not miss the gentle, porcelain beauty of her features. Nor could one miss the undeniable proof that Mrs Ralston was not as immune as she seemed. A pulse-note beat at the base of her throat, quick and rapid, belying her attraction.

He stepped back. He wouldn't kiss her, not today. She

might think he was in the habit of always kissing her. She might come to take those kisses for granted. That would do his seduction no good if he chose to pursue her. 'You know nothing about me, Mrs Ralston.'

'Or you me.' Mrs Ralston's features schooled themselves into an elegant portrayal of politeness. 'Although you seem content to speculate that you do.' Her implication was clear. She thought him a hypocrite.

She was no coward, he'd give her that. Sharp tongued, sharp witted, Mrs Ralston was not easily bested.

'Are all Americans like you?'

'Are all Englishmen like you?'

Just once he'd like to have her answer a question without another question. It was proving to be a frustratingly evasive tactic of hers.

'My cousin isn't anything like me.'

'No, he's certainly not.' It was said equivocally. Was it Henry who'd been measured and come up lacking or was it himself? They were back to Henry, where they'd started. The conversation had come full circle.

Ashe pulled out his pocketwatch and made a show of checking it. 'Since we're not likely to tell each other our secrets, this seems to be a good place to make my exit. Thank you for the tour of the garden. It was most insightful.' She could spend her evening pondering what insights he'd gleaned. 'I can show myself out.'

He hadn't gone more than twenty paces when she called out, 'When will you be returning to London?'

Ashe turned and said slowly, 'I don't have any plans to return to London in the immediate future, Mrs

Ralston.' He grinned, making her regret the impetuous question. 'Were you afraid you'd miss me?'

She did laugh at that, the same throaty sound he'd heard at dinner. 'Miss *you*? Hardly.'

Ashe resumed his departure and called over his shoulder, 'You will, though. *Adieu*, Mrs Ralston, until next time. There will be a next time. You're going to have to deal with my forty-five per cent whether you like it or not.' If he squared his shoulders a little more than usual and walked a little straighter or with a bit more swagger, it was only because he knew she was watching. She liked to look at him. He'd caught her at it several times. It was a start. At least she wasn't ignoring him, although that could be fun, too, if he had the time for it.

If the stakes weren't so high, he'd thoroughly enjoy flirting with Genevra Ralston and then taking that flirtation a step further, Ashe mused, swinging up on Rex for the ride to the village and the public house. But the stakes *were* high. He could not gamble haphazardly. This was one seduction that had to succeed. He didn't have a choice, no matter what he pretended to himself. There was no question of selling his shares and backing away just as there was no question of meekly accepting his less-than-majority ownership of his own estate's regency. His track record in seduction was impeccable. It was *her* record he was worried about, especially if she had any loyalty towards Henry.

The women he seduced were willing. His partners

understood from the start this was a game just like *vingt-et-un* or whist with its rules and progressions. It was contractually understood that his partners knew where the game ended before they even started. He wasn't entirely sure Genevra Ralston would play by those rules, or that she'd play at all in spite of her hot kisses and fast-beating pulse.

In her case it wasn't enough simply to want him. There was a fortitude to her that suggested her mind could resist the temptations of her heart. To win her, he'd need a strategy that went beyond chance meetings and the thrill of stolen kisses. It bore thinking about. It wouldn't do for the one woman he couldn't seduce to be the woman he had to marry.

But now was not the time. Thoughts of Genevra Ralston's grand seduction had to wait. Right now he had to concentrate on the evening ahead. Ashe touched the pocket of his coat. Inside were tokens of female affection, acquired from his various *affaires* in London: a ruby stick pin, a set of emerald cufflinks, a rhinestone pin. They would be enough to get him a few games of billiards at the assembly hall in town. He would start building his own bankroll for Bedevere. *He* would find the money to pay for improvements. Asking Genevra to advance him funds would only make it more obvious just how much he needed her fifty-one per cent.

Ah, there was nothing like the smell of ale and sweat to bring a man peace. Ashe breathed deeply of the pungent smells as he stepped into the back room of the public house. It might not be the freshest of odours, but it was familiar and right now that was enough. He always thought well when he played billiards. It was a lot like playing the piano. Focusing on the game freed his mind to think about other things with greater objectivity. He needed time to think and to raise funds. If luck was with him, tonight he'd be able to do both.

Like most assembly rooms and public houses in villages across England, the village of Audley sported a billiards table. This particular table, Ashe noticed, was well used to put it mildly. But Ashe had faced better players on worse and tonight he just wanted to play, wanted to lose himself in the game. Ashe scanned the perimeter of the table and found his prey, not that it had taken much. The man was frankly advertising himself as a target.

'Will no one play?' the big man behind the baize table was gloating loudly. The crowd around the table shook their heads after the last victim had been dispatched. Ashe chuckled. He'd seen players like this before. The man had no finesse. He was too obvious with his skill. The trick was to hide one's true skill until it was time to strike.

Ashe stepped forwards and launched the first salvo in his private campaign to restore Bedevere. 'I'll play you.' Tonight, he was going to make money the only way he knew how. It would be better if his usual comrades, Merrick or Riordan, were with him. They could have run the two-friends-and-a-stranger gambit on this fellow. It would have been quicker. But Merrick was

happily married in Hever with twin girls and lord only
knew where Riordan was these days. Without them,
Ashe would have to settle for quiet manipulation on
his own.

The crowd stepped back to make room for the newcomer. The heavier man studied him with disdain, already mentally dispatching him. Ashe knew what his
opponent saw. He'd planned it that way on purpose—a
younger man overdressed for this place with a pocket
full of guineas, a veritable rooster for the plucking. He
was still dressed in the clothes he'd worn to call on Mrs
Ralston. They were riding clothes, to be sure, but they
were well cut and made for an afternoon in Hyde Park.
Good, Ashe thought. *Be as cocky as you like.*

'What shall we play for?' The man eyed him with
barely contained greed.

'This.' Ashe placed a rhinestone pin on the rim of
the table, drawing oohs from the crowd. The pin wasn't
extraordinarily expensive, but it was well made and the
rhinestones had the desired effect, catching the light
from the table lamp hung over the playing space. He
could see the man's eyes flare with interest. *That's right.
Keep your eyes on the prize and you'll forget to concentrate on the game.* 'Shall we go best three out of five?'

Ashe played skilfully, losing the first two games
and buoying the man's substantial ego. He won the
next three, and then the next three. The man gave up,
but there was another to take his place. And after that,
some enterprising soul had awakened the local billiards expert in the next village over and brought him

in at dawn. That match had taken a while before Ashe claimed victory and put a thick roll of pound notes in his pocket, enough to pay wages for a month for anyone who wanted day labour at Bedevere.

He'd played longer than he'd anticipated, but once word got out who he was, there'd be no more billiards games at the local public house. Gentlemen didn't gamble with commoners. Still, there were areas around Audley Village that wouldn't hear the news for a while. If he travelled for a few games, this idea would last. But what else could he do to raise money? That sparked another, long-term idea. If he couldn't gamble at the public house, perhaps he could set up billiards games at Bedevere, after a proper period of mourning had passed, of course. When he got home, he'd see what sort of shape the billiards table was in. He suspected it hadn't been used in years. But that was for later—he'd need some ideas for now. Perhaps an auction, as distasteful as the idea was.

His mind started to whir with ideas. He could clean up Bedevere, make it look respectable enough for entertaining a few gentlemen over an evening of billiards and brandy—cards, too. He could invite the gentry—some squires, their sons, their nephews. He'd have to ask Leticia for a list of people. That meant gardens to pretty up and a few rooms to restore. The idea of restoring the gardens didn't seem so wasteful now. Perhaps for an auction there was furniture in the attics…

Ashe's mind was fully occupied when he stepped outside, cravat undone, coat slung over his arm. The bright daylight hit him full force. He squinted and lost his footing on a loose cobblestone.

'Oh!' The cry came too late. Ashe careened right into a passer-by, taking her and her packages to the ground along with him in a most intimate pile of legs and arms and thighs and skirts.

He levered himself up, aware that the sensation of being on top of this lush female was something his body didn't find entirely unpleasant—or unknown. It was quite funny, really, in the way that irony is funny. Of all the women in Audley Village, he'd managed to crash into Mrs Ralston.

'I'm sorry.' Ashe laughed, making light of the mishap. What else was left to do when one has landed in the perfect matrimonial position atop a lovely woman? On the positive side, he already knew her, which made it far better in some ways than landing on a stranger.

Apparently she didn't share his humour over the incident or his optimism. A stormy set of grey eyes met his and instinctively he knew he wasn't as sorry as he was going to be.

Chapter Eight

His eyes were *tremendously* green up close, and she couldn't imagine him being any closer than he was right now. Nor could she imagine being any more mortified. The source of her mortification didn't come from the fact that his body pressed most intimately against her in a public venue, but from her response. She *should* have been more upset with such familiarity and much less aroused. But, in all honesty, she *was* aroused and, from the feel of him, he shared the sensation. Of course it was all a great game to him, just like that ill-advised kiss in the conservatory had been.

Ashe had risen with a laugh. 'Mrs Ralston, are you hurt? Let me help you up.'

He looked taller and more presupposing than usual from her supine position on the sidewalk. He offered her a hand. She ought to take it, but her stubborn pride wouldn't permit it. She could get up by herself very well, thank you, and perhaps gather her thoughts into some sensible order in the meanwhile.

'Keep your hands to yourself.' Genevra struggled to her feet, trying to look somewhat graceful amid the strewn packages as if she collided with handsome, arrogant gentlemen on the street every day.

He tossed back his dark mane and laughed. 'And my other parts? Should I keep them to myself, too, or do you have need of them?' Genevra blushed furiously. Had he no decency? She was coming to learn Ashe said and did the first things that came to his very imaginative mind.

'Oh, hush up, and help me gather the packages.' They were starting to draw a discreet crowd. This was fine excitement in the sleepy village. Goodness knew what kind of tales would enliven dinner tables tonight.

She took a step forwards, bent to reach a parcel and stumbled, caught only by the firm grip of Ashe's hand at her arm. 'Eager for a repeat, are we?' he whispered wickedly, steadying her. 'In all seriousness, Mrs Ralston, I think you might have done yourself a minor injury.'

'You mean *you* might have done me a minor injury.'

He smiled, all white-toothed wickedness. 'Yes, *I* may have done so since it was I who fell on top of you. There's a decent inn across the street. Let's get you some tea and some rest.'

Now she had no choice but to rely on him and hobble on his arm to the inn, a *different* inn than the one he'd been coming out of, she might add. The presence of a woman's touch was evident in the Sheaf and Loaf. Blue-chequered curtains hung at the front windows and a big-bosomed, bustling woman in a clean apron was eager to seat them in a private parlour—an industrious innkeeper's wife, to be sure.

Genevra did not think her ankle was sorely damaged. A rest would be all it would take to restore her to proper working order, but in the meantime it meant keeping company with the enigmatic Ashe Bedevere.

'Will you be all right, Mrs Ralston?' he enquired after tea had arrived. She smiled over her tea cup. If he could be audacious in conversation, she could be, too.

'In the two days I've known you, you've kissed me, come to my home uninvited and landed on top of me in a public street. Truly, Mr Bedevere, I am beginning to wonder.' She was wondering quite a few things about this man these days; things she shouldn't wonder because one look was really all she needed to know precisely the kind of man he was: a man she should not get involved with.

She'd known it from the first moment he'd blown into Bedevere, travelling cloak swirling on those broad shoulders. His actions in the conservatory that night had confirmed it. Looking at him now, she should not be surprised he'd come careening out of Audley Village's more disreputable public house dressed in the same clothes he'd worn to her home yesterday afternoon. She knew precisely the kind of man he was. A smart woman knew that when a man looked like a rake and spoke like a rake, the man was definitely a rake.

'I do apologise for the mishap,' Bedevere began, giv-

ing her that slow smile of his designed to charm. She
would not let herself fall for such an obvious ploy. But
what a smile it was. It was the eyes that helped the smile
right along. Sharp and green like a cat's, the eyes glinted
with all nature of mischief. Oh, yes, she understood this
man quite well.

'You wouldn't have to apologise if you hadn't been
there in the first place.' There was a censorious tone to
her voice, although truth be told she was slightly curious to know what had kept him out all night, even if
she didn't quite approve.

'Or if *you* hadn't,' he answered easily, passing her
the plate of scones. 'I do believe it takes two to cause
a collision.'

How dare he make the accident her fault, as if she
had wanted all that male muscle to land on her in such
a fashion? '*I* was shopping, whereas *you* were coming
out of a public house at eleven in the morning.'

He laughed again and she had the suspicion he was
laughing *at* her. 'Is that a crime? You say it as if it's a
bad thing.'

'It is,' Genevra retorted. 'Just look at you. Just *smell*
you.' To her great alarm he grinned and did just that. To
her even greater alarm, she could feel herself starting
to melt. That smile was beginning to work. Good lord,
he was devilishly handsome when he grinned like that.

'Hmmm. Cigar and whisky. A little on the stale side,'
he said matter of factly. She had the impression he was
enjoying this far too much. She needed to end this avenue of conversation. Whatever he'd been up to, he'd

been up to it all night. She wasn't generalising there. His startling green eyes showed signs of sleeplessness and his clothes told their own story.

'Mr Bedevere, really.' She was no prude, but he pushed the boundaries of what could be tolerated.

'That's another thing. I do think we've moved past "Mr Bedevere and Mrs Ralston"—don't you agree?' He leaned over the table, closing the space between them. For a fleeting moment she wondered if he was going to kiss her again.

'I have a confession to make.' Probably more than one—he didn't strike her as precisely the church-going type. 'I usually call women I've, um "landed" on by their first names.' She was sure he did. She didn't miss the plurality of reference.

'Call me Ashe. It's the second time I've asked.' He was smiling again and a small rebellious *frisson* ran down her spine whether she wanted to be immune or not. He did not wait for her to offer the appropriate response. 'And I'll call you Neva,' he drawled, his eyes holding hers.

'Your aunts and Henry call me Genni,' Genevra countered quickly. Even in a morning parlour at an inn, 'Neva' sounded far too sensual on his lips. It was a name she should not permit for her own sanity, if not for protocol's sake. She'd been in England long enough to know better. An English woman of decent society would not allow it.

'Well, that's hardly original, but then again that's the

limit of Henry's imagination,' Ashe said off-handedly, leaning back in his chair.

Genevra laughed in spite of herself. 'Why don't you like your cousin?'

'Oh, no, you don't.' Ashe smiled and crossed his arms. 'No more answering questions with questions. We were talking about your name, not Henry's. We're not changing the conversation.'

Genevra sobered and leaned across the table, all seriousness. 'Mr Bedevere.'

'Ashe.'

She sighed and conceded. '*Ashe,* I can see that you're used to flirting with women and having some success there. I am flattered.' Genevra rose. Leaving was the most effective way of ending a conversation she knew of. 'However, I am not interested in whatever you're offering.'

Matrimony, Ashe thought wryly. The 'whatever' he was offering was far bigger than she suspected. He knew what she thought; he was out to make her his latest mistress. Perhaps she believed he meant to woo her fifty-one per cent out of her. She wasn't far from the mark, but he'd make an honest woman of her in the process. He wasn't such a cad to not offer marriage in exchange for her shares.

Ashe rose to stand beside her, taking her arm and effectively cutting off her lone exit. He kept his voice low. 'Are you certain? You don't know what I'm offering since I haven't made my "proposal" as it were.'

She gave him a cool sidelong look that would have done any courtesan playing hard to get proud. 'I know very well what you're offering, Ashe.'

'Really, and you still refuse?' Ashe murmured. 'I must say either your fortitude is quite amazing or your imagination is not.' Her mouth quirked into a split-second smile before she regained her composure. 'It's all right, you can laugh. I am known for my witticisms,' he assured her.

'I am sure you're known for much more than wit.' She looked him squarely in the eye. 'I am not for you. Again, I must decline your, um, "proposal." Now, if you would excuse me, I would prefer to leave alone, Mr Bedevere.'

'Ashe. We were making progress on that a few moments ago.'

'Good day, *Mr Bedevere*.' There was a stern finality to her voice.

'Good day, *Neva*.'

What a woman. Ashe let her go. She'd be back and she'd be his. Of course, he wouldn't offer her matrimony to begin with. She would reject that request out of hand and likely she'd see the proposal for what it was: an attempt to take control of the estate. He'd start small and tempt her with his gardens. She liked gardens and, with his new endeavour in mind, his had to be cleaned up. The arrangement was really quite symbiotic if presented in the right light. That light was not morning light, however.

Ashe sat back down and finished his tea. His head

was starting to pound after the long night. It did bring him a silent bit of humour to think the lovely and discreet Genevra Ralston's first reaction to his flirtation was that he offered something improperly wicked. It was a delicious bit of irony that the woman who'd scolded him for spending a night in Audley Village's version of a gaming hell had a mind that went immediately to bedding. Not that he was opposed to it. He was definitely up for it, in all ways.

What was *not* delicious was the rather lowering discovery that the one woman he needed to marry was the one woman who had outright refused him before he'd even asked.

Ashe pushed a hand through his hair, catching a whiff of his evening activities. She was right. He did smell, but a bath would have to wait. He had labourers to hire and supplies to order. What a difference a day made. Yesterday he hadn't any idea what he'd do with supplies or workers even if he could have afforded them, but today he did and Genevra Ralston was going to help him whether she knew it or not.

From his table by the front window of the public house Henry had a clear view of Audley Village's main street, lined with shops and businesses, while he ate an early lunch. At least the rabbit stew was good, something he couldn't say for his day so far. He'd come to town to 'accidentally' run into Genevra on her usual shopping day, but he'd had no luck after combing the stores.

If all had gone well, she would have been sharing lunch with him across the street at the inn instead of him eating alone at a lesser establishment with only its view of the street to recommend it. If she was in the village he'd see her.

Henry's spoon stopped halfway to his mouth. There she was, coming out of the inn, the basket on her arm full, indicating she was done with her shopping. Henry grimaced. She'd be unlikely to want to wander the shops if that was the case and, to all appearances, she'd already stopped for refreshment. His options were a bit limited. Still, he had to try. At the very least he could accompany her home. Henry hastily dug for some coins to leave on the table and hurried to follow her. But he didn't get far. Another all-too-familiar face emerged from the inn. Ashe.

Henry understood immediately what had happened. He'd not seen Genevra on her usual rounds because Ashe had beaten him to it. Henry stepped back inside the public house. There was no sense going after her now. He would merely be redundant if she'd already met with Ashe.

'Do you know that bloke over there?' A gruff presence established itself over Henry's right shoulder. A hulk of a man stood there.

'He was in here last night, playing billiards,' Henry's newfound companion said over mugs of ale. 'He cleaned me out. Suckered me, he did. He played false for a few games and then started to win and didn't stop. I left after I lost, but I hear he played all night, beating all comers. He's a sharp, that's what he is.' The man scowled into his mug.

Henry smiled. Hammond Gallagher was a poor loser. He could use that. 'That's Ashe Bedevere, the late earl's son. The Honourable Ashton Bedevere to us commoners.'

Hammond's eyebrows rose and Henry knew what he was thinking: he'd been beaten by an earl's son, there was some pride in that. Now it was time to disabuse him of the notion.

'Bedevere hasn't been around much, he's spent his time on the Continent whoring, drinking, gambling.' Henry shrugged in disapproval of such activities. 'He's only home now because of his father's death and here he is gambling when he should be in mourning and finding a way to support his dear old aunts.'

'Sounds like he might need a lesson.' Gallagher blew into his ale.

Henry hid his smile in his mug. This was what he'd been angling for and it hadn't been hard to get. Henry eyed Gallagher. Gallagher was built like a blacksmith: broad of shoulder, wide of chest. Ashe would have difficulty with the sheer mass of him if Gallagher took him by surprise.

'Bedevere is not well liked by some,' Henry began. It wasn't a complete lie. His cartel certainly didn't like him. 'I have friends who would pay if you had friends who would be interested in a little fun at Bedevere's expense. After all, he's already had fun at yours.'

Gallagher looked thoughtful for a moment and Henry knew he'd been right. Gallagher wanted a bit of revenge and the only thing holding him back was the thought of taking on a peer's son. Henry pushed some of Trent's coins across the table. 'There's more where that comes from once the job is done.'

Gallagher pocketed the coins with a nod and left. Henry thought his day was vastly improved. A good drubbing wouldn't remove his cousin from the estate, but it would certainly slow him down and right now Henry needed time—time to court Genevra, time to work out how to gain a majority control of the estate's management.

Ashe was proving more difficult to dislodge than previously imagined.

It was most disappointing. Henry'd had it all worked out. He would wait a decent interval, court Genevra, marry her and settle at Bedevere without her being any the wiser as to the real motives behind his courtship. After all the time they'd spent together over the winter, it would seem a natural course of events. Henry had hoped his uncle would have settled full custodianship of the estate on him. Coupled with Genevra's fortune through marriage, he'd have been indisputably in charge. But nothing had gone as planned.

The terms of the will made his courtship look obviously avaricious. But if it hurt his cause, it hurt Ashe's, too—perhaps even more so. Four per cent would not nearly be as threatening to Genevra as Ashe's forty-five.

Henry took a final swallow. He would not be

thwarted by the matchmaking efforts of old ladies. He'd come too far, waited too long. He'd coveted Bedevere and its hidden treasures for years. He'd spent countless hours currying favour over the last months with the old earl. He wasn't about to let it go now nor the opportunities that came with it. If he could win Genevra, he could have it all.

There was always a chance she'd say no, but he'd deal with that when it happened. There were ways to make a woman say yes.

Chapter Nine

~~~~~~~~~

'Yes, Melisande, I loved your new design for hand-kerchiefs with the Bedevere family crest. Thank you for sending it over.' Genevra looked up from her work-space in the Bedevere drawing room, her gaze return-ing again to the scene outside the wide French doors.

There was nothing particularly lovely about the view. The day was overcast and the gardens were nothing but churned-up mud. String and pegs outlined spaces where something more substantial would later replace the expanses of dirt. It wasn't the view that drew her eye, but the man who walked among the plots, stopping occasionally to clap a worker on the back and talk, his hands pointing and gesturing.

The day was not especially warm. There'd been some wind when she'd driven over, but Ashe didn't seem to notice the cold. Ashe worked only in shirt and riding breeches, the sleeves of his shirt rolled up, and he wore no waistcoat. The lack of a waistcoat left him surpris-ingly exposed, Genevra noted. There were no illusions about what might or might not be under that waistcoat. Nothing prevented her from taking in the leanness of his waist, or the muscled length of his thighs beneath the dirt-smudged breeches. The sight of him working was really quite intoxicating—probably because it was the last thing one would expect of an earl's son. Or because it was the last thing she'd expect from Ashe Bedevere.

'Genni, dear, you've stopped cutting,' Lavinia said from the easel where she sat painting a pot of early primroses.

How long had she been staring? Apparently long enough for everyone to notice. 'I've been wondering what your nephew is up to out there in the gardens.' She might as well admit to it. It didn't sound so voyeuristic when she said it like that.

'He says he wants to get the gardens closest to the house organised for spring.' Melisande's voice held a tinge of excitement, her approval of the plan evident. 'It will be lovely to have flowers again and a place to walk. It will be just like the old days. I would give anything for one last summer in a real garden.'

Lavinia shot her a sharp glance. 'Don't be so maudlin, Melly, we all have plenty of summers left in us.'

'Of course you do.' Genevra turned from the window. 'We've got so many plans for the markets and things are already better.' She gestured towards the window. 'In fact, if you don't mind, I think I'll go out and see if I can give your nephew some advice.' If he was going to go forwards with his plans for the estate without consulting her, then it was time to talk. He could not treat her as if she were an invisible partner.

Leticia brightened at the prospect. Genevra could see the wheels spinning behind her blue eyes, none of it having to do with the conditions of the estate. 'By all means, Genni. I'm sure Ashton will welcome any input you can give him.'

Genevra picked up her fur-lined pelisse from the chair where she'd draped it and headed out to the garden, careful not to look back for fear of what she'd see: smiles of matchmaking satisfaction on the faces of four old ladies. She had no intentions of satisfying them on that account, although that left her with no small amount of guilt.

It seemed deceptive not to tell the aunts about her new role in the estate, but she could only imagine how their matchmaking efforts would blossom if they knew, to say nothing of how Ashe would exploit those efforts. Ashe would throw in with the aunts and manipulate their influence to its maximum, a potentially lethal combination.

Genevra stepped around pockets of squishy mud, gingerly navigating the terrain, much like she'd have to navigate their upcoming conversation. Both she and Ashe each had time to assimilate the results and those results of the will had to be discussed. He had started this work in the garden without her permission. If this went unaddressed, who knew what other larger issues he'd attempt to supercede her authority on?

Genevra lifted her skirts, barely missing a puddle of

mud. It was definitely much easier to appreciate Ashe Bedevere at a distance where one could afford to be entranced by the masculine beauty of his physique. Up close, there was much more than a pretty face to contend with: that seductive drawl of his, those eyes, those hands that knew just how to touch a woman, to say nothing of the man who played the piano so expertly, or who carried so many mysteries behind his green eyes—why hadn't he come back sooner? Why had he ever left in the first place? What had happened between him and his father? What had he been doing all these years in London? How did all of that factor into the decision to leave him only forty-five per cent of the estate?

Perhaps it was the hope of discovering answers to those questions that kept propelling her into the gardens. Perhaps it was just the thrill that came with being in his presence. His conversation carried an edge, everything around him seemed to vibrate with an energy waiting to be unleashed. For all his roguish airs, Ashe Bedevere was turning out to be the most excitement she'd had in ages, his forty-five per cent nothwithstanding.

Ashe saw her coming and moved towards her, holding out a hand. 'Here, Neva, let me help you over that so you don't slip. We can't have you twisting your ankle again.'

'Aren't you freezing?' Genevra took his hand, shivering underneath the pelisse.

'You don't feel the cold once you get moving.' Ashe shrugged. 'What are you doing out here?'

They were three sentences in and Genevra was thinking it might be the nicest conversation they'd ever had. She hated to spoil it with business just yet. 'I came out to see why you changed your mind. The last time we'd talked, you'd thought the gardens were a waste of time.'

'I had a change of heart, that's all. I can't very well entertain with Bedevere in this condition.' He was noncommittal at best, a sure sign he was hedging. Before she could respond, he tucked her hand through the crook of his arm and began walking. 'Come see what I've laid out. It's all very simple compared to your plans at Seaton Hall, just colourful flowers and trees really, but it's what can be managed this year with spring nearly upon us. Next year, I'll do more. Right now, I want to focus on the front drive and this space off the drawing room since that's what people are likely to see most.'

'We,' Genevra put in, stopping the conversation. 'You mean "we" should focus on the front drive.' She paused, letting him digest the import of that two-letter word. 'I am the majority shareholder in the estate, whether or not either of us likes that arrangement.'

Ashe turned to face her squarely, arms crossed over his chest. 'What exactly do you mean to imply by that reminder?'

Genevra met him firmly. 'You cannot randomly make unilateral decisions about the estate, to say nothing of the finances. I need to approve of any expenditures. You must know by now the estate's monetary resources are limited. We must make judicious decisions with the funds we have, *together.*'

'This is my home.' Ashe's tic began to work. His

short sentence said it all. He wouldn't tolerate being reined in like a recalcitrant schoolboy. Neither would he tolerate an outsider asserting her authority.

Genevra softened, laying a hand on his sleeve. 'I did not ask for this, Ashe. But we are in this together for the time being.'

'What do you want, Neva?' Ashe said in silky tones.

'I want to help you with the gardens.' If she could get a partnership out of this, she would be making progress. 'Tell me your plans. Your aunts are already talking about how good it will be to walk in the garden again.'

They turned a corner and the wind lessened. 'I want to make the aunts an outdoor room of sorts here, with roses and stone benches and comfortable places to sit where they can bring their work.'

Genevra stared hard at the man beside her. Where had *he* come from? This was *not* the Ashe Bedevere who sparred so seductively with words, who challenged her at every turn with his cynicism.

'What do you think, Neva? Will they like it?'

'Yes, I think they will.'

'And will you? Will you come and sit with them in the summer and do whatever it is you do?' There was a glimmer of his seductive self stirring to life in those green eyes. It was a softer version than she was used to, but seductive all the same.

'Of course you can help me with the gardens, Neva.' She was acutely aware of Ashe's other hand covering hers now where it lay on his arm. 'I meant to ask you the other day at the inn, but you were so set on refusing my proposition, I thought it best to wait.'

This had been his proposition? Genevra suddenly felt foolish beyond words. She'd given him quite a dressing down for a proposal she'd felt would be nothing short of scandalous and all he'd wanted was some help with his gardens.

She gave a short laugh and shook her head. She couldn't quite meet his eyes. 'You must think I'm a shrew.'

'I think you're a woman alone in the world. I think you've had to learn to protect yourself in the absence of anyone else to do it for you and I think you do an admirable job.' He spoke quietly, his finger tracing another of his circles on the back of her hand.

She looked up, able to meet his eyes this time. 'I think that's the nicest thing anyone has said to me for a long time.' She cocked her head and gave him a contemplative stare. 'Are we becoming friends, Ashe Bedevere?'

He laughed. 'I hope not. Women and men can't be friends, not for any long period of time.'

'Why ever not?'

'It's the sex, Neva.'

There was the Ashe she knew. Well, thank heavens, he wasn't gone entirely. 'That's too bad. I was hoping we'd be friends.'

'No, you're not,' Ashe replied in easy disagreement. 'Friendship is safe, Neva. It's a little interpersonal limbo you can live in somewhere between not acknowledging your attraction to someone and giving full vent to it. If I were you, I'd hope for something more. Now, before you cut up at me for that—I can see that you want to—come see the old fountain and tell me what you think.'

Just like that, the friendlier version of Ashe Bedevere was back, the *safer* version. There was a begrudging truth to what he said, Genevra thought as they trudged across the garden. The safe Ashe, the compassionate Ashe she'd seen today, talked of gardens and plans. The wicked Ashe talked of feelings and hard truths and things she didn't want to admit to herself.

The fountain was dirty and dry, the basin full of dead leaves from years of neglect. 'I know it's in bad shape, but I am hoping a good cleaning will help.' Ashe reached down and scooped out a handful of brown leaves.

Genevra nodded. 'If it's like the one at Seaton Hall, the hydraulics have been turned off. A good scrubbing and a look at the pipes will solve your problems.'

'I played a lot in this fountain as a boy.' The nostalgic quality of his tone caught her off guard. She turned to face him, trying to imagine this grown man as a small child.

'Did you have a boat?' She tried to picture him in a sailor suit.

'A ship actually, a four-masted schooner. It was my pride and joy. I spent hours sailing it. Sometimes, on warm days, I'd put my feet in the water.' Ashe bent down and scooped another handful of leaves out. 'I've not thought of that for years. Alex had a boat, too. Often times we'd play together and have glorious naval battles.' His voice trailed off, leaving his thought incomplete. But she could guess where his thoughts had gone, back to those happy days running around the estate with his brother and not a care in the world.

'Whatever happened to your boat, Ashe?'

Ashe looked away from her towards the fountain. 'Henry broke it.'

'On accident?'

'No, he broke it quite on purpose. Alex gave him a black eye for it.'

Genevra idly picked at dead leaves on the edge of the fountain. 'Is that why you dislike your cousin? Because he broke your boat?' She gave a quietly coy smile, but Ashe was in deadly earnest.

'There's not one event that made me dislike my cousin. It's a combination of many events. But Alex and I were always able to handle him.'

'You're a lot like your brother,' she murmured. 'He talked often of growing up here.' She hesitated at the last. Discussion of Ashe's brother was new ground and he'd been so touchy that night in the conservatory when she'd mentioned his father. But his reaction today was far different.

'My brother was here?' Ashe's eyebrows drew together in confusion.

Genevra nodded. 'Didn't you know? Your father kept Alex here after the breakdown. He was here when I arrived in the area last June. I gathered from the aunts that he wasn't physically incapacitated in any way, his mind had just gone somewhere else and not came back.'

She could see the pain in his eyes at the thought and rushed on to alleviate it. 'Alex was always telling stories about the two of you when you were younger.' She paused, her gaze going to an invisible point over his shoulder so she wouldn't have to look at Ashe.

He had to be told. If no one had told him, she had to. 'I think that's where his mind lives now, back there in his childhood with you. He liked the story about the time you climbed the apple tree and sat up there all day eating apples until your stomachs hurt.'

A brief grin flashed across Ashe's face. 'We'd been told to go pick the apples and we didn't want to, so we decided to eat them. We thought doing it that way would make it look like we'd picked them since there wouldn't be any apples in the tree for proof. We didn't count on the stomach aches afterwards. We were so sick.'

He drew a deep breath. 'Where is Alex now?'

'He's been moved to a private institution outside Bury St Edmunds. It's a nice place where they care for people like him. Henry thought it would be best,' Genevra said. 'I'm sorry you didn't know.' She could see it was an enormous surprise to him.

Her heart went out to him in that moment. For all his audacious behaviour and flirtatious ways, he wasn't without redemption. He loved his brother. Impulsively, Genevra put a hand on his sleeve. 'I could take you to see him, if you'd like.'

He nodded without words. 'Was Alex brought home for the funeral?'

Genevra shook her head. 'No, I offered to drive over for him, but there were so many other arrangements to make and Henry thought—'

Ashe exploded at that. His quiet reserve had become a storm. 'I do not want to hear the words "Henry thought." one more time.' Alex should have been here. He should have been here to say goodbye to his father. He should have been here always, he should not have been shuffled off to strangers or put out of the way as if he doesn't exist. This was his home. He was safe here.'

He bowed his head, his eyes shut tight. She could see the tic in his cheek jumping with a ferocious effort to hold on to his control.

'Mrs Ralston, please excuse me.' He did not wait for a response. He turned on his heel and walked away from her with a rapid stride that suggested he might not reach his destination before he broke. It took all of her will-power to not run after him. She'd had two glimpses into his depths and it was rapidly becoming clear to her that Ashe Bedevere was not all he seemed. Heaven help her, such a revelation only served to make him that much more irresistible. A rake with a soul was a rare thing indeed.

Chapter Ten

How had it come to this? It wasn't the first time he'd asked himself the same question since his return. Ashe wanted to kick something, punch something, do *some* violence, so great was his anger, his outrage, his grief. But there was nothing to hit, nothing to break in the vast openness of the Bedevere parklands. All he could do was run and he did, just as soon as he was out of Genevra's sight. Boots weren't the best shoes for running, but Ashe shoved the discomfort aside and ran, letting the wind take his hair and bathe his face, letting his legs pump up and down in rapid motion in the fleeting hope that the activity would keep his emotions at bay for just a little longer.

Everything he'd kept so carefully tamped down inside him since his arrival was threatening to break loose. Hell, it wasn't threatening, it *had* broken loose after all this time. He'd held on to his control long enough to get out of Lady Hargrove's bedroom, long enough to get home, long enough to take stock of the situation. But his time was up.

His feelings, those things most of London believed he did not possess, would have their day. He hadn't had them the day he'd faced Lord Longfield at twenty paces over an accusation made at cards. He hadn't had them when he'd cut off Lord Hadley's curricle coming around a sharp curve in a dangerously mad race that could have seen him dead. But, by God, he was having them now.

Ashe had no conscious idea of where he was headed, only that he was headed away: away from Genevra Ralston and her grey eyes that saw too much; away from his gentle aunts who looked to him for support; away from Henry and his treacherous coveting; away from Bedevere and the responsibilities it posed.

Aimless as his mad journey was, he wasn't surprised when his feet stopped running to see he'd arrived at the one place on Bedevere property he hadn't been yet—the domed mausoleum. Ashe braced himself with an arm against the stone sides of the structure and bent over, trying to gather his breath. The intensity and the distance of the run had left him winded. He hadn't run out here since he'd been in his teens. He and Alex used to play out here when they'd been younger, and later they'd raced out here in friendly competition.

His breath gathered, Ashe sat down on a stone bench placed at an angle for better viewing of the mausoleum. It was a handsome building with its dome and Palladian columns. A regal resting place for generations of Bedevere males, generations that went back long before the Bedeveres were earls.

Ashe supposed that might be why he was so attached to being 'Mr Bedevere'. It had always been the family's name, just as this house had always been the family's house, although other properties had presented themselves with the earldom. In the great scheme of history, the title of Audley was relatively new come to the family, the earldom only four generations old. But Bedevere had been around nearly as long as England. Growing up, he and Alex used to fancy they were related to Sir Bedevere, who'd sat at King Arthur's fabled table. *That* probably wasn't true. But who knew? The remembrance began to calm his roiling emotions.

He wasn't ready to go inside yet. Ashe reached for a small piece of wood on the ground and pulled out his knife. He whittled while he sat, letting his thoughts wonder along whatever paths they preferred to take. Pride had done this. The real Bedevere legacy was the stubborn Bedevere pride. The same pride which had driven his great-grandfather to build an earldom was the pride which had driven Ashe from home at the age of twenty.

No doubt it was the same pride which had perhaps persuaded his father at the last to gamble with Bedevere's future. Unwilling to admit his prodigal son had not returned in time to make amends and unwilling to admit defeat in the face of economic disaster, his father had found a way to defy traditional law and push

Bedevere towards the future, uncertain as it was. It had been an enormous gamble.

His right hand began to ache from the knife work and Ashe flexed it out of old habit. The cold weather and the rough work outdoors this week, even with gloves, had aggravated it. He hadn't done his hand any favors these past few days with letter writing and gardening and playing the piano. Usually, regular activity didn't bother it, but regular activity in London was something of a subdued nature compared to the 'rigours' he'd encountered out here.

Ashe held out his hand and slowly turned it over, palm side up. A thin, pale-white line bisected the palm, a mark nearly invisible after eight years, but not forgotten. Pride had done that too.

Ashe huffed a sigh, his breath swirling like a mist in the cool air of late afternoon. His body was cooling, too. He shouldn't stay out much longer in only a shirt. He brushed his hands against the thighs of his breeches and stood up. It was time to do what he'd put off doing since the moment he'd arrived. It was time to go inside and pay his respects.

There was a certain finality to seeing a life etched in stone, chiselled into a three-line biography for descendents to linger over: name, title, date of lifespan. That finality was not lost on Ashe as he entered the marble-floored mausoleum and followed the dates to the most recent row. His father was there, of course, marked by a polished marble plaque containing the dates; February 7th, 1775–January 25th, 1834. Ashe raised his hand and traced the chiselled numbers, emotions rising. This was why he hadn't come out earlier—not because he hadn't cared, not even because he'd been busy with other important things to do for the estate and for the living. The dead could wait after all. They weren't going anywhere—but because he knew once he got here, he'd break down.

He was right.

Ashe backed to the wall where a slab for sitting had been cut in marble blocks. He sat hard, feeling the hot sting of tears behind his eyes and then he gave himself permission to do what he hadn't done in a decade.

He wept.

He wept for being too late to say goodbye. He wept for Alex, for a neglected home, for a ruined hand and a ruined dream, for all the things that might have been in a more perfect world where dreams and sons and fathers could co-exist. And when he was done, he would be ready to face again the imperfect world that was.

It was dusky-dark when Ashe stepped outside, one of his favourite times where night met day. Daylight hovered on the hem of the horizon while early stars poked their brilliant heads through the night fabric of the sky. He looked up at that sky and drew a revitalising breath and stiffened before he could exhale. Someone was here.

With reflexes honed from too many years spent in the alleyways of gaming hells, Ashe bent swiftly to retrieve the knife in his boot. He palmed it and called out.

'It's me.' A dark figure rose from the bench and stepped forwards, the clear shape of a woman becoming evident.

'Neva.' Ashe sighed and replaced the knife. 'You startled me. I wasn't expecting anyone to be here.'

'Obviously.' She shot a wry glance towards his boot where the knife was sheathed. 'I brought you this.' She held up his coat. 'When you didn't come back, I got to thinking you might be cold if you stayed out too much longer.'

Ashe shrugged into the jacket, appreciating its warmth. 'Thank you. How did you know where I'd be?'

'It wasn't hard to figure out,' Genevra said softly, those grey eyes once again seeing more than he wanted to reveal.

'Your father would have liked to have seen you again,' Genevra offered quietly as they began the long walk back. Her arm was tucked through his for balance so she wouldn't trip over the uneven ground in the growing dark.

'I'm not sure I agree. I might have hastened his decline,' Ashe said truthfully. 'I think sometimes the living require absolution more than the dying.'

'Absolution comes in many forms.'

The words brought Ashe to a halt. It occurred to him in those moments that loss and forgiveness were things she would understand. The conflict fuelled by his father's will had obscured her humanity. She was more than the physical embodiment of 'fifty-one per cent', more than someone to be manipulated.

'Is that why you're here? Is Staffordshire your absolution, Genevra?' She was a young widow, a woman who had lost a husband not long after their marriage and most likely in sudden circumstances, so goodbyes had not been possible. He thought of her comment earlier about his need for atonement. Had she guessed because of her own?

She turned away from him. 'I suppose it is,' she said quietly. 'Seaton Hall is more than absolution, it is a redemption of sorts, a redemption for other women.' She paused here and Ashe waited for her to go on. 'I haven't told anyone yet, but I plan to make it a business *and* a home for women who have no place to go and no means to support themselves. Once the place is renovated, I'll look for women to come. They can give tours, tend the garden, put on teas. I think it's the perfect genteel business opportunity.'

'Like my aunts selling handicrafts at the local fairs?' Ashe murmured with a smile.

'Yes,' Genevra replied staunchly. 'Everyone needs to have a purpose, to feel useful. No one wants to be a thing. No one wants to be helpless.'

The statement spoke volumes, Ashe thought, although he could not imagine Genevra tolerating being minimised. 'Did you love him? Your husband?'

Her husband. Philip Ralston. A handsome bounder who'd convinced a young girl he was desperately in love with her.

Genevra looked down at the ground, studying her

feet as they began walking again. She seldom spoke of Philip to anyone but perhaps Ashe would see now the kind of resistance he was up against. Philip had ruined her for marriage. She would not risk walking that path again. She was not that naïve. 'I suppose I did in the beginning before I saw him for what he was.'

'What was that?' Ashe prompted softly.

'A man who loved my money far more than he loved me, only I was too young to know it.' Even after the distance of time, it was still hard to admit that awful truth. 'My father tried to warn me, but I was too stubborn to listen.' Genevra shrugged and gave a half-hearted laugh. 'It sounds like a Gothic romance, doesn't it? Rich girl falls victim to a fortune hunter. It's hardly original.' There was more to it, of course, but she wasn't ready to share the sordid details. She didn't want Ashe's pity. It was time to move the conversation on to a different track. She'd reached the limit of what she wanted to disclose.

'I have to confess there's another reason I came out looking for you. Henry is staying for dinner. I thought you'd want to know in advance.'

Just like that, the brief magic of the evening faded.

Chapter Eleven

It could have been worse; not the most stunning accolade to attach to a dinner, Genevra thought. But at least Ashe hadn't thrown anything at Henry beyond words and vice versa. She'd been more than glad to make a hasty retreat to one of Bedevere's quiet sitting rooms and spend the remainder of her evening with a book.

She'd not planned to stay overnight, not after having so recently made a return to Seaton Hall, but the weather had conspired against her. The moderate breeze that had accompanied her drive over this afternoon had become something rather more by nightfall. Why not stay? the aunts had argued. There was no one expecting her at Seaton, and no plans that demanded her immediate attention, so here she was, tucked away with a book and hoping for some peace, something that had been in short supply since the earl's death and Mr Bedevere's arrival.

Genevra tucked her legs beneath her and opened the

book, a posthumously published edition of Ann Radcliffe's *Gaston de Blondeville*.

'Genni, there you are. I've been looking all over for you.' Henry's convivial tones broke her concentration on page five. Genevra fought the urge to let her shoulders sag in disappointment.

'Hello, Henry.' She looked up and smiled, pushing back her more uncharitable thoughts. It wasn't Henry's fault, not specifically anyway. She'd come to Staffordshire to avoid male attention and here she was with a fifty-one per cent share in an estate and two cousins circling like vultures, waiting for her to decide what her role would be in all this.

'I'm not interrupting, am I?' Henry pushed off from the door jamb and sauntered over. She wondered what he'd do if she actually answered the question.

'Of course not.'

Henry took the chair next to the sofa and pulled it forwards. 'I've been wanting to talk with you for ages, but I haven't been able to catch you alone.' He smiled boyishly, his golden hair falling across one eye. He brushed it back. 'I even went into the village on your shopping day in the hope of catching you, but...' his voice trailed off and he shrugged. 'Seems my cousin had beaten me to it.' He furrowed his brow. 'Has my cousin beaten me to your affections, Genni? Have I erred by playing the gentleman too long?'

She feared where this conversation was headed, but she'd known it would happen since the will had been read. 'Your cousin has had more important matters on his mind than flirting with a neighbour,' Genevra said lightly. It was almost true, except for that kiss in the conservatory, or the incident in Audley Village.

Henry leaned forwards in a pose of earnest. 'I must warn you about him, Genni. You don't know him like I do.' He paused. 'I know you were with him that day in Audley Village. I saw you come out of the inn and he came out a few moments later.'

'People can have tea together in a public setting, Henry,' Genevra laughed it off.

'It's never just tea with him, Genni. Do you know what he'd spent the night doing? He spent it gambling on billiards.'

That explained the stale smell of smoke and ale on him. Well, she shouldn't be surprised. She'd thought as much, but the confirmation was still disappointing.

'Genni, he's been home for a handful of days, supposedly to mourn his father and take up some form of an active role in the estate. Instead he was gambling. He's a rotter through and through, Genni.' Henry sounded genuinely aghast, perhaps a bit too much. Genevra had the fleeting notion he would do well on Drury Lane with that expressive face of his.

'Henry, I think you make too much of it,' Genevra said softly, but she wasn't convinced of that, or of Ashe being entirely a 'rotter'. She'd had glimpses of a far nobler man beneath the roguish exterior. 'I think, too, that you misjudge him. He's beside himself over his father.'

Henry snorted at this. 'Don't be misled, Genni. He could have come home sooner and maybe none of this would have happened. Now, he wants to waltz in here and claim *all* of the estate after the rest of us have propped it up in his absence.'

Genevra heard the vehemence, the envy in Henry's words. 'What of you, Henry? What do you want to claim? I don't believe Ashe is the only one with an agenda. You were upset the day the will was read. You expected more?'

'I want you, Genni.' Henry fixed her with a strong look. 'I don't care about estates. I want you and if I sound angry it is because I see you slipping away from me, slipping towards Ashe. I know I should wait a decent period before I ask, but I find I cannot risk it. If I wait any longer, I fear Ashe will steal you from me.' There was another of his dramatic pauses. She was starting to become truly annoyed by them.

'He's stolen a girl from me before, you see. There was a girl, the daughter of gentry. They're no longer in the area. I was seventeen and I was in love. We walked out a few times together, did all the things that typify young love: strolled the summer fairs, sat together at local socials. But Ashe was home from Oxford, older, richer and he took a fancy to her.' Henry shook his head. 'How could I compete with an earl's son, even a second son? I was just the nephew, visiting for the summer with a modest inheritance.

'I would protect you, Genni, from being his next victim. I would not see you thrown aside when he was done with you.'

'I don't need protecting, Henry. I can take care of

myself. But thank you for the concern.' Genevra picked up her book, signalling she'd like to start reading again, a sure dismissal. But Henry would not be daunted by the subtle manoeuvre.

'I am not asking to protect you, Genni. I am asking you to marry me. I meant it when I said I wanted you, only you. I've grown fond of you in our months together and I find that none other can compare. I'm twenty-seven and it's time to be looking to my future. I want you in that future.'

It was a pretty speech with all the requisite elements of a decent proposal—an expression of affection, of sincerity and an allusion to the acceptability of his prospects—although both of them knew she was the one with the prospects if they wanted to live beyond his mid-sized manor farm.

'Forgive my surprise, Henry,' Genevra began delicately while she searched for the right words. 'I had not realised your affections had transmuted from those of friendship.'

'I could make you happy, Genni. You're far too young to be alone in this world for the rest of your life. Surely you cannot mean to remain a widow for ever.'

'I am flattered, Henry, truly I am. But now is not the time for me to be thinking of marriage. I have Seaton Hall to finish at the very least,' Genevra hedged.

Henry smiled good-naturedly. 'You sound like you're not sure?' He reached for her hand. 'We can take things slowly. We can always announce our engagement and wait until you're ready. We should wait, anyway, with the funeral having been so recent, so you needn't feel awkward about it.'

If she'd been a different kind of woman, a woman who craved the respectability and security marriage brought with it, she would have taken Henry's offer. He was good looking, possessed of a certain charm. Some woman, somewhere, would be thrilled to marry Henry Bennington, but that woman wasn't her, not at the present at least, although she doubted that would change.

'Your offer is generous, I just can't accept at present,' Genevra said. Something stirred at the door and she looked past Henry to see Ashe in the doorway. He'd only just arrived, unlikely to have overheard the conversation, but the look on his face was thunderous. She could imagine how the situation appeared to him—Henry sitting close, her hand in his grasp, Henry looking earnest.

'I was on my way to read some post.' Ashe fixed her with a piercing stare. 'Gardener informed me a letter of some importance arrived late this afternoon from London.'

Was she supposed to have known about the letter? His look suggested he suspected she did. She had no energy left to play 'divine the secret message in my gaze'. She'd had to work too hard with Henry. Genevra rose with her book. 'I think I'll retire. Goodnight, gentlemen.' She felt Ashe's hot eyes follow her out the room. As exits went it was of the same calibre as dinner—it could have been worse.

* * *

But that didn't mean sleep came easily. The wind howled at her window and her thoughts rambled around in her head, conspiring to keep her awake well after midnight.

What had the old earl meant by leaving her such a controlling influence in the estate? She was happy enough to offer her ideas on boosting the estate's productivity and happy enough to even offer a loan. She didn't need fifty-one per cent to do that. Surely the earl had known she would have done all that anyway? But he'd given it to her none the less and now she had to honour that position by not letting Ashe Bedevere exclude her from estate business.

Only it just wasn't about the estate. She was drawn to Ashe Bedevere against her better instincts. It had been easy to refuse Henry. He had been a companion, but nothing more. He didn't stir feelings to life in her that were hot and dangerous. She didn't want his kisses, didn't want to probe the depths of his mind. But Ashe had merely to enter into a room and all of her attentions were riveted on him, as he'd so aptly demonstrated tonight.

She knew all too well how such a reaction could cloud her judgement. Ashe was most assuredly a rake, a character trait that would normally not earn him any points with her. But then there had been glimpses of a far deeper, far more decent man beneath that roguish exterior and the combination was potently compelling: the noble rogue. The woman in her wanted him unabashedly, but the business side counselled caution against such rash behaviour.

Genevra threw aside her covers. This was the second sleepless night she could lay at Ashe Bedevere's feet. She grabbed a dressing robe and belted it with determination. Mrs Radcliffe's novel had not accomplished its purpose. Perhaps there was something more suited to her temperament in the library. She grabbed a candle and headed downstairs.

The library was dark and she set the candle down to light a lamp, letting the larger lamp throw its glow on the walls. She trailed her hands over the book spines, pulling out one book after another, none of them satisfactory. Even the novels held little appeal. She decided on *Waverly* and turned to go, only to discover she wasn't alone.

A little shriek of surprise died on her lips as she recognised the broad-shouldered frame standing in the door. 'You scared me, Ashe.' An odd thought occurred. 'How long have you been standing there?'

'Long enough to know you had difficulty making up your mind.'

Genevra was glad for the protection of her robe. No doubt he'd been standing there long enough to know she was indecently clad for such an encounter too.

He advanced. 'Having difficulty sleeping?'

'Yes.' She swallowed hard, glad her voice hadn't cracked. He was a decadent wolf by lamplight, his green eyes glittering. He took the book from her hand and studied the cover. '*Waverly?* He marries the baron's daughter, the coward.' Ashe set the book on a nearby table.

'I've read it before.'

'Then you know what motivates our hero's choice. He chooses the safe course with Rose instead of the passionate way with Flora.'

Genevra was about to respond with a defence of Waverly's solid choice but Ashe silenced her with a finger pressed to her lips. 'I did not come down here to debate Waverly's notion of good choices. And we both know it's not the reason you're here searching for a book after midnight.' Challenge flared in his eyes daring her to gainsay him.

'Exactly what would that reason be?' Genevra answered in haughty tones.

'Henry's proposal has unnerved you,' Ashe asserted boldly, his eyes watching her intently for any tell-tale sign of remorse or happiness.

So Henry had told Ashe. 'I wish he had not mentioned it.' Genevra idly fingered the spine of the book where it lay on the table. 'Nothing will come of it.'

'He meant it as a warning for you and me both. Did Henry tell you how despicable I was? Did he fill your head with tales of my decadence?' Ashe had stepped closer to her during the conversation. He laughed now in the darkness, a deep, sensual chuckle.

'He did mention your reputation was less than pristine in that regard.' She was aware of his closeness, of the smell of him, clean and appealing even after a long day. Her body was starting to stir.

'I will not respond in kind by slinging arrows at Henry's reputation. It can prove itself on its own merits, which I am sure it will do given enough time.' There was an edge to Ashe's voice that implied one should be sceptical of Henry's golden-boy charm.

'I am not looking to make a marriage, not to Henry or to anyone else.' She might as well be clear on that matter with Ashe from the beginning.

'Not tonight anyway.' Ashe laughed at her defiance. 'That doesn't mean we can't explore other interesting avenues of association. Unless, of course, you are indeed committed to Henry? Are you, Neva? Are you and Henry secret lovers? Secret conspirators?'

Ashe had not liked seeing them together and he'd drawn his own conclusions. He was daring her to prove it was otherwise. 'I decide for myself. Neither Henry nor you have any claim on me,' Genevra asserted, although her body knew the latter statement to be something of a lie. Ashe did claim her attentions in a way that transcended their connection through the estate.

Ashe's long fingers reached out to stroke a cheek. 'And what have you decided, Neva? Have you decided to allow yourself the pleasure of a night? It is too late to deny it. I see the desire in your eyes, and not only tonight. I've seen it before, in the conservatory. I intrigue you and you intrigue me. I would gladly give you the one night your body is asking you for.'

Genevra whetted her lips, weighing the invitation against the challenge. Already, in the midst of this little quarrel, her body was rousing for him, her mind excited by the possibilities he promised, her curiosity provoked by Henry's insinuations about Ashe's reputation as a lover.

What would it be like to be with a man such as Ashe Bedevere, who would give pleasure without extracting a price? He was promising a moment out of time, a moment outside of the life she'd so carefully cobbled together after Philip. Maybe if she leapt, the nobler Ashe Bedevere would be waiting on the other side. That would be a man worth leaping for.

Ashe tipped her chin upwards, taking her mouth in a most decadent inducement of a kiss and she accepted, *Waverly* forgotten. Who needed a paper hero, when she had Ashe Bedevere very much in the flesh and blood and a chance for just one night to throw caution to the wind?

Chapter Twelve

Ashe released her long enough to shut the library door, the snick of the lock bringing with it a finality in the silence. Decisions had been made, consent had been given. Genevra gave the ribbon that held her hair a swift tug, letting it fall loose about her shoulders.

'Lady Godiva.' Ashe's voice was hoarse with anticipation. He crossed the room in a slow approach, giving her time to drink in the enormity of what she was about to do. His own hair was loose, creating the impression of a dark mane, framing the sculpted planes of his face, highlighting his eyes.

He did not stop beside her, but went on to kneel in front of the fireplace giving her a glimpse of his backside as he laid a quick fire. He was still dressed in his shirt and trousers from dinner, enough to be considered in dishabille, but wearing entirely too many clothes for Genevra's preferences at the moment. Then he turned and faced her, his hands at the waistband of his trousers as if he'd read her mind. In a fluid, cross-armed motion,

Ashe pulled his shirt over his head. Genevra sat down hard, suddenly aware of the chair that met the back of her knees. He was not a man to appreciate standing up. In the firelight the contours of his torso were like a map leading downwards to that most obviously male region of him. Her hands itched to trace those lines to their logical conclusion.

His hands drew her gaze once again to the waist-band of those damnable trousers. He pushed his trousers down lean hips, past muscled thighs that spoke of years in a saddle.

She clutched the arms of the chair, vaguely aware that her mouth had gone dry as all this glorious English manhood was revealed slow inch by slow inch. He gave a quick flick of his foot and his trousers were off. Completely. It occurred to her briefly that such a skilfully effortless undressing was not accomplished without practice—lots of practice. But tonight she didn't care. Tonight, he would be hers and in the morning there would be no complications because they both understood there couldn't be, not with the estate between them.

'Come, Neva,' he coaxed from the fireplace, hands on his hips, his index fingers pointing ever so subtly to the jut of his phallus. 'It's your turn—I want to see you naked.'

She rose, suddenly shy, her fingers fumbling with the sash of her dressing gown, acutely aware she'd never disrobed quite so deliberately for a man before, or stood naked before one. To undress deliberately was erotic and powerful. Ashe's eyes were hungry for her. It had not been like this with Philip. She pushed the thought away. There was no place in this interlude for his intrusion. This was her moment of pleasure. She was due this.

'No, wait. Not yet, I've changed my mind.' Ashe moved towards her, closing the small distance, enviously comfortable in his own nakedness and clearly unabashed by the noticeable proof of his arousal. Ashe placed a finger on her lips when she would protest and drew it down the base of her neck.

At his touch, heat pooled low in the cradle between her legs. He could excite her so easily. His hands found the belt of her robe, letting the halves of it fall away before he pushed it back from her shoulders.

He turned her gently, putting her back to the fire, his breath catching. 'Firelight and lawn becomes you, madam.' He did not take her gown immediately, instead he traced her against the flame, making her aware she might as well be naked already for all the covering the fine material of her nightgown afforded. He cupped her breasts, drawing the material taut against her nipples, the light friction of the fabric beneath his thumbs eliciting a tender ache that sought fulfilment. But she knew instinctively fulfilment would not come yet and that knowledge in itself fuelled her arousal.

Genevra arched against him and he knelt before her, his hands framing her hips, his thumbs massaging the low bones of her pelvis in deliciously tantalising circles not unlike the ones he'd drawn on her hands. He looked up at her, green eyes blazing, and she felt her power. She was Venus in that moment, her supplicant worshipping at her feet, seeking only her pleasure. It was heady ambrosia indeed, but nothing compared for what Ashe did next. He kissed her through the thin fabric of her gown with all the reverence due a goddess. A sharp arrow of heat sang through her, a moan of want escaping her lips.

'Sit down in the chair, Neva and spread your legs for me,' Ashe commanded, no longer the supplicant, but the wolf. There was an undeniable thrill in what he asked, in being vulnerable and exposed before him. He knelt again and pushed up the material of her gown until it bunched at her waist. His hands gently skimmed the soft skin of her thighs, his thumbs stroking the softer folds of her womanly places.

She trembled, her body begging. Then he lowered his head to her, no longer the supplicant or the wolf, but something in between: the seducer, the lover, the pleasure-giver. His breath was warm and welcome at her juncture and she sighed from the sheer delight of it. Then his tongue flicked across the tiny secret nub of her and all delight fled, replaced by something more intense, more overwhelming than anything she'd known and she was drowning in it. Her hands were in his hair as if, by holding on, she could drive him deeper into her and resolve the search for fulfilment. She was vaguely aware of thrashing now as the ecstasy began to take her, his hands strong and firm at her hips, steadying her until at last she broke against him with a sob that sounded more like a scream.

Ashe rose and gathered her to him, his arms about her, his hands stroking her back in a gentle rhythm while she recovered. He took her down to the floor after she'd quieted and they lay in stillness, her head on his chest, his arm about her, tracing shapes on her back. But he was by no means done with his seduction. His own need had not yet been slaked. His phallus rose firm and insistent in the firelight, the flames dancing on the crystal bead of moisture at its tip.

Genevra sat up and pulled her nightgown over her head, arms extended, ready at last to be naked, to have nothing between them. This was heady new ground. But if the night had taught her anything, it was that she'd known nothing of passion until now. What had passed between her and Philip had not been this. It had been fumbling and harsh. It had lacked all the beauty and release that Ashe had shown her and she was hungry for more.

Ashe's eyes were on her, as hot as any flame, watching her discard the gown. 'You're beautiful,' he whispered. 'I could look at you all night.' His hands mirrored his words, reaching up to push her hair over her shoulders so that no curtain hid her breasts. He rose up on his knees to meet her, taking her breasts in his hands, kneading them ever so gently, his thumbs circling the aureoles. His mouth found hers in a kiss that spoke of slow sensuality.

'We are like Adam and Eve in the garden,' she whispered.

'Discovering each other,' Ashe replied. The desire

in his eyes had changed from a primal smoulder to a deeper flame. They were getting to the core of the fire, the place where the flame of passion burned more fiercely now that the initial wildfire had been subdued. There was time now for exploration.

Genevra pushed lightly at his shoulders, signalling she wanted him to lie down. 'It's my turn.'

Ashe gave her a lazy wolf's grin. 'For a while.'

She started with his chest, tracing his aureoles, watching his flat nipples pucker in response. 'Is it the same for you, I wonder?' She'd hardly been aware she'd spoken out loud until she heard Ashe give a throaty laugh. His hand came up to capture hers.

'It's not nearly as stimulating. I don't mind it, of course, it's nice, but it's not as arousing for men.'

Genevra gave a little pout. 'I feel sorry for you then. You're missing out.'

'Men have other spots, my dear.' He guided her hand lower, mischief in his eyes. 'If you're willing, there are those who believe a man's sac is his sensual equivalent to a woman's breasts. I happen to be among their number.'

Genevra complied, marvelling at the weight of them in her hands. She gave them a gentle, experimental squeeze and was rewarded with a moan. There was joy here. She'd never taken a man in her hand before, never known he could be so open to pleasure, that this love-making could be a congress of equals.

His phallus beckoned and she moved her hand to

cover the sparkling tip and began a slow journey up and down its length.

He bucked hard against her once. 'I think it's time, Neva. I won't last much longer. Rise up over me, take me inside you.'

Her eyes widened at the exotic nature of the challenge. How amazing. She had not guessed. She hesitated for the briefest of moments, but Ashe was there, taking himself in hand and guiding her on to him, a wondrous 'ohhh' escaping her as he slid home. This was incredible indeed, to be able to look at him, to watch him as need took them both. His hands were at her hips, guiding her into a rhythm, her body aware of the pressure building in her once more as it had done in the chair. Release would come. She wanted to hurry it along, wanted to feel that blissful emancipation one more time.

In a sudden remarkable move, Ashe gathered her to him and rolled, taking her beneath him, their bodies not parting. Above her, the same pleasure captured him. It wouldn't be long until they were both there together. Once, twice more, she shattered and somewhere in the prism of fractured sensations, he shattered with her.

Ashe waited for the sensation to pass, waited for the momentary physical peace to fade all too soon as it always did. Tonight, it was being gloriously stubborn. It was lingering and he was happy to bask in its unlooked-for afterglow.

Beside him, nestled against his body, Genevra dozed, naked and satiated beneath a throw he'd managed to

pull down from the chair without rising up and disturbing her rest. She'd been a sensual marvel, an intoxicating mixture of bold experience and shy reserve. It was
a combination even the most practised of courtesans
could not replicate. It was insightful, too. Her husband
had failed her.

There was no issue of virginity between them, but
virgin or not, she had been untutored. He would wager
his last pound she was not trailing a string of sundry
lovers behind her. Her knowledge had not been as fully
formed as her willingness. Yet she'd taken his instruc-
tion eagerly. He knew a particular manly thrill in having been the one to instruct her on finding her pleasure.
Whatever experiences had preceded him, none had
equalled him, of that he was certain. He was counting
on that now to override her misgivings about marriage.
Tonight didn't have to exist in isolation.

Bedding an heiress was a tricky business when one
was a poor man. They were not impressed by baubles
and trinkets. They could buy enough of those on their
own. The only currency he had here that carried any
value was the pleasure he could give.

Ashe pushed such sordid thoughts aside. Yes, he had
to think about winning her, but, no, tonight had not
been entirely about that. He'd found pleasure aplenty
with her that far superseded plans and calculations or
any of the physical enjoyments he'd found in the arms
of London's more adventurous ladies.

Tonight had been about acting on an attraction that
had sizzled since the moment he'd seen her. It was a

balm to his post-coital conscience that, Bedevere aside, he would still have wanted to bed her and most definitely would still have tried. He was not in this alone either. Even without the complications of Bedevere, she would still have wanted him, would still have chosen to be with him.

But Bedevere *was* involved. Ashe knew he was betting heavily on the pleasure they'd found to count for quite a lot in the morning light, not the least being the contents of the envelope that had arrived from London.

Ashe hated himself immediately for the thought. Had he really fallen so far as to use sex as a tool to coerce a woman into a marriage of convenience? If so, what did that make him?

Genevra stirred in his arms, her body warm against his as she dozed, so very unsuspecting of the turmoil in his mind. He reminded himself it was all for a good cause. But when would the ends stop justifying the means?

Chapter Thirteen

'Genevra, would you like to tour the estate with me, this morning? The weather has turned out to be fairer than expected after last night.'

Genevra's fork stopped halfway to her mouth, shirred eggs dangling dangerously in mid-air. Had any man in the history of the world used those words to follow up a mad night of passion? *Would you like to tour the estate?*

'I need to get out and see the tenant farmers and assess their needs before spring planting gets underway,' Ashe continued from the sideboard, piling a plate high with eggs and sausage.

He was doing so much better than she at pretending last night hadn't happened. Then again, he hadn't been the one to wake up on the library sofa. He'd been gone when she'd woken. But she couldn't argue with that. It was the right thing to do. The English had protocol for everything. He couldn't very well be discovered sleeping on the floor with her. It would be far easier for her to explain having fallen asleep on the sofa should an early-morning maid walk in to build up the fire.

'Genni is just the right person, Ashton,' Leticia put in from her place at the table. 'She knows everyone. She'll see to it that you're introduced. Everyone will be glad to know it's business as usual at Bedevere.'

'I would be glad to go,' Genevra said because there was nothing else to say without looking querulous. Leticia was right. She would be the best person for it, she'd ridden out several times during the old earl's illness, but she didn't relish spending the better part of the day riding around on a bench seat next to Ashe.

There would be too many reminders of the previous night. Even now it was hard to look at him and not remember the decadent things he'd awoken in her. It was probably no less than she deserved. There was a reason curiosity killed the cat. She'd satisfied her curiosities and now she knew exactly what it was like to be with Ashe Bedevere. Those exquisite moments would be for ever etched in her mind, on her body, for the rest of her life, for better or worse.

'What are you going to do today, Henry?' Genevra asked, turning the conversation a different direction in hopes of distracting her thoughts.

'I have a meeting,' Henry offered vaguely. He made a great show of taking out his pocket watch and checking the time. 'In fact, I am nearly late. If you'll all excuse me, I need to go.'

Ashe put aside his napkin. 'We need to make an early

start as well. I'll call for the gig and have it brought around in twenty minutes.'

Genevra couldn't help but notice the aunts smiling at one another as she left to go change. No doubt this was a prime opportunity in their eyes for her and Ashe to spend time together. Perhaps they were already thinking Ashe was showing signs of interest by extending the invitation to join him. The poor dears would be shocked if they knew the truth.

'We should talk about last night.' They'd barely turned on to the road, Bedevere still visible behind them.

'We both know what last night was.' Genevra kept her eyes fixed on the road ahead.

'What was it?' Ashe said coolly.

'Two people satisfying their curiosity about each other, I think,' Genevra replied.

'A curiosity that could have resulted in a child. Surely you didn't overlook the fact that we took no precautions,' Ashe pressed.

'I very much doubt it. Before my husband died, we'd resigned ourselves to a childless marriage. It is unlikely I'll conceive.'

'I do love American bluntness.' Ashe's voice carried an edge to it. They went over a deep rut in the road and the gig lurched heavily. Genevra grabbed Ashe's arm to steady herself.

'Well, there's no sense mincing the truth and I won't lead you down a path I know to be a dead end.'

'Still, I think it must be considered. Infertility isn't always the woman's fault. Men don't like to admit it, of course. Should your hypothesis be proven wrong, Neva, I would want to know.'

It had been on the tip of her tongue to say something cutting such as, 'so you can trap both of us in a marriage neither wants', But intuition struck and kept her silent. Is that what he wanted? Did he want control of Bedevere so badly he'd risk a child to force a marriage? Would he doom himself to a relationship he didn't want? Of course, it wouldn't be a hardship for him. He'd marry her, leave her at Bedevere and return to London for his mistresses and entertainments.

Genevra spoke in sober accusation. 'You promised last night didn't have to mean anything beyond pleasure.'

'So I did.'

But it occurred to Genevra as they pulled up to the first cottage, that this was a promise Ashe Bedevere might not be able to keep.

The day sped by, filled with faces and names. Ashe shook hands with farmers, toured their fields, met their wives and children. He made list upon list, overwhelmed at the need. There were roofs to repair, fences to mend, farming implements to replace. Everyone he met was polite, but Ashe had a growing sense that things had not been taken care of at Bedevere for a very long time. The guilt he'd fought since arriving flooded back. This was his fault.

He would have to make it right somehow. He was starting to suspect making it right would involve swallowing his pride. There weren't enough billiards games in the county to bankroll these improvements. He was going to need Genevra's money.

Meeting with the shopkeepers in the village went better. Ashe positioned himself outside the inn, setting up a hasty plank 'table' across barrels and ordering ale for those who wanted to sit and talk.

One theme emerged regularly in those conversations. Business had been slow since the farmers had less money to spend, merchants were worried about their revenues. The item on their minds was the annual St Bertram's festival. Some believed it would help bring additional revenue to the village while others thought they ought to forgo the festival out of respect for the old earl's passing.

Ashe smiled. The festival of St Bertram had been a regular occurrence in Audley Village since nearly time immemorial. He and Alex had enjoyed the festival as boys. 'Is it still the first week of June?' Ashe asked, quelling the growing discussion with his question.

'Yes, and it's still the largest local fair in these parts,' the owner of the tavern put in, bringing another round of ale.

Ashe looked over the heads of the men gathered at his makeshift table. He spied Genevra with a group of women, someone's toddler on her lap. She was never very far away. She looked up, having heard the talk of the festival. Ashe chuckled to himself. She was probably already calculating how many handkerchiefs and jars of jam she could sell, God bless her American sense of entrepreneurship.

'I think the festival should go on as planned,' Ashe declared. 'Summer is a time of renewal and Bedevere is ready for that. A new time has come.' Never mind at the moment he was responsible for only forty-five per cent of that new time. No one needed to know that except he and Genevra.

Over the seated crowd, Genevra's eyes met his and she smiled her approval. It was gratifying and surprising to feel pleased at having obtained her favour, but Ashe felt them both. It had been a long time since he'd allowed himself to care what anyone thought about him or what he did. But he was caring now, a definitely new sensation.

'You made a good choice today,' Genevra offered once they'd completed their visits and turned the gig towards Bedevere. 'The festival will mean a lot to them and it's well positioned right at the end of spring planting.'

Ashe nodded, his attention only partly on the conversation. The gig seemed to be listing slightly to one side or perhaps it was his imagination and too many ales this afternoon. Too many ales? Really, the thought was laughable. He'd been in the country too long. He was Ashe Bedevere. In London, he could drink all night and not feel the effects. He doubted four ales in the middle of the afternoon was responsible for this.

Perhaps it was the road. There were ruts aplenty, left-over from winter snows and rains. 'Alex and I used to love the festival, we played all the games. Alex was a crack shot with a pistol. I don't think he lost a shooting contest since he was fourteen. Our father was so proud.'

'What about you?' Genevra ventured. 'Were you a pistol man, too?'

'No, I was a knife man.' Ashe smiled as he bragged. For the first time since coming home, it felt good to talk about the past, about his family. All those years alone in London, he hadn't realised just how little he spoke of them. 'Whatever Alex could do with a gun, I could do with a throwing knife. I wouldn't be surprised if there isn't a box of ribbons still tucked away in the attics. Our mother saved everything.'

'Your mother?'

'Yes, I had one, you know.' Ashe joked.

'It's just that no one ever mentions her,' Genevra replied quietly.

'Well, she's been gone a long time.' They were back to more painful memories now. It was more fun to talk about the festival. 'She died in a boating accident when I was seventeen. Alex was nineteen. She had been vis-iting friends over in Trentham and they'd gone out on the lake.' Her death had marked the beginning of his troubles with his father. Without her to act as a buffer between them, he and his father had failed to manage their disagreements. Not even the presence of the aunts could mitigate those quarrels.

'I didn't mean to stir up sadness.' Suddenly the gig

lurched. Genevra grabbed for the side railing of the bench, barely keeping her balance. 'That must be some rut we hit,' she gasped, recovering her seat.

Ashe shook his head. 'We would have seen a rut that big. Do you think the gig is riding lopsided?' The words were barely out of his mouth when there was a final lurch and the little cart crashed, turning on its side and taking them both to the ground.

Ashe's first and only thought in the time it took for the accident to happen was Genevra. She would take the brunt of the fall. Whatever had happened, happened on her side of the vehicle. He grabbed for her, trying to break her fall, trying to roll with her out of harm's way. Only the weight of the horse still in the traces prevented the gig from rolling once more on top of them.

'Are you hurt?' Ashe asked briskly, staggering to his feet.

'Nothing mortal, I'm sure.' Genevra replied in shaky tones, but Ashe noted she was slow to rise.

'Stay here, I'll see to the horse,' Ashe ordered. The sooner the situation was stabilised, the safer they'd be. Fortunately, the horse had had the good sense to remain still after the initial excitement of the accident passed.

'Steady there, old girl,' Ashe called out softly, taking the horse by the harness. From the horse's head he could survey the ruin. The back wheel had come off. It lay shattered in the road not far from the remains of the gig. They wouldn't be using the gig again. Ashe quickly freed the horse from the traces and led the mare away from the wreckage.

'I've got transportation!' he called down to Genevra, trying to make light of the situation. She smiled up at him and managed to get to her feet. 'Can you take the horse while I look at the gig?'

There was no reason the wheel should have come off and he wanted a better look at the hub and axle before it got dark. Ashe bent down for a closer look. He found the culprit immediately. The wheel had been loosened. It had simply rolled right off the axle itself.

'Neva,' he called out, 'did you ever take the gig out or my aunts?' It would be interesting to know when the gig was last driven and what kind of regular maintenance it was given.

She nodded. 'We used the gig for the summer and autumn fairs. We drove it quite a lot. But we haven't had it out since December.'

'No troubles with it?' Ashe stepped back from the wreck.

'None. What is it?'

'The wheel came off.' In itself that wasn't uncommon. But it was a rather bizarre occurrence for a vehicle that had been driven regularly without mishap and then lain unused for only two months. It was hardly long enough for the equipage to go to rack and ruin. Wheels simply didn't come off carriages without a little help.

It made one wonder what kind of help might have hastened the wheel's departure from its axle and Ashe didn't like the speculations he came up with or what they might mean.

Chapter Fourteen

Genevra didn't like the look in Ashe's eye one bit when they arrived back at Bedevere. The stare he gave her when she slid off the back of the horse and announced she'd be returning to Seaton Hall was proprietary and unyielding.

'I think you should stay,' Ashe said tersely. He'd been silent most of the way home, speaking only to enquire if she was all right. 'I want to speak with our groom and then you and I need to have an overdue discussion.' She didn't like the sound of that any more than she'd liked the look.

'I think I should go.' Staying would mean another night at Bedevere, which might lead to another night with Ashe. While there were appealing aspects to such a prospect, that had definitely not been part of the bargain she'd made with herself last night. Last night had been a moment's pleasure, a curiosity satisfied, but not to be repeated.

'Go inside and freshen up. I'll be along shortly. Try not to alarm my aunts.'

He was deliberately ignoring her request. Genevra's temper over the high-handed treatment rose. 'I will not be dismissed in such a manner,' she countered.

Ashe's eyes glinted dangerously, green coals waiting to ignite, his voice a low growl of authority. 'Yes, you will, temporarily. If you want to cut up at me, you can do so in the estate office in a half-hour.'

There would be no winning this. Genevra drew a deep breath to still her temper. She would temporarily cede the field. But she'd be waiting.

Ashe was prompt, early even. He was the one waiting for her in the office. Sitting behind the big polished desk, he looked every inch the peer's son. Even though time had been short, Genevra noticed he'd managed to change into clean attire. Looking at him, one would not guess he'd been in a carriage accident a scant two hours ago. She hoped she looked as well put together. There'd been time only to change her dress and re-pin her hair.

'Was your talk with the groom satisfactory?' Genevra took the seat on the visitor's side of the desk, feeling very much the supplicant come to beg crumbs from his lordship's largesse. She would not be intimidated by the big desk and the handsome man sitting behind it. For heaven's sake, she was a businesswoman. But all her mental protestations could not deny the flutter in her stomach when she looked at Ashe Bedevere.

'Somewhat,' he replied enigmatically. His tones were cool, exuding authority. He was going to be stubborn, she just knew it.

'I don't think the wheel was an accident, Genevra.'
Oh, this was serious. He wasn't calling her Neva. She
braced for the storm that was sure to come.

'The groom said the gig was in good shape when he
harnessed the horse. The groom confirmed what you'd
told me, that you had used the gig quite regularly and
it had not been sitting idle. The groom also said no one
had been near it this morning except himself. Which
makes sense...' here Ashe paused with a chuckle of
derisive laughter '...since we no longer employ a full
complement of grooms.'

Genevra furrowed her brow. 'All that seems to support the wheel *was* an accident, which, I might remind
you, is the exact opposite of what you postulated moments ago.'

'You Americans are too impatient. Let me finish.'
Ashe waved a long, elegant hand. 'What it means is
that someone tampered with the wheel while we were
in the village. The gig was out of view during part of
our visit. It would have been easy enough to do. There
would have been no one around, everyone was gathered with us.'

'All right.' Genevra folded her hands in her lap. 'If
that's true, why would someone do it?' She thought
Ashe was seeing villains where there weren't any. His
conclusion was somewhat extreme.

Ashe fixed her with one of his hard stares. 'You're
the one with a jilted suitor and fifty-one per cent controlling interest in an estate. Why don't you tell me?'

'Henry? You think Henry did this?' Genevra said in
disbelief. 'He was at a business meeting all day. I doubt

he knows the mechanics of a carriage wheel to begin with. Your cousin's a book man. He's hardly the type to get his hands dirty.'

'He's the type to pay someone to do it for him,' Ashe said succinctly. 'I don't think Henry did it himself, but I think he is likely behind it.'

Genevra shook her head. 'You're seeing the worst because you don't like him.' It was absurd really.

'Sometimes our eyes deceive us.' Ashe's long fingers fiddled with a paperweight, tracing the lines of cut glass. 'Forget about Henry's golden good looks and that boyish smile of his. Think about the facts, Genevra. You saw how angry he was when Marsbury read the will. He'd clearly expected more. He's tried to get more by proposing marriage to you. You've refused him and effectively scotched his last avenue to gaining nominal control of the estate—'

'You're spinning out of whole cloth, now, Ashe,' Genevra interrupted. This was silly. 'Why would he go to all that trouble for an estate that will not be his once Alex dies? Whatever he gains will only be temporary. You'll be the earl eventually.'

'Unless I die first,' Ashe drawled. 'Henry needs Alex alive. Whether Alex lives or dies, Henry can still wield control. Right now, it's better if Alex lives. As long as I'm alive, Alex is safe. Henry doesn't want to risk me inheriting because his control of the estate, meagre as it is, goes away.'

Genevra's quick mind grasped the implications. 'But if you're dead, Alex isn't as useful to Henry.'

'No, then Alex becomes expendable. He becomes more of an obstacle, the only obstacle that prevents Henry from having complete control and the title, too.' Ashe got up and pulled open a drawer in one of the glass-fronted bookcases lining the wall. He pulled out rolled paper and spread it on the desktop, holding it down on each end with paperweights.

'Come have a look, Genevra, and get your first lesson in English inheritance law.' Genevra rose and stood next to him, studying the lines he traced with his long finger.

'Here's my father, Richard Thomas. He has two sisters, Lavinia and Mary. Lavinia never had any children. Mary, Henry's mother, made a disappointing marriage to local gentry, Steven Bennington. They both died several years ago, leaving Henry a small property. That leaves my father's line. He's the earl. He marries, he has two sons, all seems well.' Ashe's hand traced the lines leading to his name and Alex's. 'But now Alex is mentally incapable and there's just me. Henry is next in line as the next male of the family line as the only nephew of my father.' Ashe shot her a wry look. 'As you can see, it's a fabulous game of live and let die.'

'It doesn't convince me Henry's a murderer. It just convinces me that primogeniture is complicated,' Genevra argued.

'A man's life hinges on its protocols from the moment he's born.' Ashe rolled the parchment up and put it away. 'What a man can and can't be is tied up with his birth order.' There was great hurt, a gaping chasm behind Ashe's comment. For a moment, the authoritative aristocrat gave way to the enigmatic man she'd glimpsed beneath his urbane surface.

Genevra smiled softly. 'In America, we believe a man can be anything he wants.'

'And yet you left such a land of promise.' The harder side of Ashe had returned. He motioned for her to take her seat. 'I think the point of this conversation has escaped you. Allow me to spell it out. I am in danger because I stand in Henry's way. You have refused his proposal and, by doing so, have effectively shut down his last avenue of legitimate recourse for gaining control of the estate. You are now in danger as well. If we're both eliminated, Henry gains control of our shares. What he can't accomplish through marriage, he can now accomplish only through death.'

Genevra scoffed at the notion. 'I am thankful I don't have your imagination for the morbid. Do all Englishmen sit around and daydream up myriad ways of how their families could dispatch them? What a paranoid lot you must secretly be.' She rose to go. She'd had enough of the ridiculous.

Ashe stood too and reached for her arm across the desk. 'We're not finished, Genevra. Sit down.'

'I want to get home before dark,' she protested.

With his free hand Ashe pulled an envelope from the desk drawer and tossed it on to the polished surface. 'You might feel differently after you read this.'

Genevra sat down, sceptically eyeing the letter. It was the one that had arrived from London yesterday.

A cold knot started to form in her stomach. 'Your office has the most interesting things in its drawers,' she remarked, unfolding the letter. 'Family trees, letters from London.'

'We're very thorough,' Ashe said drily.

'I can see that,' Genevra replied with equal coolness, her eyes scanning the crisp white paper. The opening sentence boded ill—'the woman in question…' which no doubt was her. He'd had her investigated.

She read the letter in quiet rage. 'I have nothing to fear from this letter. My husband is dead and that has been settled for quite some time.'

'Nothing except quite a lot of scandal should all the details be unearthed. His death was not quite as simple as stepping out in front of a dray and being run over by a twelve-hundred-pound draught horse.'

No it wasn't. He'd come home the night before in a drunken rage, blaming her for another failed business venture. He'd smashed stained glass and china. He'd come after her, too, until she'd feared for her safety. She'd spent the night at her father's. But in the morning he'd come for her, hungover and dishevelled and begging for money again. That was when she'd threatened the divorce and two of her father's men had to physically remove him from the house. She'd stood on the front steps, watching it all happen. They'd been rough, throwing him on to the street, and he'd cursed her and stumbled to his feet, only to step out backwards into a busy Monday-morning street full of delivery carts.

His family blamed her of course. They said she might

as well have pushed him herself. She'd provoked his distraught mentality. He hadn't been in his right mind, they said. She'd wanted to scream he hadn't been in his right mind for some time.

'Now you know the truth.' Her tone was icy as she laid the letter on the desk. 'You wanted to know what I was doing here—now you know. Is the truth gratifying to you?'

Ashe was unfazed by her quiet anger, which was most unsatisfying. He just sat there, looking at her with those green eyes. 'You're right, you have nothing to fear from that letter. There is nothing criminal there. But there is scandal. That scandal could be potentially embarrassing should it come out.'

Genevra clenched her fists. 'If you mean to blackmail me with this, you are a far worse rogue than I first believed.'

Ashe shook his head. 'No, I don't mean to do anything with it. I want you to realise that if I can get this information, Henry can too. I don't promise his motives will be as pure.'

Genevra's eyebrows raised. 'Pure? Perhaps you'd like to outline your motives so that I might better understand your application of pure?'

'Leave it alone, Genevra. It's enough I didn't mean any dishonour by it,' Ashe cautioned.

'No, I will not leave it alone. You had me investigated, behind my back. You will tell me why.'

'I wanted to know if Bedevere was in any danger from you,' Ashe said shortly. 'I wanted to know if you had misled my father in any way, hoping for a piece of the Bedevere pie.'

Genevra paled. 'You thought I was a fortune hunter.' She covered her mouth with a hand in abject horror. He'd implied as much in the conservatory that first evening. But hearing the words spoken so blatantly was different. It was the worst thing he could ever accuse her of being.

'I did not mean to distress you,' Ashe said. He might as well have said, 'I told you so, I told you to let it be.'

'You don't understand, Ashe,' Genevra said quietly, mastering her temper. 'You just accused me of being the very thing I abhorred in my husband.'

Well, that had gone poorly. Ashe raked his hands through his hair. No doubt Genevra was upstairs right now, packing her things and preparing a retreat back to Seaton Hall and all its dropcloths and new-paint smell. He couldn't blame her. For a man skilled in seduction, he'd certainly bumbled this. Ashe folded the letter up and put it back in his drawer.

He'd only meant to show her the danger of secrets. If Henry knew this, he could easily use it to blackmail her into marriage. This would be a scandal she'd want repressed. It could hurt business with her shipping line and it would certainly hurt her socially if she decided to enter London society at some point. Henry would not hesitate to use it as leverage.

But Genevra hadn't believed him about Henry. She

didn't think him dangerous. That was the problem. No one ever did until it was too late.

Gravel crunched on the front drive and Ashe looked out the long windows. Genevra's carriage was ready. She hurried down the front steps and the carriage pulled away. She was gone. For now. His body protested her leaving. There wouldn't be a chance now of coaxing a night of passion from her. Last night had been extraordinary, far more than a physical seduction. He'd thought of little else all day. Even while he'd listened to tenants and shopkeepers, part of his mind had been on her.

The women of the village admired her. Their approval had been evident in the way they'd gathered around her, showing her their babies and taking her into their circle. Ashe didn't think Genevra had been without a baby in her arms or a toddler on her hip all afternoon. Whenever he'd looked over at her, she'd had a child with her.

Babies raised a whole other issue. Ashe was convinced his father meant for them to marry. Had he known Genevra believed she couldn't have children? Marrying Genevra meant the end of the Bedevere line. Assuming she was right, of course. There was no question of Alex siring an heir. Any heirs would have to come from him. It would be something of an irony to sacrifice himself in marriage to save Bedevere only to have no one to save it for. But perhaps the present was more important than the future.

Marrying Genevra was fast becoming the only solution available, not only for Bedevere's well-being but for her own well-being, even if she wasn't willing to see it. He hoped it wasn't a lesson she had to learn the hard way. Marriage to him would put her out of Henry's way. She would no longer be an obstacle to the estate, all the authority would now lie solely with him. If Henry wanted Bedevere, he'd have to go through him to get it, and him alone. That meant he had to protect Alex, his aunts and perhaps most of all Genevra, whether she wanted his protection or not.

Chapter Fifteen

His week was up. Genevra had refused him and Henry thought Marcus Trent was taking the bad news rather well. Henry shifted in the deep leather armchair across from Trent's desk, trying not to prematurely breathe a sigh of relief. It was just he and Marcus today. The others were blessedly absent.

Marcus leaned forwards, elbows on the cherrywood desk. 'Then it's time to not play nice, Henry. Everything is in place for our venture. We're merely waiting for permission from the estate to start the mining process. Either we get that permission through marriage, or through some other means.'

'Some other means', Henry very well knew, meant fatal accidents. Trent's cartel had been involved with other ventures that had got off to difficult beginnings until certain 'coincidences' had marginalised or eliminated those who had been difficult. Here was a chance to impress Trent with his forward thinking.

'My cousin has offended a few men in Audley. He

won money from them at billiards. One of those men was more than glad to arrange a carriage accident when Ashe was in town this week.'

Trent's reaction wasn't quite what Henry had expected.

Trent raised bushy black eyebrows. 'And by doing so, you may have tipped your hand prematurely, Mr Bennington. In fact, it may have been downright foolish of you at this stage of the game.'

'But you just said it was time to stop being nice,' Henry sputtered in argument before Trent silenced him with a look. One did not argue with Marcus Trent.

'Violence isn't the only way to coerce,' Trent said with a pointed look. 'While you've been failing to secure our heiress, I've been researching. Mrs Ralston was of little interest to me before your uncle's death, but circumstances have demanded I pay attention to her.' He touched his temple with his index finger. 'Lesson one, Mr Bennington, is to always know one's opponent. What are their weaknesses, what are their strengths? Mrs Ralston's weakness is her past, as is most people's. Have you ever asked yourself why a rich American would come to Staffordshire and bury herself in the country when she has enough money to go anywhere and do anything?'

No, he'd never wondered. Genevra had simply presented herself as a widow looking to make a new start away from America. Up until this week, he'd assumed a new start would include a new husband. But apparently she had no proclivity to marry again. That had been a surprise. Didn't all women want to marry? Even rich ones? He felt foolish now. Even when she'd refused him, Henry hadn't thought about the reasons why.

Henry's silence was answer enough. 'I can see the thought didn't cross your mind. Thankfully, for all of us, it did cross mine.' Trent gave him a patronising smile. 'My sources in London tell me her first marriage was nasty and her husband's death nastier. She stood on the front steps and watched two footman all but shove the poor blighter into the path of an oncoming delivery dray. He was killed instantly.' Trent shook his head as if in disapproval. 'I'm certain it wasn't *exactly* like that. But still, if such aspersions were to get around, it would be damaging for her.' He slid a brown paper envelope to Henry. 'It's all in there. I think Mrs Ralston might find marriage more palatable, especially if it ensured permanent protection from such rumours.' Trent cocked his head. 'She's not indifferent to you, is she, Bennington? I thought you'd said the two of you were good friends.'

'No, she's not indifferent,' Henry lied. His pride could not bear to admit otherwise.

'Good. She might be amenable to such an overture coming from a friend. But I wouldn't wait too long, Mr Bennington. I hear your cousin was seen with her in town.' Trent leaned back in his chair, studying his nails.

'This is your chance, Mr Bennington, for revenge. Steal his woman, steal his estate. It's what you've been waiting for all your life and I am serving the opportunity up to you on a very nice platter.'

Henry nodded his thanks and rose to leave. Trent was indeed providing him an invaluable service. He was well aware that Trent's plans, Trent's consortium, Trent's money had greased the way this far in the plan to mine the wealth of Bedevere. He was also aware Trent wasn't a man who gave such favours for free. Trent would receive a fair share from the mining venture, but Henry couldn't help but wonder if Trent was after something more. Henry pushed such deep thoughts aside. Perhaps it didn't matter. Trent was entitled to play whatever games he liked as long as Henry got what he wanted and that started with an afternoon call to Genevra.

Bad news was supposed to travel in threes, but the post proved it could travel in twos just as effectively. Genevra's hand shook as she set down the two letters. Neither was good. Henry had sent a note asking permission to call that afternoon.

In light of the note's tenor and his recent behaviour, she was beginning to rethink the reasons for Henry's sudden desperation. Lately, Henry had been far too keen on pressing a friendship into something more even after she'd tried to scotch those efforts as politely as she could. Henry was a changed man since the earl's death and she worried what he might intend by requesting this meeting.

The second note was from Ashe and it had arrived only hours after her return on stiff cream-coloured paper bearing the Audley seal. The wording was for-

mal; Mr Ashton Bedevere wished to call tomorrow afternoon on Mrs Genevra Ralston at her convenience
to discuss a proposal of mutual benefit to them both.

If the note had come from a different man, or under
different circumstances, she would not be worried. It
would be perfectly understandable that he'd want to
speak of business and the estate, maybe even to discuss
the use of a loan. After a week of assessing the situation,
the usual man would be ready to embrace the realities
of their partnership. But she did not fool herself into
thinking Ashe was the 'usual man' and that meant she
had no idea what he wanted with this request to call.
They'd parted in anger over an issue that had been part
business in its origins, but had quickly become personal
in its outcomes.

Genevra looked at the hands of the clock. It was
barely eleven. She had two hours. All she could do
now was wait and perhaps change her dress, a small
but useful distraction.

Genevra had dressed carefully in a dark-blue receiving gown trimmed in white lace. Her maid had
arranged her hair in a sophisticated twist, creating the
image Genevra was looking for: a respectable woman,
confident in her own abilities. She had just put on her
tiny pearl earrings when Henry was announced. She
smoothed her skirts and drew a deep breath. So it began.

Henry waited for her in the drawing room, looking
polished and well groomed in buff breeches and a coat
of blue superfine. His gold hair was brushed to a fine

sheen and he'd brought her flowers, a rare treat in the last weeks of winter.

Genevra took the flowers, wary of what they might be a prelude to. 'They're lovely, Henry. I'll have them arranged in a vase and set them in here. They'll look beautiful in this room. Wherever did you find daffodils so early?'

'A friend of mine has a hothouse,' he supplied with a glib smile. 'The house is coming along splendidly, Genni. Are there other rooms that are done as well?'

'My bedroom and the kitchen. But the downstairs is scheduled to be completed within the month.' Genevra sat and smoothed her skirts. The conversation felt stunted.

Henry must have agreed. He cleared his throat. 'Thank you for agreeing to see me. Might we sit?' He looked eagerly towards the chairs, his nerves apparent in his stiff manners. He was playing the anxious suitor once more to perfection. The realisation hit her again as it had her last evening at Bedevere—Henry was quite a role player. What other roles had he played over the course of their association? The friend? The loyal nephew rushing to the side of his ailing uncle?

Genevra marvelled that she hadn't seen it before. Henry was a consummate actor. She'd seen his many faces, but she hadn't yet really seen him. The realisation stung with the tang of betrayal. If it was true, he'd willingly duped her and duped the aunts. The only one not taken in had been Ashe. Genevra knew a moment's alarm. If Ashe hadn't been taken in, did that mean Ashe was right in his less savoury conclusions about Henry as well?

'Genni, this is more difficult than I thought,' Henry began and her sense of alarm ratcheted up a notch. 'I know that you refused my initial offer of marriage, but I have hopes you'll reconsider in light of new information that might change your circumstances.' He said the last gently with the tones of the friend, but his eyes held a hard glint that belied the tenor of his voice. She was learning to read him, to see the little chinks in his façades she should have seen before, but for which she had no cause to suspect.

'What new information, Henry?' She fought the urge to clench her hands in her lap. This revelation worried her greatly, but she dare not show it. Ashe's warning came back to her: if Ashe could discover her secret, what was there to stop Henry from doing the same?

Henry lowered his eyes, seeming to debate with himself over the words to use. He began slowly as if he still grappled for words. 'It has come to my attention that your husband's death is surrounded with unsavoury details.'

It was Genevra's turn to assume a role. She looked down at her hands. 'His life was unsavoury, it is no surprise his death was, too.' Henry would have to make his accusations more blatant than that if he wanted to scare her. How brave would Henry be?

'The unsavoury details are about you, however.' Henry pushed in a spurt of boldness. 'I am sure you would not want to fall victim to such rumours even if they were unfounded. Through marriage to a respected family, you would be protected from such nasty repercussions. No one would dare to gainsay the Bedeveres.'

So Henry knew. It was quite enterprising of him really, and highly out of character for the man she'd thought she'd come to know over the winter. Genevra gave him a sharp stare. 'Are you trying to blackmail me into marriage, Henry?'

'Genni! How can you think such a thing?' His shock appeared genuine, or perhaps it was embarrassment over having been called out on his improper game.

'Well?' Genevra pressed. 'Let's call it what it is. You were politely refused and now you think to regain your position through less palatable means.'

Henry rose, his face suffused with anger, his jaw stiff. 'I came here to make you an honourable proposal of marriage and you treat me like a dog.' He slapped his gloves against his thigh in a gesture of agitation. 'Has my cousin already poisoned you against me? I warned you he would, but that warning, like my offer, has fallen on deaf ears,' Henry sneered. 'Maybe you think to wait on an offer from Ashe, the great Mr Bedevere himself. You'll probably get one. He's that desperate to hold Bedevere against me. He didn't care a jot for the estate until he discovered I had a toehold in it. He'll marry you, for Bedevere, for money, but not for love. He'll never be faithful. He's a tomcat if ever there was one. I don't think you're the kind of woman who could tolerate that, yet when I offer you a decent marriage, you scoff at it.'

Genevra rose. This angry Henry thought to intimidate her with his height. She would not scare so easily. She kept the low table separating the chairs and the sofa between them. 'I'd like you to leave now,' she said in even tones.

This Henry-chameleon who stood before her disturbed her with his ability to switch in and out of roles so adroitly. This Henry was a stranger to her and one she did not trust. He'd come here the suitor, but had abruptly become an angry man.

Henry advanced on her, the table proving to be a useless barrier. There was no place to go. Genevra squared her shoulders. She reminded herself there were servants about.

Henry's hand reached out to caress her cheek. 'You're the answer to Ashe's prayers. He wants to marry you for the money and the estate. He'll bed you and leave you. But I would protect you from that and whatever else, my sweet.'

Genevra slapped his hand away and repeated, 'I'd like you to leave now.'

'You can't make me, though.' Henry's blue eyes glittered with a hard cruelty as he dragged her to him with a fierce grip about her waist. Genevra struggled.

He gave a cold smile and held her fast. 'Perhaps if you had a taste of what you'll be missing you might change your mind about marriage. I can make it good for you. Ashe isn't the only lover in the world.'

Genevra shoved at him hard, fists pummelling his

chest, but she gained little ground against him. She'd not realised how strong Henry was.

'Leave the lady alone, Henry. She's made her intentions clear, as have you,' came a dangerously cold voice.

Ashe.

Henry let her go so swiftly she nearly fell to the sofa. 'This is none of your business.'

'A woman in distress is always my business. We seem to have done this before, Henry.' Ashe moved from the doorway to the centre of the room, his eyes locked on Henry although his words were for her. 'Are you all right, Neva?'

'Yes.' She was breathless, watching the two men circle one another. Her drawing room was too small for the both of them. She had visions of her newly redone room being smashed to bits.

'You do remember the squire's daughter, don't you, Henry?' Ashe said in cool, mocking tones.

A knife appeared out of nowhere in Henry's hand. Genevra stifled a scream, but Ashe was fast. In the same fluid move she'd seen at the mausoleum, Ashe retrieved his boot knife. It stalled Henry momentarily.

'Quite the equaliser, Coz.' Ashe was all cold focus as he palmed his knife. 'I'm not afraid of a fight. I believe I won the last one.'

Oh, lord. They were going to fight over her, with knives, in her drawing room. She did not want this, but she was powerless to stop it. She was no coward, but only a fool would come between two men with knives. Genevra stifled a gasp and retreated as far back on the sofa as she could lest she become a casualty of the cousins' war.

Henry's gaze shifted a fraction. 'This is unseemly conduct for a gentleman and I will not engage in it.' It was a coward's strategy, taking refuge in the high road.

Genevra breathed a bit easier. If Ashe had any sense, he would give Henry this polite *congé*. Ashe sheathed the knife back in his boot and gave Henry a hard look that chased him from the room without even a goodbye.

It was only then that Genevra realised Ashe had come to call looking resplendent. White breeches were tucked into high black boots polished to a gloss. His greatcoat was brushed with buttons polished, and, beneath it, a blue coat trimmed in heavy gold braiding graced his broad shoulders. A ruby stick pin was stuck in the snowy cravat that peeped elegantly over the vee of a silk waistcoat. The sight was breathtaking even under these circumstances.

Ashe noted her lingering gaze. 'Wearing my station, as the expression goes.'

Ah, and setting the tone of the meeting as well. From the formal note to the formal attire, he meant for this to be an official visit, which worried her even more. What could he mean by this?

'My apologies, Neva.' Ashe made her a short bow. 'A beautiful woman often brings out the worst in men.'

'As does money,' Genevra said with a certain sang-froid now that she'd recovered her wits. 'I'm not naïve enough to believe you and Henry were fighting over me.' No, they'd been fighting over her money with the knowledge that whoever controlled her controlled Bedevere. It was something they'd all known, now it was out in the open.

Ashe remained undisturbed by her declaration. He settled himself in a chair and fixed her with his mossy eyes. 'Good, then you will understand why it is now absolutely imperative that you and I marry with haste for our mutual benefit.'

Chapter Sixteen

'Do you believe me now about Henry?' Ashe asked once the shock had left her face. 'Henry will blackmail you down the aisle, all for his own avarice.'

'Then that makes two of you,' Genevra said coldly.

'I will not be classified with the likes of him.' Ashe's tic began to twitch at her words. 'I come to you with honesty. He came with protestations of love and the trappings of romance, both of which are a lie. A man in love does not importune a lady the way he did today. I am hiding nothing from you, Neva. I am not masking my proposal as anything more than what it is, a business venture. Once I am legally in control of Bedevere's trusteeship, Henry will have no reason to bother you. You will be safe. You will be a countess-in-waiting for your efforts.'

Painted like that, it sounded like a very tempting offer indeed until one remembered all that Ashe gained in exchange: money and control of his estate and control over her. She was in England now. Their marriage laws when it came to property rights for women were very different. Marriage to an Englishman would demand some compromise on her part.

'Such an offer demands the surrender of my freedom,' Genevra challenged.

'It secures your protection,' Ashe countered.

He was crazy to think she'd give up her freedom to a man she'd known barely a week. Then again, she'd kissed him on the acquaintance of a few hours and had done much more on an association of days.

'I hardly know you,' Genevra stalled.

Ashe gave her a wry smile, his eyes half-lidded. It was a sensual look that said he knew her secrets. 'You know enough, I think, to know marriage to me would hardly be an onerous chore.' Genevra felt her face burn at the reference to their one night, a night that wasn't supposed to matter.

'Think about it, Neva. How will you thwart Henry on your own? Even if you manage to escape the repercussion of his nasty rumours, he will come again, next time with violence perhaps. Actually, there is no perhaps. He came with violence today, you saw that. What he cannot take by subtle manoeuvres, he will attempt to take by force. Henry is a predictable creature.'

'That is no reason to trap ourselves in marriage.'

'It's only a trap if you don't see it. There is no trap for us, Neva. We know exactly what we're doing and exactly what we'll get.' Lord, he was silky toned and his arguments as slick as an eel. It all seemed so probable, so sane when he laid it out like this. But in the end, it all came down to one thing—did she need protection from Henry's threats badly enough to risk her freedom? No, that wasn't fair. There was more than protection at stake, there was an estate to consider as well. It had been given into her care. What would serve it best? Uniting with Ashe or remaining his adversary?

'You and Henry seem to think I have only two options: him or you. There is a third option, however. I could turn over my shares to you, leave Seaton Hall unfinished and go live somewhere else. I could wash my hands of the entire mess your father left behind.'

It was an empty threat. Even as she spoke the words, she knew it would be leaving too much: leaving her dream of helping other women become independent, leaving the aunts and walking out on her promise to the old earl. In sum, leaving would make a hypocrisy of all she thought she'd stood for. She could not make others independent if she could not do that for herself.

'I think you torture yourself unnecessarily, Neva. You'd never have been with me if you hadn't trusted me.' Ashe reached for her hand, pressing a kiss to her knuckles and then turning it over to press a slow kiss to her palm. The fires started to stir, challenging her objectivity, her reasons.

Henry's warnings rang in her head—Ashe was a tomcat, he'd never be faithful. Most certainly he'd not pledged to be any of those things today. He'd pledged only to be a source of pleasure and protection. Yet when he kissed her hand like that, she wanted him to be so much more even while she knew he saw this marriage as nothing but an expedient means to an end.

There was a wicked gleam in his eye as Ashe relinquished her hand as if he knew he was gaining ground.

Genevra rose and began to pace, trying to re-establish her objectivity. Henry had tried to force her compliance today—he might even have been behind the carriage accident. She had to admit that sawed spokes weren't accidental. Henry was a desperate man. Could she really expect to stay in Audley and remain unscathed from his efforts? 'It's not exactly the kind of marriage proposal a girl expects to hear.'

'Can I take that as a yes?'

There was no choice. If she meant to stay in Audley and see her plans to fruition, if she meant to stop running, she would need help. Ashe had proven most willing and able to offer protection today without protestations of love. That had to count for something. So, for the sake of her dreams, for the sake of a promise to a dying earl, Genevra said, 'Yes, I suppose you could.'

'I am well honoured by your acceptance,' Ashe said with a stiff formality required of the occasion. Inwardly, he breathed a little easier, but only a little. He would truly celebrate once the marriage was done and Henry was no longer a threat to her or to Bedevere. It had angered him beyond measure to see Henry's hands on her when he'd arrived and the anger had been surprising.

Ashe recognised it would have infuriated him no matter who the woman was. He might be a profligate rake, but he only dallied where he was welcome. Henry, on the other hand, knew no such restraint. But the anger that had rocketed through him today had been different, it had been deeper, more possessive, and it had shocked him with its ferocity. Henry had been accosting *his* wife-to-be. Ashe had known relief when Henry had drawn a blade, it had given him an excuse to draw his own and let go some of the feral energy coursing through him.

'Neva, there is a last thing I'd ask of you. I'd like you to accompany me back to Bedevere so we may tell the aunts our good news. They will want to make plans—it will be best if you're there to guide them.' He gave her a conspiratorial wink.

Genevra answered with a smile that softened her whole face, 'They don't know about the will, do they? They will think this is a love match.'

He leaned back in his chair, stretching his long legs, ready to do some teasing now that his initial anxieties had passed. 'Yes and yes. But I think we can offer a reasonable facsimile of their expectations, don't you, Neva?'

She favoured him with a blush. For all her sharp wit and shrewd insights, he could still get to her. Ashe was finding he liked that quality about her. She wasn't as worldly wise as she often pretended, but she was not beyond a little humour of her own. 'When shall the wedding be, Ashe? Shall we play the romantic lovers to the hilt and marry in haste or shall we wait a decent period because of the funeral?'

'I think in haste would suit best given the circumstances. Even the king will understand the need to secure the succession. The potential of a babe in the Audley cradle within the year will forgive a multitude of sins.' The sooner she was under his protection, the better.

'I have told you there is little possibility of children—' Genevra began, but Ashe cut her off with a sharp shake of his head.

'You don't know that for certain. There's no sense in bringing it up. It does not help our cause,' Ashe cautioned. 'We can marry within the week, I think. I need to procure the special licence and I want my brother here for my wedding, if it's possible. With your permission, we will leave in the morning to get Alex.'

'You want me to come?' Genevra was clearly surprised by the request.

'Four hours in the carriage will give us time to become better acquainted,' Ashe said with a levity he didn't feel. It would give them time to talk but, in truth, Ashe was worried about what he'd find when he saw Alex. He'd never fully understood what had happened to Alex. He'd been too horrified over the news to properly pursue it. It would be a help to have Genevra with him if the situation was worse than he imagined. She'd been here a short while with Alex. She would be familiar to him, perhaps even a comfort.

They departed promptly at eight in the morning, taking the travelling coach, hitched with the four horses remaining at Bedevere for just that purpose. Bury St Edmunds was too far to risk going unprepared for the weather, which promised only to be inconsistent despite the blue skies that oversaw their departure.

The journey would take two days if nothing went wrong. Genevra had done the calculations in her head. With luck and good roads, they'd arrive around one in the afternoon, perhaps earlier. Ashe would be able to go straight to see Alex. They'd spend the night at an inn, visit Alex one more time in the morning and make the return trip home with or without Ashe's brother. The schedule would be grueling, but Ashe had been clear he didn't want to spend more time away from Bedevere than he needed to.

Genevra tried to keep herself busy with reading. But sitting across from Ashe Bedevere and remaining entirely aloof was a nearly impossible feat. She'd already lost her place five times for sneaking a look at her handsome husband-to-be. He was dressed today in tight buff breeches and high boots that showed off his legs to perfection in the confines of the coach. She couldn't help but notice his long legs, stretched as they were between the two opposing seats. Long, strong legs, with well-defined thighs, giving way to the coat of blue superfine and turquoise waistcoat beneath. He was always immaculately turned out, even for travelling.

The sixth time she looked, she got caught. 'What are you staring at so intently and so often while you pretend to read your pamphlet?' Ashe drawled, that teasing, arrogant smile of his on his lips.

'I'm merely contemplating some of the material I've been reading. It provokes much thought.'

'Well, while you've been contemplating the wonders of—what is it?—' Ashe leaned forwards and tipped her pamphlet up '—Ah, the wonders of knot gardens by Mr Hayman—I've been staring at you. I think I have the better of it, frankly. Agricultural tracts have never held any allure for me.' His tone made it clear, however, what did indeed hold an 'allure'.

This was the Ashe Bedevere she'd come to know, perhaps the Ashe Bedevere that would make up the bulk of their convenient marriage. It made her wonder if the Ashe who'd spoken of reminiscences in the garden or so fondly of shooting contests at a country fair had been a figment of her overactive imagination.

'Is everything a seduction to you?' Genevra countered.

'When it comes to you,' Ashe said boldly. 'Do you want to know what I was doing in my mind while I stared at you?' It was a rhetorical question. She didn't get to answer. 'I was playing this decadent game with your hair. I was wondering how many pins I could pull out before all that glorious hair came tumbling down.'

The temperature in the coach seemed to skyrocket. He was wreaking havoc with her senses, with her body. His voice, his touch, his presence, all commanded her attention. She couldn't simply ignore him and it disturbed her. Deep down, she didn't want to ignore him. She liked his naughty banter with its witty innuendos. Ashe kept her on edge, kept her looking forward to his next outrageous suggestion. Life with Ashe around had been more, well, more exciting.

That frightened her. She hadn't come to England looking to fall in love. She'd been looking for precisely the opposite. She'd wanted to get away. She didn't want to fall for anyone. But falling for Ashe Bedevere would somehow be worse.

'What are you afraid of, Neva?' came the seductive whisper. 'We are to be married. Lust won't be a sin any more.'

'You, Ashe. I'm afraid of you. I think you can turn a girl's head without her even realising it and that's a frightening thing indeed.' Genevra stiffened her resolve. 'Our marriage is based on convenience, not on romance. You're too dangerous to a decent woman's heart. I've told you before I'm not interested in what you're offering.'

'Yes, but we were talking about gardens then, Neva.' Ashe's green eyes sparked with mischief. He was enjoying this far too much.

'Most of the world's problems came from a garden.'

'Only Man's. Man is the only part of creation to have fallen, Neva, and some of us have fallen further than most.'

There it was again, that glimpse. Just when she was convinced he was one-hundred-per-cent pure rogue, he gave her a glimpse into the very human depths of himself and created chaos out of her preconceived notions. Genevra picked up her agricultural tract and focused on it with exaggerated attention. If she wasn't careful she'd be falling right along with him. Marriage might protect her from Henry, but what would protect her from Ashe?

They made good time, pulling into Bury St Edmunds an hour ahead of schedule. Ashe settled them at the Fox, an inn at the east entrance to town and closer to the place where Alex was housed. The Fox was a nice inn with heavy oak timbers and panelling in true Jacobean style. Plain and unassuming, what it lacked in luxuries it made up for in cleanliness. Ashe secured two rooms upstairs and gave instructions for the horses to be stabled. He would rent a small gig from the livery for the short trip to see Alex.

'You've checked your watch three times in the last minute. It won't make the horses come faster,' Genevra scolded playfully while they waited in the courtyard for the borrowed gig to arrive.

Good lord, he was nervous, Ashe admitted to himself. He had no idea what he'd find. Where had Henry housed Alex? Was it some raving-lunatic asylum? What was Alex like now? Would Alex even know who he was? That probably scared him the most. He supposed he harboured hopes that Alex could give him answers to all his questions. It was hard to imagine Alex's mind being gone.

The gig had arrived and they made the short drive to the home a few miles outside the city. Ashe's worries eased slightly as they approached. The home was an old estate, well kept with a neatly trimmed yard. The house itself seemed to be in good repair.

Inside, they were welcomed. Ashe gave the man at the door his card and they were ushered into an old library converted into an office by a matron dressed in a clean grey-and-white uniform. Then they waited. But not for long.

The door opened and a bearded man in an austere dark coat and simply tied cravat entered. 'I'm Dr Lawrence, Mr Bedevere, what a pleasant surprise to see you. Audley doesn't have many visitors.'

'I must apologise for the abruptness of my visit,' Ashe said. 'I've recently returned home and I did not want to delay in seeing my brother.' He was glad to note that the hospital had shown Alex the proper reverence and adopted the use of his official title when referring to him. He wondered if it meant anything to Alex, though.

'Does he understand our father has died?' Ashe asked, taking a seat opposite Dr Lawrence.

Dr Lawrence shrugged. 'At times. But not always. What can I help you with today?'

'I want to see him and I want to hear about his condition. It has not been fully explained to me. I would also like to discuss the possibility of having Alex come home with me.' At the last comment, the doctor stiffened ever so slightly. He covered it hastily with a condescending smile, but Ashe had noticed.

'I think those are laudable sentiments, Mr Bedevere. However, I think once you understand the nature of his condition, you will realise it is best to leave him here where he can be under professional supervision. We have others like him, others from families not unlike your own. He is in good hands.'

Ashe studied the man. Dr Lawrence had been good natured and open, but the mention of taking Alex home had changed him into a man of great wariness. Ashe could see it in his eyes. He chose to let it go for the moment. He would not help his cause by alienating Dr Lawrence too soon.

'Tell me about my brother.'

'Lord Audley has been with us since November. It is a shame we didn't have him right away after the breakdown. We might have been able to do more for him. But, as you know, nearly three years had elapsed and there is little hope for any further recovery. Instead, it has become apparent that he is prone to recurring breakdowns.'

'Breakdown? Define that for me,' Ashe prodded. He was interested in causes right now.

'Nervous breakdowns are triggered by a stressful event in a person's life. From what Mr Bennington shared with us, it is likely the trigger was the Forsythe scandal or perhaps the family's failing financial situation in general. Unable to face up to his financial responsibilities, Lord Audley's brain simply stopped functioning. He was despondent, he didn't answer when spoken to, he stopped eating. He lost all time orientation.'

Dr Lawrence paused, his voice lowering. 'Mr Ben-

nington shared with me that one night he found Lord
Audley with a gun. His intentions were quite clear.

'I must be straightforward with you, Mr Bedevere.
Your family did an admirable job caring for him as best
they were able even after that incident. But when your
father began to fail last autumn, there simply wasn't the
time or ability to look after them both and your brother's condition appeared to worsen. He would have periods where he wouldn't know who he was or what his
circumstances were and this created an intense paranoia on his part. He'd begun taking long walks and not
know how long he'd been gone. There were occasions
when he'd become lost and had to be searched for. Mr
Bennington and four ageing aunts couldn't manage the
dual responsibility. Mr Bennington put your brother
here, because he has become a danger to himself.' '

'I would like to see him.'

Dr Lawrence nodded and rose. 'Please follow me.
You must understand he lives mainly in the past now.'

Ashe asked Genevra to wait in the foyer. He wanted
to meet Alex alone. Dr Lawrence led him upstairs and
down a hall. 'Your brother has access to the entire house
and grounds, but we have a companion assigned to him
so that he goes nowhere alone.' He stopped at a big,
bright room at the end of the corridor. 'I'll leave you
for a few minutes.'

Ashe stepped into the room. It was white and clean
and stark in its features except for a little vase of yellow
flowers on a small table, but Ashe's gaze spared little
consideration for those details. His attention was fo-

cused on the lanky figure standing in the big bay of the window looking out over the lawns, his back to Ashe.

Alex was much as Ashe remembered him: a thinner rendition of himself. Even growing up, Alex had sported a more slender physique, a poet's build. It wasn't a weak man's build, but he'd never had Ashe's powerful shoulders or muscled thighs. Alex had been strong in other ways. He was an astute thinker and a compassionate human being. He would have made a good earl.

Alex turned from the window and saw him. Ashe's breath caught. He looked so *normal*. Ashe wasn't sure what he'd expected. Shouldn't a crazy man look a certain way? He supposed he thought one should. But Alex was dressed in a patterned-blue waistcoat and trousers, polished boots and a pristine white shirt. He looked no crazier than the next man and Alex hadn't known he was coming. It gave him hope.

'Alex,' Ashe said simply.

Alex's brown eyes registered recognition. 'Ashe. I knew you'd come.' In a moment Alex's long legs had covered the distance of the room, Alex's arms enveloping him in an embrace. 'Thank God, you've come at last,' he said in quiet but firm tones. 'You have to get me out of here.'

Chapter Seventeen

'Get me out of here.' It was what insane people said all the time. Alex was prone to periods of extreme paranoia. Dr Lawrence had told him it was customary. Still, Ashe couldn't bring himself to share that bit of information when the doctor had come back for him. He'd said simply it had been a good visit and that he'd come back tomorrow. Other than that bit of paranoia, Alex hadn't demonstrated any more outwards signs of mental debility.

He told Genevra as much over dinner at the Fox that evening. 'Of course, we didn't talk of anything upsetting other than Father's death.' He poured her another glass of the excellent red wine. They had a private parlour and dinner was proving to be a delicious meal of venison stew and freshly baked bread. A mincemeat pie waited on the sideboard for dessert. 'Perhaps he can handle little things without becoming overwrought.' There was a pathetic amount of hope in his voice. There were no cures for these kinds of ailments. He didn't do himself any favours in pretending there was.

'I'm glad the visit went well.' Genevra took a bite of the stew, the candlelight limning the delicate curve of her jaw. She looked like a veritable angel in the flickering lights.

His angel.

Or his devil.

He had won her, for better or worse, for Bedevere, for his aunts, for Alex. He needed her money for all of them. For them, he'd bought her the only way he knew how—binding her to him with passion and seduction, even if he feared it would cost him the last of his pride and the last of his soul. He could talk about protection all he wanted, but once the concern over Henry was retired, he would be left with only the pleasure he could give her in bed to keep her bound to him. He'd have to look that man in the mirror every morning, knowing he'd found his price.

'I will go back and see him tomorrow.' Ashe rose to fetch the pie. He'd given explicit instructions that they be left alone while they dined. 'Will you be all right on your own for a few hours?'

'I'll be fine. I'd like to explore the market and see if there's a merchant who would be willing to take some of your aunts' designs for the summer.' Genevra reached to take the pie and knife from him with a laugh. 'Let me do that. It's a pie, not a pig. You're butchering it, Ashe.'

Genevra passed him a slice of pie and he was struck by the domesticity of the moment. Little things like that had not mattered much to him before. This idea of someone doing something for him who wasn't a servant was quite novel. He wondered if this was how it was like for his friend Merrick and Alixe. Of course it would never really be that way for him and Genevra. They *had* to marry. Merrick and Alixe had married for love.

It occurred to him, as he finished his pie, that he wished it could be different. If he had seen her across a ballroom in London, if he had been able to marry anyone he chose, he might have been tempted by her beauty, her grace and her wit to fall headlong into a decent romance. It was a shame he'd not find out what it would be like to come to her honestly as a man in love.

This was a new revelation to him that perhaps a heretofore unacknowledged part of him had secretly wished to marry for love, in spite of the realities he'd long ago accepted. Even second sons, *especially* second sons, had to marry where the money was.

'You look deep in thought. Are you thinking about Alex?' Genevra rose to clear the dishes, another intimate, domestic act.

'No.' Ashe sighed and pushed back from the table. It would do no good to tell her he wished it could be different. Instead he said, 'Thank you for coming. Alex seemed quite well today. I've changed my mind about tomorrow, I think he'd like to see you. We can tell him together about the wedding.' He smiled mischievously. 'It would mean giving up your tour of the market and franchising my aunts' handiwork.'

Genevra gave a light laugh. 'Ah, I see you're start-ing to accept the idea.'

'Tolerating the idea.' Ashe chuckled. 'Since there's no dissuading you from it, I've decided to tolerate it.' This was a good moment, a hopeful moment. In time, their marriage might be full of more moments like this where they weren't merely two strangers thrown to-gether by circumstance.

'It's late, I should go up.' Genevra gathered the last of their dinner things and set them on the sideboard next to the remaining pie.

'I'll walk you up.' Ashe rose. He smiled at her wari-ness. He could see she wanted to protest his offer. Going up alone would preclude any seduction. She'd be safely ensconced behind a locked door before he mounted the stairs. And that would not do tonight for either the rake in him or the husband-to-be.

The rake in him argued this was a perfect opportu-nity. They were here, alone, at an inn with no one but Genevra's maid and the coachman for chaperons. Who would know if he went to her bed or if she came to his? And with nuptials pending, who would care? The soon-to-be bridegroom in him saw it as another chance to remind her that she could trust him. They might marry without the benefit of romance or common knowledge but he would not be a cruel husband, he would not be another Philip.

'It is not necessary. Stay here and enjoy your brandy,' Genevra offered generously.

It was on his lips to answer, 'When I could be upstairs enjoying you? Never.' But tonight was not an evening for glib words. 'Tonight is not for being alone, I think, Neva,' he said in quiet tones. The last two days had been full of strain for them in separate ways. She'd witnessed Henry's duplicity firsthand and faced the reality of her options. For himself, he'd reunited with his brother and secured a marriage, neither event without its own turmoil of emotions. It was time to seek solace for those emotions.

'Very well, you may see me up.' Genevra's voice was as quiet as his as they exited the private parlor, a sure sign she understood.

Ashe kept his hand at the small of her back up the stairs. At her door they stopped. She fumbled for her key. 'Allow me.' Ashe deftly took the key from her and fitted it to the lock, swinging the door open. The room inside was lit by a carefully laid fire. One of the inn's maids had been here recently.

'Do you have everything you need?'

'I think so.' She looked up at him, her grey eyes luminous, her thoughts transparent behind them, her pulse racing at her neck. She was not unaffected either by the domestic intimacy of their dinner or their companionship on the long carriage ride.

She wanted him. Ah, Ashe understood her reticence downstairs immediately. She wanted him, not as a result of any flirtatious games he'd invoked at dinner, because he'd invoked none, nor did she want him as a means to satisfy a growing curiosity like she had in the library at Bedevere. She wanted him simply because she did and that was very gratifying indeed. For him. For her, Ashe thought, such a realisation would be frightening, a clarion call to caution. She would worry he would use such knowledge against her as Philip had. She would worry such a wanting would make her weak in this fledgling partnership of theirs.

He understood those feelings all too well. They were not that different than his own. God help him, tonight he wanted her for reasons that had less to do with securing his inheritance and more to do with a being a man desiring a lovely woman. He tilted his head to capture her mouth in a slow, lingering kiss at the door.

'Neva, I'd like to come in,' he said in hushed tones against her ear. Tonight, he would show her with his body what he could not tell her in words. He could feel her body tremble against him as she made her brief contemplation and decided.

'Yes,' she whispered.

There was no going back now, perhaps there never had been. Perhaps she'd been fooling herself all along about the one night in the library. It had never really existed as a moment out of time. Genevra stepped into her chamber, feeling Ashe's body move behind her, hearing his elegant hands shut the door. Tonight he would be her lover. She had no illusions about what he'd requested. He wasn't coming in to check for rats. He was coming in to share her bed and she could not pretend she'd not thought about it throughout the day.

It might possibly be the most audacious thing she'd

ever done. This would not be like the library, rash and
unplanned. She'd not gone downstairs that night thinking she'd encounter Ashe and let him seduce her. Tonight was premeditated. There could be no excuses for
rash behaviour afterwards.

Genevra turned and faced him, her hand reaching
for the hairpins. She tugged once, twice and her hair
fell. 'Two, the answer is two.'

Ashe gave a low growl, all manly appreciation. His
eyes glowed with the intensity of coals. 'Allow me to
do the rest. Let me undress you, let me worship you.'

Genevra gave a throaty laugh. 'Shall you play
lady's maid?'

'Oh, no, I shall play the supplicant. No lady's maid
has ever undressed you like I shall.' He managed the
tiny buttons down the back of her dress with alarming efficiency, pushing the sleeves of the gown down
her arms with a gentle thrust that sent goose bumps
of pleasure coursing through her. His lips skimmed
her bare shoulders, his hands holding her firm at the
waist, his thumbs deliciously close to the undersides
of her breasts.

She moaned in frustration. She'd become greedy for
his touch in such a very short time. He kissed her neck,
nipped at her ear. His hands moved up at last to cup her
breasts, caressing and teasing through the fabric of her
chemise until they felt heavy with desire in his hands.
Only then did he reach to gather up the cloth of chemise
and tug it over her head. Genevra wiggled her hips and
let the gown slide to the floor. At last she was bare and

free. She turned in his arms and his mouth met hers in a fierce, possessive kiss.

It was her turn now to undress him. She reached for the cravat and tugged, laying waste to his efforts at an intricate knot. She drew him out of his coat, then his waistcoat, her hands fumbling at the buttons in her haste.

'I thought it was only women who dressed in layers,' she teased. She had not imagined undressing him to be frustrating, but she had not imagined her need being so great. She was well aware her body thrummed for him, that his caresses had driven her to a perfect state of readiness.

Genevra tugged on the tails of his shirt, pulling the length of fabric from the waistband of his trousers. Ashe stepped back and finished the shirt himself. 'Look at me, Neva.'

Again, he was magnificent in the firelight, his torso limned by flame, his musculature defined by shadow and light. Genevra's fingers itched to trace the lines of those muscles and the tantalising path they drew leading to the waistband of those trousers. She swallowed hard as his hands followed her eyes down. He boldly cupped himself through the tight trousers, making her fully cognisant of his arousal.

He pulled at his boots and pushed at his trousers, his eyes never leaving her. It was the most erotic undressing Genevra could imagine. He was displaying himself for her, letting the disrobing heighten her own desire until she was nearly overcome with it and he missed not a moment of it. He was entirely conscious of the effect.

He came to her, gloriously naked and brazen. He drew her into his arms, the hard length of his phallus pressing against her unabashedly. There was no pretence or modesty between them. The bed was at her back, she could feel it against her knees. He urged her on to it and straddled her, his haunches taking his weight. He looked like an American native in the firelight as he rose above her with his dark hair framing his face.

'You're beautiful, Neva,' he whispered hoarsely and she revelled in the power of knowing she could trigger this depth of desire in a man who could have any woman. She was Eve in that moment, or perhaps Lilith.

His mouth found her bare breast, sucking and coaxing her nipple into erect hardness. She arched against him, her body begging for more, begging for the intuitive release that lay beyond even this pleasure.

He moved his mouth to her navel and feathered it with a breath. 'If we had wine, I could show you a trick,' he murmured, his breath warm and arousing on the surface of her skin. She shuddered delightfully. Just the mere decadence of the suggestion was enough to set her on desire's edge.

Her hands stroked the muscled length of his back, cupping his buttocks, urging him to that most private place between her legs. At last he came, the moist tip of his phallus nudging at her entrance, his knee spreading her legs wider still for him and she welcomed him.

There was more they might have done, more play they might have had, but they were ready for each other and the dance had gone on long enough for tonight.

He rose and thrust and she took him in with a cry that bordered on joyous. He thrust again and again and she joined him in the rhythm his body created within her. Her hips rose to match him, her legs wrapped about him, holding him, her hands raking his back in abandon. He was fierce in his possession, their desire riding him hard, and she met it equally. They were in the throes of a magnificent madness. Suddenly the madness crested and then it broke all around her, shattering into a million fragments of desire achieved and passion spent.

Ashe lay beside her, unquestionably as depleted as she. His breathing was ragged and his skin held the sheen of sweat in the firelight. She rested her head against the strength of his shoulder, their breathing slowing at last. And then, without words, she slept.

Chapter Eighteen

As a rule, Ashe hated mornings. They were bright and littered with realities. This morning was no different. He stretched and waited for the regrets to flood with the sunlight, but none came. He waited for his mind to chastise; he'd allowed himself to get caught up in sentiment last night. Beside him, Genevra slept soundly, no doubt exhausted by the evening activities. He'd taken her again twice more in the night, the last right before dawn.

He should feel something, but he felt nothing of the usual recriminations, only an alien sense of deep contentment such as he had felt in the library. Only this time, it was far more intense. He also felt a sense of resolve. It was the sense of resolve that propelled him out of bed. Alex was waiting, counting on him to return. Ashe made a quick *toilette* and dressed before waking Genevra. He would slip downstairs and arrange for the carriage, giving her the privacy of the room to make her morning ablutions.

Ashe sat on the side of the bed, pushing back her tousled hair to wake her. Even in sleep, she was a beauty beyond compare. 'Neva, we must get up.' She moaned a little at the intrusion. He was tempted to let her sleep, but decided against it. He wanted her with him. If Dr Lawrence tried to forcibly prevent Alex from leaving, Ashe wouldn't have time to stop by the inn and pick Genevra up.

Genevra stretched and rolled on to her back, the sheet slipping to reveal the swell of a breast. His body hardened. If there hadn't been the business with Alex this morning, he'd gladly have slid back into bed. But the sooner he dealt with Alex's situation, the better. What else might Alex tell him if put to the question? How much of it would be driven by the paranoia of his condition and how much of it was real? He kissed Genevra's brow with a final admonition to get up and went downstairs before his body could launch an effective counter-argument.

Alex was dressed for the day and having breakfast when they arrived. Dr Lawrence had not been pleased to see them, nor had he been pleased with Ashe's request for a private meeting after the visit. But Alex had been ecstatic over his return and that he'd brought Genevra. They pulled up chairs to the table and the three of them sat down to a breakfast of tea and pastries.

'We have something to tell you,' Genevra began after they'd all fixed their plates. Alex looked up from his food with interest and wariness.

'I hope it's not more bad news. The aunts are all fine, aren't they?'

Ashe was pleased by the response. Alex remembered everyone, was able to be concerned about them. Alex had always been alert to the needs of those around him. Such a quality would have made him a grand earl.

Genevra reached out a comforting hand. 'It's nothing like that. They're fine. It's good news, actually. Ashe and I are getting married just as soon as we can and we'd like you to be with us for the wedding.'

'You're taking me home.' The emotion of the simple statement nearly broke Ashe. He'd come as soon as he could. There'd been so much to do right away at the estate. But he wished he'd come sooner—the books, the will, the bills, the garden, even courting Genevra, be damned.

Ashe stood up and walked to the window to gather himself. He let Genevra chat with Alex about the aunts and Bedevere and the plans for the garden. When his emotions were under control he returned to the table.

'Congratulations, brother.' Alex's eyes sparkled with genuine affection. 'Finally, there's a woman who can settle you down.' He winked at Genevra. 'Has he told you all about his wild escapades in Italy or how he held Vienna in thrall with his piano playing? He even performed at Schonbrunn Palace.'

Genevra shook her head in mock seriousness. 'He has neglected to mention much of that to me. But he has played for me at Seaton Hall. He is magnificent.'

'I'm standing right here, you know,' Ashe put in.

Alex meant well with his stories, but Ashe didn't want him to tell too many. That was all in the past and not all of it was as rosy as Alex painted it.

Genevra tossed him a smile and moved towards the window. 'I'll give the two of you a moment to talk.'

'Alex, do you know why you're here?' Ashe asked, taking his seat again.

Alex set down his cup and sighed, hanging his head. 'I am not well, Ashe. They tell me on occasion I am given to bouts of paranoia and despondency where I don't talk to anyone and I think everyone is conspiring against me.'

Ashe leaned forwards. 'Is now one of those occasions? Do you think you're in your right mind?'

Alex held his gaze with solemn dark eyes. 'Yes, I am absolutely in my right mind for the time being. But I never know when an episode of madness might come upon me. That's why I must stay here.'

Ashe's heart cracked at the admission. His brother had always been so confident, so certain of himself. Now, he was shadow of that former self. 'Henry says you are a danger to yourself and to others.'

'Ha! Henry. What does he know? He says and does whatever is best for Henry. You know that.' For a moment Ashe glimpsed the old fire.

'Henry said there was an incident with a firearm.'

Alex snorted at this, very much like his former self when Henry would challenge him with absurd untruths in their youth. 'It was hardly an incident. If I'd known what he'd make of it, I'd have shot him then and there and saved all of us the trouble. Next time I will.'

The fire of his statement riveted Ashe. 'What trouble would that be?' Was this paranoia speaking or a genuine plot being uncovered?

Alex leaned towards him across the table. 'The trouble over Bedevere. Who is to rule Bedevere if I am unable? They call me the earl and I suppose nothing can change that except my death. That doesn't serve Henry. He can commandeer Bedevere as a trustee as long as I live. Heaven forbid I die, then you're the earl and Henry loses all claims.'

'Bedevere is broke—why does Henry want it at all?'

Alex lowered his voice. 'It's for the coal. He believes he'll mine Bedevere and make a fortune. I found out right before I got ill. He's spent two years amassing investors and biding his time.'

'And the Forsyth scandal?' Ashe's suspicions were on high alert. The coincidences were starting to mount. Very soon, he'd have another look at the books. Maybe with Alex's memories to fill in the gaps, the odd entries would start to make sense.

Alex shook his head. 'Dr Lawrence says that must have been my first fit, although no one realised it. I have no recollection of ever having authorised those investments. I had the running of the household. Father was unable to do much of anything. It's my signature on the receipts, but I don't recall having done it.' The eyes that held Ashe's were serious, earnest and entirely sane. How could he doubt his brother?

Suddenly Alex grabbed his forearm. 'Ashe, you do believe me? You are taking me home for good, not just for the wedding?' The gesture stank of desperation and Ashe's hopes fell. How was he to know if these were the ramblings of a man who needed care or a man who'd been marginalised and pushed out of the way by a scheming cousin who coveted his estate?

It didn't matter. Alex had never failed him. Ashe owed him this. Ill or not, Alex was coming home. Ashe covered Alex's hand with his own and bowed his head until their dark heads met across the little table. 'You're walking out of here with me today. I promise. The Earl of Audley belongs at Bedevere.' Then he called to Genevra, 'It's time to go. Take Alex straight to the carriage. I'll settle things with Dr Lawrence.'

The interview with Dr Lawrence did not go well. Lawrence was visibly upset by the decision to remove Alex. He made all the usual arguments: Alex needed care, he needed doctors, one never knew when a fit might take him, he was a danger to himself. Ashe met each of them with a sharp emerald gaze and crossed arms.

In the end, Ashe simply said, 'Who pays your bills? Mr Bennington?' Dr Lawrence paled at the mention of that particular fact. It had been a logical but lucky guess. Ashe pressed his advantage. 'If so, I doubt you'd want those monies scrutinised. If I looked too closely, I might discover something much akin to bribery in those payments.'

That silenced him. Ashe smiled coldly. 'I thought as much.' He also thought the terrified Dr Lawrence would have a letter posted to Henry within minutes of their departure. The other concern was whether or not Dr Lawrence would recover some modicum of courage such as it was and try to stop their departure from the city. For both those reasons, Ashe wanted to be well away with all haste.

He joined Genevra and Alex in the carriage and gave the signal to be off. If their leave-taking resembled a getaway more than a departure, so be it. Ashe didn't trust Dr Lawrence any further than he could throw his knife and that was about twenty feet.

The trip home was blessedly uneventful. Alex sat in relative silence, drawn carefully into conversation by Genevra. She chatted of the improvements being made at Bedevere, of Ashe's plans for the gardens and of the aunts' new designs for the summer fairs. Occasionally he would nod and smile, but for the most part he held himself rigid as if his good fortune would be shattered at any moment.

Ashe watched them both: the woman he'd marry and the brother who needed him. What an odd family he was assembling. After years without one, he now had a family of ageing aunts, an ailing brother and an American bride. A very odd assortment indeed. Each in their own way were counting on him. He wouldn't have it any other way. A primal desire to protect rose in him. With Alex coming home, everyone who was entitled to that protection would be under one roof: his. He would not let them down.

Henry was waiting for them when they arrived in the late afternoon. They'd no more than pulled into the drive than Henry was down the steps, livid with rage. Ashe grimaced as he stepped down from the carriage. He could guess the source of Henry's fury. Henry hadn't been there the night he'd announced his betrothal.

'What were you thinking to take Genni with you?' he thundered the moment Ashe's feet touched the gravelled drive. 'Have you no sense of decorum? People will talk. She will be ruined.'

'We are to be married, cousin. No one will mind if we travelled together for Genevra to pick up a few essentials for the wedding.' Ashe could not resist a cold smile as he delivered the news. He reached into the carriage to hand Genevra down. 'Do wish us well.'

'I cannot believe you left with nothing but a maid,' Henry charged Genevra.

'And my clothes,' Genevra said just to be perverse. The spirit of her made Ashe laugh, but he could feel her grip on his arm tighten under the furious look Henry gave her.

Henry was scandalised. 'Genni!'

'Oh, for heaven's sake, Henry, it was hardly a holiday,' she scolded lightly. Ashe knew what the brave front cost her. Just days ago, Henry had tried to force his attentions upon her. She would not soon forget or forgive the imposition. If Henry didn't voluntarily leave

Bedevere before supper, Ashe would 'suggest' it. His protection started now.

Ashe glared at Henry. He might have banished Henry right then if Alex hadn't intervened. 'It seems I am one of those wedding essentials,' Alex said congenially, stepping down on his own. 'It's good to see you, Henry.'

Henry's anger over Genevra was nothing compared to the pale rage on his face when Alex emerged. He'd not expected that, Ashe thought.

'What have you done?' Henry turned his anger back to Ashe.

'I have brought my brother home where he belongs,' Ashe said sternly. 'If I were you, I'd be more concerned about what you've done. Now, if you'll excuse me, I want to see my brother settled.'

Ashe was intoxicating like this, Genevra thought quietly, making her way to her borrowed chambers at Bedevere, all his authority unleashed as it had been the first day she'd seen him. She would let the family settle Alex. She had thoughts of her own to settle and she needed distance from Ashe's potent sensuality. Her room at Bedevere was the best she could manage. There was no question of going to Seaton Hall. Henry's gaze this afternoon had been venomous. She didn't want to be caught alone and Henry's recent behaviours suggested he wasn't beyond such tactics.

Whether she wanted it or not, Ashe's protection was becoming very necessary. But it came with risks of it own.

Up until last night she'd believed she could have her fantasy with Ashe and remain detached. She would satisfy her curiosity and nothing more. It was becoming more difficult to do that in practice.

She had not guessed they would share something so monumental between them not once, but twice. Nor had she guessed the depths of loyalty he carried. Bringing home his brother was not the action of a man who thought only of himself and his pleasure. It was not the first time she'd glimpsed this about him. But his choice with Alex had certainly solidified that such behaviour was not an anomaly. It would be easier if it was.

It would be far easier if Ashe Bedevere had turned out to be precisely the man she'd thought he was: a rake, a gambler, a seducer of women. Instead he'd turned out to be something far worse; he turned out to be a man she could love. That could make for a disastrous, lopsided marriage. Ashe had made it clear he would protect her and pleasure her, but he'd never promised he'd love her.

Still, there were small things to be thankful for. Ashe informed her as they went into supper that Henry had left the premises on a more permanent basis. Supper was a simple meal, but one full of celebration. Henry was gone, Alex had returned and a wedding loomed on the near-horizon.

By the end of dinner, the aunts and Ashe had decided it should take place on Friday, just two days away. Such haste was probably best, Genevra concurred. There was no need for lots of plans. The family was in mourning and she and Ashe knew what the wedding really was even if the rest of the family didn't: a convenient merger. Such an alliance didn't need to be heralded with ribbons and roses and other wedding fripperies. She would send to Seaton Hall for a good dress she had in mind for the occasion and that would be the extent of her preparations.

The happy little group adjourned to the music room where Ashe played for them on the old Broadwood piano while the aunts chattered excitedly about Bedevere weddings past. Genevra listened to their tales with half an ear. She was more interested in the man who played the piano. What was it that Alex had said today? Ashe had played at Schonbrunn? It occurred to her she could ask Alex for more of the story, but that seemed hypocritical. If she wanted to know, she should ask Ashe himself, especially after her tirade over Ashe's investigation of her background.

Alex rose and went to the piano. Genevra followed his movements with her eyes. He murmured something to Ashe. Ashe stopped playing and shuffled through the sheet music until he found what he was looking for. Genevra was aware of Leticia setting aside her needlework in expectation.

'The boys are going to sing like they used to,' she said in an excited whisper, nudging Melisande and the others to the attention. 'Alexander has a lovely tenor.'

What followed was grand fun. Ashe and Alex entertained the group with lively songs that made the aunts laugh and they closed with a sad rendition of 'Barbary Allen' that left a tear in the aunts' eyes. Even Genevra found herself wiping at wet eyes as the last notes faded. Ashe's gaze caught her out as they all rose for bed. Their eyes met and held and Genevra understood. He would come to her soon.

Chapter Nineteen

Ashe was coming. Her body thrilled to the idea even as Genevra's mind counselled against it. She should send him away, give him some nonsense about wanting to wait for the wedding before they were together again. But that was ridiculous. Her body didn't want to wait even two days.

She realised in retrospect that he'd been priming her for this all night in subtle ways. His hand had lingered at her back when he'd seated her for dinner. His eyes had held hers a bit longer than necessary during the meal. He'd been flirting all night in small ways, heightening the anticipation that they would continue what they'd started at the inn. Perhaps he was already setting the pattern for their marriage.

It had most definitely worked. Here she was, dressed in a satin nightgown in record time and all put pacing the floor when she knew he couldn't possibly venture to her room until the house was settled. Impending nuptials or not, it wouldn't do to be caught sneaking up to her room.

Genevra hoped the house would settle soon. Perhaps she should make a list of all the things that needed doing, all the plans she'd need to co-ordinate for her own estate from here. She went to the little writing desk and pulled out paper and ink. She'd just begun the task when the scratch came.

A slow smile crept across her lips. He was here. Genevra rose and smoothed her gown for good measure. 'Come in.' There was a small catch to her voice that belied her anticipation. If she sounded more eager than she preferred, she could be forgiven for that. Ashe in dishabille was a sensual sight designed to arouse the staunchest spinster.

He carried a small black canvas bag in one hand and was dressed for the night in a blue-paisley banyan and slippers, but not much else if the view of smooth skin at his neck and chest where the banyan vee'd was to be believed. A tremor of desire shot through her at the thought of him naked beneath the robe. How daring, too, it had been of him to take such a chance wandering the house dressed like that.

'I see we are of like minds.' Ashe's eyes slid over her form, hot appreciation evident in his gaze, her body responding instantly.

'Only I'm not wandering the house,' Genevra teased. 'Is Alex settled?'

'He is very glad to be back in his own rooms.' A faint

smile hovered on Ashe's lips. 'I stayed and talked with him a while. It's why I'm a bit later than I expected.'

'No apology needed. He is your brother—'

Ashe shook his head in interruption. 'It's been a long day, right now I want to set all that aside. I just want you.'

I just want you. Those words could atone for a variety of sins. But Genevra was careful to understand them for what they were. She was his escape. There was both compliment and insult in that. Was this the pattern he wanted established in their marriage? Would he come to her after a long day and lose himself in her body while keeping his thoughts locked away?

He came to her now, ready to be lost, his hands resting possessively on her hips, his mouth engaging hers in a light caress that aroused and promised, while still saying 'not yet' in the most tantalising of ways. 'Give me a moment to make everything ready,' he whispered against her neck.

He left her and strode purposefully to the delicate white table beside her bed. He placed the bag on it and began setting out items: small stoppered vials, a tiny shallow-bottomed pan and a small wire stand. He turned back to look at her with a wolfish smile. 'Sit. You're welcome to watch and to imagine what we might do with these things.'

Genevra watched intently, giving her mind permission to move her earlier misgivings to a far corner. Ashe's movements were too mesmerising to concentrate on much else. There would be time for those contemplations later. He removed the chimney from her lamp and set the stand over the open flame. With deft hands, he adjusted the flame and settled the shallow pan above it, creating a burner, carefully pouring in liquid from his bottles. With another man, the process might be merely scientific, but he had the uncanny ability to turn the act of warming liquid into something sinfully decadent. He put his nose over the little burner and inhaled deeply, his eyes shut, his dark lashes long and sensual against the sweep of his cheek.

He exhaled and she could smell it, too, the scent of lavender tinged with the spice of lemon slowly filling the room. He faced her and held out an inviting hand. 'I am ready for you, Neva. I've thought of nothing else a good part of the day.' *When he wasn't thinking of his brother, or ousting his cousin from the family seat, or dealing with recalcitrant doctors,* came the unbidden thought, quickly pushed aside but no less powerful for its brevity.

His eyes were on her and she rose, determined to make good use of his attention. If escape was where they started, she would accept that for the time being and move on from there. Genevra slid the thin straps of her nightgown down her shoulders and gave a graceful shrug that sent the satin garment slithering to a pool at her feet.

'Temptress,' Ashe growled his approval, his hands going to the belt at his waist and making quick work of the garment.

Her breath caught at the male beauty on display. She

had seem him naked before, but only in firelight. In brighter light, too, he did not disappoint. He smiled in comprehension. 'Tonight, there will be plenty of time to, ah, shall we say, "appreciate" one another. Come lie down, Neva.'

She felt sure those four words were uniquely designed to render her incapable of any sensible thought. She gladly complied. It was clear he had something planned for her although she could not guess what it was. She was well aware that she was entirely at his mercy while she was naked and sprawled on the bed, a realisation that made her more uncomfortable than she cared to admit. Last night she'd felt in control, a partner. She did not feel that way now. 'What are we doing?' She eyed him suspiciously as he retrieved the pan from the burner.

'Are you nervous?' The bed took Ashe's weight as he sat on the edge.

'Yes,' she said frankly.

He smiled, all traces of the wolf gone, but he made it clear he would not brook any balking. 'We won't do anything you don't like. We'll begin with a massage and I guarantee you'll like it very much. Let me start with your feet.'

Oh, she did like it! The warm oil on her skin was a wicked pleasure made even more so by the slide of his hands on her body, expertly rubbing and pressing as they moved up the length of her: feet, legs, thighs, buttocks. Was there anything as heavenly as this? As *decadent* as this? Lying naked with a man, his hands on her body, soothing and coaxing, readying—the ultimate foreplay. When he reached her back, he levered himself over her, careful to avoid giving her his full weight. She could feel the heavy brush of his sac as he massaged her back.

'Where did you learn to do this?' She was amazed she could form any words at this point.

'In Venice.' His hands were at her shoulders now, his thumbs at the base of her neck. 'It's quite an art, mostly an eastern one.' She could believe that. It was far too sinful for stuffy old England to embrace wholesale.

'Venice sounds wonderful, then,' she murmured, not wanting to think of who might have taught him the art or where precisely in Venice he'd acquired it.

'Venice *is* wonderful. East meets west—it's the gateway to the Adriatic, to Istanbul, to Egypt. Britain is just starting to see its potential, although others in the east have long recognised it.' He could make even a lecture in geography sound sinful.

He leaned over her, pushing her hair to one side, his voice low at her ear. 'Shall I take you now, Neva?' His phallus nudged at the place between her legs and her buttocks rose instinctively to meet the request. This was new and unfamiliar territory, but her body knew what to do and she'd abandoned her inhibitions at the first caress of his hands.

His arm was about her waist, holding her steady, lifting her to him and then he was in her, his entry swift and sure until she could feel him deep inside her, her body flowing around his intimate presence. This was the pleasure she'd waited the day for, the pleasure that kept her at Bedevere. Pleasure seemed far too bland a description for the sensations rocketing through her anew at each of his powerful thrusts. She gasped and moaned, reaching for the penultimate release. The thundering pulse of his phallus assured her it was not far off for either of them.

In a fleeting moment of clarity before the shattering liberation of climax took her, the thought swept her ever so briefly; this was not merely sex, a messy act of physical gratification, this was *art*.

Whoever had taught her had not thoroughly tutored her. There was a spark of pride in knowing that he was truly the first to awaken real passion in her. It wasn't perhaps the most refined of thoughts to have after such a critical moment, but it had popped into his head none the less, a random tangent that had resulted from contemplating the woman beside him.

Ashe propped himself up on one arm and traced lazy circles around the tip of her breast. 'Will a Friday wedding suit you, Neva? It occurred rather belatedly to me that you might have some friends to invite. We could wait a few days for their travel.' Now that Henry was physically off the property, Ashe could afford the luxury of a slight delay.

'No,' Genevra said simply, but the negation aroused Ashe's curiosity.

'I can hardly believe such a beautiful woman has sprung from wholecloth in the midst of Staffordshire.'

She laughed, the delightfully enticing smoky sound that promised a man a lot more than she knew. 'Hardly wholecloth. You know I'm American. It wouldn't be prudent to invite my family. We haven't the time.'

'Oh, so you do have a family,' Ashe said in teasing tones. His drawings moved to the other breast. It was hard to believe she was entirely alone.

'Did,' Genevra said slowly. 'There was my father and I for a long time. He passed away shortly after Philip's accident. Then there was no one to speak of. I have an uncle who grows hops outside Boston. We are not so close any more.' The scandal, Ashe guessed without asking.

'Is that why you came to England? Because there was no reason to stay?'

'Something like that. It seemed like a good challenge.'

'And you like a challenge? Apparently I do, too. Getting you to talk about yourself is becoming a Herculean feat,' Ashe joked.

'You're not the easiest either.' Genevra rolled to her side, dislodging his hand and propping herself up. 'Why did you leave Bedevere?'

Ashe groaned, but it was more playful than tortured. He flipped on to his back, hands behind his head. 'Second sons are supposed to leave, to get out of the heir's way so there's no dissension. I'd always understood that. In a way, I even welcomed that. After Oxford, I was ready to take my gentleman's education out into the world and see what I could become.' He sighed.

Genevra watched the rise and fall of his chest. 'It's not the leaving I regret, Neva, it's the not coming back.'

Genevra moved a finger in patterns on his chest, copying his earlier gesture. 'Why is that? Does it have to do with Vienna?'

Ashe shook his head and gave a short laugh. 'Alex talks too much. I'll tell you some time, but not tonight.' He offered an apologetic smile, but no answers, no absolution for her curiosity. Neva would have to wait to learn his darker secrets. Some things were harder to admit to when one cared what someone thought. It was a stunning revelation to make for a man who'd spent most of his adult life not giving a fig what others thought of his exploits.

He still didn't care what London thought of him, but he realised he cared what Genevra thought. What would she think if she knew what he'd been doing when his father died? About the quarrel? About Vienna? Would knowing those things affirm for her he was just as bad as she believed him to be? Or would she see the man he was starting to become since he'd arrived home—a man whose past did not necessarily predict his future. He did not regret his past entirely, but neither would he let it drag him down with its limits.

'I'll tell you something about me, one of my most shocking secrets.' Genevra's voice pulled him away from those thoughts. She was teasing, of course, he could hear it in her tone.

'I like to make money,' she announced. 'And I'm good at it.' The announcement carried its own shock value. She knew men in London who would be genuinely alarmed. In their world, gentlemen didn't make money and neither did well-bred ladies. 'Last year, I doubled the shipping company's profits with my investments overseas.'

She paused. Ashe could practically hear her gathering her thoughts. 'You could make money with Bedevere,' she began tentatively.

'I'll get the tenant farms back on their feet in time for spring planting.' He'd not planned to think about Bedevere while he was in bed with Genevra.

'No, not farming,' Genevra insisted. 'Although that's fine, too. I mean with the house and the garden. In the spring and summer you can open the house and garden up for tours. We can make scones and serve tea. We can advertise in the guidebooks. I'm doing it at Seaton Hall this summer, giving it a trial run.' She sounded so earnest, so enterprising.

'Where do I live while people are swarming my home?'

'You'll be in London at least part of the time, I suspect.' Was she fishing for something there? He heard the hedge in her tone. Did she think he'd go up to town and leave his American wife in the country? He'd not thought of that. It would be one more thing to work out. Genevra would need to be introduced to society eventually. He didn't relish the prospect, not because he didn't believe in her capability to pull it off, but because he didn't necessarily want her encountering the more sordid elements of his life.

'Maybe I'll choose to stay in the country,' Ashe said for the sake of argument just to see what she'd say.

'Or you can lease the Audley town house if you decide to stay here. There are families visiting London for the Season that wouldn't mind renting. Either way, you should consider it. You cannot be in both places at once and there's no sense in one residence remaining idle.'

Ashe laughed. 'Neva, did anyone ever tell you it's not sexy to talk about money after making love?' He was rewarded with a warm hand on his stirring phallus.

'You don't seem to particularly mind,' she whispered coyly.

'You're the one who does that to me, not the money, I assure you.'

She straddled him, leaning forwards to let her breasts brush his chest. She kissed him full on the mouth, her hair falling about him like a curtain. His body was rousing, ready for the next bout.

'It's better not to know too much all at once, don't you think?' He reached for her ear lobe, sucking hard on the tender flesh. 'I like it this way—pleasure without expectations, without complications.' She moved a hand between his legs again and he gave up the fight. It wasn't a hard fight to lose. She liked it this way, too—being enjoyed for simply being a woman, not an heiress. The problem was it couldn't stay that way. In time, Ashe feared she'd want more than his body. She was that kind of woman; the kind who chose to love fully and would expect that fullness to be reciprocated. Could he be that kind of man? He'd known from the outset this marriage would involve setting aside his pride. He had not expected it to involve love, even one-sided love, but that was fast becoming a consideration and a complication all rolled into one.

Chapter Twenty

It was fast becoming the time to not play nice. Henry hoped the cartel would see recent developments as Ashe's fault and not his. If there was any nastiness, Henry preferred it be directed at Ashe. Trent, Samuels, Bardsworth, Ellingson and Cunningham were all assembled and anxious. He eyed the group of investors with great trepidation. For the second time in a span of weeks he had to face them with bad news.

'Your Mrs Ralston is set to marry your cousin in the morning,' Trent began. 'It's not what we talked about.'

He made it sound as if a minor mistake had occurred, like a tailor producing a waistcoat in a slightly different shade than what had been agreed upon, but Henry was not fooled into believing his complacency. There was a very real danger to himself here if he did not deflect it.

Henry opted for the high road of righteous indignation. 'My cousin is worse than ever. He's thrown me out of the house.'

It wasn't the strongest course of action. He'd hoped

to paint Ashe in a malicious light, but the complaint only weakened his position.

Cunningham looked up. 'Now you have no direct access to him and no way to keep an eye on things.'

By things, Henry knew Cunningham meant the books. The last disaster would be for Ashe to discover the errors in the ledgers and his perfidy there. It would be enough to get him locked up or transported, neither of which option suited him. It would also be enough to expose the cartel's interference in the dealings.

'Bennington hasn't mentioned the other piece of news,' Marcus Trent drawled from the head of the table. 'Tell them, Bennington, how Bedevere brought his brother home.'

'Damn it!' Ellingson exploded from the other end of the table. 'Can you do nothing right, Bennington? First you lose the heiress, now this. The crazy loon might tell Bedevere something of use and Bedevere might believe him, whether he's crazy or not.'

Henry forced himself to remain outwardly calm. Inside, however, he shared Ellingson's explosive feelings. Here at the last it was all falling apart. If it did, he would pay dearly with his freedom and quite possibly his life. Newgate or a prison hulk would be the least of his worries if Trent and company got to him first.

Henry tried a desperate deflection. 'We must act quickly. It's not too late to salvage this. We need to shift our plans from minimising the players to eliminating the players.' It would all be easier if Ashe were simply removed from the situation. The time had come for him and his investment partners to revisit more drastic means of minimising Ashe's role in the estate's future. The future of Bedevere lay below ground, not above it. That just might be where Ashe's future lay, too.

'Perhaps a kidnapping,' Samuels spoke up, his narrow eyes thoughtful and malevolent. 'We could use your fellow in the village, Bennington, the one that did the carriage wheel. Perhaps we could exchange someone for mining rights. The earl? The bride? I've always fancied doing a bridal kidnapping.'

Trent shook his head. 'Bedevere knows we can't harm his brother without ruining Henry's claim. Our threat would have no bite. As for the bride, who knows what Bedevere would or wouldn't do for her? He's marrying her for money, not love. Why would he exchange her for his estate? It's counter-intuitive to his plans.'

'Death, then,' said Cunningham. 'Bedevere simply has to die. Soon.'

Trent gave a casual shrug as if he planned executions every day. 'Both of them. With the brother out of the way, Bennington's the earl. It makes sense. It takes away the chance that Henry's crimes in the ledger might be discovered.' He winked at Henry and Henry felt cold. 'Forgery is still a nasty crime to be convicted of, isn't it, old chap?' Trent said it as if it were a lark. To him it might be. It wasn't his head on the chopping block if he was discovered.

The whole investment wasn't supposed to be this complicated. It was supposed to have been a simple matter of taking over Bedevere, of taking advantage of circumstances. Henry had never guessed it would lead to a discussion of murder or him becoming the earl in quick succession. But he was powerless to stop it—why should he when it came with a title? That was a powerful carrot to dangle in front of him indeed.

Henry was a selfish creature. If he had to choose between Ashe and himself, he'd choose himself, but he'd be damned if he was going to pull the actual trigger. 'I think we need to have a professional do it,' Henry put in. He was done taking risks for the moment.

'Cunningham'll do it.' Trent nodded towards the thickset man with small eyes. Cunningham grinned. 'Yeah, I'll do it.' He cracked his knuckles with no small amount of glee. 'If we can't kidnap a bride, we can at least shoot a groom.'

Trent smiled. 'And you, Henry, will be the bait to draw Ashe out.'

Henry felt cold fingers walk down his spine. 'Oh, don't worry, Henry,' Trent drawled with impatience. 'Confession is good for the soul.'

'Any last confessions, little brother? You're about to be a married man,' Alex joked in a little antechamber at the side of the chapel.

'I don't think we have that much time. Genevra should be here any minute.' Ashe looked past his brother's shoulder one more time, distractedly watching the door at the chapel's entrance. It wasn't quite ten o'clock.

Technically, Genevra still had another ten minutes. What was she doing right now? Was she coming downstairs at Bedevere? Climbing in the carriage? Was she already on her way? Was she having doubts and wondering what she'd done? Perhaps she was thinking she could manage Henry and his threats on her own, that her freedom was too high a price to pay for protection.

Alex's hand gripped his shoulder. 'Don't worry, she'll be here. Everything will be all right.' Alex smiled. 'She likes you, you know. More than likes you. She wants to know you, Ashe.'

'She knows what must be done.'

Alex nodded. 'Still, she's not a woman who does things against her will. She would not marry you if it didn't suit her.'

That was what worried Ashe the most. What did he know of marriage and having a wife? He'd hardly kept a woman over two weeks, let alone a lifetime. Failing was not an enjoyable prospect, but neither was the alternative. What if he did fall in love with his wife? Then the risk of disappointing her would be far greater than disappointing someone who didn't hold his affections.

Vicar Browne motioned for them to take their places. Ashe drew in a deep breath. The carriage must have been sighted. Salvation was in sight. Genevra hadn't run, although he had no reason to think she would have.

Alex embraced him one last time. 'The next time I do that, you'll be a husband and within time a father.' The wistfulness in his voice could not be completely hidden.

'It should be you, Alex,' Ashe whispered. But it would never be Alex. Alex would never marry.

'I will be a doting uncle and very happy. Let yourself be the same, Ashe. You carry too much guilt with you. Don't think I don't see it. I am your brother and I know you better than anyone. Let yourself be happy.' Alex stepped back from their embrace and smoothed the shoulders of Ashe's morning coat. 'There. You're ready.'

Ashe squared his shoulders and took up his place, Alex beside him, at the front of the little chapel. The chapel had played witness to generations of Bedeveres; his own parents had married here, he and Alex had been baptised here. His father's last service had been here. Leticia's own wedding had been here. He was cognisant as he stood at the front of the church, with his covey of aunts looking on, how auspicious the place and occasion was to them. Life passed through this little stone chapel.

His aunts might be the only guests in attendance, but they had not let the event go unmarked. A pristine cloth covered the altar. Silver candlesticks burning new wax candles sat on that altar, bracketed by two vases of hothouse flowers. Genevra would not look back on her wedding day and say it had been devoid of any decoration, even if it had been devoid of guests and the great pomp that would have, *should* have, accompanied the wedding of a lord under other circumstances.

The door to the church opened. Genevra stood there, looking for something, looking for him. She found him, smiled and began the short walk down the aisle, composed and elegant in pearly-grey satin. The satin of her gown hugged the contours of her form, emphasising the slimness of her waist, the gentle curve of her hip as she moved towards him.

'She's beautiful—you're a lucky man, Ashe,' Alex whispered, following up with a surreptitious poke to his ribs. But more notable than her loveliness, she walked the short aisle alone.

Ashe thought she might well be one of the bravest people he'd ever known. She was alone in the world except for nominal family in America. Yet she'd thrown her lot in with his and chosen to march towards a very uncertain future.

Ashe reached for her hand and drew her to him. She was pale despite her composure and her hand trembled within his. He hoped she wasn't having regrets already. There would undoubtedly be some. English society would not look upon this marriage with kindness and it would be difficult for her initially. She was an outsider, married only for her money. London would not let her forget it, although he would do his best to smooth the way when the time came.

For now it was enough to know that she was out of Henry's reach. The papers had been signed yesterday in Marsbury's tiny office. Genevra was as legally safe as he could make her. She was no longer an official shareholder in the regency of the estate. Henry had not been seen since he'd left, but that didn't mean he was undefeated.

A jolt of pain shot up Ashe's leg momentarily and he barely bit back an 'ow!' Genevra had squashed his instep with her slippers. He speared her with a disbelieving look. What bride stepped on her groom's foot doing the service?

'I believe this is your part,' she whispered, an enquiring smile on her very kissable mouth.

'Do you, Ashton Malvern Bedevere, take this woman to be your lawfully wedded wife?'

Genevra stifled a nervous laugh. His middle name was Malvern? She hadn't known. This was sheer madness, marrying a man whose full name she didn't know. Then his green eyes held hers as he repeated the vows and the craziness seemed well justified, rational even.

This wedding was very different than the one she'd had with Philip. The comparison came unbidden and unwelcome—she didn't want to think of that earlier occasion on today of all days, except that the contrast was so glaring. That wedding had borne all the trappings a wedding should have, and borne them in extreme. There'd been fifteen urns of flowers lining the church in Boston, pews full of the city's finest, and her dress had been imported from France. The preparations had taken months. In the end, it had been for naught. Philip hadn't loved her. Had never loved her, only feigned deep affection, and she'd been too naïve to know the difference.

Today was a simpler, more honest occasion. Ashe hadn't pretended to love her, hadn't whispered nonsensical flattery in her ear, but she knew from the start what she was getting: a man who would protect her from scandal, a man who was not entirely without feeling for her, a man who took his responsibility to his family with seriousness. That would have to be enough.

Ashe slid a ring on her finger and bent to kiss her. It was done now, enough or not. Marry in haste, repent at leisure, came the unbidden thought as his lips found hers. With Ashe Bedevere as a husband, that could be fun indeed.

But that would have to wait a few hours at least.

There had still been some wedding traditions to perform. They'd spent the day at Bedevere, lingering with Alex and the aunts over a delicious wedding breakfast before delivering tokens of the wedding to the few servants on hand. More would be hired within the week, of course. Now that she was the ostensible mistress, Genevra would see the place fully staffed as quickly as possible. It would be her first official task.

Afterwards, Genevra had changed into a walking gown and she and Ashe strolled through Audley to celebrate with the villagers and farmers. Ashe tossed pennies to the children in the village square and Genevra laughed at their delighted scrambling.

The shadows lengthened and at last it was time to turn for home and their wedding night. There'd be no wedding trip, but it was understandable. With Alex newly home, the funeral still lingering, and Henry out there somewhere licking his wounds, a trip seemed poorly timed.

But, Genevra discovered, Ashe was not without his resources. 'Where are we going?' she queried as they turned away from the house and headed down towards the little lake.

Ashe winked. 'The summerhouse. My aunts tell me

you've not been there yet.' But that was all he'd say on the subject.

Dusk and lanterns showed the structure to advantage and Genevra gasped softly when she saw it. 'Oh, Ashe, it's beautiful.'

She had not ventured out here before. It was not a place for winter visits and Ashe's father had been too ill to walk so far in any case. Ashe held the door for her and she slipped inside. The building was a three-walled structure with a bank of windows looking out on to the lake. In the summer the windows opened completely. Filmy white lengths of curtains hung at the windows and the room was comfortably furnished with *chaises*, chairs, small tables and, most importantly, a box bed. An armoire stood along one wall full of supplies: blankets, clean sheets and drawers for clothes.

'I might not want to leave,' Genevra confided.

Ashe was behind her, his hands settling at her waist, firm and possessive. An undeniable thrill ran through her at the thought: *I am his.*

'Perhaps we should try it out, though, before you decide,' Ashe suggested. 'There's bread and cheese and a bottle of wine on the sideboard.'

She turned in his arms, eyeing him with teasing scepticism. 'What shall it be first, Mr Bedevere, bread and wine or bed?' She warmed to his playful teasing.

'Why do we have to choose?' Ashe replied naughtily. 'Bed and wine are a delightful combination if one knows what they're doing.'

'And I suppose you do?'

'Oh, yes, I most certainly do.' Ashe stepped back, a seductive smile on his lips. 'May I be so bold as to say you might find yourself overdressed for the occasion? I think you'll find something more comfortable behind the screen.'

Genevra ducked around the screen that shielded the box bed from the rest of the room. There was a trunk at the bed's foot and she found it well stocked. Genevra pulled out a satiny dressing robe in white, trimmed with elegantly embroidered green flowers. Melisande's work, she thought with a sentimental tear. The old dear had outdone herself on the robe. She took out a second robe, a man's banyan, and laid it out for Ashe. She changed quickly, listening for Ashe beyond the screen.

It didn't take him long to appear, tray in hand, his green eyes burning with approval at the sight of her. 'Now it seems I'm the one who is overdressed.' She heard the desire in his voice. He set the tray down, his hand going slowly, deliberately, to the cravat tied at his neck.

He pulled it loose and drew it off. Then came the coat, the waistcoat and the shirt, leaving his chest bare to her scrutiny. 'You're doing that on purpose,' she accused playfully.

He looked at her with hot eyes. 'Maybe. Is it working?'

'You know it is.' Her husband was a fine specimen of male virility. Muscles defined his arms and his torso right down to the long lean length of his hip and thigh.

He sat for a moment to pull off his boots and shrug out of his trousers.

Genevra sucked in her breath. The strong planes of his back and the curve of his buttock as he bent to retrieve the bottle from the tray were positively enticing. 'Wine, my dear?' He held up the bottle, divinely unbothered by his nakedness.

'What about the bread and cheese?' This was shaping up to be unlike any picnic she'd ever experienced.

'There'll be time for that later. Now, take off your robe and lie back for me.' She did as she was told, carefully setting the robe aside.

He came to her, straddling her hips, his phallus teasing her where it brushed against her skin with promises of what was to come. 'Allow me to pour the wine.' With elegant grace he pulled the cork and trickled a few drops into her navel, running a trail up to her breasts. She gasped at the audacity of it, the absolute eroticism of it.

'Shh, be still or it will spill,' Ashe cautioned with a wicked smile. Then he bent his head and drank, and licked and sucked until she thought she'd go mad from the sensations he roused in her.

She thrashed a bit as he sucked the last of the wine from her breast, the sensation too much to contain. 'Remind me to tie your hands to the bed next time, my restless one,' Ashe murmured against her skin. 'Do you think you'd like that?' He sat up and shifted his position, moving lower until she had no illusions about what he intended next. Surely he didn't mean to… 'Ashe?' The one word carried her hesitation.

'Don't worry, Neva, you'll like this, I promise.' He'd been right on that account before. His head bent to that most private part of her, his tongue making good on the promise until she cried out her pleasure. Only after that did he cover her with his length and sheathe himself inside her and create pleasure for them both.

As wedding nights went, they were off to a good start and the sun hadn't quite set yet.

They managed to get to the bread and cheese an hour later, curled up on a double-sized *chaise* by the windows. Ashe poured a glass of wine for her. 'A toast is in order. To my wife, who has made me a happy man on this day and shall make me happier in the years to come.'

The toast was short but perfect, the words thoughtful. Emotion stirred. It would be easy to love this man, easy and dangerous. He couldn't hurt her if she didn't love him. But the chasm between 'just sex' and love didn't seem as broad as it use to be. If she wasn't careful, she could fall. The wicked rake was also a very good man at heart. She wondered if she'd be able to trust him with hers or whether she'd have any choice in the matter when the time came. She rather suspected she'd wake up one day and find it had simply become his without her consent.

Ashe reached for the bottle of wine and sloshed it a bit. 'There's half a glass left.' He made to pour it into her glass.

'No, I have a better idea.' Genevra gently took the bottle from him and came around to his side of the *chaise.* She knelt before him, untying the banyan and spreading the halves wide so that he was revealed in all of his male splendour. He was already half-aroused and she gave a seductive laugh, running her thumb lightly over the head of his phallus in preparation. 'I have it on good authority wine is good for other things besides drinking.'

She spilled wine along the ridge of his member and very slowly lowered her head to him and took him in her mouth with deliberate intimacy, tongue licking and coaxing. Her hands, braced on the insides of his thighs could feel his muscles tighten as his pleasure heightened. She heard a groan, deep and guttural, in his throat and then it was over, his hands tangled in her hair as he sought his release.

'Neva, you'll be the death of me,' Ashe whispered hoarsely.

'There are probably worse ways to die.' She smiled, revelling in her power for a moment. Whatever else might plague their marriage, the bedroom would not be part of it. This would be the one place where they'd have equal ground and equal pleasure of one another. Surely that counted for something. Marriages had started with less.

Chapter Twenty-One

Ashe leaned against the stone balustrade of the back veranda, savouring the surprising warmth of the day and taking in the rarity of the scene spread before him. The sun was out, teasing about the possibility of an early summer, and Genevra was home early from the village, a rare occurrence indeed. She sat with his aunts on the newly finished stone patio, reading while they were busy with needlework. It was a peaceful scene, much as he'd envisioned it when he'd planned the patio.

Ashe would liked to have said marriage was just as bad as he'd ever imagined it would be; that he'd knowingly traded his freedom for financial security and was now feeling the sting of being yoked to a harpy for the rest of his life.

The truth was, marriage to Genevra was working out just fine in its early weeks. Genevra was already vastly familiar with the workings of the household and Ashe realised for the first time how indispensable she must have been for the aunts during the past winter.

She had known few servants were left and had set about hiring more. Within a week, Bedevere was staffed as it had been in the years of Ashe's childhood. There were footmen running errands, maids polishing banisters, grooms in the stable and gardeners, well, in the gardens.

She'd been unstinting with funds, too. As soon as she could she had turned over a large sum of money to him for the welfare of Bedevere. He'd paid the outstanding debts and bought farming supplies for his tenants. He had commissioned more work on the gardens and set about buying horses for his newly staffed stables.

After the string of bad luck that had plagued Bedevere over the years, this was a heady time for the struggling estate and for him. He'd been without regular funds for years, living on his reputation. It had been something of a struggle to keep his rooms on Jermyn Street and to keep up appearances with his wardrobe. Now, money was no object, thanks to Genevra, whose generosity he saw everywhere he turned at Bedevere, but whose actual presence was much absent.

Without a wedding trip to intervene between the wedding and taking up the reins of the household, they'd settled into a schedule almost immediatcly. He saw his wife in the mornings over breakfast and the newspapers. They would adjourn to the estate office to discuss business, which Genevra would cover in a brisk manner, running through her itemised lists of things she was doing and things that needed doing in the near future: the attic needed cleaning out, several pieces of furniture needed bringing down, there were new window treatments and furniture to order, a decorator was coming from London with a store of silk wallhangings for the public rooms.

Three days a week, she was off to Seaton Hall to oversee the last of the interior renovations and some of the energy that radiated throughout Bedevere was gone. The other two days, she spent in the village helping Vicar Browne with those in need. She'd become the perfect lord's wife: busy and efficient, running his home, supporting her charities, and acting as his liaison in the village so that he could carry out his other responsibilities.

There were plenty of those. She wasn't the only one with a filled schedule. He spent time with the farmers learning how best to maximise Bedevere's crops. He'd thought he'd hear about how bad the harvests had been the last few years.

Poor harvests seemed to suggest themselves as a reason for Bedevere's failing fortunes. But harvests had been adequate. Many he talked to blamed the lack of proper equipment and poor maintenance of the land itself; a fence that had crumbled and not been repaired had let livestock in to trample cornfields; a dike had collapsed, leaving flooded crops in its wake. Someone had quietly sabotaged Bedevere in subtle ways. Ashe's first thought was Henry, but he could not prove it. Not yet.

But for all he'd learned, he wasn't making any progress in solving the financial mystery that haunted Bedevere. Crops had been set up to fail, the coffers had been emptied. By whom and why? If it was Henry, why? How had he done it? Ashe was sure the answer was in the ledgers somewhere, but he didn't know where to start or what to look for. Ashe came home each evening, tired and frustrated, wanting his wife and the few hours of peace she brought. He had her in the nights. But in the mornings, she was gone again.

He knew many men who wouldn't complain of such an arrangement. Three months ago, he would have been one of them. Three months ago, he'd been a different man.

That man had spent his nights carousing in all manner of establishments, perhaps going weeks without bedding the same woman two nights in a row, his fortunes dependent on the turn of a card, the roll of a billiard ball, or the right invitation. This man, the new Ashe, was more concerned about spring planting, about restoring the gardens outside his home, and about his absent wife. His old crowd in London would not know this new man. He wasn't even sure he did.

Genevra looked up from her book and saw him. She was lovely today in a sky-blue gown trimmed in white lace, a straw hat to match. She waved and motioned for him to join them. Ashe started down the shallow stairs towards the patio. The only complaint he had about his wife was that he was slowly but surely falling in love with her. He'd promised himself he wouldn't allow it to get that far. He could respect her, he could admire her, he could find her lovely, that was all. But he was failing at it. By now his initial passion for her should have bottled its edge as it had done with so many other

women before her. Instead, he found himself counting the hours until nightfall when she'd be his, not the
village's Lady Bountiful, not the aunts' companion or
Alex's. Just his. Perhaps he could persuade her to take
a walk and he could steal a march on evening.

He had eyes only for her and the knowledge of it sent
a thrill down Genevra's spine as Ashe approached. He
bent to kiss her on the cheek, so very chaste and husbandly compared to the passionate lover she encountered in the night.

'Do you like the patio, Aunts?' Ashe settled himself
next to her on one of the benches, his thigh brushing
her leg. 'The roses will bloom before long and it will
smell wonderful out here in the summer.'

After a decent interval of small talk, Ashe reached
for her hand. 'Aunts will you excuse us? I want to take
Genevra for a walk in our glorious afternoon. Perhaps
we'll walk down by the stream.'

The aunts smiled at one another and Genevra knew
they didn't believe him. She blushed. The old dears
were romantics at heart and she guessed the directions
of their thoughts.

'Your aunts think you're stealing me away for an
afternoon tryst,' Genevra said once they were out of
earshot.

'They're good guessers.' Ashe laughed, not the least
bit ashamed of his transparency. She liked that about
him. He made no apologies for what he did or what he
wanted. For the time being, that was her.

He wanted her. How long that would last was any-one's guess. It was almost too good to be true. When she wasn't careful, it was too easy to forget it was her money rejuvenating the estate. Of course he wanted her—she held his welfare in her hands. Without her, he would be nothing. No, not quite nothing. Ashe Be-devere would never be nothing and, for a little while, he was hers.

She had to protect herself against the time that would come when he'd need her money a little less, or when he grew tired of her and sought someone else. A rake like Ashe wasn't used to monogamy. It had only taken Philip two months before he'd acquired a mistress. Out here in the countryside, Ashe might take longer, but it was still just a matter of time. She kept herself busy so that when that time came she might notice it a bit less.

'What is it, Neva? You look like a cloud passed over your sun,' Ashe scolded, helping her over some stones in the path.

Genevra shook her head. 'Nothing.' She'd been caught thinking. She needed deflection. 'How are things going with the ledgers? Have you made any progress?' She knew the estate's finances were an agony to him. He wanted to know what had happened, but that was one area in which she had no knowledge to offer him. When she'd first made the aunts' acquaintance last sum-mer, much of the damage had already been done and of course no one ever showed people their ledgers.

Ashe pushed a hand through his dark hair. 'I don't want to think about it on such a nice day. It's a very dark topic. If I discover what happened and who did it, I am obligated to bring them to justice.'

Genevra shot him a querying look. 'Do you think the culprit is other than Henry?'

'There's always the possibility that it was Alex. Certainly, no one expects me to prosecute my brother in his condition.'

'Have you asked Alex? Surely he'd tell you? He knows you wouldn't harm him.'

Ashe shook his head. 'I haven't. I'm a coward, Neva. I haven't wanted to trigger a fit. I've enjoyed having my brother, having him here with me healthy. I can almost pretend he's going to be all right.'

Genevra smiled softly. This was the first time they'd talked of something personal since the wedding. Perhaps they were making progress of a different sort. 'Maybe I can help. I would be glad to look over the books with you if Alex can't. Who knows, there might be something I remember.'

'You have so many other activities right now. I don't want to bother you.' He was slipping away from her again. Genevra could feel it. The vulnerability of a moment earlier was vanishing.

'I'm your wife. You can let me help. I want to help,' she protested.

'I'll manage it, Genevra,' Ashe snapped, making clear the conversation was finished.

She walked in silence beside him, fuming over his behaviour. How dare he shut her out? 'Has there been any news of Henry?' Genevra ventured once she had her temper under control. Perhaps some of the walk could be salvaged.

Ashe shook his head. 'He's most likely at his farm.'

'Will he stay there?' Genevra queried.

'If you're asking are our worries over, the answer is maybe. You don't have to worry. You're safe now. If he wants anyone, it's me.'

That was the last straw. Really, the man's arrogance knew no bounds. 'That makes you happy, doesn't it? It's all on your shoulders. The rest of us can't interfere,' Genevra ground out. The man was infuriating.

'No one else need be placed at risk,' Ashe said simply. 'Ah, we're here. The stream. Alex and I spent countless summers sneaking away down here.'

He was about to launch into a story of boyhood adventure, but Genevra wasn't satisfied. 'We're not done with the previous conversation. I don't want you to shoulder all the troubles alone. I want to be more than your banker, Ashe.'

Ashe stiffened as if slapped, his gaze fixed straight ahead on the far bank of the stream. 'I've never treated you as just my banker.'

'You just did.' Genevra turned to go. Tears threatened. She would not let him see her cry, not over this. He'd never professed to love her. Whatever hurt she'd incurred was her own fault. She'd let herself believe so many things when she'd known better.

Ashe's hand seized her arm. 'Genevra, be fair. I never once—'

Genevra wrenched her arm away. 'No, not once, *al-*

ways, Ashe. You have consistently shut me out. You're bothered by the ledgers, but you won't let me help. You won't tell me what's on your mind half the time. I don't know why you fought with your father, I don't know why you stayed away for so many years. I don't know anything. You make love to me at night and I write you banker's drafts during the day and you expect that to be enough. It's not.'

Ashe sat down on a large rock, looking weary, all the teasing from minutes ago gone. She'd said too much. 'I'm sorry,' she began, but Ashe waved her away.

'Sorry for what? Sorry for the truth? It is the truth, you know, Neva. But I can't give you any more. Not right now.'

Maybe not ever, Genevra thought. She should have contented herself with her fantasies and make-believe. He didn't love her and she'd pushed him to say as much which only served to make things awkward, not better. Whoever thought honesty was the best policy had never been in love with a man who didn't quite love you back.

Genevra sat down beside him, trying to forget the ugly conversation. 'So, you and Alex used to come here as boys?' She looked overhead at the wide tree limb. 'Too bad there isn't a swing. This would be a perfect place for one.'

Ashe shot her a wry look. 'It is the perfect place and there used to be one. If you look closely, you can still see the remnants of the rope up there.'

Genevra squinted and followed Ashe's finger up into the leafy boughs. 'What happened?'

'Henry. He was always pulling pranks on Alex and me. Pranks was his word, not ours. At first, they were just malicious jokes, but as we got older the pranks got more serious. I think this one was the worst. The rope was sliced so that whoever was on the swing would fall when they swung out over the water. In the summer, you had to swing out to the middle of the stream before you dropped. The water was too shallow closer to the bank. If you dropped too soon, you could hit rocks, which was what Henry wanted.'

Genevra peered down into the water, trying to make out the rocks. 'You can't see them in the winter or spring when the stream is full,' Ashe explained.

Genevra stiffened visibly in shock over the revelation. 'Was anyone hurt?'

'A distant cousin. He broke his leg and has not walked properly since. The accident kept him out of the military, out of a livelihood. The cousin was a second son with hopes of a commission in the cavalry.'

'That's a terrible story. What happened to Henry? Was he punished?'

Ashe leaned closed, his voice quiet and intimate. 'We couldn't prove it. Ropes fray, especially ropes outdoors in the weather. Henry's very good at not getting caught, Neva.'

'Maybe you'll never discover what happened in those ledgers. Maybe it would be best to just move forwards.'

'And maybe if I do that, history will repeat itself. I can't take that risk, Neva. I have to know. If it's Henry, he has to be caught this time or he won't stop until he has it all. Don't you see, Genevra? The less you know, the safer you are. If it is Henry, and if he suspected you knew something that could ruin whatever scheme he's planning…'

He had shut her out to protect her, she could see that now, misguided though his plan was. Such a plan would have to be rectified. It wasn't love, but it was a start.

Genevra didn't let him finish. She placed a finger on his lips. 'If you brought me out here to seduce me, you'd better get on with it or risk disappointing your aunts.'

Chapter Twenty-Two

It rained the next day, just to prove it wasn't quite spring yet. The weather kept everyone inside, which suited Ashe perfectly. It was high time to tackle the ledgers, with help. Genevra's sharp words at the stream yesterday had given him pause for thought. On his own, he was no closer to resolving the mystery of where the money had gone than he was when he'd first arrived. It was also becoming clear that this was the last and perhaps most critical piece to resolve before his home-coming could truly be complete.

Ashe announced his intentions for the day at break-fast, earning an approving nod from Genevra, and the three of them sequestered themselves in the estate of-fice, prepared for a long day. Ashe took up residence behind the big desk while Alex and Genevra stationed themselves near the fireplace with a low table between them, perfect for sorting papers.

'Are you sure you're up to this, Alex?' Ashe asked one more time before they started.

'I will be fine. It will be good to know if I am to blame or if someone else took advantage of the situation and used me as a scapegoat,' Alex said staunchly. Ashe admired his brother's courage in that moment. Alex had never been one to shirk his responsibilities and he wasn't avoiding them now.

Ashe spread his hands on the desk's surface. 'All we know is that it is likely someone behaved irresponsibly with the estate's finances. According to the ledgers, items were sold for far less than their actual worth. We want to look through the receipts for those bills of sale. The receipts will tell us who the items were sold to and perhaps even the actual sale amount.' Although, if it was Henry, and if Henry was smart, he'd keep the two prices consistent, perhaps issuing a receipt to the man he charged and making a separate receipt for the Bedevere records. Still, a receipt would have a name and they could always contact the new owner.

Sorting through the receipts was a daunting task. There were boxes of them and progress was slow. It was something of a needle-in-a-haystack-style search. Amid the receipts for daily living expenses and regular estate bills, they were looking for the odd sale.

Halfway through the pile, Ashe was beginning to despair. Maybe there was no receipt. Perhaps his assumption had been erroneous from the start. Then his hand stilled on a bill of sale. He read it twice to be sure. They'd had a few false alarms already. It was the receipt for the horses. His gaze dropped to the bottom of the page, searching for a signature. But the name he found wasn't either of the names he'd been expecting. The signature scrawled at the bottom was his father's.

'Alex, look at this.' Ashe handed the paper to his brother.

'In November.' Alex checked the date. 'It's likely I was gone by then. Father took a turn for the worse in November and Henry was eager to have me out of the way. It was a very difficult time.' Alex paused. 'I wasn't well in November, not that I remember any of it.' Ashe could see how difficult the confession was for Alex to make. He turned to Genevra, hoping to spare Alex.

Genevra picked up the receipt and shook her head after a moment's study. 'Your father could not have signed it. He was very ill and wouldn't have been interested in doing any business in the first place. But even if he'd wanted to sell the horses, he couldn't have physically signed a bill of sale. By that point, he'd lost the ability to use his right hand. He could not have written his name with that amount of precision.'

She checked the date again. 'You were not here, Alex. At least on account of the horses, you can rest assured they were not your doing.' There would be record of that, Ashe thought. The place where Alex had been kept would have a note of his arrival. That only left Henry. But it raised another question.

'How did Henry pay Dr Lawrence?' Ashe asked. 'There's no mention of payments in the ledgers and I haven't seen any receipts to that extent, yet Dr Lawrence gave quite the affirmative response when I asked if Mr

Bennington paid his bills.' He hoped Genevra would know. Henry had been living here full time by then.

'It was never discussed.'

Ashe drummed his fingers on the desk top, thinking out loud. 'Henry doesn't have that kind of money. His income is comfortable, but he's not that charitable. I can't see him depriving himself of his worldly pleasures to pay Dr Lawrence.' In fact, too much of this didn't fit Henry at all. It was all too carefully planned. The receipt for the horses matched, confirming either that separate receipts had been made or the items in question had been sold for far less than their worth. The only chink was that his father could not possibly have signed the receipt.

A devastating thought occurred to him: the will.

The date had been much later than November. Marsbury had the original, but Ashe had a copy of it for his records. Ashe dug in the desk drawer. 'Here, look at this.' He spread the papers out for Alex and Genevra to see. 'Father's signature is barely legible here, it's hardly more than a scribbled line.'

They found other receipts, all signed with his father's name in legible, impossible precision, but no sign of any monies having been sent to Dr Lawrence. Ashe drafted letters to the buyers, politely asking to verify the amounts paid for their items, but their answers weren't mandatory. The big question still remained unanswered: why would someone deliberately bankrupt the estate? Especially if that someone was Henry and had hopes of taking it over.

* * *

Ashe pushed back from the desk well into the afternoon. He'd come back to one thought time and time again throughout the morning. 'I think it's time to consider the possibility that Henry isn't operating alone.'

Alex looked thoughtful. 'Who?'

Ashe shrugged. 'I don't know and I don't know why. But they could be the ones who paid Dr Lawrence, which is why we have no record.'

'We also have to consider more than the receipts,' Genevra put in. 'These receipts are just the tip of the proverbial iceberg. Household items were being sold, but that alone wouldn't bankrupt a healthy estate. Whatever has been done here, has been going on for a few years. This doesn't explain where the usual income went from rents and crops.'

Ashe nodded in agreement. What they'd done today was merely pick the low hanging fruit. It was a start, but there was so much more they didn't have. They didn't even have Henry's name on a document to prove he'd been skimming money from the sales. If he'd actually sold the items for the recorded prices, then he was guilty of nothing except bad judgcment in the eyes of the law.

Ashe rose. 'We're done for the day. Keep thinking of anything you might recall.'

He needed some time alone. It was still raining outside. A walk was out of the question, so he headed to the music room and took refuge in his piano. Today had been more emotional than he'd expected. He'd not thought looking over receipts and bills would affect him so strongly. But he'd been wrong. Seeing his father's signature on the will again, and hearing Genevra mention how his faculties had failed him, were potent reminders of mortality. If a man like his father could deteriorate, so could they all.

Ashe ran his hands over the keys, letting physical memory take over as he played so his thoughts could wander. He'd come to grips with his father's death that night at the mausoleum, but he'd not come to terms with the dying. He was starting to realise they were two different things.

He felt a presence rustle behind him, soft hands at his shoulders and the smell of lemongrass.

'He was alone. Both of his sons had left him.' Ashe spoke his thoughts out loud.

'Not entirely alone.' Genevra spoke quietly. 'He had his sister and his wife's sisters with him.'

'And you,' Ashe said.

'And me.' She was humble, but his father must have come to care for her a great deal. He'd pinned his estate's hopes on her and his father had not been misguided in that. Ashe had seldom known his father to make mistakes, as hard as that was to admit growing up. His father had been right about practically everything. His father had not been wrong now choosing Genevra, not just for Bedevere, but for him.

'Thank you for letting Alex and I help today.' She moved away from him and he turned to follow her progress to the window.

'Was it bad at the end?' Ashe went to join her at

the window. This was the conversation she'd wanted to have in the conservatory that first night, but he'd not been ready for it.

'He'd been failing for months.' Genevra sighed and leaned back against him. 'His doctor said he'd had a series of strokes over the past three years. Each one left him a bit more debilitated. He'd recover a little and there would be good days, but in the end it was just too much. He couldn't walk, couldn't write, speech was difficult.'

'I cannot imagine him that way.'

'Then don't. Keep him in your mind the way you remember him most.'

'I remember the last day I saw him. It was in this room. My bags were packed for Italy and the carriage was ready, even though we'd fought over my going. Father wouldn't have his son leaving in an old gig, disagreement or not.' Ashe caught himself smiling at the remembrance. His father had been duly proud of his station in life and had encouraged his sons to never forget what they'd been born to.

'He walked into the room and I thought, "Oh, no, here we go again." But all he said was, "Don't let yourself become less than you are." At the time, I only saw his words as another way of voicing his disapproval over what I intended to do.'

'What was that?' Genevra's body was warm and comforting against him and he tightened his grip about her waist. He'd not talked of this with anyone for years but it felt right talking with her now. He wanted to tell her.

'I wanted to be a pianist. I wanted to study in Vienna, I wanted to go to Italy and study piano-making. I wanted to make the grandest pianos of them all.' Ashe shook his head, remembering the numerous quarrels he'd had with his father over it. 'But that wasn't a dignified calling for a son of my father. The son of an earl, heir or not, did not put himself on stage performing, or dirty his hands in any form of carpentry. I'd been raised my whole life to understand that I would seek my career outside Bedevere. Bedevere was for Alex. But there were limits to what that career was supposed to be. Pianos weren't on the list. Unfortunately, I couldn't see myself in the military or behind a pulpit, God forbid.'

Genevra laughed softly with him. 'I don't know, you might have been a very popular vicar to say the least. The pews would have been full of women every Sunday. You might have done the Church of England a great service.

'But, you went anyway?' Genevra sobered and prompted him to return to the story.

'Yes, there were four of us that set off together on our Grand Tour. We went to Vienna first and took rooms on the Lanterngasse. I studied privately with a master there, but I was young and cocky and too talented for my own good. Suffice it to say, there were those who were jealous. One night, not long after I'd played at Schonbrunn, I found myself set upon by common street thugs after a performance. They'd been paid, of course, by those who thought I was rising too quickly.

It only took a sharp shard of glass to put paid to any future career hopes.'

Even now, years later, he could feel the pain of the slice that had ended his career, recalled the helplessness he'd felt in that alley, outnumbered five to one. Genevra was caressing his hand, turning it over before he could stop her.

'Is this it?' Her index finger traced the thin white line bisecting his palm. 'I'd never noticed it before. It healed well,' Genevra murmured.

'Thanks to a woman in Venice. We left Vienna immediately, but infection had set in and I took ill with a fever as we travelled. We got as far as Venice when we decided we needed professional help. She saved me.' Ashe winced. That part of the story was probably not suitable for a wife's ears. Genevra didn't want to hear about Signora de Luca. His friends had gone on after a while to other parts of Italy, but he'd stayed a long time with her, trying to piece together the remnants of his dream.

To her generous credit, Genevra did not pause on the mention of the good *signora*. 'Does it pain you? I think it must. I've noticed you flexing your hand on occasion. I thought nothing of it until now.'

'Only if it's overworked. I learned I couldn't build pianos, though.'

'What would you have built?' Genevra asked.

Ashe chuckled. 'I haven't thought of that for ages. I was going to build pianos with eight full octaves that thundered in a concert hall.' He sighed. 'It was too much strain every day. I also couldn't train or study with my former intensity. It was over. So, after a while, I rejoined my friends in Italy and I came back to England.'

'But not to Bedevere?'

'No.' This was the hard part of the story. He'd been too ashamed of his failure, too ashamed of the way he'd left to face his father. 'A twenty-three-year-old man's pride is a terrible obstacle, Neva.' It was also an obstacle that had grown more insurmountable as the years passed. He'd seen his brother occasionally when Alex had come up to town. But he'd not seen his father again.

'Your father would have forgiven you.'

'For leaving? Perhaps.' But for the rest? For deserting Bedevere, for deserting him? For becoming less than what he was? Ashe wasn't so sure. He wasn't certain he deserved it anyway.

He placed a kiss on the long column of Genevra's neck. 'I've never told anyone that story before. Not even Alex.'

She turned in his embrace to wrap her arms about his neck. 'I'm glad I'm the first,' she said, taking his mouth in a soft kiss, his body rousing at her touch.

'Do you know what else I've never done?' Ashe whispered.

'I can't imagine.' Her grey eyes were alight with teasing mischief. She boldly reached for him, finding the core of him and tracing its length through his trousers until he groaned.

'Careful, Neva, or I won't last until I get you to the piano.' His need was consuming him now as he lifted her to the piano. He needed to bury himself inside her, needed to feel her legs wrapped tightly around him. Her money had saved Bedevere, but *she* could save him.

Chapter Twenty-Three

'It has been a month and you've done nothing!' Henry's anger made him brave as the cartel sat at the long reading table adorning Marcus Trent's library.

'You are impatient, Bennington,' Trent scolded. 'How much bad luck do you think the Bedevere family can withstand before people start to question the reason for it?'

'The longer we wait, the better the chance becomes Bedevere will get a look at those ledgers and figure out something is wrong,' Henry argued. 'We already know he's started.' Thanks to Genevra's hiring flurry it had been relatively easy to place a man in the household who could monitor any interesting activity at Bedevere. He'd reported last week that Ashe had been combing the books and letters had gone out to names Henry recognised as purchasers of some of the goods he'd sold.

'If he's only looking at receipts, Henry, there's little to worry about. All he'll discover is your very poor sense of business.' Marcus waved away Henry's concerns.

Henry nodded, debating whether or not he dared to interrupt again. He'd sold the goods initially to continue breaking Bedevere. He'd not cared what price he got for them. It was all part of the plan to make the estate desperate, so desperate that whoever was in charge would welcome the opportunity to turn the parklands into a coal mine. But there was more to find in the ledgers if Ashe kept digging and Henry could not let it go unaccounted.

'If I might mention the other?' Henry began delicately. 'There's also the money "lost" on the "bad investments".' It wouldn't take Ashe long to start sniffing down that path. Most of the Bedevere funds had been drained that way. He'd signed Alex's name to most of them, most notably the Forsyth deal. The Forsyth deal had been real enough, but the other bad investments hadn't existed. They'd been fronts for Trent's cartel. The Bedevere coffers were now being used to fund the mining effort in part.

'Your name isn't on any of the deals,' Marcus said glibly. 'It's the young earl's name.'

'Signed by me,' Henry protested. 'Now that Alex is home—' The danger of discovery rose exponentially, but he didn't get to say that. Cunningham broke in.

'Now that the earl is home he can't be controlled by us any more. Dr Lawrence can't simply sedate him when he gets too assertive.' Cunningham glared.

That wasn't fair. It wasn't his fault Ashe had brought Alex home. Henry tried a different argument. 'We all have money tied up in this venture. The longer we drag it out, the longer we delay our profits. A month ago we'd agreed to take decisive action and we've done nothing.' A few heads nodded.

'All right, here's what I propose.' Marcus Trent rubbed his hands together and began to plan. 'We will try to buy him with his own money.'

'There are two gentlemen downstairs who wish to see you, sir,' Gardener announced in quiet tones.

Ashe looked up reluctantly from his game of chess with Alex. 'Do they have an appointment?' He didn't recall anything being scheduled on his calendar. 'Did they say what they wanted?'

'No, sir,' Gardener answered.

'Are they really gentleman, Gardener, or are you merely being polite?' Ashe gave a wry smile.

'They are businessmen, sir,' Gardener said without a trace of condescension, but the implication was there all the same. They weren't gentlemen and they were calling without a letter of introduction or an appointment. It was all very curious and out of the ordinary.

'I'd best go down and see them.' Ashe stood up, reaching for the jacket he'd discarded earlier. 'We'll finish when I get back. Don't touch anything, Alex. I know exactly where all my pieces are.'

'Maybe I should go with you.' Alex rose, too, but Ashe halted him.

'That's not necessary.'

Alex sat with a smile. 'It's probably not. Nobody

wants to do business with a crazy man.' He laughed it off, but the remark stung Ashe.

'It's not that. I was thinking of your safety. I didn't like the idea of you and I in a close room together with strangers.' Strangers who had no appointment.

'And the doctors say I'm paranoid,' Alex joked. 'It is possible, Ashe, that Henry has given up and is happy to remain on his farm. It's been a month and no news of anything nefarious.'

Ashe finished adjusting his jacket. 'I reserve the right to be sceptical on that account, Brother. Gardener, give me five minutes in the estate office and then show them up.'

Gardener had been right. The two visitors weren't gentlemen, although they tried very hard to be in their tailored clothes. But they lacked the accents that marked the upper class and that certain air of aristocratic hauteur. By the look of them, they were wealthy and that was the extent of their recommendation.

'Mr Bedevere, thank you for seeing us,' the larger, dark-haired man effused. 'I'm Marcus Trent and this is my associate Arthur Ellingson.'

Ellingson shot an eager look at the decanters lining the sideboard, but Ashe didn't take the hint. He'd offer them a seat and a few moments of his time, but that was all. 'Sirs, I haven't much time this afternoon so I'd appreciate it if we could get straight to your business,' Ashe said in aloof but polite tones.

'You might be in less of a hurry after you hear what

we have to say.' The one called Marcus chuckled. Ashe fixed him with a cold stare.

'It just so happens we know there is a significant deposit of coal on Bedevere land, a deposit, if mined correctly, that could keep the pockets of future earls lined for generations. We'd like to buy the rights to mine here for a significant fee of twenty thousand pounds and an offer of fifteen per cent of the profits once mining begins. It's a very generous offer.'

'I am sure it would be if I wanted to turn my estate into a mine.' Ashe's tone was glacial. 'But I assure you, I do not, never mind the fact that I have no idea how you've come by such information.'

Ellingson jumped in. 'I have charts, sir. You needn't worry about the authenticity of the information.'

'That's not what I'm worried about.' Ashe stood. 'Good day, gentlemen.'

'Don't be so hasty.' Trent met his gaze with a steely stare of his own. 'You'd hate to regret passing on this opportunity.'

'Is that a threat, Mr Trent?' Ashe did not mistake the intention of his words.

'Let's just say you can contact me if you change your mind.'

Or have it changed for him. Ashe understood this type of man all too well. 'I won't.' He called for Gardener to show the men out. He didn't want these two so-called businessmen lurking on Bedevere land longer than needed.

* * *

'Where's Mrs Bedevere, Gardener? Is she home yet?' She'd gone down to the village to help a mother with a new baby.

'She hasn't returned yet, sir.'

'Send her to me at once,' Ashe said tersely. He'd breathe easier when she was home, safe. The pieces were starting to come together. It was supposition only, but what if Henry knew about the coal? It gave him a motive to see Bedevere penniless. A penniless estate would be tempted to take the offer and, if Henry were in charge of the estate, he'd take that offer. Twenty thousand pounds was a small fortune in exchange for simply walking away from Bedevere not to mention the eventual fifteen per cent. It would be a comfortable allowance.

That was where he was different than Henry. Henry saw only the profit. Ashe saw the legacy of preserving the estate. Even if it hadn't been for Genevra's money, Ashe knew he would not be tempted. Staffordshire was full of industry and mining and he knew well the sight of ugly industrialism. Staffordshire was also full of rural beauty. Not all of the county had been industrialised yet and he far preferred it to a factory landscape.

The door to his office opened and Genevra breezed in, her hair in slight disarray from her hat, her cheeks pink from her drive. 'You'll be glad to know they're all doing well—' Then she stopped suddenly, her exuberance fading. 'What is it, Ashe?'

'There's a cartel that wants the rights to mine Bedevere for coal.'

'Henry?' Genevra sat down quietly.

'It makes sense.' Ashe outlined his theory. 'I have refused them, of course. I don't need their money.'

'But they're not likely to take no for an answer,' Genevra supplied.

'No. I do believe we'll be encouraged to rethink our position.' Ashe understood all too well this visit had been a warning and a chance, a last chance to throw in with Henry's plans or face his cousin's revenge.

Chapter Twenty-Four

This was how they'd do it: Henry would send a note to the house for Ashe. He wanted to talk and clear the air. Would Ashe please meet him at the mausoleum? The tone of the note would make it obvious this was to be a confession. If Ashe had no idea what Henry wanted to confess, all the better. But Henry very much feared Ashe would have at least an inkling. His cousin had spent too much time holed up going over ledgers not to suspect something was wrong even if he didn't know exactly what it was.

It wouldn't matter after today. He could tell Ashe he'd stolen the crown jewels among his myriad sins and there'd be nothing Ashe could do about it. Ashe would be dead before he left the mausoleum. A paid man would be waiting in the foliage to take a prime shot and catch Ashe unawares while he and Henry talked. Then Trent would quietly kill the man who had shot Ashe and no one would be any wiser. People didn't come looking for men who could be hired for murder. The shooter would not be missed and Ashe's death could be ruled as many things: suicide, a gun handling accident, perhaps even an accident perpetrated by his crazy brother. Henry liked that option best. It would give him an excuse to put Alex back under the care of Dr Lawrence.

The note had been sent. Even now, it should be sitting on the front table at Bedevere, waiting for Ashe's attention just as Henry would be waiting for him. Plans were in motion, even a little surprise Ashe would know nothing about if all went well. In a few hours this would be over and Bedevere would be his.

Ashe was late. Alex checked his watch again and paced the foyer. It was a languid pace, a stroll really. He wasn't upset. They were supposed to go walking this afternoon, a chance for brothers to talk. But Alex had seen him sitting on the lawn with Genevra enjoying a day of rare weather. When he'd looked out later, they'd been gone. He didn't mind. His restless brother was happy at last. And in love, although Alex didn't think Ashe even knew it. He would realise it soon enough and that gave Alex great comfort. Ashe would be content and that contentment would make him a fine trustee of Bedevere and a fine earl.

He'd not spoken of it with Ashe and hadn't planned to until he absolutely must, but he thought he didn't have long left in this world. There'd been a young doctor at the place where he'd been kept who'd confided his opinion of Alex's condition to him. Dr Lawrence hadn't agreed with such a bleak prognosis and had banned any further discussion, but it had made sense to Alex. The nervous breakdown had been a prelude, a sign of something larger. The depression, the despondency, the fits of forgetfulness, all typical. The young doctor had called it a disruption of his neurological system. He wasn't crazy. That was the good news. It had sustained him the months he'd been away. But his condition would eventually lead to death. With luck he had a year.

Alex could feel the small changes already. It was nothing drastic, but he could feel his energy ebbing throughout the day. Some days, he could feel his thoughts slipping away before he could grasp them. Some days, his speech slurred on occasion. Some days his hand shook.

And some days, like today, he was just fine. Today was a blessing. He worked hard on those days. He'd worked hard today, writing everything he meant to tell Ashe against the days and the times that would come when he wouldn't remember the answers his brother was looking for.

Alex paused by the front table. A folded note lay on the silver salver. Invitations were a rare commodity at Bedevere these days, but he imagined a time not far off when Genevra and Ashe would inspire a plateful of invitations. Bedevere would thrive again and Ashe's children would run up and down the halls and sail their boats in the fountain.

Alex picked up the note. It was addressed to Ashe, but there was no postmark to indicate it had come from

London or elsewhere. Whoever had written it had been local. No one in the house would write a note when they could just as easily speak with Ashe at dinner.

A fearful intuition pricked at him. Henry. Henry was out of the house now, driven off by his anger over Ashe's impending marriage. A note would be the only way for Henry to directly reach Ashe. Before his conscience could cause too much trouble, Alex flicked open the note. His eyes scanned down to the signature—*your cousin, Henry.*

Alex read each line carefully. The weasel was up to something. Henry wanted to talk? To confess? There wasn't enough hours in the day to hear that confession. The request seemed uncharacteristic. Henry wasn't exactly the penitent type. Alex carefully refolded the note and put it back. Whatever Henry wanted with this meeting, he was up to no good. His coal-cartel colleagues must be getting nervous. Henry had to know his 'business partners' would turn on him if he didn't deliver on his promises. He would have to give them something.

Thoughts clicked. Henry would give them Ashe. With Ashe dead there would be no more contest for the trusteeship of Bedevere. Only Ashe and Henry held any shares in Bedevere. A cold chill rushed through Alex. Ashe was walking into a trap. Henry didn't mean to confess. He meant to do murder.

Alex made a quick decision. He would go in place of Ashe. Henry didn't want him dead. Not yet, anyway. But first, he had to get something from his room.

Forewarned was forearmed. A 'crazy' man with a gun was bound to scare anyone and Henry had always been a coward.

'Sir, your brother has gone out walking alone.' Ashe nodded. Alex had been well since his return, but Ashe had made it explicitly known he wasn't to roam the estate alone. It was his fault. He was late. He was supposed to have gone out with Alex. He'd thought Alex would wait.

'Do you know which direction?' Ashe asked. The receipts could wait. 'How long ago did he leave?' Alex couldn't be that far ahead of him, he was only twenty minutes late.

'Ashe,' Genevra said tersely, 'read this.' She passed him a note. 'It was here on the table, but I think this might explain where Alex has gone.'

Ashe read the note, his fist clenching around the paper until it crumpled. 'Gardener, find my pistol.'

'Bring one for me, too, if you have them to spare,' Genevra said matter of factly. Gardener didn't flinch at the request. Gardener was doing better than he was.

Genevra turned to him. 'I'm going with you. If Henry plans to do evil out there, you will need me.'

'No, Neva. I cannot risk you,' Ashe said firmly. He would not put Genevra in harm's way intentionally. 'I need you here in case Alex comes back.' He couldn't quite give voice to the rest of the reason. He needed her here to be witness to the circumstances if he didn't return. If Henry had something horrible planned and he didn't come back, Genevra would be the one who had to seek justice.

Gardener clattered the down the steps, guns in hand. Ashe gave Genevra a final glance. Her grey eyes were dark and the stoic set of her jaw suggested she guessed at the unspoken reasons. She put a hand on his sleeve. 'Be careful.'

Ashe felt as if he was riding out to do battle. When had it become so ugly? When had this become so sinister? Henry's malice ran deep, far deeper than anyone had given 'lazy' Henry credit for.

His horse covered the distance to the mausoleum in no time. He dismounted a fair way from the destination. If something nefarious was afoot he didn't want to risk announcing his presence. He approached quietly, his pistol in hand discreetly at his side. If he'd guessed wrong and Henry had honourable intentions, he'd look utterly foolish coming armed.

But Ashe saw immediately his initial assumptions were correct. Alex stood in the clearing facing Henry, his voice carrying in the clearing before the mausoleum. 'You're surprised to see me.'

'The message wasn't for you.' Henry was nervous. His eyes darted everywhere and his feet shifted anxiously from foot to foot. Something was wrong. Ashe looked about trying to see what Henry hoped to see. Was there someone hidden in the bushes?

'I know.' Alex began to circle Henry. Alex had always been able to manage Henry. Watching him now brought back memories from childhood when Alex had been the only one who could bring Henry to justice for his cruel pranks. 'It made the message that much more interesting. What in the world did you need to tell my brother that it had to be done in private out here, so far from the house?'

Alex prowled like a cat. Henry's eyes followed him around the circle. Alex did not relent. 'Did you mean to tell him you forged your uncle's signature on several bills of sale? Or perhaps you wanted to tell him you forged *my* signature on the funds you took from Bedevere for the Forsyth investment?'

'You're a raving lunatic, no one will believe you. Dr Lawrence will say it's part of your paranoia,' Henry snarled. 'All the knowledge in the world won't save you.'

'And nothing will save you.' Alex brought his arm up, levelling a pistol at Henry. 'We're both lost souls, Henry. How does it feel?'

Henry paled. Ashe watched in fascinated horror. Alex had seemed almost fragile since his return, but today he was strong and commanding, the way Ashe remembered him, except now there was a cold edge to that command devoid of Alex's usual compassion. Ashe waited, not wanting to intervene until it was necessary.

'You won't shoot me,' Henry challenged, but his voice wavered as if he didn't believe it himself. Ashe didn't believe it either. Alex would shoot him. The coldness in him left Ashe in no doubt. The bigger issue was whether Ashe should let him do it.

'Of course I will. I'm "crazy". A crazy man with a

gun is a very frightening thing. One can never tell what they'll do.' Alex paused, his eyes narrowing in consideration. 'Or maybe I'm sane after all. Which is more terrifying because then you can be sure I know exactly what I'm doing. I will give you one chance, Henry. I want a signed confession from you about the forgeries and I want you to resign yourself from any attempt to control Bedevere.'

Henry looked petulant. 'Maybe you're not the only one here with a gun. Maybe there's a man in the woods waiting to fire.'

'On me?' Alex made an exaggerated show of amazement. 'I'm a peer of the realm. Is that what you'd planned for Ashe? To have someone shoot him unawares when he came to meet you in good conscience?'

Ashe looked about the grove. If a shooter recognised him, that could still happen. It was becoming imperative for all their safety that the elusive hidden man be found. There was a slight movement on the periphery of the clearing and Ashe saw what he'd been looking for.

Within in moments, Ashe had manoeuvred behind the would-be assassin. It was the work of seconds to render the man unconscious. Ashe decided it was time to show himself. He picked up the man's gun and stepped forwards.

'Your man has been neutralised, Henry.' Ashe smiled. 'I have personally rendered him useless. It hardly seems sporting of you to have planned such an unpleasant surprise for me. Now, about that confession

Alex has offered you. I suppose that offer is looking better and better.'

Henry was deathly pale now, all his plans in sudden shreds. 'That confession is my death warrant. You know the penalty for forgery.'

'As did you when you began all this,' Ashe reminded him.

'I'll shoot you now if you prefer,' Alex offered.

Ashe wondered if his brother would do it. He seemed in deadly earnest. He didn't relish watching Henry gunned down in cold blood at the family grave site. 'I think he means it, Henry. Come to the house, write out the confession,' Ashe urged.

Henry's face suddenly lit with something akin to hope as if he'd just remembered something. 'That might be difficult.'

'Why is that?'

'Because Bedevere is burning,' Henry said with malicious glee. 'You can smell it.'

The wind shifted and Ashe smelled the smoke for the first time. Alex vaulted up behind him on Rex and they were off, Rex driven hard by Ashe's own panic.

They saw the dark billows of smoke looming over the house as they took the last rise. 'Dear Lord,' Alex breathed, his grip on Ashe's waist tightening in horror.

It was only part of the house, Ashe noted. Already, he could see the workers from the road rushing towards the house. If he could get a bucket brigade going, there was still time to save the main wing. There had to be. Everything he loved was down there. Genevra was down there.

* * *

'Mrs Bedevere, there's a man here to see you.' Gardener found her in the music room where she'd taken up vigil after Ashe had ridden out. All she wanted was for Ashe to come back safely, for the issue of Henry's perfidy to be resolved once and for all.

'Who is it, Gardener?' The last thing she wanted was to receive guests and make small talk while she worried over Ashe.

'He is one of the coal people, madam.' Gardener's voice carried a tone of disapproval. Clearly, Gardener felt the man was not fit company. 'He called here once before to meet with Lord Bedevere.'

Genevra fingered the smooth butt of Ashe's pistol. She did not want to worry Gardener with other suppositions. Genevra had kept the pistol with her—the afternoon had been strange. What if this was a man who'd come with news about Ashe or some new threat from Henry? She hurried downstairs, the gun hidden effectively from view in the folds of her gown.

She didn't like the man on sight. He introduced himself as Mr Trent, a man of business, but he didn't look respectable in spite of his expensive clothes. He didn't carry the air of a successful businessman—there was something too sinister about him for that.

'What do you want?' she asked unkindly.

He chuckled at her coldness. 'You must be Mrs Bedevere. Mr Bennington told us you were quite the spitfire. He was right. Bennington knows his women. My business is with Mr Bedevere. Is he here?'

'You know he is not,' Genevra guessed. 'He's with Bennington. There was a note, as I am sure you're well aware.'

Trent leered with satisfaction. 'If he's with Bennington, he's dead already.'

Genevra held her ground. She would not give in to the fear those words invoked. This man meant for the words to upset her. She wouldn't give him the satisfaction. Henry wouldn't kill Ashe, he wasn't that brave. 'I doubt it. Mr Bennington has shown himself to be a fool on more than one occasion.'

'Don't worry, Mrs Bedevere. Henry didn't have to do the shooting. We hired a professional to do that. You're right, Bennington doesn't have the ruthlessness to do it in cold blood.'

Genevra's bravado faltered. Did this Mr Trent know that Alex had gone as well? A professional would not hesitate to shoot both of the handsome Bedevere brothers. There was a moment when she could imagine them lying dead at the mausoleum, taken by surprise with no chance to defend themselves. But then she thought of the night she'd gone to wait for Ashe there, how fluid his movements had been when he'd pulled his knife from his boot, how he'd sensed her presence before she'd announced herself. Surely no one would take him by surprise.

'I don't believe you,' Genevra replied smoothly. 'Mr Bedevere is a tough man to kill.'

'If you're right, he'll be in time to save you. If you're wrong, then you can both be together in the afterlife.'

He raised his hand in a signal and Genevra watched in dismay as three other men filed into the hall. 'I'll manage the chit, you fire the building. Make sure it takes.'

'No! You cannot burn this house,' Genevra protested, her anger rising.

Trent struck a match and watched it flare. 'I assure you I can. It's my match.'

No one was going to burn Ashe's beloved Bedevere while she lived and breathed. With a steady arm, Genevra raised the pistol from its hiding spot against her skirts. 'It's my gun.'

'You've only got one shot and I've got a hundred matches.' Trent was a cool customer, unfazed by the pistol barrel. Her eyes held his. She let him see every ounce of her determination. She'd give him no reason to doubt this woman would fire the weapon and at this range she would not miss.

'You can't light matches when you're dead.'

'Then my men will light the match. You can't shoot us all.'

'Are you so eager to die for a stick of wood?' Genevra challenged.

But her bravado was short lived. 'I've had enough, boss.' One of the men spoke. 'I've got a pistol, too. Let me shoot her and be done with it.'

'Cunningham.' Trent swivelled his oily gaze towards the man who'd spoken. 'Always the thinker. Well, what do you say, Mrs Bedevere? Are *you* eager to die over a stick of wood?'

Everything that happened next seemed to slow. A

shot rang out from above in the stairwell and Cunningham fell, a rose of colour blossoming on his chest. Another shot fired from Trent's men, she turned to see Gardener fall in answer. 'No!' Genevra screamed. She remembered too late to fire her own pistol. Trent rushed her, grabbing for her gun arm, his hand imprisoning her wrist until the gun fell to the floor.

Trent dragged her upstairs past Gardener's prone form. She screamed, she kicked, she struggled, but there was no one to hear, no one to help. The day labourers were working on the fences along the road. The aunts, thank the lord, were in Audley Village and it was cook's day off. There was only Ashe and Alex if they were still alive.

Trent shoved her into a bedroom and slammed the door. He looped a length of rope over her hands and secured her to a bedpost. 'Hopefully, Henry will prove as foolish as you believe and Mr Bedevere will come racing home in time.' He laughed harshly. 'But then I'll be here, waiting on the front steps, and I won't fail like Henry.'

Genevra spat at him. It was a vain gesture. He swiped at the spittle on his cheek. He leaned close, his breath fetid with garlic, and took her mouth in a bruising kiss. 'I wish there was time for more. I could teach you the merit of obedience, my spitfire. You'd be worthy of my bed.'

Genevra glared. He laughed at her defiance. 'We'll see what you think about that when the smoke reaches you. My bed might sound like a good bargain for your life.'

He slammed the door behind him, but not before Genevra caught the smell of smoke rising from downstairs. Bedevere was burning and she was alone. She tugged at the bonds around her hands, assessing their strength. The bonds held. If she couldn't break the ropes, maybe she could break the bed post. She threw weight into it, but the strong mahogany that had served generations of Bedeveres held firm.

It wasn't until the first fingers of smoke curled under the door that she truly began to panic. There was a real possibility she'd die before she could tell Ashe she loved him.

Chapter Twenty-Five

Ashe flung himself off Rex, his pistol at the ready, Alex beside him. It reminded him of all the times they'd fought imaginary foes of the Round Table, Alex always at his back. But this was no child's game.

A man stood sentry at Bedevere's entrance. Before Ashe could speak, Alex raised his pistol and fired. The man fell, but not before Ashe saw a second too late what Alex had seen in time. The man dropped a knife, his arm arrested in the early stages of a throw. If not for Alex's cold-blooded assessment, he'd have died on the steps.

Another man rushed them from the side of the house. Ashe swept up the dropped weapon and sent it into the man's shoulder. The man sank to the ground and Ashe wasted no time pressing a boot to his neck. 'Where's Mrs Bedevere?'

The man growled and Ashe pressed harder, reaching for the knife in his own boot. The knife had the desired effect. 'She's in the house, on the second floor.'

The man coughed. 'But you'll be too late, for all the good that will do you.'

Alex was beside him. 'I'll take care of this swine, Ashe. Get Genevra, I'll be behind you in a moment.'

Ashe left Alex with his pistol and raced into the house. A body lay on the floor of the hallway. Another of Henry's so-called friends, he guessed. The smoke was rising fast. He was on the stairs and already choking. There were flames from the small front parlour. They must have set the curtains on fire. That posed a danger. Those flames would go straight up through the ceiling and into the second floor.

There was another body at the top of the landing. What had happened here? Then Ashe recognised the form. Good God, it was Gardener, shot straight through the heart. Who the hell had shot the butler? Rage tore through him. Ashe fell to his knees, impulsively looking for signs of life. It seemed incredible that, two hours ago, Gardener had fetched his pistols and now lay dead in a burning house. He had to find Genevra. She would not die for him, too.

'Genevra!' He staggered to his feet, struggling for breath. If she was hurt, she might not be able to answer. Ashe threw open each door he passed. The third door revealed success.

The smoke was thick in this room and Genevra had fallen slack against the bed frame, overcome. 'No, no, no, no, no.' Ashe fumbled at her neck for a pulse. 'Neva!' He shook her. He would not be too late, it wasn't possible. 'Neva!' He took his knife and sliced the ropes. She fell into his arms, the merest groan escaping her lips.

Ashe slid his knife into his boot and lifted her into his arms. The staircase was engulfed in smoke. He hoped there were no flames at the bottom yet. There was no other choice.

He heard someone call his name. 'Up here! Alex, I'm up here.' His voice was fading. With the last of it, he managed a warning. 'Get out, Alex, it's too dangerous. The stairs won't last.'

Something nearby cracked and crashed. He couldn't see it. Ashe hurried on to the smoke-shrouded staircase, Genevra heavy in his arms. He turned her head against his chest trying to protect her from the smoke.

Alex emerged on the stairs, having disregarded the warning. 'We'll take the servants' backstairs at the end of the hall. There's no chance this way. The hall below is engulfed.' Alex pushed him back up the stairs just in time. They'd gained the landing when the whole case gave way, effectively trapping them on the second floor. Alex led the way down the long hall, fearless and sure. The air was clearer here. The backstairs were as yet untouched. Alex held the door and ushered Ashe before him.

'You're a crazy fool, Alex, coming in like that.' Ashe panted as they reached the bottom and spilled out into the vegetable garden. He laid Genevra down, relieved to see signs of life as she stirred in response to the clean air.

Alex doubled over, catching his breath. 'I could see

the staircase was in jeopardy of collapsing. I knew you
would try it. You didn't know the other way was clear
and it was the shortest path to an exit.'

'You could have been killed,' Ashe scolded.

'You still might be. In fact, I think it is a surety.'
Ashe turned. Henry, the cousin of nine lives, stood in
the gateway, gun in hand. 'I think it's time I did my own
dirty work.' There was madness in Henry's blue eyes.
Pale and bedraggled, he'd managed to find his own
way back to the house. Ashe had no doubt his cousin
meant fatal business. It was the only way this could
end now for Henry. His cartel was shattered, Henry's
secrets exposed.

Ashe bent for his knife, but he knew it wouldn't be
fast enough. Gun would beat knife in this contest. He
had the knife in his hand and threw from a crouch, hoping the throw would be accurate. A shot fired. There
was a yell, a scream. Neva! Then he was falling, thrown
off balance. He waited for the burning sensation of the
ball to take him. None came.

Ashe scrambled to his feet, searching, but there was
no enemy. Genevra was scrabbling to her knees, half-
crawling, half-falling towards a form on the ground.

'Alex!' Ashe rasped in horror.

'He threw himself at you when Henry fired,' Genevra
gasped. She was tearing at Alex's shirt. Henry lay still
a few feet away, Ashe's knife in his chest and Henry's
bullet finding deadly purchase. His brother had given
his life for him. Ashe knelt by Alex, closing his hands

over Genevra's where she'd pressed a hastily made pad to the wound. His throat tightened.

'Ashe.' Alex's voice was a mere whisper. Ashe bent forwards, his ear to Alex's lips. 'You're the earl now, little brother.' Alex coughed.

'We'll get help.' If he was talking, maybe there was some hope, Ashe thought wildly.

'No, just stay with me. It won't be long now.' Alex was calm. 'I've written it all down for you if the fire didn't take it. You know most of it already.'

Ashe gripped his brother's hand. 'You shouldn't have done it. You shouldn't have thrown yourself away like that.'

'I hadn't long left, Ashe.' Alex struggled for a breath. 'It's much better this way.' He managed a smile. 'Father loved you, he forgave you for leaving. Make sure you forgive yourself.' His grip tightened on Ashe's hands. Pain and fear flashed in his dark eyes.

'Remember what we used to say when we played, Ashe? The king is dead, long live the king.'

'I remember.'

A lone tear trailed out of the corner of Alex's eye. 'The earl is dead, long live the earl.' Then the fear was replaced by peace as Alex breathed his last.

'So passes the fifth Earl of Audley,' Ashe said solemnly. Genevra held his gaze, unbothered by the tears on his cheeks. 'Long live the earl,' she softly echoed Alex's words.

He pulled her to him, revelling in the feel of her body, of life. 'When I saw the smoke, all I could think of was I was too late to tell you I loved you. I should have told you weeks ago, but I was too stubborn to admit it.' He pushed his hands gently through her hair, tilting her face up to his.

'I love you, too, Ashe. I think I loved you from the first.' She kissed him softly.

Ashe laughed. 'No, you didn't, Neva. You slapped me across the face for insolence.'

'Well, maybe you're right about that.' She smiled wearily and didn't protest when he bent to carry her away from the heartbreak that lay in the garden and into the future.

One year later

Ashe paced the back terrace, surveying the expanse of parkland and gardens. Rebuilt, redecorated, Bedevere had never looked so well, or perhaps it was his own happiness that painted everything with a rosy veneer these days. Ashe could not recall having ever been this content in his adult life, not even when he'd been playing piano in Vienna. He shifted the bundle in his arms ever so gently.

'Fatherhood becomes you,' Genevra said softly, shutting the veranda door behind her. 'Is he asleep?' She peered into the blanket at the little face. 'I missed him too much today.' It had been her first day out of the house since little Alexander had been born two months ago.

'How is Seaton Hall?' Ashe asked. It had become operational a few months ago, Genevra's dream of a place for women to run their own business fully realised.

'It's fine. I am happy to say they're ably running things on their own. They hardly need me at all.'

'That's good.' Ashe bent to kiss her. 'There are plenty of us who need you here.'

'That reminds me, I have a surprise for you.' Genevra smiled. 'Come walk with me.'

Baby in one arm, his wife on the other, Ashe let Genevra lead him through the garden to the fountain. It still wasn't working. After the fire, there'd been plenty of projects to oversee that took precedence in order to make Bedevere livable again.

Genevra gave a nod of her head and the fountain sprang to life. Water plumed high into the air, arcing gracefully into the wide basin below. 'Happy birthday, Ashe,' she whispered. With a gesture of her hand, people began to emerge from behind the trees—the staff were there, his aunts were there, Markham Marsbury was there.

'I'm sorry we missed it last year. I didn't know.' Genevra shrugged apologetically. She moved to take the baby from him, but he declined.

'No, I want to hold him a while longer.'

'You'll be the only lord in England to actually raise his own child,' Genevra teased.

Ashe grinned.

'What are you thinking?'

'I'm thinking what a difference a year makes.' Last year had been full of loss. He'd lost his father, his brother, even a chance to make amends, but he'd found Genevra and he'd found peace. The future lay in his arms and stood by his side.

'I have a gift for you.' Genevra reached for an awkwardly wrapped package at the base of the fountain. 'Now you'll have to let me take the baby.'

Ashe obliged and undid the wrapping. Beneath the paper was a model four-masted schooner. He was speechless for a moment. 'It's perfect, Neva. Does it float?'

'Put it in the fountain and find out.'

There were those who believed Ashe Bedevere was the greatest pleasure of the Season, but he knew better. The best pleasure was being loved by Genevra through all the seasons to come, and there would be plenty of them if he had anything to say about it. Ashe Bedevere was home.

* * * * *

MILLS & BOON

HISTORICAL

Awaken the romance of the past

Escape with historical heroes from time gone by. Whether your passion is for wicked Regency Rakes, muscled Viking warriors or rugged Highlanders, indulge your fantasies and awaken the romance of the past.